MARC OLDEN
GAIJIN

J

JOVE BOOKS, NEW YORK

GAIJIN

A Jove Book/published by arrangement with
Arbor House Publishing Company

PRINTING HISTORY
Arbor House edition / June 1986
Jove edition / December 1987

ISBN: 0-515-09194-4

Jove Books are published by The Berkley Publishing Group,
200 Madison Avenue, New York, NY 10016.
The name "JOVE" and the "J" logo
are trademarks belonging to Jove Publications, Inc.

PRINTED IN THE UNITED STATES OF AMERICA

10 9 8 7 6 5 4 3 2 1

Gaijin

Alexis never saw his hands move, never saw the knife. But she felt him grab a handful of her hair, jerk her head back on her neck and then there was this terrible pain on the right side of her head and she couldn't stop screaming.

The *gaijin* held Alexis's bloodied right ear between his thumb and forefinger. He looked at it for a few seconds, then dangled it over her head. "Anyone refusing to answer a question put to them by a samurai was punished thusly. Silence indicated you were a deaf man and therefore had no ears. An appropriate discipline, I should say . . ."

Also by Marc Olden . . .
Dai-Sho

In memory of Raymond Maldonado

Acknowledgments

Diane Crafford for being there; Richard Pine for a job well done; George Coleman for being the right editor at the right time.

PART ONE

Heiho no Metsuku.
The eyes in combat.

In seeing things, there are *kan* and *ken*. Penetrating the true nature of things is *kan;* seeing surface phenomena is *ken*.

—MIYAMOTO MUSASHI,
Gorin no Sho

One

Alexis Bendor sensed danger.

When she awoke from her nightmare it was almost dawn.
She looked through the sliding glass doors of her bedroom at
a rain forest of ferns and giant philodendrons. Something
familiar. Just the thing to pull her from the horrors of a bad
dream.

She heard the cooing of doves gathered under the redwood sun deck. The birds were hiding from a sudden storm,
now starting to taper off. These doves were her favorite,
small birds called barred doves, which formed couples
that remained forever faithful and roosted at each other's
side by night. Cooing doves and a steady rain. Welcome
sounds.

Alexis sat up in bed. Sixty-three years old and getting
crackbrained in her old age. Of course she was alone.

The nightmare, her worst in years, had been about Rupert
de Jongh. Even wide awake her heart wouldn't stop pounding. Her hand shook as it touched the pulse on the right side
of her neck. Lord above. It was positively throbbing.

With the back of her hand she stroked the smooth old scar
tissue where her right ear used to be. She flinched at the pain.
You'd think the wound was still healing.

A shrink would have said, "My advice to you, Mrs.

Bendor, is to stop dredging up memories from the black storehouse in your mind. I recommend several sessions at $150. Guaranteed to cure what ails you.''

The rain stopped. Alexis looked through the glass doors at dozens of birds now rising from the rain forest to soar against a rust-colored sky. Wings snapping, the doves flew from under the sun deck and pursued the flock. Four doves. Four was the number of agents in Alexis's spy team in February 1945, the year the nightmare had begun.

She had been scheduled for a safe war. Do her time in Washington breaking enemy codes and face nothing more terrifying than a run in her seamed stockings. But in 1945, twenty-five-year-old Alexis had come to the attention of the OSS, which was interested not only in her decoding abilities, but in her ability to speak Japanese. And in what she knew about Rupert de Jongh, a rather unusual Englishman.

The tall, blond, and almost pretty Alexis Waycross, her maiden name, knew a lot about Mr. de Jongh. Credit that to her curiosity and love of challenge. During the war, field agents and Allied contacts worldwide had flooded Washington with information on Japan. Some of it, a lot of it, went unnoticed. Too much material and not enough trained personnel to correctly collate and analyze it.

Alexis, born to scrutinize and go mousing, took it upon herself to examine some of the data, particularly anything dealing with Rupert de Jongh. De Jongh was a traitor and traitors fascinated her.

Mr. de Jongh was not your everyday traitor. He was an English aristocrat turned samurai. Absolutely mesmerizing.

He was called *gaijin* and in him Japan had what could only be described as a blue-chip spy. Reports crossing Alexis's desk compared him to Wilhelm Stieber, the intelligence genius who had served Bismark and who was the most admired of German agents. And to Sidney Reilly, the notorious double agent who at various times had worked for the British, French, Russian, and Japanese secret services.

The *gaijin*, however, exceeded them in his cruelty, his unrelenting savagery and cold-bloodedness. He had tortured and murdered too many Allied agents, while surviving the attempts on his own life. De Jongh, damn him, had been blessed with either good luck or good judgment.

He was a member of the Kempei-Tai, Japan's secret police, and had obtained copies of British, American, French,
and German cipher machines, which he showed Japan how to
adapt for its own use. This was a giant step in developing
Japanese cryptography, aiding de Jongh's adopted country in
closing the distance between it and the Western powers,
which had been far ahead of Japan in this area. But even de
Jongh couldn't win them all. The Japanese alphabet contained
over two thousand hieroglyphics and almost sixty letters, too
many to adapt to a cipher system. So they sent their codes
in Roman letters, a break for Western cipher experts like
Alexis.

She also pounced on another de Jongh tactic. Like all
Japanese agents, he clung to the idea that the Japanese language was too complicated for foreigners to understand its
many shaded meanings. Alexis, however, took pride in dis-
abusing de Jongh of that notion. With unalloyed glee she broke
his cipher, then read and understood the nuances in his messages. De Jongh was unaware of this until the FBI arrested
two Americans acting as Japanese spies and working out of a
Miami stationery store.

De Jongh became Alexis's pet project, a particular piece of
business close to her heart. She compiled a file on him, first
for her own information, then at the request of her superiors
and OSS. She obtained de Jongh's photograph and family
history from London intelligence sources, in return sharing
her dossier with them. The photographs of de Jongh practicing judo, kendo, and Japanese archery were just one indica-
tion of how thoroughly Japanese the Englishman had become.
He spoke Japanese, played Japanese musical instruments, did
beautiful calligraphy, and wrote haiku. And there was his
primary accomplishment, one unheard of for a Westerner:
complete acceptance at the highest military and social levels.

Alexis, through persistent research and investigation, knew
more about the *gaijin* than any intelligence agent did. Now it
appeared that de Jongh was about to surface in Geneva.
Source of this important information: "Richard Wagner,"
code name for the top Allied spy in the Berlin Foreign Office.
De Jongh, Wagner said, was supposedly coming to Switzerland to learn if the Soviet Union intended to break its peace
treaty with Japan and declare war on her. Stalin had long held

an appetite for Japanese territory. With Japan preparing for invasion by American forces, now was the time for Stalin to reach out and fill his plate with the spoils of war from the Far East.

But de Jongh, Wagner warned, was devious. His true reason for coming to Switzerland was to gather intelligence on the secret peace offers Nazi leaders were quietly making to the Allies. Himmler, Goering, Goebbels, and others had individual peace plans, all aimed at saving themselves from retribution. Each plan was being offered to America, the Allied leader. And all contained the same demand, that Germany be left with her government intact in order to join the West in a holy war against Communist Russia. If Germany was preparing to abandon her ally Japan, de Jongh wanted to know.

We're heading for certain victory, the OSS told Alexis. What we want to do is speed it up. Eliminating de Jongh is one way of doing that. Someone has to go to Switzerland, someone who knows de Jongh, his ciphers, and who speaks Japanese and German. Alexis would be given some OSS training, but not much. No time for that. Then she'd be flown to London to familiarize herself with America's operations in Switzerland. In London she'd also touch base with the British taking part in this mission. A joint Anglo-American team would listen in on de Jongh's code and after that the British would try to take him prisoner. An Englishman, Michael Marwood would be the liaison between American and British intelligence in Zurich. It was important to the British that de Jongh stand trial as a war criminal. If he resisted, they were quite prepared to kill him on the spot.

Nothing would have stopped Alexis from volunteering. She had never been more anxious to do anything in her life. This was her chance to see action and not just hear about it. All she had to do was sneak into Switzerland and eavesdrop on de Jongh, as she'd been doing for years. Maybe give the British a hand in cutting off his wind. Then she'd spend a day or two in Bern getting debriefed by the OSS, followed by a return flight to London. No reason for there to be any trouble. A firmly neutral Switzerland insisted that Allied and Axis agents behave themselves or be deported.

Talk about luck. A chance to be in on the excitement

before the war ended. To be a part of the greatest adventure
of all time. Jesus, how lucky could a gal get.

Geneva. February 1945. The brutal interrogation of Alexis
and her team began immediately after their capture by de
Jongh. Late one afternoon the three Americans and one Englishman were picked up by SS posing as Swiss policemen
and driven to a secluded dairy farm several miles outside the
city. The farm was in a shallow valley lush with pine and
linden trees and within sight of the snow-capped French Alps.
It belonged to Peter Schulman, a Swiss-German who was an
ardent admirer of Heinrich Himmler. A few minutes in
Schulman's chalet was time enough for Alexis to pick out the
barrel-chested farmer's most prized possession. It was a framed
and prominently displayed photograph of himself and Himmler taken twenty-three years ago at a Munich costume ball.
The round-faced, chinless Himmler was dressed as "Abdul
Hamid, the Sultan of Turkey." Schulman, in turban and
blackface, and a step behind, had come as Himmler's slave.

De Jongh, on the other hand, carried himself like a gran-
dee, a man of mark. He was smaller than Alexis had imagined, with blond hair, blue eyes, and the clean good looks of
the Duke of Windsor. A natty dresser like the Duke, too.
High-waisted, double-pleated pants held up by suspenders.
Box-pleated and belted Norfolk jacket. Green sweater, purple
tie with a wide Windsor knot, red pocket handkerchief, and
gray fedora hat. Alexis had expected someone in a kimono,
with a samurai topknot and *dai-sho*, the warrior's long and
short swords, tucked in his belt.

In addition to de Jongh and Schulman, Alexis's captors
included two Japanese, three SS, and one German intelligence officer. All deferred to de Jongh. The intelligence
officer, Alexis noticed, deferred reluctantly. He was Arthur
Kuby, a tall, blond, hook-nose man in his mid-twenties, with
the precise speech of an upper-class Prussian. A whispered
remark behind the hand, from Kuby to de Jongh, brought an
icy reaction from the turncoat Englishman. Through tight lips
he told Kuby to mind his own business. Alexis guessed Kuby
had said something about the problems involved in taking
Allied agents prisoner in neutral territory. Surely de Jongh
had to know there would be retaliation from both the Swiss
authorities and Allies. But if he knew, he didn't give a damn.

As far as Alexis could see, there were only two women in the chalet: Schulman's plump, gray-haired wife and a lovely Japanese teenager, whom Richard Wagner had identified as de Jongh's traveling companion. She was, Wagner said, the only living creature for whom de Jongh showed any tenderness. Woe be unto anyone who harmed the youngster, who was only fifteen years old. She was a former *karayuki,* one of thousands of Japanese girls sold into prostitution overseas by relatives in need of money. Almost all were forced to work in military brothels set up by the Japanese army as it expanded throughout Asia. Kasumi's parents had handed her over to procurers for three bags of rice.

De Jongh asked the questions, directing all of them at Alexis, speaking in German, Japanese, and English. He commented upon her linguistic skills, knowledge of Japanese culture, and cipher skills. Alexis thought he reeked of manners and good breeding. He carried himself like someone who'd been trained in the proper forms of social conduct, but that was part of the deceit. De Jongh was whoever he wanted to be and nothing you expected him to be. Alexis had no illusions about the man; when he decided to stop playing Lord Fauntleroy and go after the answers he truly wanted, he'd crucify her and the others. De Jongh pulled out a pocket watch, studied it briefly, then announced it was time for an object lesson. Everyone to the barn, if you please. Women stay behind, save for Miss Waycross. She was to accompany the men to Schulman's barn.

"By the way," de Jongh said to her, "it appears I've broken your cipher. Puts me in the victory column, I believe."

Alexis shook her head. He was lying. Her ciphers were unbreakable. She was the best. No one was supposed to outwit her. No one. *But she and her team had been captured.*

De Jongh looked up at the beamed chalet ceiling and tapped his chin with a forefinger. "Let's see if I have this correct. You keyed your cipher to the pages of the German farmer's almanac. You used the call letters *T*-slash-*Y,* then added two numbers and a single letter. The letter, of course, was changed each time you transmitted. Your traffic was between here and Bern. And to Zurich as well. And I believe you have also been in contact with some Germans across the border, misguided souls who feel that Hitler has perhaps outlived his usefulness."

He snapped his fingers and pointed to several items on a small table. Alexis's ration card, forged identity papers, a small bottle of Benzedrine tablets she used to keep awake. A cyanide capsule she was to have taken upon capture. "You aren't good enough, Miss Waycross. It's that simple, really. This is, if I may say so, a most dangerous game we play here. Most dangerous. Involves many unforeseen things. No matter how often the technicalities arise in discussion and no matter how neatly you file away the answers in your little brain, the truth is you are always on your own. Theory, I'm afraid, rarely holds up in this sort of business. And theory seems to constitute your resources, from what I can observe. One must banish theory. Reality is forever intruding. Survival. Now that's a whole different kettle of fish. It owes much to a quick mind and a great deal of luck and nerve. As far as I can make out, you come up short in all areas."

He fitted a Player's cigarette into an ivory holder. "Mr. Marwood, God rest his soul, won't be joining us. He has been dealt with, of course, so look not to him for deliverance. I understand he was to be a party to my disposal. Ah, the vagaries of fate. Now. That object lesson I mentioned. Let's toodle over to the barn, shall we?"

The object lesson. Alexis had read about de Jongh's cruelty. Nothing, however, had prepared her for what was to happen in Schulman's barn. De Jongh took his cigarette holder from his lips, looked at a tall, stoop-shouldered SS man with hairy nostrils, and pointed to Julian Conroy, a young Pennsylvania schoolteacher who had been in OSS less than a year and was scheduled to be married in the spring. Alexis had been invited to the wedding.

The tall SS man coughed up phlegm, spat, then took a snubbed-nose Walther PPK from his overcoat pocket and shot Conroy in both feet. "Gracious," the SS man said with mock seriousness. "Our friend's wounds are too serious to be treated." The other SS knew their roles. They agreed. Much too serious. One stepped forward with a gas mask and placed it over Conroy's face to silence his screams. "What can I do?" said the tall SS. "I must help our friend." He then took an axe and amputated Conroy's feet. Alexis threw up. Willis Speed, the youngest member of her team, began to weep. "He'll bleed to death within an hour," the SS man said.

De Jongh's cold blue eyes never blinked. He took a deep drag on his Player's, blew smoke at a stack of baled hay, and pointed the holder once more. At James Milnes, a twenty-six-year-old Welshman who'd been a rising young opera singer before the war. Later Alexis wondered if Milnes acted out of panic or in the belief he could escape. In any case, he ran. Broke loose from the two SS holding him and sprinted for the barn door. De Jongh caught up to the Welshman in three steps. He spun Milnes around and kneed him in the groin. As the British agent doubled over, de Jongh grabbed him by the lapels of his leather jacket, crouched and whirled around in one motion until his back was to Milnes. Yanking down with both hands, de Jongh threw the Welshman over his right shoulder. Milnes flew high, arms whirling, legs entangled. He landed heavily on his left side and cried out as a bone snapped. He cried out again as de Jongh drove a heel into the base of his spine.

Grunts of approval and admiration from the SS. Schulman smiled and applauded. *Wunderbar.* The Japanese exchanged looks. One lifted a corner of his mouth in a small smile. De Jongh was *bushi*, a warrior. A Westerner with the soul of a true Japanese. De Jongh squatted, picked up his cigarette lighter, and brushed it off. He looked at the SS and said Milnes was still alive. Continue.

Alexis, her eyes swollen with tears, looked away. They're dying because of me, she thought. Because that bastard broke my code.

An SS with receding blond hair and pointed chin stepped forward holding a pitchfork. He turned the groaning Milnes over on his back and carefully placed the pitchfork handle on the Welshman's throat. Then the SS man stood on the handle, legs apart and arms out to the side for balance and rocked side to side until Milnes was dead.

The SS man smiled at de Jongh and said this is how we did it in the camps. Jews, gypsies, Russians. Within seconds they all seemed to develop permanent throat trouble.

"Interesting," de Jongh murmured, turning back to talk to Alexis. She was to spend the night in the barn with her remaining associate, Willis Speed, a soft-spoken Georgian who'd been all-American in basketball at Georgia Tech. De Jongh begged their forgiveness; they would be under guard and without their clothing. Baring a body was a prelude to baring the soul. Nudity had its psychological effect and de Jongh was sure they were aware of this. It added to a prisoner's feeling of powerlessness, but sad to say, these things were unnecessary. They had to be prepared for tomorrow, when de Jongh would expect complete and truthful answers to all queries. He would know if they were lying. Truth was like fire; neither could be resisted.

"I'll take it upon myself to contact your OSS cohorts," de Jongh said to Alexis. "You're supposed to check in twice daily, I believe. At noon and eight at night, am I correct? I should be able to concoct some fanciful tale about your having spotted me and how you're setting about tracking me down. Do try and get some sleep, the both of you. Tomorrow promises to be rather a hectic day. *Bon nuit.*"

Alexis thought, we've got a chance. When he sends my code he'll hang himself. Every code had a precaution against misuse or against the sender being forced to operate against his will. Alexis, like most senders, always included a deliberate mistake. If that mistake was missing, it was a signal that something was wrong. Including or excluding a single letter or changing the order of words were other signals indicating trouble. De Jongh might be clever as a fox, but he knew none of Alexis's precautions. They were known only to her and her receiver. Maybe he'd broken her cipher, but the second he started using it he'd seal his doom. The OSS would know it wasn't her and come running. All Alexis and Willis had to do was stay alive and hope their side reached them in time.

The night in Schulman's barn was the worst of Alexis's life. Tied hand and foot, the naked American agents shivered in a stall near the open front door. No blankets, on de Jongh's orders. For warmth, Alexis and Willis covered themselves with straw as best they could and huddled near a sleeping black-and-white cow. Both slept with their backs to kerosene lamps placed on the ground. They dozed fitfully, guarded first by a pair of SS in black leather overcoats, then by two Japanese who talked until the sun came up.

Morning. A smiling Willis told Alexis he'd enjoyed sleeping with her, though these weren't the ideal circumstances and he'd always been the romantic type, the type who would bring a lady breakfast in bed. He was trying to cheer her up. And keep his own fear under control. The ropes had cut off circulation to their hands and feet and the cold had left them cramped. Willis was sick to death of smelling the damn cow. Both noticed that the bodies of Conroy and Milnes had disappeared.

Willis started to say something and stopped. Alexis followed his gaze. De Jongh, Schulman, the Japanese, and the three SS were halfway between the barn and the chalet. When de Jongh paused, they all did. The Englishman looked up at the sky, said something, and the rest of them laughed. The ground between the chalet and barn was lightly covered in snow, but only de Jongh wore boots. He wore knee-high rubber boots and looked every inch the gentleman farmer out for a morning stroll.

Arthur Kuby remained on the balcony of the chalet. He was talking to Kasumi, who ignored him and kept her eyes on de Jongh. De Jongh looked toward the chalet and asked Kuby to please join them. The German intelligence officer touched his fedora to Kasumi and left the chalet. Alexis thought he didn't seem in a hurry to get to the barn.

She whispered to Willis, "Our people are on the way. Remember that. De Jongh made a mistake contacting them. They know it's him and not me and they're on the way."

"Can't get here too soon for me," drawled Willis. He wasn't too keen on this hotel. Room service was piss poor and he'd about had it with inhaling cow pies.

De Jongh and the others entered the barn and stood in front of the prisoners' stall. Only de Jongh had shaved. He smelled of fine cologne and wore a Panama hat, which was out of style but looked stylish on him.

He stepped forward, pulled up his trousers at the knees, and squatted near Alexis. "Forgive the lack of preliminaries, but I'd like to get down to brass tacks, if you don't mind. Let's start with Richard Wagner's real name. Please tell me who this chap is who's been funneling information to your people."

I don't have to be brave for long, Alexis told herself. Just for a minute or two. She thought of Conroy and Milnes and she held de Jongh's gaze and said nothing.

He remained squatting, fingers linked together. "I'm waiting, Miss Waycross."

Silence.

Alexis never saw his hands move, never saw the knife. But

she felt him grab a handful of her hair, jerk her head back on her neck and then there was this terrible pain on the right side of her head and she couldn't stop screaming.

De Jongh held Alexis's bloodied right ear between his thumb and forefinger. He looked at it for a few seconds then dangled it over her head. "Anyone refusing to answer a question put to them by a samurai was punished thusly. Silence indicated you were a deaf man and therefore had no ears. An appropriate discipline, I should say. Now once more. Richard Wagner. His name, please."

Willis Speed said, "Goddam it, leave her alone. I'll tell you his name."

"No, you won't tell me his name," de Jongh said. "Because if you say another word without my having addressed you directly, I shall cut out your tongue. My question is directed to Miss Waycross. I advise you to remain silent."

Alexis, face and hair covered with her blood, tried to get away from de Jongh by crawling under the cow now standing and chewing its cud. De Jongh said, "Tsk, tsk," and grabbed the rope around her ankles, dragged her toward him on her stomach, and cut her on each buttock. This, he told her, was a torture called *Ling-chez*. Death of a thousand cuts. Chinese, he said, with a long history. There were numerous variations. The one he was about to apply to her involved twenty-four cuts, no more, no less. And always administered two at a time.

Richard Wagner. His name.

Alexis kicked at him with her bound feet and missed. "You are the spirited one," de Jongh said. He turned her over and on her back and jammed a hand down on her mouth. Not to insure silence, but to keep her head in place. Then he made a cut in the center of each eyebrow. Not deep, not long. But painful. And he told her in advance what he was going to do.

Forearms. A three-inch cut on each. Not deep, but agonizing.

Breasts. A two-inch cut atop each.

Alexis's eyes turned up in her head. She passed out.

When Alexis came to it was dark and snowing lightly. Her mouth was taped. The smell of manure, animals, and kerosene lamps meant she was still in the stall. She came wide awake, however, when she realized she was tied to Willis

Speed's corpse. He lay stomach down in the straw. Alexis was face down on his cold body, arms and legs roped to his. She screamed, but the sound stayed trapped in her throat. She pulled, twisted, and tried to free herself. The ropes held fast.

The sound of footsteps entering the stall made Alexis redouble her efforts to escape. But she succeeded only in tearing skin from her wrists and ankles. A gloved hand touched her shoulder. Gently. A terrified Alexis stopped struggling and waited. There was warm breath near her ear. "Arthur Kuby," whispered a male voice in accented English. "I should like very much to do a deal with you."

He removed a glove and pulled the tape from Alexis's mouth.

Kuby used a penknife to free her, then dropped his leather overcoat on top of her and looked through the barn opening at the lighted chalet. He turned to see Alexis crawl away from him and cringe in a corner of the stall. Kuby, now in a hurry to get all of his words out, spoke in German. He began by telling her of the man he had just killed. The SS man who had been guarding her and who had chopped off her friend's feet. Kuby had never killed anyone before and had found it difficult. Not for moral reasons, but because it was physically hard work. He, too, had used the axe, so as not to make noise. Unfortunately, the human body was so durable. Kuby had to give the SS man quite a few strokes before the man ceased to be a problem. The corpse was hidden behind the feed bin.

Kuby now had two choices. Run back to Germany, where the war was lost and people dreaded each day and feared the advancing Russians above all. Alexis would be left to take the blame for the dead SS and could expect no mercy from the man's companions. Kuby's second choice, the one he preferred, was to cut a deal with the Americans. For this he would need Alexis. He'd already helped her; in return she could act as his passport to the OSS.

"Where's de Jongh now?" Alexis asked.

"Should be arriving in Geneva any moment. Your comrade, Mr. Speed, attempted to save your life by giving him Richard Wagner's real name. I would advise you not to look at Herr Speed. De Jongh did things to him that it is best you do not see. Wagner's identity is so important that de Jongh did not feel safe putting it on the air. He decided to personally

drive to Geneva with an SS and one of the Japanese, and pass
on the information to the German legation there. Your ear, it
is all right?''

Alexis brought up her hand, but didn't touch the wound.

Kuby said, ''De Jongh cauterized it for you. He wanted
you to live until he comes back. He has a strong hatred for
you, I must say. It is as though you have done him some
intense harm. Have you done such a thing?''

''I broke his code and got some of his people in America
arrested.''

''*Ja*. I see.''

Alexis shook her head and whispered, ''They didn't come.
They didn't come.'' Why hadn't they seen the mistake in de
Jongh's use of my cipher? She blinked. Unless they had
simply overlooked it. De Jongh had gotten away with using
her cipher. He had had incredible luck and gotten away with
it. She began to weep.

Kuby looked at his wristwatch. ''We haven't much time.
What about our deal?''

''Deal?''

Kuby said he had information the OSS might be interested
in. Information on the Russians, on the Japanese attempts to
negotiate a new peace treaty with the Soviet Union and keep
her out of the war. On German scientists who were hurriedly
attempting to split the atom and create a mysterious new
bomb with awesome destructive possibilities.

Also, if Alexis could get to the chalet she might be able to
reach her people in time to warn Richard Wagner.

Alexis asked how many men were in the house. One SS,
one Japanese. Schulman and his wife. And the Japanese girl.
A very lovely girl and quite different from any female Kuby
had ever met. Exotic, quiet, and totally submissive. Kuby
found submission very attractive in a woman.

Alexis said, ''We'll have to kill them.''

Kuby seemed taken aback. ''Perhaps. *Ja*, perhaps. It is
dark, but not dark enough to hide you if you were to come to
the house. I could walk to the house without any trouble, but
I am not sure if I can handle three men.'' He shook his head.
''I think of the trouble I had killing one man.''

Alexis pushed herself to her feet and put on Kuby's leather
coat. She fell back against the stall, eyes closed. After a few

seconds she said, "We'll get them to come out in the open. Catch them off guard."

She looked at Kuby. "We'll set fire to the barn. Schulman will come for sure. The others will come out to see what's happening."

Alexis wanted a gun.

Kuby disappeared behind the feed bin, then returned with the dead Nazi's Walther. Did she know how to shoot? Alexis took the gun from him and looked away. Her arm dangled at her side and she said nothing.

Schulman was the first to run into the barn, waddling ducklike into the smoke and calling on God to protect his property. Alexis crouched in the stall with Willis's dead body and let the Swiss farmer rush by her. Then she stood up, aimed at his back and pulled the trigger twice. Schulman stumbled forward, then fell face down.

Two shots outside of the barn made Alexis whirl around. When she stepped outside, the SS man was lying on his side in the falling snow and the Japanese had his hands raised. Kuby, his pistol aimed at the Japanese, hesitated. He was confused and rapidly losing control.

The Japanese man looked very young, a small, thin figure with long feminine eyelashes and a round face. He'd run out of the chalet without a coat. Or gun. Just pants, rubber boots, and what looked to be the top of a pair of longjohns. Alexis brought up the hand holding the Walther and shot him point-blank in the face. When he fell she moved closer and emptied the pistol into his body.

Alexis heard Mrs. Schulman cry out for her husband. It was a cry that recognized something was wrong, but at the same time didn't want to know. Alexis ignored her. Instead she stared at Kuby, who tried not to tremble. But when he put his pistol in his jacket pocket his hand shook. For he knew that if Alexis's gun were not empty he would now be a dead man.

She walked past him without speaking, the falling snow bits of lace in her bloodied, matted hair. Her steps were halting, her eyes glazed. The empty pistol, however, was still in her hand.

Two

At sunset the *yakuza* leader Yamaga Razan stood behind bamboo blinds in his Waikiki flat and watched the Feast of the Dead. He thought of a woman who had been dead almost forty years. In all of that time he had never stopped loving her.

He stared at the ancient rites now being performed in a neighboring park by *Bon* dancers, Japanese Buddhists in gray kimonos and white headbands. Under glowing paper lanterns they chanted and danced to guide the dead back to earth for a brief reunion with the living. Later the lanterns would be floated on water, lighting the dead's return to the netherworld.

Razan stroked a scar on his bare left shoulder and watched the dancers circle a bamboo tower to the sounds of gongs and flutes. A racially mixed crowd had grown around the *Bon* dancers until they could hardly be seen. Hawaii, the racial melting pot. Whites, Hawaiians, Filipinos, Samoans, Chinese. And Japanese. The *yakuza* leader shook his head in disapproval.

To him Hawaii was a disturbing intermixture that produced low cultural and moral standards. Its people were not living in harmony so much as nervously coexisting together for economic and political survival. Razan preferred the racial purity of Japan, a homogeneity that had given that nation an unquestioned solidarity, not to mention a remarkable identity as a society and as individuals.

Hawaii, the galaxy of cultures. Hawaii, the social rainbow. "Flapdoodle and twaddle," his mother would have said. Straight from Gilbert and Sullivan, whom she had taught him to love. A line from 'The Gondoliers' came to mind—*When everyone is somebodee, then no one's anybody*.

Razan had not wanted to come to Hawaii. The trip, his first outside Japan in years, had been forced upon him. Leaving the country for a secret meeting with the Americans, however, was the key to holding together his *yakuza* group, and guarding his "island," his territory in Japan and the Far East. He was running against time and change, the deadliest of opponents.

Within his own group the younger members no longer had the absolute respect and loyalty for the *oyabun*, the leader, that was once the rule. Violence and money alone kept them in line.

And there was a rival gang leader, the brutal, ambitious, and younger Uraga. A gang war had broken out last month between Uraga and Razan, a murderous and implacable conflict. Thousands of *kobun*, soldiers, were involved on each side and casualties were high. Razan himself had barely survived an assassination attempt. To the victor went control of Japan's lucrative drug, pornography, gambling, and loan-sharking rackets and the supreme role in the underworld, a position long held by Razan.

Police and press had come under public pressure to stop the fighting when innocent bystanders were killed. By guns. In this war, the worst Japanese crime that had been seen in some time, the traditional weapons of swords, knives, lynching, and fire were not enough.

Guns, however, were prohibited in Japan and the severe laws against them were strictly enforced. As a result, hundreds of *yakuza* had been arrested. Underworld finances had also come under scrutiny. For the moment the romantic mystique that drew politicians, entertainers, and sports figures to the underworld no longer existed. Even top corporate executives, who used Yamaga Razan and other *oyabun* to keep shareholders in line at stock meetings, now preferred to do without *yakuza* services.

Since World War II, Razan had seen enough underworld

conflicts to know that this one was different. "The profits have never been as high," he told a lieutenant, "and never as tempting. The young, such as Uraga, all have the courage of their greed. All are happy to be rich and are willing to take the consequences."

Because his power and will were one, Razan arrived at a solution. Similar pressures ten years ago had forced him and other *yakuza* to expand abroad, to Asia, Australia, and above all, to Hawaii, golden meeting place of East and West. And to the American mainland, to take their share of Japan's phenomenal business success there. Police in Hawaii gave them trouble, forcing the *yakuza* to operate mainly in the Japanese community, which could be easily cowered by threats of violence. And on the American mainland Razan and other *oyabun* were restricted both by police security and fear of clashing with the American underworld. It had even been necessary to pay financial tribute to certain American groups before being allowed to pass narcotics through their territory for sale among Japanese. To date the *yakuza* had been allowed a very small slice of the gigantic cheese wheel that was the United States.

Survival was not enough. From the current gang war Razan had learned the importance of nothing less than an equal partnership with the American underworld, one to include legitimate enterprises as well. It would also have to include American politicians. He was going to take the dare of the future and make it his greatest achievement. He would crush the pulseless swine Uraga and in the process become the most powerful *oyabun* Japan had ever seen.

Yamaga Razan was in his mid-sixties, a slight, long-nosed man with an icy elegance and thick silver hair. This evening he was barefoot and wore only a *fundoshi*, a length of white cloth pulled between his legs and wrapped several times around his hips. His body was virtually covered with tattoos, multicolored dragons, flowers, birds. His back was blue with the portrait of a vengeful sword-wielding samurai, a design painfully applied to his flesh over a period of months with special bamboo tattooing needles. Only his face, neck, hands, and feet remained unstained. Both little fingers were missing.

He was *oyabun* of Japan's largest *yakuza* group, a syndicate called Shinanui-Kai, fire of the mysterious origin, with more than eleven thousand men in branches throughout Japan and abroad. He wielded power with absolute energy, maintaining his position through force and terror. He possessed discipline and intuition and in all things acted with unwavering self-assurance. As *oyabun* he acknowledged no will but his own, and was as brutal as his needs required.

If age had weakened Razan's body, it had brought him increased psychological insight and an unyielding conviction in his ability to succeed at anything he undertook. Even those who hated or feared him agreed that Razan was a born leader, one able to command and enforce, one to whom other men surrendered their destinies.

Such an unusually strong will set him apart from others and made him an intruder in the world of mortal men.

An outsider who had never been photographed and who was never seen in public.

And who had an unexplainable and mystical perception into all that was Japan. Razan was an outsider with uncommon understanding. His spirit grew stronger each year and it was said that he could sense hidden enemies, see into the future, and predict the moment of one's death. Some even said he was impossible to kill.

Razan turned his back on the *Bon* dancers and walked across a room empty of all decorations and furniture, except for straw mats on the floor and lighted paper lanterns hanging from the ceiling and rice paper walls. His eyes were on a small fire burning in a brazier in a corner alcove. Neither this apartment in a high-rise he owned nor his seven homes in Japan were elaborate affairs. All were severe and light in the Japanese tradition and contained nothing he did not find beautiful or useful.

In his slender hands he carried a black pine box, its lacquered surface grainy with powdered gold. The box contained a doll's head and a dagger given Razan by Admiral Yamamoto, planner and executor of the daring raid on Pearl Harbor. The doll's head had once belonged to a *hina-ningyo*, a set of fifteen dolls depicting ancient nobles and members of the Japanese imperial family. It was all he had to remind him of the woman he still loved.

At the alcove he knelt, placed the box to one side, then began work on the Ikebana flower arrangement that had been her favorite. It was a casual design, a windswept grouping of pink roses and a single branch of evergreens. He knew exactly what to do with each flower, each branch, just as he knew the exact angle at which each piece should be placed. What had begun as conscious thought in his early study of the way of the flowers had after years become instinctive.

Half an hour later Razan had shaped flowers and greenery into three strong lines leaning far to the right, lines representing heaven-man-earth, the three levels of the cosmos. Supreme beauty. Subdued elegance. Achieved through the greatest restraint and with a minimum of material.

Now to complete his offering to the woman.

He lit incense sticks in front of the flowers, then reached into the black pine box for the dagger. Its handle was covered in sharkskin; the silver pommel was topped by a gold-embossed letter *Y* and the blade was sharp enough to draw blood with a mere touch.

Knife in his right hand, Razan closed his eyes and pressed the flat of the blade against his forehead. *The woman*. He opened his eyes, gritted his teeth. *Now*.

With his left thumb and forefinger he pulled his top lip away from the upper gum. His right hand squeezed the handle of the dagger. A second's hesitation. Then Razan cut into the gum just above the teeth.

He stiffened with pain. His nostrils flared, whitened. Veins leaped against the skin of his temples and neck.

The blood belonged to his oath but he swallowed it, for he believed that doing so was beneficial to his health. With the dagger now in his left hand he lightly tapped the tip of his right finger with the cutting edge. He waited. When the fingertip was bright with blood he gently pushed it under his top lip, touching the gum wound. Holding the finger against the half-inch cut he lightly clicked his teeth together thirty-six times to calm his mind and slow the bleeding.

Razan returned the dagger to the box and picked up the doll's head. With his blood-stained finger he stroked the round face, eyes, forehead, mouth.

"For a samurai," the fiery Yamamoto had told him, "the first center of power, the serpent power it is called, lies at the base of the spine. It contains a channel of control that climbs up the entire spine and travels across the skull to end at the upper gum. Meditation on this center revitalizes a warrior's body, calms his mind, gives him immense inner strength. It gives the warrior unshakable, yes, unshakable confidence in his ability."

An oath sealed in blood from the serpent power and the sword hand. Nothing was more sacred.

Geneva, Switzerland. 1945. It was the last time Razan was to see her. In a hotel room in Carouge, the city's medieval district of fountains, pubs, and tree-shaded squares, he held the weeping sixteen-year-old girl in his arms. "Don't talk such nonsense," he said. "You are not going to die. Hear me. I say you are not going to die. I shall complete my mission, then we will return to Japan—"

"I shall never return to Japan." Her sadness was heartbreaking. "I shall die away from my country. I know this is true."

"Listen to me. I shall see to it you do not die. No one will harm you. I promise you this."

She touched his face with a small hand. "Promise that you will carry a lock of my hair back to Japan and bury it there. Say you will do this for me. I ask nothing else."

"I—"

"I beg you, Razan-san." She started to fall to her knees in front of him, but he held her up. He could not, however, stop her tears.

And in the end, because he knew he would love her for as long as forever was long, he made the promise to her in blood taken from the serpent power, a promise he then failed to keep. Something done that could not be undone. *The woman.* Her name was in the shadow of his soul and he read it night and day.

In his Waikiki apartment, Razan wiped blood from his small mouth with a white silk cloth and glanced over his shoulder at the window facing the park. Soon the *Bon* dancing would stop, then the Buddhists would carry the lighted paper lanterns to one of the park beaches and float them out to sea. He had lit lanterns in the apartment for the woman, as he would have done in Japan. In Japan he, too, would have floated lanterns on water. Perhaps in Yokohama harbor, or on Tokyo's Sumida River, or on the ornamental pond lined with moss behind his Osaka home.

For a few seconds he was caught up in the net of memory,

in a delicious sadness that left the thought of the woman as the only reality. She had left her mark on him forever.

Razan reached out to touch a pink rose and in that instant he knew he was going to leave the apartment with a lantern. Immediately. Cross the street and have the lantern blessed by one of the Buddhist priests. Then carry it through the park until he came to Queen's Surf Beach. Until he reached the sea. He would float a lantern for her as he had every year since her death.

A meeting with the Americans here in the flat was scheduled for eleven o'clock tonight. Razan had over three hours until then. Even walking with a cane as he did would allow him to make it to the beach and back in less than an hour. He needed the woman's help, for the dead were the most venerable of spirit-gods and controlled good and bad fortune. In Japan, the dead were more important than the living and always had to be kept alive in memory.

Razan left the alcove, alerted his bodyguards, then went to his bedroom, where he dressed and weighed the risk of going outside. While Uraga's *yakuza* group, Ginkaku-ji Gumi, Temple of the Silver Pavilion, was active in Hawaii, none of the members had ever seen Razan. Only two of Razan's *yakuza* lieutenants in Honolulu had ever met him, while in Japan hardly anyone even knew he was out of the country. A quick trip into the park, then back. A simple matter. Two armed bodyguards would accompany him. For added protection he would bring the Korean, who was napping in the flat and smelled of garlicked vegetables, and who would also attend the meeting.

Razan finished dressing in a dark summer suit, white shirt, and black tie, then returned to the alcove. Here he broke off a single pink rose, attached it to a paper lantern and looked around to see the bodyguards and the Korean waiting near a sliding door.

No one spoke as they left the flat. Razan wanted it that way. Silence was a discipline. Silence allowed the woman to grow within him.

In the humid twilight Alexis Bendor and members of her jogging club neared the end of a mile run in knee-deep water off Queen's Surf Beach. They were training for the Waikiki Rough Water Swim, held each September, a two-mile run in

deep water from Sans Souci Beach to Duke Kahanamoku
Beach. She was third behind Ramon, the leader, a skinny,
young Filipino in a headset and purple T-shirt reading *Don't
Think—Veg Out*.

Alexis enjoyed running, but Ramon was a fanatic. He did
little else besides attend cockfights and customize his car. For
a change, however, the strong pace he was setting did not
bother her. It helped take Alexis's mind off her son, Simon,
who was a day late in returning from Japan. There had been a
chance of his getting killed there, but nothing Alexis could
have said would have stopped him from going. Simon had to
pay off a debt to a woman who had saved his life. Alexis's
hatred for this woman who had sent Simon to Japan was
inexhaustible.

Good ole Ramon. Didn't slow down after running out of
the water. Led Alexis and the others across an almost empty
beach and into Queen's Surf Park. Past beachboys in cutoffs
playing volleyball, past blinking fireflies hovering at the base
of royal poinciana trees, past laughing Hawaiians reeling in
giant kites out of a darkening sky.

Sweet Jesus, thought Alexis. The bastard's really going
through with it. Going to make us do the Kapiolani jogging
track, another mile and three-quarters.

Tiring and starting to feel a cramp in her right calf, Alexis
dropped three runners behind Ramon.

Dear God, don't let Simon die in Japan.

"What worries me," she had said to her son, "is that
maybe you're doing this for the wrong reason. Let's face it,
buster, you do love to hold the tiger by the tail, you know."

Simon was a professional thief and had told her that in
times of extreme danger he was capable of doing things that
were ordinarily impossible. Only when taking risks did he
really feel alive.

He took her hands in his and squeezed. "There's more to
this one than walking a tightrope without a net. I owe Erica
for saving my life and that means she owns a piece of me.
Now, if I don't get that piece back, I'm going to end up
hating her and I don't want that. Gratitude's a heavy load to
carry, especially for me. Okay, so you don't approve of
Erica—"

"I didn't say I didn't like her."

"Alexis, Alexis. This is me, remember? You look at her

sometimes like you want to rip her lips off. I wish you two would get along. She likes you.''

"I'm sure you give her enough love for the both of us. Meanwhile her sister's in deep shit and you could get killed trying to pull her out.''

Simon looked away from his mother. "I don't have much choice. If it wasn't for Erica I'd be dead. Her sister's going to be dead, too, if something isn't done soon to get her out of Japan. Our government won't help and the Japanese government doesn't care.'' He looked at his mother. "The hardest thing for me to do, kiddo, is stay here and watch it happen.''

A tearful Alexis took him in her arms. "Erica giveth and Erica taketh away. I suppose in the fullness of time I could learn to love her, but at the moment she's not worth putting my hand in the fire for. It'll go against the grain to have you sent back to me in a body bag. I plan on taking it goddam hard. Show me a good loser and I'll show you a loser.''

He grinned, gently brushing his fist under her chin. "I'll be fine, don't worry. I'm just like van Gogh. Whatever you tell me goes in one ear and stays there.''

No formal goodbyes. No face-to-face farewells. Simon might have survived, but Alexis never would have made it. She would have collapsed, fallen apart in front of him. She loved her son too much. One morning she awoke in the luxury home they shared on Honolulu's Mount Tantalus and knew he was gone. Barely able to breathe, she got out of bed, slipped into a housecoat, and hurried down the hall to his room.

Empty. Bed made. Dawn coming in through the sliding glass doors of a bedroom looking onto a Norfolk pine sun deck that Simon had built himself. Everything in its place, a room as exact and as precise as Simon himself. The papers he left behind were neat, too, in three rows on top of a white wicker desk facing a picture window. Alexis stared down at them through her tears. Simon's will, insurance policies, keys to safety deposit boxes, property deeds, checkbooks. And a letter to his attorney, witnessed and notarized, appointing Alexis coexecutor of Simon's estate.

For a long time, she sat on the edge of his bed and stared east over the dew-slicked rain forest. Toward Japan.

Alexis Gladys Bendor was sixty-three, an exceptionally tall

woman with a sharp watchful face, gray eyes, and dyed blond hair held in place by a headband she had braided out of Jade vines. In the July heat she wore a cutoff gray sweatshirt, white shorts, running shoes, and a pedometer strapped to her thigh for an exact record of her daily mileage. She had lived in Hawaii thirty years, was a widow, and owned a bookstore in a Waikiki shopping center. During World War II she had been a brilliant cryptoanalyst. It was a job that had left her feeling superior to most people, not because of knowing secrets, but because she was doing work that not one in a thousand could do.

On the jogging track in Kapiolani Park she watched Ramon slow down to a trot, then begin walking. Praise be. The run was over. Time to head home, get out of her wet clothes, and into a dry martini posthaste. But not before warming down. Ramon's law.

He led them in a slow stroll along the inside of the track, leaving the outside to joggers and other running clubs. A passing runner called Alexis's name and she lifted an arm in weary greeting as he sped past her into the dusk. Her landlord. A thirtyish overachiever who had come to Hawaii from Maryland only six years ago and now owned $200 million in island real estate. Two heart attacks, plus Alexis's urging had convinced him to drop sixty pounds, cut back on his twenty-hour workdays, and start running.

Alexis herself had been frightened into running. High blood pressure, overweight, a two-and-a-half-pack-a-day smoking habit, and a lump on her right breast that had scared her shitless. The lump had turned out to be benign, but the five days she had waited to learn this had been the longest five days of her life.

That's when Simon had taken charge. He knew how to handle her. Neither of them liked being told what to do. Both were stirred by their own impulses and had a pride that placed them at a distance from other people. And each loved the other dearly.

He started with bribery. If she stayed off the weed a year, a new Mercedes. At the end of six months, a thousand dollars for every pound she had lost. He would outline an exercise and diet program and see her through it. Simon himself followed a rigid workout and nutrition program, maintaining a state of physical fitness equal to his days as Hawaii's high school gymnastic champion.

Daily Alexis gulped down vitamins by the handful, carefully measured her grams of protein on a tiny scale, and developed a taste for carob brownies and meals without red meat. She kicked the weed cold turkey, lost twenty pounds (collected from Simon on that), and saw her blood pressure drop to that of a woman half her age. The ringing in her ears stopped, her sciatica eased off, and her occasional double vision disappeared entirely.

Ramon's warm-down finished. Short walk, some stretching, and it was goodbye until tomorrow evening. Alexis left the track with Leonard, a stocky Portuguese museum guard, and Gloryette, a former Tennessee schoolteacher. Now increasingly worried about Simon, Alexis let Leonard and Gloryette do most of the talking. Both were discussing the merits of *pakalolo,* Hawaii's home-grown marijuana.

From what Alexis could gather, the two had tried them all—Kona Gold, Puna Butter, Kauai Electric, and the most potent of all, Maui Wowee. Well, marijuana was Hawaii's biggest cash crop after all, surpassing the money earned by the sugar and pineapple industries. Neither Alexis nor Simon ever touched the stuff. God, Simon didn't even believe in aspirin.

"Hey, over there." Leonard pointed to the crowd.

Alexis squinted into the twilight and nodded when she saw the paper lanterns strung near a giant banyan tree. *"Bon* dancers."

Gloryette shivered. "Creepy is what it is. Dead comin' back to life and all. My daddy always said that when you die somebody's always glad you're gone."

"Chanting's stopped," said Leonard. He grinned. "Hope it wasn't something we said."

Trailed by Leonard and Gloryette, Alexis walked toward the *Bon* dancers and their audience. "They're getting ready to bless the lanterns before floating them on water," she said. Feast of the Dead. Feast of Lanterns. She visualized Simon's face and in it the two men she had loved, both of whom were now dead. She trembled as she caught herself wondering if Simon were still alive.

As the Buddhist priests silently blessed the lanterns, the

crowd became quiet. Except for a raucous group of Australian tourists.

Alexis squatted down to massage her sore calf. And froze in place. At first she thought it was her imagination, that by thinking too much of Simon she had unhinged her mind. Remaining close to the ground, she listened carefully, listened with her ears and mind. Then grew frightened. As if in a dream she rose slowly from the ground and turned toward the sound, the absentminded gesture of a ring tapping against the head of a cane.

Stunned, Alexis stared at the man who was doing the tapping. He was behind Leonard, *right behind him.*

With her terror now came anger. In seconds her nerves were strung tight and she became like a tiger.

Her head snapped toward the boisterous Australians and she screamed, "Goddam it, be quiet! Shut up, shut up, shut up!"

The hysteria in her voice paralyzed them. Others in the crowd stared at her; a few edged away. Leonard's jaw dropped. Gloryette slowly reached out for Alexis, finally deciding to risk touching her, gently, on the shoulder. Alexis heard whispers, heard her name being called, but she and the man with the cane had now locked eyes.

The tapping . . .

Alexis remembered one of the first rules of cryptology. *Each code sender has an individual touch, one as distinctive as fingerprints and as impossible to duplicate.*

She looked past Leonard to see Rupert de Jongh staring at her. Older, yes, with a few lines in his face, and he leaned on a cane. But he had the same cold elegance, long nose, blue eyes. And amused smile.

He was flanked by three Orientals, one of whom held a lighted paper lantern. Two were Japanese with flat haircuts and hard, unsmiling faces; the one with the lantern was missing a pinky finger. The third Oriental was a small Korean with large ears and a baggy, gray suit. He wore an expensive Rolex on each wrist. Alexis knew him. What was his name? *What the hell was his name?*

De Jongh and Alexis stared at each other. Did he recognize her after almost thirty-nine years?

And then his hand went to his right ear. Alexis flinched and reached out for Leonard's arm. He asked if she was ill,

while Gloryette took her elbow and tried to guide her away
from the crowd. But Alexis stood rooted to the spot, refusing
to budge. Instead she and de Jongh eyed one another as she
lifted her right hand and patted the hair hiding the scar tissue
where her right ear used to be.

The silver-haired de Jongh nodded silently. Recognition.
Alexis felt him stare into her very soul with the same powerful life force that had terrified her almost forty years ago.
That terrified her even now. The Korean averted his face and
with his back to Alexis now angrily whispered to de Jongh.

The sense of danger hit Alexis like a kick in the stomach.
She wasn't supposed to see de Jongh, nor see him and the
Korean together. Alexis looked away to say something to
Gloryette, but no words came out. She turned back to stare at
de Jongh, but the Englishman and the Orientals with him had
disappeared.

And Alexis knew that she was the hunted once more,
stalked by the man called *gaijin*.

Three

Simon Bendor stood in front of a wall of floor-to-ceiling windows in the bedroom of his condominium and gazed into the darkness at his own reflection. He watched himself carefully wrap bandages around his bare rib cage. He wore white jeans and *zoris,* the rubber sandals that were a popular Hawaiian beachwear. There were bloodied scratches on his forehead and left cheek.

Bandages tied, he massaged his aching left elbow. More reflections in the tall, gray-tinted windows: a mirrored wall and an Elizabethan-style four-poster bed behind him, with bloodstained bandages lying near one of the bed's oversize pillows. Looking at the bandages made him feel as though he had been hurting forever. Pain made for a very long day.

The condominum was on the thirty-fifth floor of a new Columbus Avenue high-rise, with a spectacular view of Central Park and the city's skyline. To keep the view as uncluttered as possible, Simon had done without curtains and instead had framed the huge windows with hanging moss, tall palms, and giant ferns. The furnishings were a careful mixture of English and French antiques, with a handful of new pieces selected for him by his mother. Simon had her telephoned minutes ago. She wasn't home and she wasn't at the bookstore.

He walked from the window to the bed, sat down near a pile of blood-stained bandages, and closed his eyes. Bone tired. Jet lag. Left side starting to throb again. Flopping back on the bed, he massaged his aching eyes with his fingertips. He had rescued Erica's sister, Molly, from the *yakuza* in Tokyo and now both women were in the apartment with him. The rescue was the closest he had come to getting wasted since Nam.

He opened his eyes. Change that. Closest he had come since the night he first met Erica.

Simon Bendor was in his mid-thirties, five foot nine and wiry, with the blond, green-eyed good looks of a cold angel. He was a thief. He had been one since finishing his Vietnam tour with a special CIA unit ten years ago. In that time he had stolen over $100 million in jewels, cash, antiques, collectibles, and bonds. He worked alone and at night, carried no weapons, and avoided all confrontation. Intelligent and bold, he maintained the outstanding physical condition that had made him a record-setting high school athlete. He was addicted to stealing, not for the money, but for the excitement.

He refused to steal or fence stolen goods in Hawaii. It was home and there was enough uncertainty and expectation in life without bringing any to his front door. Hawaii was sanctuary, a place to enjoy the lemon odor of white hibiscus as he drove along the winding road leading to his mountaintop home. Hawaii was jogging on a lava bed 150,000 years old and basking in winters with a low temperature of 71 degrees. Hawaii was dining in restaurants built around miniature waterfalls and fish ponds, while gazing at the most beautiful sunsets in the world.

He stole in New York. And along the mainland's East Coast. He owned a twelve-room Manhattan condominium, a Honolulu home, and real estate in Hawaii and on the mainland. He also owned a health club in Honolulu and one in Manhattan. His stock portfolio was a good one, thanks to his mother's knowledge of the market, and he was a partner in a Honolulu antique shop owned by a friend, a Japanese-American named Paul Anami.

The business investments left Simon covered for tax purposes. Taxes were the dues he paid for peace of mind.

In the bedroom he forced himself to open his eyes. Of course. Have Paul telephone Alexis. Let him track her down. But first dispose of the blood-stained bandages and look in on Erica and Molly. He left the bedroom, the bandages balled in his hand, and walked along a thickly carpeted hallway, then across a sunken living room until he reached the kitchen. Here he tied the bandages inside a black plastic garbage bag but decided against the incinerator. There was always the chance the bag might get stuck in the chute going down, or be discovered by someone working in the basement. Simon would dispose of the bag himself, away from the building. No one could guard his secrets better than he.

He left the kitchen and walked to the guest bedroom nearest his, where he stood listening at the door. Erica and Molly were asleep. Both women had been exhausted; an emotional reunion had drained them even more. Simon looked down at the light coming from beneath the door. Molly had been shaken by what had happened to her in Japan. In three weeks there she came to fear the darkness and now could not sleep unless the lights were on.

Simon cracked the bedroom door and peeked inside. The sisters slept on twin brass Victorian daybeds, which Alexis had purchased on London's Portobello Road. Erica Styler, the oldest, slept nearest the fireplace. She was dark-haired with brown eyes, in her early thirties, slender and almost as tall as Simon, and had fallen asleep on top of the covers wearing one of his robes. She was a professional gambler, the most skilled woman poker player in the game and as ruthless as any man. Simon had been drawn by her fearlessness. Before Erica he had deliberately shut out love and so it surprised him when he realized how quickly he had fallen in love with her.

Molly January, the January was a stage name, slept in the bed facing the window. She was in her early twenties, a childlike blonde with a waifish face on a woman's body. Eighteen months ago she had been a $250-a-week hairdresser in Queens. Now she called herself an actress and bounced back and forth between auditions in New York and Los Angeles, picking up only the occasional small job. Simon thought her without talent and too undisciplined to get the necessary training. She was self-centered, quarrelsome, and obstinate in the belief that she was destined to lead an exceptional life.

Last month Molly had gotten lucky. Or so she thought. A Los Angeles talent agent named Victor Pascal had booked her in Tokyo. She was to work in a new club as a singer and dancer, with a promise of modeling work on the side. But there was a word for Pascal's promises. Industrial-strength bullshit. When Molly arrived in Tokyo the only job waiting for her had been as a hostess in a cheap nightclub owned by the *yakuza*. And they had not hired her to sing or dance.

Her letters to Erica told of being threatened for refusing to become a prostitute and perform live sex shows. It became worse when Molly rejected the sexual advances of a *yakuza* boss. He flew into a rage, yanked her hair, and kicked her. One club hostess then gave Molly a warning: give in to this guy if you want to live. He had already killed two foreign girls who hadn't done as he ordered.

Nor could Molly leave Japan. The club owners had taken her passport "to protect it from thieves" and were also holding back most of the money due under her contract. There was no telephone in her flat and she and the new girls were prevented from using telephones at the club. They were watched at all times. She needed help and there was only Erica. Erica, after trying and failing to get Molly out of Japan, turned to Simon.

"I feel afraid," she said to him. "And I feel guilty as well. I was supposed to take care of her. Now look where she is."

Simon thought, You can't help her, but she can damn sure drag you down.

Erica reached into her purse for a sugarless mint, a new nervous habit since Simon had convinced her to give up smoking. "I promised my parents before they died that I'd watch out for Molly. She was always getting into trouble. Eventually I developed what I thought was an easy way to deal with her. Just throw money and hope she goes away. My life centered around the card table. Wasn't room there for anybody who wasn't a player."

"Stop kicking yourself. You did your best. Didn't you tell me that Molly was always a little short on brains?"

"My dad always said she would plant eggs to get chickens. Not too smart, my sister. But you know something? Will you tell me just who the hell these fucking people are who think they can trick a woman into leaving the country, then turn her into a whore because they feel like it?"

She almost lost control. Almost. For a few seconds she was vulnerable and afraid. She looked at her purse and Simon knew what she was thinking. The gun. Like other gamblers she sometimes carried large sums of money and with it a licensed .357 magnum. Twice Erica had shot men attempting to rob her.

Simon took her in his arms and kissed her hair. "Get me a passport-size photograph of Molly if you can. If not, just give me what you have. I want it as soon as possible. We have to make up a passport for her. One more thing: no more letters or cables to her. And stay away from consulates and the agent who sent her to Japan."

"I don't understand."

"If you warn Molly I'm coming, you'll be warning whoever's watching her. At the most I'm giving us both two days to take care of a few things, then we're going to see Paul."

"Paul Anami? I thought you always worked alone."

"I do. It's a rule I've never broken and never will. But Paul's Japanese and he knows the *yakuza* from firsthand experience. If we're going to the senior prom, we'd better learn how to dance."

Paul Anami sat in his office behind the antique shop and read Molly's letters to Erica. When he finished he reached down to pick up a sleeping Akita puppy and place it on his lap. For a few seconds he stroked the plump animal's broad head. He had begun breeding them as a hobby. Eventually the hobby had become a profitable sideline. He was now the leading breeder of Akitas in Honolulu, selling puppies for an average of $2,000 each.

Anami looked at Erica and Simon sitting in front of him and said, "Blond hair, round eyes, big boobs. Very popular with Japanese men. Three things Japanese like to do when they come to Hawaii: fire guns, gamble, and have a blond prostitute. Guns are illegal in Japan and blondes are rare. Gambling? Well, you can find that anywhere in the world.

"What they did to your sister happens all the time on the mainland. Phony ads in show business trade papers telling girls they can make big money and become an international star by working in Japan. It's the *yakuza* operating through unscrupulous American talent agents in Los Angeles, San Francisco, Phoenix, Dallas, other cities. Hard to resist a job offer when you're a young, pretty girl starting out in show business. It's usually the ones who can't make it in America who get caught up in this scam. Please forgive me. I mean no insult to your sister, but these are the facts."

Paul Anami continued stroking the Akita. The Japanese-American was in his mid-thirties, a spare little man whose solemn face still retained a youthful softness. Only his darting eyes betrayed the uneasiness lurking behind a gentle charm. Simon was one of the few who knew that Anami, a close friend since their high school days, was being treated for nerves. Under his calm exterior the antique dealer was tense and highstrung.

He was dressed in a pale green caftan, smelled of Paco Rabanne, and wore a gold Maltese cross around his neck. There were several thin jade bracelets studded with amethysts on one wrist. His slanted eyes were hidden behind rimless blue-tinted glasses, and all his fingernails were bitten to the quick.

He said to Erica, "You mentioned that the Japanese consulate in Los Angeles did nothing."

"In a polite way, of course. Told me it was not government policy to get involved with the work problems of foreigners in Japan. It's obvious they don't want foreigners working in their country and if they get in trouble working there, shame on them. I received five minutes of the consulate's time, then it was out the door and don't bother coming back."

"Japanese have little respect for foreign women," said Anami. "They enjoy seeing them sexually humiliated. Sad to say, Japan is a racist society. The American government wasn't much better, am I right?"

"Sympathy. And that's it. You meet some heavy-duty people playing poker and one of them put me in touch with a State Department official. This tightass had the nerve to tell me that my sister wouldn't be the first stranded tourist to concoct a little scam in order to get a free ticket home."

Anami leaned forward and picked up the top letter. "Ah, America the beautiful. My father told me that in the internment camps some of the Japanese-Americans actually sang that song. How's that for patriotism? According to this, Molly's return address is in the Roppongi district." He looked at Simon. "Your old stomping grounds."

"I made two R and R trips to Tokyo," said Simon. "After Nam, Japan was heaven on earth. Roppongi was popular with GI's because there was always someone around who spoke

English. Clubs, discos, pizza joints, sex shows. Great place. Molly says they might move her somewhere else.''

"That bastard Pascal," said Erica. "Him and the scuzzo working with him. Nora Barf."

"Bart," said Simon. "Nora Bart."

Erica snorted. "She and Pascal promised Molly she'd make a thousand dollars a week in Tokyo. Promised her a round-trip ticket in advance. But the day Molly and the two other girls were due to fly out of L.A., Pascal and *Miss Barf* show up at the airport with a one-way ticket for everybody. Gave the girls some lame excuse about a mixup and how it would be all straightened out once they got to Japan. As far as I'm concerned, I'd be delighted if an elephant were to use Miss Barf as a tampon."

Erica's smile was as cold and as hard as a key. "In one letter, Molly calls Pascal 'Dickbreath.' If I ever run into him I'm going to cut it off. With the rustiest pair of scissors I can find."

Anami opened a desk drawer, removed a small bottle of pills and put two in his mouth, washing them down with mineral water. "You've never met Pascal?"

"No. I had a friend in L.A. check him out. Marilyn, that's my friend, she says Pascal used to be in show business himself. A singer."

"And . . ."

"And Marilyn says Pascal's a sleazeball. A chronic liar. Year doesn't go by that the guilds and unions don't have him up on charges. Sexual harassment, bad checks, overcharging on commissions. Charging for auditions, which are actually free. Selling ads in nonexistent trade publications. The man's so greedy he'd eat the hair off a dog."

"According to Marilyn," said Simon, "Pascal and Nora Bart left for Toyko day before yesterday. His office is on the Sunset Strip. He has one receptionist and she leaves at 3:30 every day."

Anami looked down at the Akita as it chewed his thumb. "So what's breaking into his office going to get you?"

Simon tapped his temple with a forefinger. "You sharp, bruddah. Very *akamai*. Very smart. Mr. Pascal used to be an entertainer, we're told. A singer who never made it. Which means he's got an ego. Which means he's still got photographs of himself on the premises. A quick peek at his desk diary and I should be able to learn where he and Nora Bart are staying in Tokyo. My plan is to find Pascal and make him tell me where Molly is. I figure he ought to know. After that Molly and I are going to get the hell out as fast as we can.''

Anami placed the Akita on the floor, then reached for a folder on his desk. He opened it to reveal a typed two-page report. ''Okay, let's talk about the *yakuza*. These are the minutes of the last Chamber of Commerce meeting. I'm a member of that august body, though I sometimes wonder why.''

He pushed the report toward Simon. ''Almost eight hundred thousand Japanese a year visit Hawaii and the mainland. They spend a billion and a half dollars. That's a lot of *kala*, a lot of money. It's also a very big reason why the *yakuza* are on the islands and the mainland. They've forced their way into the Japanese tour business here, San Francisco, Los Angeles, and other American cities as well. Everything from sightseeing tours to Japanese bars, from souvenir shops to some of our better-known Waikiki hotels. *Yakuza*-owned lock, stock, and souvenir T-shirt.''

He leaned down to stroke the Akita. ''They launder a lot of money here through legitimate fronts. Plantations, condominiums, restaurants, bars, banks. Same thing on the mainland. They move dope in and out of Hawaii. Easier to get it into Japan from here than to bring it, say, from Southeast Asia into Japan. They buy guns here and on the mainland.''

Anami sat up in his chair and looked at Simon. ''This means you can't bring Molly back here to Hawaii, assuming all goes well and you do get her out of Japan.''

Simon looked up from the report. ''Jesus, I should have thought of that. I had planned to let her rest at my home here for a few days. But you're right, she might be recognized.''

''By a *yakuza* courier who travels between Japan and Hawaii. By someone who remembers her from a *yakuza* club in Tokyo.''

Anami looked at Erica. ''She can't stay with you in Las Vegas either. The *yakuza* are very big on gambling junkets to Las Vegas, Atlantic City, London, the Caribbean.''

''No shit,'' said Erica. ''You can't gamble without running up against *them* sooner or later.''

''The junkets are operated in connection with American organized crime,'' said Anami. ''The *yakuza* deliver the players, who lose money to 'the boys' and are forced to borrow from the *yakuza* at horrendous rates of interest. Everybody wins, except the gamblers.''

Anami leaned back in his rattan chair and stared at a revolving ceiling fan. "The *yakuza* have loan companies called *sarakin*. Means salary-finance. Truth is, these companies are little more than loan sharks and it's all done in conjunction with the banks. The banks advance the *sarakin* millions of dollars and are happy to do it, bruddah. Know why? Because banks can only charge 14 percent interest a year. *Sarakin* can charge the earth and, believe me, they do. That's why it's become a national scandal in Japan, where the *sarakin* can hit you for 150 percent interest a year or more and do whatever they want to get the money back.''

He looked at Erica. "They murder people who can't pay back, burn their homes, force women into prostitution, beat up old men. I have a Japanese friend over there, he's in prison now. He killed a taxi driver, someone he'd never seen before. Did it so he'd be sent away where the *yakuza* couldn't get him. Last year an old couple in Kyoto borrowed money to pay medical bills. When they couldn't repay a *sarakin* company, the *yakuza* held the old woman's feet in the fire. She was eighty-three. They made her husband watch. He died of a heart attack.''

A nervous tic started near Anami's left eye. "They killed my parents.'' It was a few seconds before he could go on. "My parents immigrated from Japan to California. San Diego. That's where I was born. They were interned and after the war they came to Hawaii to start over. My father did well as a fish exporter, but he had always planned to retire to Japan. When the time came, he did. Took some of his money and invested in a very big Tokyo electronics company. That's when he ran up against the *yakuza*. That's when . . .''

He reached for the pills, swallowed two more, and cracked his knuckles. "They call it *Sokaiya*, a form of corporate blackmail practiced by the *yakuza*. For a price they promise not to disrupt stockholders meetings and to see that nobody else does either. Sometimes they buy a single share of stock, then sell it back to the corporation for a very, very high price. That way the *yakuza* can claim they're only receiving payment for shares they own and not for head breaking. Anyway, my father questioned certain payments made by the corporation. Payoffs, bribes, that sort of thing. Well, the *yakuza* goon squad tried to shut him up. My father refused. Lots of arguing, threats, then finally the head breakers took my father from the meeting by force. Next day he was dead. Police said he'd been drinking and rammed his car into a truck.''

He patted Erica's hand. "Make it easy on Simon. Do exactly as he tells you, understand?''

"Yes.''

Simon closed the folder and dropped it on Anami's desk. "Paul, I'd like you to get me a schedule of passenger ships and freighters leaving Tokyo next Monday and Tuesday.''

Erica's eyes widened. "That's three days from now. Can you find Molly and get her out that fast?''

He looked over his shoulder, then grinned at her and Anami. "Let you two in on a little secret. Casing the joint is overrated. It's also dangerous as hell. All it does is give people more chance to spot you. The less time I spend in Tokyo, the better. In all probability, we'll come out by plane. But I always like to have a back door.''

"You'll have that list later today,'' said Anami.

"How's Alexis taking this?'' asked Erica. "I know she's not too fond of me. Still can't figure out why, unless she just doesn't like lady card players. Funny thing. She's one lady whose friendship I'd like, but just can't seem to get.''

"Alexis understands why I have to go,'' said Simon. "Like Popeye, I am what I am. Far as you and her are concerned, give it time. She'll come around.''

"I hope so. Your mother's very special. And so's her son.'' Erica moved closer to Simon until their faces touched. "I used to think that whenever you became fond of someone you gave them all they needed to use against you. I don't feel that way with you. Take care.''

It was the closest Erica, a self-contained and very private woman, had ever come to telling Simon she loved him.

The two were about to leave Anami's office when he gently caught Simon by the elbow, pulling him away from Erica. When she was out of earshot, the antique dealer said, "When?''

"Leaving tomorrow morning.''

"I thought it would be soon.''

"Los Angeles for a few days, then Tokyo. I'll tell Erica over dinner tonight.''

Anami touched Simon on the forearm. "Watch yourself over there. If they get their hands on you, they won't go easy. If they catch you, well, all I can tell you is they never forget. Remember that, Simon. They never forget."

The Tokyo heat bothered Victor Pascal even more than the city's crowds and noise. By late afternoon the temperature was in the high eighties, so he told Nora Bart, fuck it, they were going back to the hotel where there was air conditioning and a pool.

Back at the suite, Pascal decided to check out room service before taking a swim. Have drinks sent up, maybe something light to eat like a salad or a dish of ice cream. Anything, so long as it was cool. Nora would want to order, too. The woman ate more than Pac Man and still never gained weight.

She entered the suite behind him, arms filled with packages, and happier than a pig in shit because they had finally gotten the chance to go shopping. Three days in Tokyo and all they had done in that time was meet with Kisen and his people or wait around for the meetings to happen. Kisen had insisted they be on call at all times. He was the highest-ranking *yakuza* Pascal and Nora had ever met, a humorless man who demanded instant obedience. When that prick told you something, you listened.

In four years of working with *yakuza* Pascal had yet to meet the boss man, the *oyabun*. Even Kisen, as coldblooded as they come, seemed highly respectful of his mysterious leader. Pascal had once mentioned getting together with the *oyabun* for drinks, and all Kisen had done was sneer and say that such a meeting would take place only if Pascal were to "stumble and offend." In other words, when Pascal fucked up. Then he would see the *oyabun* for the first and last time. Point made.

But after a one o'clock meeting today Kisen had told Pascal and Nora they were free until evening, when they were to join him for dinner and more talk on Pascal's new role in the *oyabun*'s American expansion. An excited Nora then dragged Pascal to boutiques and shops along the Ginza and finally to a *depato*, a huge department store near their hotel. Inside they had fought their way from floor to floor in a store so large that it contained God knows how many restaurants, several supermarkets, and a couple of rooftop museums. *Museums.* Not to mention a few hundred thousand customers.

Pascal made at least two trips a year to Japan on business and each time the crush of people seemed to get worse. Thousands of buses jammed top to bottom with riders. Sidewalks flooded with millions of elbowing, pushing, shoving Japs. Subways with cars of passengers packed in like sardines. Streets solid with trucks, cars, motorbikes, and bicycles. The crowds, traffic, and noise were bad enough. Add the heat and in the end Pascal was wiped out.

In the hotel suite he stretched his arms overhead and breathed in cool air. Now this was more like it. The peace and quiet of four large Western-style rooms with a bar, fridge, closed-circuit television in English, and a view overlooking a landscaped Japanese garden three floors below.

Victor Pascal was in his late forties, a mulatto who disliked being called black and who not so jokingly referred to himself as "light, bright, and damned near white." He was a large, handsome man with straight black hair, a pencil-thin mustache, and an anxious smile, which weakened his good looks. His world revolved around women, with whom he was brutish and pleasing by turns. He supported himself by using and cheating them as it suited him, yet still could not do without their admiration and affection.

Like others, he had been exploited by the entertainment industry, but in the end he had failed because he had always sought the most pleasure in life and the least pain. He could sing pretty good, but in Hollywood there were a lot of good singers waiting tables, parking cars, and pumping gas. That's when he became a dangerous manipulator of other people's lives. This was his second talent, being able to talk trash to women, to con them into believing anything. In Hollywood, lying to a bitch was a way of life and Pascal did it as well as anybody.

What's your name, mama, and what's your pleasure? And if I have to send your ass to Japan for a job that ain't there, ain't no big thing.

The *yakuza* paid top dollar for blondes, fresh young pussy, no old meat. And they also paid Pascal for being a mule between California and Honolulu, for carrying handguns to Hawaii on so-called business trips. On return trips he would bring back cash, to be picked up in his office by a Jap who usually never smiled and damned sure had no time for small talk. Sometimes Pascal did a dope run from Honolulu to Los Angeles or San Francisco and that's when he came close to getting gravy stains on his underwear. Thinking about the feds catching you with two kilos of heroin in your shoulder bag would make anybody shit in his pants.

It was too late for Pascal to complain. With the *yakuza*, once you were in, you best go along with the program. He knew of two Americans who had wanted out. One had been dumb enough to threaten to bring in the cops. A week later he was found on his boat in the marina, hanging from a shower head. Suicide, said the harbor patrol. The second guy died in a cabin fire when a heater exploded. Accident, said state troopers.

The smart thing to do was keep quiet all the way to the bank. Just stay cool and come away with some nice money. That's what Pascal's current trip to Japan was all about. He stood to get richer because the *oyabun* planned to expand operations in Hawaii and on the mainland. It all had to do with a new arrangement involving some heavy-duty mob people from New York. Without knowing all the details, Pascal knew it involved drugs, gambling, guns, and legitimate businesses. Being a part of something this big was scary, but at the same time it excited him to be a player.

In the living room of their hotel suite, Pascal watched Nora Bart flop back on a white leather couch, kick off her shoes, and begin massaging her feet. He enjoyed watching her. She was never self-conscious. The bitch had no shame, which was one reason he kept her around. She was cheerfully immoral, with an underlying hardness that made her invaluable to him when it came to taking care of business.

Nora Bart was thirty, a thin, pretty woman with punkish short hair dyed a light pink and the lean, muscled arms and legs of a dancer. When Pascal met her she had been on the fringes of Hollywood, a sometime aerobics teacher, waitress, dance extra in music videos, supermarket clerk, and when all else failed a bisexual hooker peddling her bodacious ass to both sexes. He liked her croaky voice, her style and nerve, and her willingness to do anything for money.

Pascal slipped out of a black silk shirt made darker by perspiration and dropped it on the floor. Nora would pick up after him. He fingered the three gold chains hanging from his

neck, then raised a hand overhead and placed his nose near
one armpit. He recoiled in mock horror. "Goddamn. Smells
like something crawled up in there and died. Know something, baby? If I owned Tokyo and hell, I'd rent out Tokyo
and live in hell. Hey, do me a favor and check out room
service. Have them send up a couple bottles of Perrier, lots of
ice, and some vanilla ice cream. You . . ."

Nora wasn't listening. She was looking off to the right,
staring bug-eyed at something. It was enough to make Pascal
go up side her head for not paying attention, until he followed
her gaze and almost jumped out of his skin. Holy shit. A man
wearing the uniform of a U.S. Army captain stood in the
bedroom doorway. Big as life. The man was medium height,
had dark hair, a mustache, and wore oversize sunglasses. He
also wore surgical gloves and in one hand he held an eight-by-
ten glossy.

Pascal had no way of knowing that the photograph was of
him taken eleven years ago. In it he was smiling, wore a
tuxedo, and sat straddling a chair back to front, hands carefully folded on the back of the chair to show off a gold
bracelet and three gold rings. The captain studied the photograph, looked at Pascal, then folded the glossy twice before
sticking it in a back pocket.

He walked toward Pascal as laid-back as you please. "Both
of you on the floor. Facedown, hands behind your neck. Stay
cool and nobody gets hurt." His voice had a Godfather-type
huskiness to it. Pascal knew nightclub comics who got that
sound by stuffing cotton in their cheeks.

Pascal, however, was rapidly getting over being afraid.
The dude was probably drunk or stoned on some recreational
drug and had managed to get into the wrong room. And was
now coming on like one of the truly weird. Well, Pascal was
bigger and the guy wasn't flashing any piece. Push come to
shove, Pascal could easily trash this sucker.

"Fuck is this, some kind of joke?" asked Pascal. "You in
my room, Jack, and I don't lie down on the floor for you or
anybody else."

The captain grinned. And kicked Pascal in the shins. The
talent agent doubled over with pain, reaching down with both
hands for the injured limb. In the time it took Pascal to touch
his ankle, the captain trashed him. One step and the Captain
was behind Pascal, strong hands on the talent agent's bare

shoulders. Then Pascal felt himself being yanked backward.
Yanked hard. Right across the captain's outstretched left leg.
For a second Pascal hung in the air, thinking this shit ain't
happening to me, then he hit the floor hard, felt the ache in
every bone, and could only lay there, the wind knocked out
of him.

The captain leaned over and with the fingers of his right
hand squeezed the stricken man's larynx. A slight twist and
Pascal gagged. In his soft-harsh voice the captain said, "If I
have to tell you again, it's going to hurt a lot more. That's not
a threat, pimp, it's a promise."

The captain looked across the room at a silent Nora Bart
sitting primly on the couch, ankles crossed, hands folded in
her lap, taking it all in without any outward show of fear. She
seemed to find it interesting. Then without a word she got up,
walked over to Pascal, and lay down by his side. For a few
seconds she propped herself up on one hip and elbow, quickly
glancing at Pascal but gazing longer at the man in uniform.
Finally, she turned over on her stomach, but not before
looking at the captain with blatant sexual interest.

After Pascal rolled over to lie facedown, the captain rose
and walked to the bedroom, returning with a small brown
suitcase. He opened it, took out handcuffs, and cuffed the
couple's hands in back of them. Next, he walked to the house
phone and, with his back to Pascal and Nora, dialed the front
desk. Neither of them saw him remove cotton from his cheeks
while he waited.

Then, "Yes, this is Mr. Pascal in 305. We're about to take
a nap. I'd appreciate your holding all calls until further
notice. Yes. All calls, without exception. Thank you." He
hung up, replaced the cotton in his mouth, and returned to his
suitcase. From it he removed a roll of adhesive tape, tore off
two sections, and carefully placed them over Nora Bart's
mouth. Then, laying the roll of tape aside, he took a handkerchief from his suitcase, crushed it into a ball, and with the
thumb and forefinger of one hand pinched Pascal's nostrils
closed. When the mulatto opened his mouth to breath, the
captain shoved in the handkerchief.

As Pascal shouted against the gag in his mouth, the captain
tore off two sections of tape, turned Pascal over on his back,
then placed both pieces of tape over the holes in the mulatto's
nose, deliberately smoothing down the tape until the nostrils

were airtight. When he had finished the captain sat back and calmly watched Pascal panic.

The mulatto's face became discolored, turning blue, then red. His eyes bulged and he bucked and twisted on the floor. The captain grinned. After several seconds he reached over and pulled the handkerchief from Pascal's mouth.

The mulatto loudly sucked in air. His chest rose and fell. He had never been so terrified in his life.

"One time," said the captain. "You dick me around, the handkerchief goes back in and stays in. Molly January. She still living in the Roppongi district?"

Pascal blinked tears from his eyes and nodded. "She there. She there. Don't put that thing back in my mouth no more. Don't do that."

The captain took the tape from Nora's mouth. "Is Dark Gable here telling the truth? Because if he's not, we play hanky-panky again."

Nora nodded and kept on nodding, her small face scraping the rug. "She's still at the same place and working in the same club. Tomorrow they're moving her. Tomorrow."

The captain turned his attention back to Pascal. He dangled the wet handkerchief over the mulatto's face, swinging it back and forth like a pendulum. The terrorized Pascal jerked away from its touch. "She there, man, I swear on my mother she there."

The captain took the tape from Pascal's nose. "If she isn't, I'm coming back. And just to make sure you don't run out on me—"

His hand went into the suitcase and came out with a small black case. When he opened it Pascal groaned. "Oh, shit, man, not that."

The captain held up a hypodermic, thumb on the plunger. He grinned as though this was the most fun he'd had in quite a while. "Something to ease your troubled mind. Nappy-poo time, everybody."

"Hey man, I don't like no needles. I—"

The captain jabbed Pascal in the right bicep. When the mulatto was unconscious the captain stepped across his body and looked down at Nora Bart.

"How long will I be out?" she asked. Her croaky voice reminded him of June Allyson.

"Couple hours."

"Okay." Chipper as a midwestern cheerleader. Then, "Mind giving it to me in the leg? I mean the thigh. I have this problem. Like I bruise easy and sometimes it doesn't go away for weeks. I take vitamin C, but it doesn't seem to help. Like I don't want marks on my arms, 'cause like it shows. I mean I wear sundresses a lot. You have to in this weather. You mind?"

He pushed her skirt up to her buttocks. Nora Bart was not wearing panties. And in the middle of one shapely cheek was a small tattoo of a skull with a snake crawling in one vacant eye and out the other. The captain raised a single eyebrow and injected her just below the buttock. When he pulled down her skirt she giggled. "Will this give me the munchies? We scored some grass in Hawaii last time we were there. Maui Wowee. Hey, all we did after that was eat. Like really pig out. Officer . . ."

Her voice faded. In sleep she looked years younger and as harmless as a fawn. All she lacked was jammies and a Cabbage Patch doll.

Minutes later the captain cracked the front door, looked into the corridor, and when it was empty he stepped outside. He locked the door behind him and pocketed the key before hanging a DO NOT DISTURB sign from the knob.

Then he picked up his suitcase and, humming Billy Joel's "An Innocent Man," walked toward the elevator.

Weeping silently, a hollow-eyed Molly January entered her small, squalid apartment that evening. She was followed by a thickset Japanese with a scarred forehead and a *yakuza* pendant hanging from his neck. He paused long enough to bark a command to a pair of bodyguards, who bowed their heads and remained in the narrow, ill-lit hallway. One pulled the door closed, then each positioned himself on either side of it, arms folded across a muscular chest.

Inside, the scarred Japanese switched on the light and grunted. Molly hated that sound. It was a show of arrogance, the same as cracking a whip. The sound meant pay attention, give way to me. Immediately.

"Why you no clean apartment?" he asked. "Is dirty here."

She stood with her back to him. "It was dirty when you brought me here. Far as I'm concerned it can stay that way forever."

Grunt. "Tomorrow you go to place, three, four hours outside Tokyo. Many men there. Farmers, men in factories, fishermen. You dance for them, you make fuck with them. It not so nice as Tokyo. Very, very dirty. *Hai.* These men, they no wash. They beat you if you no obey."

He slapped his chest with his palm. "First, you learn obey me. You take off clothes. We make fuck."

In the July heat Molly felt herself get the chills. The nausea began. He was going to rape her, as he had done yesterday and the day before. He had been brutal and contemptuous, sparing her nothing, and when it was over he had taken her back to the club and boasted to hostesses and *yakuza* of what he had done. His name was Kisen.

Molly felt her stomach begin to heave. Bitter, hot fluids sped up into her throat. Slapping both hands over her mouth, she ran into the tiny bathroom and dropped to her knees in front of the toilet. She threw up immediately. When she finished she fought for breath.

She turned and saw Kisen taking off his clothes. His beefy body was alive with tattoos from shoulders to knees, a sight so repulsive to her that she crawled across the filthy floor and slammed the door closed. She fell back against the tub and closed her eyes. No more, no more.

Two days ago Kisen had threatened to scar her face on the spot if she did not dance naked at that rat hole of a club in Roppongi. He had actually held a knife to her cheek and waited for her answer. Thoroughly unnerved, Molly had given in, thinking this was the worst he could do to her, and knowing in her heart it wasn't. He had done more, and with that had come shame, bringing its own wounds.

On the bathroom floor she drew her knees to her chest, gripped them tightly, and listened to the street noises coming through a single tiny window. She was living in a slum, with blocks of boy prostitutes, sushi bars, street stalls, fast food joints, and Turkish baths, which were nothing more than massage parlors.

It had taken no effort to despise Tokyo, with its cramped, smelly streets without names, its houses without numbers, and its thousands and thousands of telephone lines reminding her of prison bars, reminding her that she was trapped in a misery with neither beginning nor end.

It was a nightmare and she was alone. The two girls she

had flown over with had been moved somewhere else by
Kisen. Greater than the loneliness was the pain of thinking of
home, of Erica.

"You come out. *Now.*" Kisen.

Molly opened her eyes and as she turned to look at the door
a hand was clamped over her mouth, while a strong arm kept
her in place on the floor. Her screams went unheard. *She
couldn't move.* There was someone's warm breath near her
ear and a voice whispered through her terror, "Don't scream.
Keep quiet. It's Simon. *Simon.* Erica sent me."

He had been hiding in the tub, behind the shower curtain,
and now climbed out where she could see him. He kept one
hand over her mouth.

She frowned. Dark hair, mustache, army uniform. Dark
glasses. He wasn't Simon. And yet . . .

Yes. Molly whimpered and clutched at him. He put a finger
to his lips, took both hands away from her now, and motioned her to sit still. He looked around the bathroom. It was
dinky and grungy, not much more space than three or four
telephone booths strung together. Simon could stretch his
arms out sideways and touch the stained walls. Hadn't been
cleaned, really cleaned, in months. It smelled like a bouquet
of assholes.

Simon reached past a wide-eyed Molly and into the tub,
found the stopper, and shoved it into the drain. He turned on
both faucets as far as they could go, then rose to stand in
front of the dirty basin. Molly had left a hair dryer and an
electrical transformer on the basin's edge near the tub. Both
were plugged into a wall socket above a cracked, grimy
mirror. Simon turned on the hair dryer and when it started to
slide off the edge he placed it in the basin, where he'd hidden
a hypodermic under a washcloth. Should be enough noise to
hide the sound of Molly and him talking.

He crouched near Molly, placed his lips to her ear, and
asked her if there was anyone downstairs waiting for the man
in the next room. *Yes. A driver.* Anyone else? *No, just a
driver.* Were the men in the hallway armed? *Yes. They're
bodyguards. There's a* yakuza *gang war going on.*

Questions finished. Now for Molly's instructions. Simon
spoke clearly, keeping it simple. Molly wasn't all that bright.
No sense making it difficult. When he finished he asked her if

she understood. She nodded her head. For both their sakes
Simon hoped she was telling the truth.

He helped her to her feet and grinned to show her that it
was going to be all right. She started to smile, but gave up
midway through the effort. She did, however, begin taking
off her clothes. As ordered. It was when she got down to her
panties that the bathroom door burst open and a naked Kisen
stood glowering at her. "Why you no finish?"

Molly quickly looked over her shoulder for Simon.

He was gone.

She raised a hand to her mouth, uncertain what to do next,
unable to remember what Simon had told her.

Kisen grabbed her breasts and dug his fingers into her
flesh. Molly screamed and backed away from him.

Simon, spread-eagle with his back against the low ceiling,
hands and feet pressed against opposite walls, watched the
tattooed *yakuza* drop a hand to Molly's pubic area. Simon
didn't like it. Molly was not doing what she should. She was
to lure the tattooed man into the bathroom, then get the hell
out herself as fast as she could. That was the reason for
stripping nude, to entice him closer to Simon and the hypodermic and away from the bodyguards.

He shouted over the hair dryer and running water, "Molly,
goddam it, *move!*"

Everything happened at once. Kisen looked up. Molly
shoved past him and, breasts flopping, ran. Simon dropped
from the ceiling.

For a large man, Kisen reacted quickly. The instant Simon
landed on him, the *yakuza* threw himself backward, painfully
slamming the thief into the basin and mirror. The collision
sent broken glass slicing into Simon's left side. There was a
sharp pain in his left elbow before it went numb. And astride
Kisen's back he watched the time-worn basin snap loose from
rusty pipes and fall into a tub almost full of bathwater,
carrying with it the droning hair dryer and the transformer.
And the hypodermic.

Instantly, the water crackled and hissed, sending steam
rising from its surface. Then it began to bubble noisily and
grow hotter, snapping like pieces of wood breaking at once. It
leaped and convulsed with an ugly life of its own. Active with
electricity, the water was now as deadly as the naked man
trying to kill Simon.

Kisen reached over his left shoulder and clawed at Simon's eyes, missing them, but scratching him on the forehead and cheek. Before the *yakuza* could strike again, Simon slammed his cupped hands into Kisen's ears.

As the naked man shrieked and stumbled forward toward the toilet Simon landed crouched on the floor. Kisen, however, gave him no time to rise to his feet. Without turning his body, the *yakuza* looked over his shoulder and lashed out with his right leg in a vicious back kick. Simon threw himself left, hugging the wall. Kisen's calloused foot missed his head by less than an inch. Simultaneously, the naked man cried out to his bodyguards, ordering them to kick in the locked front door. And kill the intruder.

Simon heard the front door being torn apart. In seconds they would be inside. He hadn't planned on fighting three men at once or facing guns. If the shooters caught him here, it was all over. The time to gamble was now.

With the back kick Kisen spun around to face Simon. In the cramped space each could have reached out and touched the other. Simon touched first. He picked up pieces of the broken mirror in his gloved right hand and underhanded them at Kisen's face. When the *yakuza*'s hands came up in self-protection, Simon hooked a right fist into his testicles. As Kisen doubled over, Simon leaped to his feet and drove his bent right wrist into the *yakuza*'s throat.

Kisen gagged, staggered backward, then lost his footing on the wet floor. Arms flailing he fell into the churning bath water and screamed instantly. As he thrashed about wildly the screaming became shrill and piercing. His skin quickly reddened, his eyes bulged, and he lashed at the water, sending it flying in all directions. Then he went rigid and appeared to almost levitate out of the tub before sinking deeper into the water. He went limp. His right arm and leg dangled over the side.

The front door gave way with a crash. Guns in hand, the bodyguards rushed in, calling to Kisen and looking left and right. Simon moved quickly and according to plan. He dropped to the wet floor, reached under the tub, and pulled out the smoke grenade he had hidden there. It had an eight-second fuse. He yanked the pin, counted three, then tossed the grenade into the living room at the bodyguards, a gentle arc of a throw that saw the grenade bounce off a wooden table and land on a sagging couch.

The bodyguards tensed, their eyes following the grenade's flight as though it were a bouncing ball in a sing-along. When nothing happened, they split up. One headed toward the bedroom, the other for the bathroom. Simon's hand was under the tub again, this time for a gas mask. What the hell was taking that grenade so long?

Then he heard the soft *plop* of the grenade going off, saw the smoke quickly spread out and fill the living room. His heart was fluttering, but he grinned. Sometimes you eat the bear, sometimes the bear eats you. Today Simon was about to eat the bear.

On the floor he rolled over on his back, ripped off his dark glasses, and fitted the mask to his face. Air pollution in Japan was so serious and life threatening that gas masks were sold everywhere.

He got to his knees and froze. The dark shape of a choking, weeping bodyguard filled the bathroom doorway. His gun hand dangled at his side and he kept his other hand over his nose and mouth. He definitely saw Simon. He started to bring the gun hand up, and Simon tensed to receive the bullet. But the gun fell to the bathroom floor and the man staggered backward into the doorjamb. In seconds he collapsed to his knees, then fell forward into the living room on his face. Not today, bear. Not today.

Simon stood up, cradled his left arm, and walked on top of the prone bodyguard, up his spine, and into the smoke-filled living room in time to spy the silhouette of the second shooter. He watched the man trip over a fallen lamp and land on top of a table. The table gave way under his weight, dropping him to the floor. He lay on his side vomiting and weeping, legs churning as though riding a bicycle in slow motion.

Roasting in his gas mask, Simon walked to the room's only closet and opened the door. Molly was crouched in a corner near his suitcase. She had put on a white blouse and pale gray skirt and was barefoot. She also wore the gas mask Simon had hidden there for her. In the mask she looked like a large blond bug with tits and painted toenails.

"Let's go home," he shouted.

In the smoky hallway he held onto her hand and the suitcase containing their passports, change of clothing and money, and headed toward the back exit. Behind him Molly complained about her mask being hot, about having no shoes on, about having left something or other behind. Simon found the strength in his bad arm to jerk her hard, a strong hint to shut up and keep moving. She did.

At the end of the hallway, just before the staircase leading down to the back exit, they passed a toothless old man with a wispy beard. He stood in the doorway of his cheap flat holding a tiny dog and a bowl of noodles he had been feeding the dog. The old man's mind was half gone and he wasn't sure what the smoke was. It could be fog, which he had always loved as a boy. Or it could be snow, his wife's favorite. But she was dead now, though he sometimes talked to her.

The old man wondered if he had truly seen a foreign woman being dragged along the hall by an American soldier carrying a suitcase. Life, he had learned, was all illusion and disillusion and we were ill used every step of the way.

But then the smoke filled all of the hallway. He heard other tenants shouting, for much of Tokyo had wooden housing jammed close together and it was wise to fear fire. He began to cough, but he didn't want to leave his room, his only home, so he stepped inside and slammed his door and hugged his small, nervous dog. He brought the animal to his lipless mouth and kissed it, but the dog continued to bark.

In his Manhattan condominum Simon closed the door on Erica and Molly's bedroom, then returned to the master bedroom. Alexis must be climbing the walls by now. Better find Paul and have him speak to her. Simon took his address book from a night table, sat down on the edge of the four-poster, and after attaching the scrambler to his telephone dialed.

Paul Anami was relieved to hear his voice. "How'd it go?"

"Like egg white on a doorknob. Smooth all the way." Simon told him everything, leaving out only the death of the *yakuza* chief. No sense worrying Paul over nothing. Simon had covered his tracks going in and out of Japan. It would take some kind of luck to ever find him. And unless Molly was awfully stupid, they'd never find her either.

"So you had no problems," said Anami.

"Nothing I couldn't handle. Me and Captain Kirk. Going

boldly where no man has ever gone before. Remember, tell Alexis everything's okay.''

"That's what I want to hear. Maybe they'll forget about you over there. All they lost is a woman, a foreign woman at that. Which is about as low as you can get in Japan.''

Simon looked down at his bandaged ribs. No, he wasn't going to say anything about the man in the bathtub. Simon had paid his debt to Erica and could now go back to living for himself, which meant giving no more thought to what had happened in Japan. He had his own approval. What more did he need?

Four

A sense of perversity had led Rupert de Jongh to buy a home in this seaport eighteen miles south of Tokyo. The city had a noticeable foreign presence—consulates, business offices for multinationals, an old Chinatown, American country music clubs. The sort of setting that de Jongh, as a *yakuza* leader and a Westerner, might be expected to avoid. True, he bore a Japanese name—Yamaga, after the man instrumental in developing *bushido*, code of the feudal warrior; Razan, after the philosopher and adviser to the Tokugawa shoguns. And he had literally shed his blood for Japan. Still, he refused to allow anyone to define him or say what he should do. He was the *gaijin* and he did as he pleased.

De Jongh's home was a red-brick Victorian mansion on the Bluff, a pine-covered hill overlooking Yokohama harbor. Despite the presence of a few wealthy Japanese, the Bluff was traditionally the foreigners' district, an enclave of Western businessmen, diplomats, and well-to-do missionaries. From a bedroom window de Jongh could see the Foreign Cemetery, final resting place of those avaricious oddballs who comprised the first foreign traders, diplomats, and soul savers to set foot in Japan. He had a relative buried here, a nineteenth-century sea captain on his mother's side. In the great tradition of British eccentrics the captain had used two of his dead wife's

vertebrae as salt and pepper shakers, while carrying around
the rest of her bones in a perfumed bag.

The Foreign Cemetery was certainly cold storage at its
most picturesque, drawing hordes of camera-clutching tourists
to photograph its gravestone inscriptions and stroll its parklike
grounds. The Oriental part of de Jongh saw it less as a
curiosity than as a reminder of mortality. A string around
one's finger, indicating that death was the final answer to all
questions. As he grew older he wondered whether life or
death was the bigger surprise.

At sunrise Rupert de Jongh went down to the private
archery court beneath his Yokohama home to practice kyudo,
Japanese archery. He wore the traditional costume of a long
blouse and long skirt, both made of dark blue cotton. There
was a buckskin glove on his right hand and he was barefoot.
Attended by two *kobun*, he shot arrow after arrow at a pair of
fourteen-inch targets attached to wooden posts sixty feet away.

Shortly before noon de Jongh fixed the last arrow to his
bowstring. He was using a Japanese bow, eight feet long and
made of laminated bamboo and cedar wood. It had been
toughened by fire to give it a combination of strength and
flexibility. The arrows, three feet long and tipped with eagle
feathers, were carried in a slim cloth quiver hung from de
Jongh's right hip.

An iron discipline gained in forty years of kyudo, Zen, and
judo allowed him to maintain the correct archer's position.
Body erect and sideways to the target. String back and bow
held at arm's length, then raised slowly overhead and held in
place. Then lowered slowly once more, gloved hand pulled
well behind the ear. Once more hold the position. Wait.
Concentrate until body and mind were one, until bowman,
arrow, and bow became a single unit.

Then the arrow was released, not forced. And the essence
of kyudo, the mental alertness called *zanshin*, was achieved.
In kyudo one learned the secret of victory in combat, which
was to psychologically dominate the enemy at all times, to
deny him the opportunity to strike first.

De Jongh had called a meeting of his most important
subchiefs for noon today at his home in Yokohama. It was a
meeting he would have to dominate if he were to survive as
their leader. To do this meant first fortifying his spirit with
kyudo. And so he had risen at dawn, gone to the narrow,

windowless room beneath his mansion, and fired arrow after
arrow until he was arm weary and exhausted. It had become
necessary for de Jongh to again show his *yakuza* that his
strength had no limitations.

The murder of Kisen two days ago by a Westerner was a
serious threat to de Jongh's rule as *oyabun* of the Shinanui-
Kai. In its own way it presented a sharper danger than
meeting Alexis Waycross in Hawaii. Kisen's death, if not
avenged immediately, could topple de Jongh from power
overnight. The burly subchief had been a beloved lieutenant.
De Jongh owed his life to Kisen, who had once thrown
himself in front of the Englishman to protect him from a
sword-wielding attacker and been slashed across the forehead.
Kisen had also been the first to warn him of treachery and
insubordination. Such men were irreplaceable.

To save face and retain respect among his followers, de
Jongh had to find Kisen's killer and destroy him. An *oyabun*
who did not protect his men soon lost their allegiance. At
today's meeting the *gaijin* intended to show that he would go
to any lengths to exact satisfaction for Kisen's death.

Of course he did not intend to ignore Alexis Waycross, or
whatever the lady now called herself. If she could convince
the Americans that he was still alive she could be extremely
dangerous. Much too durable, our Miss Waycross. Patience
made her capable of accomplishing anything. And God knows
she had reason enough to hate de Jongh, a hatred he was
certain would prove to be a keen and lasting one. She could
be counted upon to inform any existing war crimes commission that Rupert de Jongh did not conk out in 1945, that he
was still very much alive.

Her interference could mean an end to his new alliance
with the La Serra brothers, leaders of a major New York
crime family. And with that would come an end to all plans
for expansion in Hawaii and on the American mainland. De
Jongh had felt it wise to leave Hawaii within minutes of
accidentally running into Alexis Waycross. He had canceled
an important meeting with the La Serras, a Korean CIA
official, and a Hawaiian police lieutenant on de Jongh's
payroll. The lieutenant had been charged with finding Miss
Waycross and disposing of her.

Red-faced and perspiring, de Jongh pulled back on the
bowstring until it was nine inches past his right ear. This was

his last arrow. He had been in the archery court for almost seven hours and in that time had not touched food or water. Even in today's *doyo* weather, dog days, the hottest time of the year, he aimed for spiritual and physical perfection, refusing to allow the soreness in his body to drag his mind down. With his last arrow he stood as erect as he had with the first, waiting, the pain in his arms close to unbearable. But still he would not release the arrow. Not until he sensed, truly sensed that his body and mind were one.

He had no idea how long he waited. Nor did he know exactly when the arrow was released. But he heard the snap of the string and felt the bow spin around in his left hand. Then for a long time he remained motionless, eyes on the target and the last arrow sticking from it and he felt himself as mentally strong as he had ever been in his life.

De Jongh turned to look at the two *kobun* who silently served him. Their duties had been to hand him full quivers when he needed them and rush across the dirt floor to clear the targets. Yes, they respected him. But de Jongh saw something else in their faces. They feared and revered him as well. They knew that few men of any age could fire a hundred arrows in the exact and powerful manner called for in kyudo.

It was an incredible spiritual and physical feat, one the *kobun* would never again see in their lifetime. *Hai*, they had seen the *gaijin* shoot before, but never with such forcefulness and domination.

He was invincible, possessed of an unconditional authority. He was the *gaijin*.

Under his gaze the *kobun* dropped to their knees, foreheads touching the dark soil. After a few seconds de Jongh, eyes glazed, walked between their prostrated bodies until he reached a small wooden bench near an earthen wall. He sat down facing the staircase leading upstairs to the mansion, his small hands coming to rest on the long bow lying across his knees.

The meeting with his subchiefs, scheduled here in the archery court, was five minutes away.

De Jongh stared the length of the archery court at two men tied to the wooden posts that had held his targets. They were the bodyguards who had failed to keep Kisen alive. They had also let his killer escape. One bodyguard wept, pleading for his life. The other stared quietly at a lightbulb above his head, perhaps composing himself for death, perhaps too stupid to realize what was about to happen. It mattered little to de Jongh. It was obvious that anyone who could have prevented Kisen's death was as responsible as he who had caused it.

In the archery court, a dozen *yakuza* subchiefs and a handful of *kobun* stood behind de Jongh and looked on silently, eyes moving from him to the doomed bodyguards.

De Jongh stood erect, bow in his left hand. The quiver on his right hip contained only two arrows. Someone cleared his throat. Another man, an asthmatic, wheezed loudly and reached for a pocket spray. Several mopped perspiration from their faces and necks. Two looked at the ground.

Most of de Jongh's lieutenants were trustworthy. Those who weren't he called "marginals" and they were the ones who needed converting, the ones who would be quick to see Kisen's murder as a sign of the Englishman's weakness. De Jongh was about to give the marginals something to reflect on.

He jerked an arrow from the quiver, knocked it a third of the way from the bottom of the bow and brought the bow up, all in a single motion.

The arrow was released so fast that the men watching were shocked into a deathly silence and immobility.

The arrow hit the twisting, pleading bodyguard in the right temple and drove through his skull, pinning his head to the post behind him. His jaw dropped and he went still instantly. He hung like a man crucified, bright eyes on the companion to his left.

De Jongh stood motionless and eyed the second man, who had now closed his eyes. After a full minute the *gaijin* snatched the second arrow from the quiver and again did everything with lightning speed.

The arrow whistled as it sped down the court. And smashed into the bodyguard's nose, into his brain, snapping his head back sharply into the post. He collapsed forward, pulling at his bonds, jerking the arrowhead out of the wood behind him. Blood from his shattered face poured onto the dark earth at his feet.

De Jongh eyed the dead men impassively and after a time he turned and walked toward his subchiefs. They made a path for him. He continued walking until he reached the small bench, where he sat down, bow across his knees. The *yakuza*, silent and subdued, drifted over to form a semicircle around him. When they were all in place de Jongh said, "I spoke only a few words at Kisen's funeral, leading some of you, perhaps, to feel that I failed to regard his passing as a serious matter. Those of you who know my heart know I cherished our brother and loved him deeply. Therefore I prefer to let my actions speak for me. Kisen will be remembered. And so will the man from the West who killed him. This I swear to you as *oyabun*."

De Jongh removed his damp headband and wiped perspiration from his neck. "I have called this meeting for another reason as well and that is to dispel the notion that my Hawaiian trip was a failure."

He watched their faces. Oh, they were eager now. Attentive. Not a surly expression among them. And all very respectful. *Metus improbos compescit non clementia.* Fear, not clemency, restrains the wicked.

He began by admitting to his subchiefs that he had indeed been forced to leave the islands earlier than planned and all because of an old enemy. But that had not stopped him from pursuing the alliance with the La Serra brothers, leaders of a major New York crime family. De Jongh, since returning to Japan, had simply used his New York liaison, his godson, to keep in contact with the Americans. The godson, a Japanese businessman living in Manhattan, had seen to it that everything proceeded as planned.

Details. Guns, of course. The La Serras would supply as many as needed, delivering them to Hawaii. It would be up to de Jongh to get the guns into Japan.

Heroin. De Jongh's *yakuza* would supply the La Serras, not with one or two kilos as in the past, but with dozens of kilos. The Japanese had the world's best source, the Chinese who controlled the opium traffic in Burma, Laos, Thailand, "the Golden Triangle." De Jongh was to get the heroin as far as Hawaii, where the La Serras would take delivery and move it to the mainland. Top dollar to be paid the *yakuza*, who were to receive a bonus; no more tribute on heroin smuggled into the United States for sale in the Japanese community, where they were to have a free hand.

"This means our smuggling routes into America are guaranteed," de Jongh said. "The La Serras are in a position to see to it that we encounter no more American threats or interference. Nor will our profits stop there." He paused for effect. "They have agreed to take a minimum of a million methamphetamine tables a year."

Murmurs and grunts of approval. As well there should be. Methamphetamine, called "speed" by the Americans, was Japan's most frequently used illicit drug. And a great source of profit for the *yakuza*. Factory workers in World War II had been forced to take it, a way of making them strong enough to work the inhuman hours demanded by the Japanese war machine. Today it was Japan's secret shame that its "economic miracle," its postwar prosperity, rested in large part on workers still consuming this particular drug.

In the archery court, de Jongh turned to his right and spoke to a man named Soto. Small and handsome, Soto was almost oedipal in his love for his mother and was brilliant enough to play several games of chess at once. He had not hesitated to kill his own brother, a fellow *yakuza* who had betrayed him. Soto had been chosen to replace Kisen as de Jongh's second in command.

"You will handle the drug business," said de Jongh. "This means you will work closely with Kangnung. But do not forget that he is to take orders from you. You are *yakuza*, he is not."

Soto dropped his arms to his side and bowed from the waist. Kim Doo Kangnang was the Korean CIA official who had been with de Jongh in Hawaii when they had suffered the misfortune of running into Alexis Waycross. Kangnang was also a longtime *yakuza* drug courier and bagman.

Soto, as Kisen's replacement, would be in charge of a subgang containing a number of Koreans, who in fact formed ten percent of all *yakuza* mobs. Koreans sometimes caused problems and Soto would have to be careful. They were Japan's largest and most discriminated against minority, an uncouth, low-class people deserving of the description "the Irish of the Orient." Sad to say, de Jongh and the rest of the underworld had to live with them. The rotten sods had nowhere else to go.

Koreans had been imported to Japan in World War II as slave labor and never allowed to rise above that stigma. No matter how long they or their descendents lived in Japan, all were systematically denied citizenship and benefits. Even second- and third-generation children born in Japan could not become citizens and were forced to register as aliens. A Korean was lucky if he found a menial job. More than a few became entertainers, prostitutes, shoe shine women. Discrimination forced them into ghettos, and the Japanese population at large shunned them as they would lepers. A Korean had no chance to amount to anything in Japanese society.

Which is why the young Korean toughs leaped at the opportunity to work with the *yakuza*, who themselves were outsiders. Kisen, to his credit, had ruled his Koreans with a firm hand, keeping them and the Japanese from each other's throats. Soto would have to do the same or answer to the *gaijin*.

Then there was the matter of the marginals, who had hung on de Jongh's every word. They had to be watched because they had been secretly contacted by Uraga in an attempt to intimidate them into pledging loyalty and royalties to him. If he succeeded in causing them to defect it would be a major blow to de Jongh's authority and prestige. To date, none of the marginals had come forward to make a clean breast of things. De Jongh had a feeling that before the day was over they would see the error of their ways.

"We shall double the number of gambling flights to America and the Caribbean," said de Jongh. "Needless to say, the La Serras will do their best to accommodate our customers. I don't have to remind you that this means a potential profit for our *sarakin* companies that should be pleasing to all. And it is my decision that we increase the interest on our loans by a single percentage point. I'm certain I have your agreement on this."

Smiles. Greed, after all, was the moving spirit of civilization.

De Jongh gave them more. They were to be involved with the La Serras in disposing of automobiles stolen in America and shipped to the Far East. If the La Serras secured permission to build an Atlantic City casino, the Japanese were to have an interest in it. In return a $200 million hotel now being constructed in Honolulu by de Jongh's group would take in the La Serras as a small but silent partner. This would give the Americans a foothold in Hawaii, something the Mafia had been unable to do up until now.

Yakuza money, washed through front companies and foreign banks, would be made available for certain La Serra investments, starting with the construction of condominiums in Atlantic City, New York, and Florida.

"Most important," said de Jongh, "will be our unrestricted use of banks controlled by the Americans in three of their states. This will allow us to move our money from here to America without coming under the scrutiny of authorities. I'm certain you understand what I am saying. Specifically, it makes our business with the Hong Kong people that much simpler."

De Jongh had not told the La Serras the full extent of his operations. Why should he? Keeping secrets allowed you to rule others; that same secret, once revealed, could end up ruling you. And so he had told the Americans nothing of what he termed his "Hong Kong secret." His *yakuza* group would be moving huge amounts of cash from the British Royal Crown Colony to Hawaii and America. Astronomical amounts, in fact, and none of it belonging to de Jongh.

His organization was merely the courier, the suitcase for money on deposit in Hong Kong, considered to be increasingly unsafe for such deposits as the year 1997 drew closer. That was the year China was to claim Hong Kong back from the British after some 150 years. Goodbye to a nineteenth-century treaty forced upon the Chinese at gunpoint by Queen Victoria's tricksters.

Meanwhile Hong Kong stocks were plummeting to earth like birds shot from the sky. Property values were collapsing with equal rapidity. Money, which the Chinese said gave a man thirty years more of dignity, tended in crisis to act in a most undignified manner. The mere thought of the impending Communist takeover was sending Hong Kong's money men to bed with the vapors.

Enter the *gaijin*. He had moved money around the world in the past, his own and that of others. So Hong Kong's money men had contacted him about their problem and he had agreed to move their funds to a safer climate. It would be no small task.

"Something you might find amusing," de Jongh said to his subchiefs. "I was left with the impression that the La Serras might make life in America difficult for Uraga." Pause. "And his supporters." He smiled at the marginals. None could hold his gaze.

"A final matter," he said. "Raymond Manoa is to run for

public office. It was my wish, of course, that he do so. I see him winning quite easily. He will be running for the Hawaiian state senate. His victory will be ours."

Raymond Manoa was the Hawaiian police lieutenant whom de Jongh was to have met before Alexis Waycross tossed a spanner in the works. A strange man. A heroic police officer with many commendations for bravery. A Hawaiian with a reverence for the islands and its traditions, which made him popular with native Hawaiians who were disgusted with seeing real estate developers destroy Hawaii's beauty.

But the outwardly pleasant Mr. Manoa had a dark side, one rooted in island superstitions and in past confrontations between his family and ruling whites. A thin veneer of civilization hid a bestial nature. De Jongh had charged Mr. Manoa with finding Alexis Waycross and eliminating her.

In the archery court the Englishman answered questions, then rose from the bench, signaling the end of the meeting. He led them from the archery court and through the house, then into a walled garden behind the mansion. Some of the subchiefs drew sunglasses from their pockets; others shaded their eyes against a white-hot sun. No matter. De Jongh would soon take their minds off the heat.

He walked them along the garden's winding path of stepping stones. He had planted the garden himself, designing it around a red-lacquered teahouse once belonging to the great Hideyoshi. The warm air was sweet with evergreens, orchids, azaleas, irises, chrysanthemums, and rare plum blossoms, all fed by a small stream running from beneath a corner of the house. De Jongh had also planted lemon and dwarf bamboo trees, pruning their branches, shrinking roots, and grafting trees together until their gnarled and twisted shapes represented the Japanese innate sense of nature.

He did not stop in the garden. He led his subchiefs to a door in a far wall, which he opened, standing aside to allow his subchiefs to precede him. He waited several seconds before joining them.

They were crowded into a small courtyard empty except for a naked Victor Pascal. He was spread-eagle on a ten-foot square piece of galvanized iron propped against a courtyard wall. His face was swollen, bloodied, and a swollen, blackened tongue filled his open mouth. At the sight of de Jongh and the Japanese he slowly moved his head and begged for water.

Barbed wire wrapped around his wrists and ankles held him in place. The worse agony came from the heat, which had turned the iron into a giant frying pan. Each movement by Pascal tore away pieces of his flesh. De Jongh knew what the heat and metal could do. It was a torture he had watched the Kempei-Tai, Japan's Gestapo, apply to captured British and American fliers in World War II.

A *kobun* entered the courtyard carrying a bucket of fresh water and placed it at Pascal's feet. Then the *kobun* backed away from the hot iron, bowed to de Jongh, and stood near him, arms folded across his chest. At the sight of the water, Pascal pulled at the barbed wire binding him and croaked. And through his delirium saw a creased photograph of himself floating on the water's surface. Tuxedo, gold jewelry by the handful. Smile for the ladies.

De Jongh tilted his head to one side and studied the unshaven, bleeding Pascal. "The photograph was found in the bathroom where Kisen died. Brought to Japan by the American army officer, I should imagine."

He turned his back on the mulatto. "I have allowed the American woman, Miss Bart, to live. For the moment. When she has concluded her part in the search for this 'army officer' . . ."

It wasn't necessary to finish.

De Jongh left the courtyard first, followed by the others. At the ornamental pool he stopped to dip his wrists in the water and cool himself. He would offer his men nothing to drink or eat today. Let them leave with strong impressions of what they had seen here in the *gaijin*'s home.

When de Jongh stood up and turned, three men were waiting to talk to him. Nervous. Unable to hold his gaze. The marginals.

Collecting themselves, each bowed and kept his head down. Only the eldest spoke. *"Oyabun,* permission please to speak."

"Concerning what?"

Silence. Then, "It is about Uraga."

"Ah, yes, Uraga. *Hai,* let us talk about Uraga."

Five

OXFORD, ENGLAND
1937

On a mild October evening an eighteen-year-old Rupert de Jongh was climbing a flight of stairs in a shabby rooming house on Holywell Street, willing himself not to drop the portable Gramophone he carried in his arms. Wouldn't do to shatter the bloody thing before he had a chance to hear his new Art Tatum and Duke Ellington recordings. De Jongh, a second-year student at Oxford University, owned a marvelous collection of works by Negro Americans, the sort of music your average Englishman called savage and decadent and refused to allow in his home. Typically dim-witted British reasoning.

His new Gramophone had been on order for months. Until now he'd been forced to borrow one belonging to a fellow student, a sexually indeterminate Communist in the room opposite him. Unfortunately, this meant listening to the Commie hold forth on dialectic materialism, while calling de Jongh "comrade" and telling him how smashing he looked in gray flannels.

Yesterday, the Commie had left for the United States to work with the American Student Union, which had followed Oxford in passing a resolution "not to support any war which the government may undertake."

Hitler, Mussolini, and Japan's leaders were talking of a Rome-Berlin-Tokyo Axis. Other nations publicly admitted they were afraid and had begun to rearm. War, the concentration of all human crimes, appeared imminent and inevitable.

But not to de Jongh. It was all so irrelevant. A spot of bother here and there and all of it happening far from the quadrangles of Oxford. Not to worry. Things always sorted themselves out in the end.

De Jongh's time was better spent listening to swing music or punting on the Thames or competing in the university's fencing club, where he was quite expert with saber and foil. There was also his membership in the dramatic society, which by tradition concentrated on the plays of Marlowe and Shakespeare. And he could take pleasure in an occasional slap and tickle with an accommodating female student, the two of them rolling about in the university's favorite trysting place, the tall grass of St. Hilda's College.

Life would turn serious soon enough. His father, Lord Clarence Geoffrey de Jongh, shrewd, ill-tempered, and charming, had followed the prescribed educational path for the upper classes. It went without saying that he expected his only son to do the same. Eton, Oxford, then the Grenadier Guards. Then a bit of foreign military service, followed by a place in the de Jongh holding company, with its large blocks of stock in a nationwide chain of chemist shops, a motor coach company, London's third largest department store, and a real estate corporation with land in England, Ireland, and Wales.

Piss on it, thought Rupert de Jongh. No one in his right mind could be interested in business, which was little better than swindling, thank you. All so boring, really. Business would kill him long before any war did. He had more energy than he could ever use as a businessman. His was a fire not easily controlled.

Gramophone clutched to his chest, he reached the top of the staircase and turned right, walking along a narrow hallway whose floorboards squeaked like mice. Too late he remembered that he should have purchased candles, his only source of light after sunset. His digs also lacked a bathroom, no small inconvenience, and his one window was missing a pane of glass. The bed had a few broken springs and the entire floor sloped noticeably to the left. Definitely not the Ritz, but somehow refreshing after the aristocratic clutter of his parents' seventeenth-century Jacobean home in Hertfordshire.

Though in need of repair, the ramshackle rooming house was not without its advantages. It was within walking distance of several of Oxford University's sixteen colleges. And to de Jongh's unbounded delight, for he was an avid reader, the house was only yards away from the Bodleian Library, one of the greatest in the world. Two and a half million volumes at his disposal, and on top of that, the library received a copy of every single book published in Britain. Sheer rapture.

Perhaps the house's most exciting feature was its landlord, a shiny-eyed, bearded alcoholic with a withered arm and a tendency toward stammering fits. He was said to be the bastard son of a public hangman and a Rumanian murderess, a parentage giving him a celebrity status among Oxford students exceeding that of the most brilliant dean.

De Jongh was about to enter his room with his Gramophone when he stopped to listen. Singing coming from the Commie's digs. New tenant and guests, most likely. Japanese from the sounds of them and all drunk as a brewer's fart. Bloody wogs attempting to sing, of all things, English madrigals. Deplorable what they were doing to the delicate harmonies of "Phyllis, I Fain Would Die Now." Deplorable, yet rather charming in its own way.

Voices aside, the sound of their native instruments was quite pleasant. De Jongh felt as though he'd heard them before, but that was impossible, of course. Bit of déjà vu.

Why did the instruments sound so disturbingly familiar?

He entered his own digs, placed the Gramophone on the bed, then walked across the hall and knocked on the door.

There were three of them. Young males no older than twenty, all sitting and drinking on the floor of a room no less pathetic than de Jongh's. All three decked out in the fashions favored by young Englishmen of the time: chalk-stripe flannel pants, sleeveless knitted pullovers, black-and-white wingtips. A battered metal teakettle of rice wine was heating on a hot plate in front of them. Near the hot plate were two dishes of salted dried fish sprinkled with grated relish.

Two of the Nips were cousins, the birdlike Omuri and the shy, myopic Inoki. They were reading history at Corpus Christi College and lived several blocks away on Merton Street. Both were friends of the new tenant, Naiga Kanamori, a chunky, handsome nineteen-year-old with a quick smile and a cool confidence that stamped him as a leader. All were second-year students like de Jongh. Bloody odd the way he took to them all right away. Lord knows he wasn't the type to make friends easily. But he liked these chaps, particularly Kanamori, a would-be playwright and the son of a wealthy and titled Japanese businessman.

Fueled by several cups of warm rice wine, de Jongh attempted to instruct them in the proper singing of madrigals. No luck there. Game lads all of them, but they lacked the necessary command of the English language. All words containing an *R* proved insurmountable. Not that it mattered, since a good time was had by all, de Jongh especially. He sang in a pleasing tenor and they applauded mightily. They sang and he, well, he encouraged. And they all ate salted fish, drank rice wine, and laughed together, and when another student pounded on the door, demanding quiet so that he could study, de Jongh called him a cunt and told him to get stuffed.

Evening. They lit candles and incense and as the mood turned quiet the Japanese played their native music for de Jongh. Omuri played a small hourglass-shaped drum, which he placed on his right shoulder and struck with the fingers of his right hand. Inoki, slanted eyes closed behind thick glasses, played a thirteen-string Japanese zither, plucking it with the thumb and two fingers of one hand.

Kanamori was the best musician of the three; he played a three-stringed banjolike instrument with a sweet sadness that brought de Jongh, not the emotional type, to the brink of tears. De Jongh had heard this music before. *Where?*

When Kanamori finished playing, de Jongh asked him for the instrument, calling it by name. *Shamisen*. It was not a word he was expected to know. Had he admitted to being a Japanese scholar or having some interest in Japanese music, there would have been no reaction from the three Orientals. It was Kanamori who held up a hand to silence his countrymen. No questions of the *gaijin*. Not at this moment.

De Jongh lovingly stroked the *shamisen*'s long wooded neck and catskin-covered sound box. He'd held one before. *But when?* He picked up the triangular ivory plectrum used by Kanamori and began to play, plucking the strings slowly. He stared straight ahead, eyes glazed. His playing was Japanese. Sad but pleasurable. And with a lyrical quietness.

Something was happening inside of him. He was shuffling the index cards of his memory and creating a new mind. One drawn toward Japan. The idea left him frightened and excited.

He finished to a strange silence. Kanamori's face was wet with tears. When he spoke his voice was choked and husky. "Do you know what you have just played?"

A dazed de Jongh shook his head.

"It is called *gagaku*," Kanamori said. "Ceremonial music from the Imperial Court of Japan." He leaned toward de Jongh. "From the Heian period. Twelve hundred years ago."

De Jongh had played the music flawlessly.

"Karma," said Kanamori. "It is the reason one is born again and again, as a greater or lesser man," he told de Jongh. "Karma is the unending process of action and reaction. What is called the eternal causal law. Past actions determining present actions. Present saying what the future will be."

How else to account for the differences between people in matters of health, ability, and wisdom, he said. How else to explain a young Englishman's ability to play an instrument he had never seen until today.

"You have special knowledge of Japan," Kanamori said. "You are *henna-gaijin*. Perhaps more."

He picked up a folded napkin, wrapped it around the handle of the battered teakettle, then poured sake for de Jongh, Omuri, and Inoki. He did not, however, pour for himself. Instead he replaced the kettle on the hot plate and looked at de Jongh.

I know what to do, de Jongh thought. It is for me to honor him.

He picked up the kettle and filled Kanamori's cup. Among Japanese it was considered bad manners for a man to pour his own liquor.

A smiling Kanamori lifted his cup in a toast to de Jongh. *"Henna-gaijin,"* Kanamori said. Omuri and Inoki repeated the word. All three bowed their heads. De Jongh felt a chill, knowing they had done the correct thing in bowing to him, but not knowing why.

The Japanese waited until he sipped first. It was a gesture of respect due a leader.

*   *   *

De Jongh's friendship with Kanamori fortified both of their lives. It was understood from the first that each could expect much from the other. Kanamori thought they must have been brothers in a past life. Until now de Jongh had found it difficult to show affection to anyone, save his mother. But such was his warmth and regard for Kanamori that he allowed himself to be totally influenced by him.

Because of Kanamori, de Jongh now knew what he wanted and set about striving for it. He wanted the soul of a Japanese.

Kanamori said there were barriers preventing any non-Japanese from knowing Japan. But they could be broken if de Jongh learned to speak Japanese, no easy task since the language consisted of three alphabets, one of which was *kanji*, the picture writing from China. A truly educated Japanese knew at least five thousand *kanji* characters, as well as the two phonetic alphabets of forty-eight symbols each.

De Jongh was not discouraged. He lost no time in making arrangements with a university tutor for private language lessons. Within a month de Jongh was able to converse adequately in Japanese with Kanamori, Omuri, and Inoki. The astonished tutor said that in twenty-five years of teaching and study, he'd never encountered a more gifted student.

To learn Japanese history and philosophy, de Jongh haunted the Oriental department of the Bodleian Library. He ignored his regular Oxford classes to spend entire days reading about Japan, beginning with the eighth-century Nara period and going up to the Showa era, which had begun eleven years ago with the coronation of the young emperor, Hirohito. De Jongh's studies and conversations with Kanamori, however, did not teach him as much as the study of his own mind.

Because Kanamori's father was something of a mystic, the young Japanese had an advantage in understanding de Jongh. All knowledge lay in the mind, Kanamori said. The mind, therefore, was de Jongh's key to penetrating the mystery that was Japan. No knowledge comes from outside, Kanamori said. It was all inherent in man and what a man knows was really what he discovered or unveiled by taking the cover off his own soul, a mine of infinite knowledge.

De Jongh was pleased to receive a letter from Kanamori's father, a baron who traced his ancestry back through twenty-one unbroken generations. The baron thanked him for his kindness to his son and the others. He also encouraged de

Jongh to do all in his power to learn his true identity. In this search, wrote the baron, the external world was simply the suggestion, the occasion to set one to studying his own mind. Like fire in a piece of flint, knowledge exists in the mind. Suggestion was the friction that brought it out.

As for the friendship between de Jongh and Kanamori, the baron wrote that each seemed to have found a second self. And when de Jongh visited Japan he was to consider the baron's home as his own.

The more de Jongh learned about Japan, the more dissatisfied he became with England. Its fashions now appeared monotonous, its customs tedious, and its weather appalling. God knows, he'd never been comfortable with the Protestant religious code and its belief that nine out of ten human acts were despicable. And was there a more dismal spectacle than a world wearing black suits in imitation of the British upper classes?

Japan. The very word conveyed a sense of something transcending the expected and the mundane.

Henna-gaijin. Not something to be discussed with the family over tea and scones or opened up for discussion with his few English school chums. It would have to be a secret between de Jongh and his Japanese friends, though on occasion one even had to be careful around them. He once accused Kanamori of being *tatemae,* triggering the first bit of ill feeling between them. All Japanese simultaneously maintained two ways of dealing with the world. *Tatemae* was the superficial approach. One stuck to externals and dealt only with appearances. *Honne,* on the other hand, was a Japanese's true thoughts, an attitude revealed only in close friendship or after knowing someone for a long time.

The word *tatemae* had simply popped into de Jongh's head, God knows how, and he'd said it without thinking. Turned out he'd been correct about Kanamori. His friend had indeed been hiding his true thoughts. Blame it on the habits of a lifetime. But it was embarrassing to be criticized for it by a Westerner, a *gaijin.* And in front of Omuri and Inoki. There was a lesson in this for de Jongh: refrain from saying the first thing that comes to mind. And do realize that there will be times when Kanamori and other Japanese *would* see him as an outsider and not *henna-gaijin.*

*   *   *

De Jongh was invited to join Kanamori, Omuri, and Inoki in judo practice, held in the basement of the rooming house. Judo was a combination of wrestling and gymnastics, with two fighters attempting to off-balance, then throw one another. Following the throw both struggled on the mat, trying to apply a stranglehold, armlock, or a hold-down that had to be maintained for thirty seconds. Practice also included *atewaza*, striking of the body's vital points with hands, fingers, elbows, feet, and knees. De Jongh became so obsessed by judo that he dropped all other sports to concentrate on it.

For mats, they used old mattresses and rugs. Kanamori, with his rank of *nidan*, second-dan black belt, led the workouts. He, Omuri, and Inoki wore judo costumes—white cotton jackets, trousers, and a belt. De Jongh wore an old blazer and a battered pair of corduroy pants. Later Baron Kanamori mailed him a judo costume, along with a rare and valued textbook by Jigoro Kano, founder of judo.

If Kanamori was the most skilled, de Jongh was the most aggressive, attacking his opponents unceasingly and with a ferocity difficult to fend off. Kanamori's nickname for him was *oni*, demon. When there was no one to practice with, de Jongh practiced alone, spending the time learning to fall safely and easily. If he had no fear of being thrown, then he could risk all on his *kake*, his attack.

In judo, Kanamori told him, you must seize your opportunity. You must avoid mistakes and you must destroy your enemy at all costs. Defeat your enemy and not yourself. Concentrate and never weaken. This is the way of *budo*, the martial path. It was more, thought de Jongh. It was a wisdom to be treasured as long as one lived.

Until Kanamori, de Jongh had been indifferent to the blackballing of colored students by Oxford's more exclusive social clubs. Why concern himself if the university's all-white, all-male brotherhoods continually rejected Indians, Africans, and Orientals?

De Jongh himself was a member of two well-known clubs— the Gridiron, which accepted only public school graduates, and the Carlton, which had its own wine steward. Why join when he considered most of the members to be little more than chinless wonders and upper-class twits? Because his father had been a member in his school days and had prodded his son into doing same. So now Rupert de Jongh occasionally found himself in the company of young aristocrats whose idea of unbridled merriment was to smash restaurant crockery, wreck their rooms, and drink themselves into a paralytic stupor.

Still, there was an undeniable prestige in belonging to such clubs and de Jongh saw no reason why Kanamori shouldn't apply for membership. Kanamori's family was *kazoku*, nobility descended from court nobles, feudal lords, and samurai. The family also had money and political influence. Kanamori himself was attractive, had good manners, and spoke English, French, and German. He was also a musician and a promising playwright, with an encyclopedic knowledge of Shakespeare and Shaw. Above all, he was de Jongh's friend.

But no matter how hard he tried, de Jongh could not get the Gridiron or the Carlton to lower their color bars. Kanamori was blackballed and de Jongh was advised to choose his friends more carefully in the future.

De Jongh's reaction was to send letters of resignation to both clubs, stating his refusal to be dictated to by cretins who couldn't pick their noses without sticking a finger in each eye. This action insured him of more than a few enemies. Students now went out of their way to avoid him. He was a leper with a bell around his neck to clear everyone out of his way.

One unsigned letter shoved under the door of de Jongh's room accused him of having committed an act so wicked that it would destroy the university. A more violent confrontation involved three rugby players. They attacked de Jongh and Kanamori one evening outside of an Oxford restaurant, but were easily defeated through judo. De Jongh broke one attacker's arm so severely that the forearm bone tore through the skin. Although there were no more such attacks, the hatred toward de Jongh and Kanamori did not let up.

It reminded de Jongh of the thrashings he'd received from snobbish Etonians because his mother had been an actress in musicals. Damn the English upper classes and their tweed souls. Nothing but bloody hypocrites, the lot of them. Always insisting on being reasonable with each other, but in private they were nothing but liars, drunks, and whoremongers. Including his own father, who'd been unfaithful to de Jongh's mother from the outset of their marriage.

Kanamori took the rejection with good grace saying that man can plan but only fate may complete. To show his appreciation for what de Jongh had tried to do, he presented him with a *bonsecki* that he had personally made. This was a miniature dry landscape, white sand and rocks arranged on a black lacquer tray to represent mountains and the ocean. De Jongh placed it in the window of his room, where in the morning sunlight the tiny sand waves appeared to rise and fall.

De Jongh's Hertfordshire home, called Bramfield House after the nearby village where Thomas Becket had been a twelfth-century rector, was also the scene of racism aimed at Kanamori. The perpetrator was none other than the corpulent and bearded Lord de Jongh, who refused to shake Kanamori's hand. And who let it be known through his wife that he would not dine with the family for the next few days.

"He's furious, love," Lady Anna de Jongh said. "Claims he wasn't told your friend was Japanese."

"Was and is," Rupert de Jongh said.

"Your father says that when you mentioned you were bringing one of the chaps home for the weekend, he thought—"

De Jongh snorted. "Him think? Not bloody likely. And he manages to take offense at everything. Look, I'm damn sick of the treatment Kanamori's getting in this country. I've promised him a pleasant weekend, and by God he's going to get one if I have to burn this house down. All the lord of the manor has to do is be civil until Kanamori and I return to university. Now if he can't find it in his heart to do so, then he and I shall have one awful row. And I wouldn't count on him getting the best of it."

Lady Anna, who'd noticed her son's increased confidence, tried to head off any conflict. "Darling, please leave things to me. Would you do that for your dear mother? I shall personally see to it that your friend enjoys his stay with us. Welcome is the best cheer, don't you think?"

She was as good as her word, this small, pretty woman who wore her blond hair in a pageboy cut and dressed in slacks, the American fashion rage popularized by Marlene Dietrich. Accompanied by her son, she led Kanamori through rooms hung with tapestries and rich wallpaper and filled with furniture covered in embroidered fabrics. She politely answered Kanamori's many questions about the history of the beautiful home and showed him its greatest treasure, one of the two shirts worn by King Charles I at his execution in 1649, to keep from shivering on that bitterly cold day. The king, Lady Anna said, did not want to appear frightened.

She took her son and Kanamori on walks through woodlands and along Roman roads to view Tudor cottages, ruins, a moated Norman castle, and a village that still kept a whipping post and medieval stocks in its square. Kanamori was delighted with all he saw and heard. And there was no end to his questions. He asked Lady Anna about the recent marriage of Britain's former king Edward VIII, now Duke of Windsor, to the American divorcee Mrs. Wallis Simpson. He wanted to know what the English thought of Hitler and if Winston Churchill was a warmonger and would ever be returned to power. Was it true that Rudyard Kipling, who died last year, had been the world's highest-paid writer and if Britain wanted peace, as its leaders claimed, why were all citizens being fitted for gas masks?

The Japanese, de Jongh told his mother, were God's most curious people. Their desire for information of any kind was insatiable. He casually added that he had switched his course of study at Oxford from economics to Oriental history. And he would soon visit Japan at the invitation of Kanamori's father.

Lady Anna said de Jongh's father wouldn't like this Japan business. You know how he feels about—she almost said wogs, but caught herself. De Jongh politely ended the conversation by saying he had the right to choose and had exercised it and that if he had to clutter up his skull with mistakes, he insisted they be of his own making.

Shortly before de Jongh and Kanamori's arrival at Bramfield House, Lady Anna had suffered an accident in the kitchen. She had knocked a pot of hot oil on herself, burning her left arm and hip. Both wounds were painful and hadn't healed. She was said to have slipped on a wet kitchen floor, but it was known that she had become something of a drinker. De Jongh blamed his father, accounting for a growing coolness between the two. Lady Anna drank because of her husband's infidelity. And she drank because it hurt to be snubbed by his family and friends, who thought he had married beneath him. She also drank because she was lonely. Her husband had forbidden her to associate with anyone from the theater or to invite her relatives to Bramfield House. In a cruel move to cut her off from the past, he had recently thrown out Lady Anna's treasured collection of rare theater programs, posters, costumes, and photographs. Rubbish and claptrap, he called them.

Kanamori could do nothing for Lady Anna's troubled marriage, but he could do something about her burns. At sundown one evening he and Rupert de Jongh searched the woodlands for frogs. When they had found eight or so, they returned to the house where Kanamori took over the kitchen and boiled the frogs into grease. He applied the grease to Lady Anna's burns. She felt an immediate relief. And there was a visible improvement in her wounds that same day. In gratitude she and her son presented Kanamori with an ornate pocket watch that chimed the quarter hour and had a gold sovereign for a watch fob.

If Lord de Jongh was feared by his wife and servants, he was not feared by his son. Success, position, and money had given Lord de Jongh a self-assurance, but dear God, it was nothing like the composure exhibited by his son. What on earth had gotten into the boy? Frightening to admit that you could no longer lead your own son by punishment or persuasion. Bloody bastard had outgrown his father as he would a pair of cheap trousers.

The day before Rupert de Jongh and Kanamori were to return to Oxford, father and son accidentally met alone at the top of Bramfield House's magnificently carved wooden staircase, where a year before her death a feebleminded Elizabeth I had scratched her initials on the banister with a ring. "Understand you're planning a visit to the Far East," Lord de Jongh said.

A nod from his son. Nothing more.

The father said, "Do make sure not to bring any more of *them* back with you. We have all the laundry men we need in England."

The look from his son was one the elder de Jongh would always remember. It was enough to make one's hair stand on end. And it revealed something about his son he had never seen before. In that look was the power to destroy.

To hide his fear Lord de Jongh excused himself and walked downstairs, leaving his son alone on the landing. At the bottom of the stairs the father's courage returned and he said, "Perhaps you should roam abroad in the world and get that arrogance knocked out of you before coming to work for me. I daresay a change of climate might mean a change of soul."

His son's smile was feral and cold-blooded. Yes, that was the word. *Cold-blooded.* "I'm certain it will," he said to his father. "I'm quite certain it will."

Two months later de Jongh and Kanamori flew to Tokyo, arriving in the Japanese capital on a gray New Year's Eve morning. De Jongh was immediately treated to a demonstration of Baron Kanamori's power and prestige. At customs all foreigners had to undergo a detailed written and oral questioning, luggage search, and physical examination that included testing of urine and feces. As they had for hundreds of years, the Japanese remained an insular people who guarded their borders with an iron-fisted security.

De Jongh, however, was excused from all scrutiny. He was treated as though he were Japanese. An important Japanese. He and Kanamori were met by the baron's private secretary and an army major, who escorted them past white-gloved customs officials to a waiting motor car in front of the terminal. The secretary was a short, fat young man named Hara Giichi, who had a perpetual smile, extraordinarily small ears, and a club foot. The major was Jiro Takeo, burly and slovenly, with food stains on his jacket, broken, yellow teeth, and the breath of a farm animal. He wore a special badge of a star surrounded by leaves, indicating he was attached to the Kempei-Tai, the secret police.

Major Takeo led the way through the terminal, with people hastening to clear a path for him. De Jongh noticed that Giichi was visibly uneasy in Takeo's presence. Kanamori greeted the major with a certain reserve and seemed visibly relieved when he didn't get into the car with them. De Jongh found Giichi congenial enough, but Major Takeo came across as a nasty piece of work. He glared at de Jongh and gave him a bone-crushing hand shake before swaggering back into the terminal. Disappointed no doubt at not being allowed to play the hooligan with the baron's Western visitor.

De Jongh didn't tell Kanamori, but he thought the major was a swine.

*   *   *

The chauffer-driven car passed through Tokyo on its way north to the baron's home in Kanazawa, described by young Kanamori as an attractive provincial town in the Japanese Alps. They would spend New Year's Day there before returning to Tokyo. De Jongh, keyed up and hungry for anything Japanese, hoped Kanazawa was more exciting than Tokyo, which he found gloomy and ponderous. Too bloody quiet by far.

Kanamori said the quiet was actually Japanese self-control, developed from living hundreds of years in crammed, flimsy houses, which allowed no room for privacy and individualism. Self-control born of fear because severe punishments by generations of samurai had guaranteed obedience to even the harshest social code. De Jongh said it was interesting that much of Japanese life had always been maintained by force.

Tokyo, he learned, wasn't one city but a collection of cities, villages, and towns. Modern buildings side by side with a maze of winding alleys lined with low, wooden houses. There were even a number of farms within the city limits. In Japan, the old and new existed side by side. The past and present were intertwined.

De Jongh said he'd never seen both crowds and traffic so hushed and free of noise. And there were no colors running riot in Tokyo as one might find in Europe or in other parts of Asia. Everyone wore black, gray, and khaki. Murderously dull, if you asked him.

Where in God's name were the kaleidoscopic kimonos he'd seen in books and museums? After a while he came to look upon an occasional glimpse of white-gloved traffic policemen and white-covered taxi and rickshaw seats as a shocking "color." Such a passive city. Quite disappointing, really.

But as the car left the city it circled a small park where a crowd of young men with flags, placards, and banners had surrounded a bus and were singing at the top of their lungs while clapping in rhythm. Nodding their heads in rhythm as well. They sang with an overwhelming feeling. De Jongh knew he was witnessing a strong, forceful devotion to *something*.

To what?

A word from Giichi and the car slowed down. De Jongh watched the singing go on for a minute or two longer and when it ended the crowd cheered, threw both arms in the air, and cried, *"Banzai!"* Long life to the emperor. They had worked themselves into a frenzy. Damn alarming to see. De Jongh had never witnessed such fanaticism in his life. Frightening. Yet impressive.

Giichi tapped the driver on the shoulder. As the car pulled away, the secretary began to explain to de Jongh in halting English what they had just seen. De Jongh interrupted, politely ordering Giichi to speak Japanese. A bow of the head and the secretary continued. The crowd was giving a rousing send-off to a busload of students who had been conscripted into the army. Japan was at war with China. Soon she would be at war with the West. With Britain and America. A silent Kanamori and Giichi awaited de Jongh's reaction.

He looked at the Japanese for a few seconds, then said what was in his heart. Things cannot be helped even when they can be. Giichi asked if war comes do you not fear for your life? De Jongh said that once a fire has been lit who can order it to burn this and not to burn that? After this Giichi remained silent for most of the ride. And whenever de Jongh spoke the secretary listened carefully, leaving no doubt in de Jongh's mind that Mr. Giichi was mentally preparing some sort of report on him.

Kanazawa was as lovely as young Kanamori had said, with narrow, winding streets that had remained unchanged since the seventeenth century. A heavy snowfall only added to its beauty. The snow, however, left Kanamori less than enthused. He disliked the cold intensely, preferring Tokyo, where it never snowed and pretty girls could be counted in the hundreds. The only thing he liked about Kanazawa was Kenrokuen Park, one of the most beautiful in Japan. He was mesmerized by its artificial waterfalls, rivers, pools, and cleverly designed running streams.

As they drove past the park, de Jongh said he had walked here when it had been Lord Maeda's private garden, when the Maeda clan ruled Kanazawa. Lord Maeda himself had honored him for faithful service. The lord's gift to de Jongh had been a beautiful white horse.

Kanamori and Giichi knew that the Maedas had ruled the city in the seventeenth century. But both men made no comment.

Then Kanamori asked de Jongh if he remembered what had happened to the horse.

De Jongh said, "No. Perhaps it will come to me later." His heart was beating abnormally fast. So many things seen, then forgotten. And dimly remembered once more.

Baron Kanamori's home faced Kenrokuen Park and was a mansion of graceful beams, *shoji* screens, ancient ceramics, and a priceless collection of woodblock prints. De Jongh initially had trouble accepting the spartan elegance of the rooms, but he soon dropped his Western expectations and viewed the mansion through Japanese eyes. What was a bare room with a single piece of furniture now became a room with sliding screens, floor mats, wall scroll, tea cabinet, and a single vase of flowers. Perfectly tasteful. Nothing else need be added.

De Jongh's sole complaint concerned the temperature. The mansion was cold enough to freeze the balls off a brass monkey and apparently he was the only one bothered by it. Heat, such as it was, came from a small hibachi in a room corner. A hibachi only half filled with burning charcoal and ashes. The living room fared somewhat better. It was heated by an *irori,* a hearth sunk into the floor. This was as close as the Japanese came to a fireplace. No chimney. Just a large square hole in the center of the floor. Supposedly, the smoke escaped through a hole in the roof. More often than not it remained in the room to burn one's eyes and trigger a coughing spell.

Baron Kanamori was in his late fifties, a wispy little man with a large head, close-cropped white hair, and the unblinking, predatory stare of a hawk bearing down on its prey. His considerable fortune came from oil tankers, the manufacture of iron ore and cigarettes, and the importing of rice from Formosa and Korea. He had the proud bearing of a man whose ancestors had been samurai in the service of emperors, shoguns, and warlords. His black kimono bore the family crest of a silver fox and two gold empress trees.

De Jongh was, of course, apprehensive about meeting him. After all, the old boy was said to be a mystic who went days without food, meditated sitting under a waterfall in Kenrokuen Park, and spent hours kneeling before a blank wall in silent contemplation. According to young Kanamori, who was vague about specifics, his father was an associate of top military and political figures. The baron was also tied to various secret societies, some patriotic, some involving the martial arts. De Jongh didn't ask if this included ties to the *yakuza*. He simply assumed it did. It was an open secret to anyone who knew about Japan that the *yakuza* were bully boys for hire, primarily used by conservative businessmen against liberal politicians.

Young Kanamori said, "My father's most outstanding quality is his perseverence. He is single-minded and tenacious in all things. Japan is his first love, perhaps his only love. He will do anything to protect it. All of us—my mother, my sister, and I—have been told that one day we may have to give our lives for Japan."

De Jongh wondered if the baron wasn't a bit unbalanced. Off his chump, as it were.

Young Kanamori eventually told de Jongh about the secret societies. The Black Dragon, White Wolf, and the Brotherhood of Blood were patriotic groups, as were the martial arts clubs. They dated back to the nineteenth century and had begun by collecting intelligence on Japan's greatest foreign enemies, China and Russia. Later they extended their information gathering to all of Asia, Africa, Europe, and America. Membership included cabinet ministers, industrialists, military officers, journalists, students, intelligence agents.

To de Jongh's mind this made Baron Kanamori some sort of unofficial spymaster. A hard-core nationalist who believed that the military caste should again rule Japan as it had before the restoration of the emperor in the nineteenth century.

Young Kanamori spoke about the *yakuza* reluctantly. He was an idealist; it was very difficult for him to accept gangsters as a necessary part of the political process. But he had a duty to support his father and that meant not questioning him on the use of the *yakuza*. Baron Kanamori insisted that the *yakuza* had a major role to play in Japan's destiny. Japan was on a collision course with China and Russia for control of the Far East. Britain and America were also potential foes; they had Pacific colonies and wanted more. Unless Japan established its right to rule in its corner of the world, she could end up a conquered nation. To avoid this, she would need the help of all her people. *All*.

De Jongh found such a concept fascinating. The *yakuza*, vicious and disreputable, were somehow involved in national politics. Remarkable. Rascals and scoundrels found their way into Britain's government, but strictly on an individual basis, not as part of a conspiracy. The *yakuza* invariably got its way through intimidation and force. They were people who had nothing to lose. De Jongh envied their ability to go about their business minus any shame or guilt. He wondered if Baron Kanamori was an *oyabun*. It was one of several questions he wanted to ask the Japanese industrialist.

But in the smoky, chilly living room it was Baron Kanamori who asked questions of de Jongh. The first questions were silent ones, involving only the eyes. The Englishman had never been stared at with such intensity in his life. After a few seconds, the baron dismissed his secretary and son. He also told his son that he and the *gaijin* were not to be disturbed.

When they were alone the Baron took de Jongh's face between his small hands, hands that were abnormally warm. De Jongh almost pulled away, then decided no. Better see this thing through. Find out once and for all if he belonged here or in England.

The baron slowly ran his fingertips over de Jongh's forehead, eyes, ears, mouth. De Jongh felt his initial nervousness begin to fade. Yes, there was something different about the little, white-haired man, but not to worry. He definitely meant de Jongh no harm. De Jongh actually felt composed, totally undisturbed. The baron wanted to know all there was to know about him. By touching de Jongh he was stroking his soul. He was reading his inner consciousness and touching the vital spark.

The baron said a single word: *bushido.*

De Jongh held his gaze and said that it was the warrior's code. Loyalty to the lord, bravery in battle. And honor before life itself.

The baron exhaled. He was satisfied. "You have arrived just in time. Japan has need of you, *gaijin*. We must hurry and teach you what you already know."

Baron Kanamori, his son, and de Jongh left the mansion an hour before midnight and drove toward the sea, to a valley temple three miles away. They were to spend New Year's Eve working with Shinto priests, to bring blessings on the Kanamori family during the coming year.

The night had grown colder and there was a full moon. The snow had begun to fall again, the richest, whitest snow de

Jongh had ever seen. Inside the bare temple the three of them lit candles and assisted dark-robed priests in selling talismans and fortunes to long lines of worshippers. The worshippers had also come to ring the temple bell and offer prayers for the coming year. In the freezing air, surrounded by sounds of bells and wooden drums, de Jongh had never felt so happy. And at peace.

Dawn. The number of templegoers grew smaller. With an hour break before the crowds returned at sunrise, de Jongh and the Kanamoris joined the priests at the hibachi. They warmed their hands over its glowing coals, ate rice cakes, and sipped the first sake of the year. The darkness lifted and de Jongh could see the falling snow through open temple doors. Cherry trees in front of the temple had been wrapped in rice straw coats to protect them against the cold. The Japanese revered trees, believing them to be living things with souls. Snow and cherry trees formed a combination of heartbreaking beauty. De Jongh could never be completely English again.

Nor did he have to be told the significance of being in the temple on this particular night. For him, the new year meant a new life.

He looked down into the hibachi, at its seductive and subdued light. He was drained, physically exhausted, but where he wanted to be. In Japan.

Priests began to chant and it was a few minutes before he realized that the chanting had a meaning for him. *What has been, shall be. What is done, shall be done. Yesterday, today, forever.*

De Jongh closed his eyes, felt himself falling asleep on his feet, and opened his eyes wide. The priests were gone. And so was young Kanamori. De Jongh and the baron were alone at the hibachi.

They talked until it was light, until crowds again filled the temple. The baron drew de Jongh's past out of him, leaving de Jongh with a pride in his previous lives as a samurai, court noble, poet, and musician. Leaving him also with an uncontrollable desire to remain in Japan.

Suddenly the baron said, "Join me, *henna-gaijin,* in a prayer for my son." The baron had become solemn. His shift in mood caught de Jongh off guard. Something was wrong.

Baron Kanamori said, "Naiga will soon enter into rest."

At first de Jongh thought he had misunderstood, that he had not heard correctly because of the crowds. But the sad look on Baron Kanamori's face told him there had been no mistake.

De Jongh said, "How do you know?"

"I know, as I know about you. Naiga has fulfilled his karma, which was to bring you to me. He is now through with this world."

"But why must he die?"

The baron looked into the hibachi. "Because of you, *gaijin*. Because a blood sacrifice is needed to bind you to Japan. Because you can do the things for this nation that he cannot. Come to me, *gaijin*, when my son has died."

Oxford.

On a cold, damp February evening de Jongh and Kanamori attended the newly opened George Street cinema. It was their second trip to the ornate movie house in three days. Kanamori was infatuated with the pictures, particularly the Hollywood variety. He was even more ecstatic about the cinema itself, one of only two in Oxford and the most exciting thing to hit the university town since last year's exhibition match between Fred Perry, three-time British Wimbledon champion, and the great American champion Donald Budge.

On the whole de Jongh enjoyed the flicks, but the George, as locals called the new movie house, was too overdone for his taste. The lobby had a fountain with spurting colored waters, a lounge with an orchestra, and three restaurants. The theater ceiling was decorated like a night sky, complete with moving clouds and twinkling stars. In addition to a first-run film, there was a stage show and an organist.

This evening de Jongh and Kanamori sat through a stage show that featured singing dogs and a tap-dancing hermaphrodite. Kanamori was delighted by all of it. De Jongh's verdict: horrendous. Things picked up with the showing of Gary Cooper in *Mr. Deeds Goes to Town*. But even as de Jongh sat in the dark and watched Cooper give away a $20 million inheritance, his mind was on a greater adventure.

He had remained in Japan two weeks longer than planned. His father was incensed, and de Jongh also fell behind in his Oxford studies. But he had stayed in Japan because of *Yamato Damishii*, the spirit of Japan. It was a phrase not easily defined; it was simply something to be felt and understood. The Japanese did. And so did de Jongh. Call it a spiritual strength, something the Japanese believed would sustain them through any year. *Yamato Damishii* united the entire nation, committing every man, woman, and child to total war, if need be, in defense of a country they loved with a passion that defied words.

The West wanted Japan out of China and a Japanese pledge against any future aggression in Asia. Unless Japan complied it could find itself under great economic pressure. Britain and America had spheres of influence in Asia and the Pacific, giving them valuable territories and natural resources, which they did not intend to share with Japan. Asian colonies tied to the West meant no raw materials for Japan's growing industries. The choice: submit to the West or acquire raw materials through conquest.

De Jongh had witnessed and experienced *Yamato Damishii*. Japan's choice would be conquest and he wanted to be a part of that great adventure.

When the cinema closed at 11:00 P.M., de Jongh and Kanamori found a High Street restaurant that was still open and had a late supper. They talked of films and Japan. For de Jongh it was one of those few times when all thoughts of the baron's prophesy about Kanamori's death had mercifully slipped his mind.

After dinner they stepped into a street that was dark and practically deserted. Public transport had stopped and a single student cycled past them on the way to his digs. Oxford was a small town; a short stroll in the night air and they would be back at the rooming house.

They started walking and in seconds saw the light and their elongated shadows in front of them. De Jongh looked over his shoulder. Behind them a car was moving in fast, roaring through the streets as though driven by a demon. Or a drunken student. De Jongh motioned Kanamori away from the edge of the sidewalk and closer to the shops. Let the bugger drive by and don't give him too tempting a target.

When the car was just yards away, it leaped on the sidewalk behind them and began to scrape a brick wall, leaving a shower of sparks in its wake. The car hit a dustbin, grazed a lamppost, and knocked over sandwich boards serving as shop signs. A horrified de Jongh realized the car was deliberately trying to hit them.

Everything happened quickly. He caught a glimpse of the car, a yellow Daimler. Then he was blinded by its headlights and was flying through the air. Kanamori had violently shoved him off the sidewalk and clear of the Daimler. De Jongh landed painfully in the street and followed his instinct, which said keep rolling, get away from the car. He rolled until he slammed into the gutter on the far side.

Still on his back, he saw the Daimler speed along the sidewalk, dragging a screaming Kanamori beneath its front bumper. Inside the car someone yelled in triumph. There were at least three passengers besides the driver. And then the Daimler passed over Kanamori's body, swerving onto the street and leaving the body in front of a sweets shop.

Horn blaring, the Daimler raced up the High Street, red taillights receding and finally disappearing in the darkness.

De Jongh pushed himself to his knees, collapsed, then crawled toward Kanamori. He became aware of injuries suffered in the street fall. Head and left ankle hurting unmercifully. Face cut and bleeding. Pain in the left side. Had it not been for Kanamori, de Jongh would have been much worse off. Much worse.

But he had seen the car. And he knew the identity of the bastard who had been at the wheel.

De Jongh reached Kanamori and almost fainted at the sight of him. The Daimler had torn off Kanamori's legs, scraped off much of his clothing and turned his face into something unrecognizable. The area around the Japanese was so slick with blood that de Jongh almost slipped to the ground. Kanamori's mouth was a black hole in a blood-drenched skull; when he tried to speak, nothing came out. He reached up for de Jongh with an arm covered in bloody rags.

In the upper-floor rooms overlooking the street, lights came on. Windows opened. People in night dress looked out and called down, demanding to know who was causing all the trouble.

A weeping de Jongh took Kanamori into his arms. He felt a misery so overpowering that he knew he was about to be physically ill. In an amazing show of strength Kanamori gripped one of de Jongh's hands until de Jongh thought the bones would break, and then he died.

It took four constables to pull the hysterical de Jongh from Kanamori's mutilated corpse.

De Jongh suffered a concussion, twisted ankle, facial lacerations, and cracked ribs. But he left his hospital bed and testified before a police inquiry that the owner of the yellow Daimler was an Oxford student named Denis Addison. De Jongh added that he and Kanamori had bested Addison and two of his rugby teammates in a punch-up near a Merton Street restaurant. Addison, it seems, had now taken his revenge.

But in his testimony Addison claimed the Daimler had been stolen two days before Kanamori's unfortunate accident. And when the accident occurred Addison had been at a private party in Christ Church meadow some distance from the High Street. Numerous witnesses were prepared to come forward and testify to this. Yes, he'd had trouble with de Jongh and his Japanese friend. They had given him a severe arm injury, which had forced him to drop out of all school athletics. He blamed the fight on Kanamori's resentment at having been blackballed from the university's private clubs. Rupert de Jongh, said Addison, had instigated the fight in support of his Japanese friend.

Addison's father, a newly appointed admiral of the fleet, called on the old-boy network to support his son. And so Oxford authorities investigating Kanamori's death began receiving character references, telephone calls, and other communications on behalf of young Addison. They came from the House of Lords, Whitehall ministers, the Ministry of Defense, and Church of England officials.

It was Lord de Jongh who gave his son a shocking bit of news about the "accident." The police report on the stolen Daimler was false. The car had actually been reported missing thirty minutes *after* Kanamori's death. Rupert de Jongh asked if the police were deliberately lying. "Of course," his father replied. "Who in God's name do you think is going out of its way to protect the boy?

"You'll have to bite the bullet on this one, laddy buck," Lord de Jongh told his son. "And don't count on the little tale I've just told you ever seeing the light of day. I promise you it will stay buried for some time to come."

In the bitter argument that followed, Rupert de Jongh named Kanamori's true murderers: English wealth and privilege. His father called him an ass for placing the death of a single wog above the institutions of your country. And how could the de Jongh family be on speaking terms with the Addisons and others like them if this Kanamori business wasn't allowed to fade away?

Son or no son, unless young Mr. de Jongh came to his senses and renounced the late Mr. Kanamori, Lord de Jongh was prepared to cut off all monies and assistance starting immediately. Break off all contact with the press and the Japanese embassy in London and stop trying to convince them to look into this so-called murder. "You haven't been quite the same since returning from the Far East," Lord de Jongh said. "You're a white man, by God. Act like one."

Choose, he said. England and family. Or dead scum.

When Kanamori's body was shipped home to his family in Japan, de Jongh accompanied the coffin.

He was never to set foot in England again.

SEA OF JAPAN
SEPTEMBER 1944

On a freighter bound for Korea, Rupert de Jongh leaned against a derrick mast and watched a teenage Japanese girl use a folding fan to simulate several visual and emotional effects. She was quite good. Blessed with supple wrists, expressive hands, and the gift to make others see beauty. She stood near a lifeboat, performing for a dozen young Japanese girls seated at her feet. De Jongh had interrupted a morning stroll about the deck to watch her.

His eyes followed the fan. A cigarette in his mouth remained unlit. The fan was an eagle in pursuit of her empty hand, a wounded sparrow. Positively mesmerizing. The girl was as good as any professional dancer or kabuki performer he'd ever seen. And the sole bright spot on this revoltingly ugly vessel.

The SS *Ukai* was a small freighter sailing out of a port near Kanazawa and calling at ports in Korea and China. It was little more than a leaky rust bucket, with holes in the deck, broken railings fore and aft, and cargo hatches that reeked of fish, animal carcasses, and urine. There were only six cabins, all located astern behind one large room on the bridge, which served as wheelhouse, chart room, and radio room. Those cabins were cramped, with malfunctioning toilets and clanking steam pipes. The cuisine was an inescapable horror.

The twelve-man crew could only be described as vicious and foul. They were a mixture of Koreans and Japanese, a collection of loud-talking, brawling drunks who rarely bathed. Their captain was a fortyish Korean, a flat-faced and toothy little man named Pukhan. De Jongh knew him to be violently covetous, with a history of discreditable acts involving young girls. Sailing with Pukhan, and de Jongh had made a few trips with him, meant putting up with his servile and fawning ways. The captain, alas, was a toady. De Jongh had once seen him continue to flatter a general who had spat in his face. A disgusting little man, really. Amusing to watch him come to attention on the bow of the *Ukai* and salute passing Japanese submarines, destroyers, cruisers, and aircraft carriers in the Sea of Japan.

De Jongh lit his Senior Service, enjoying the hard-to-come-by British cigarette, and watched the teenager turn her fan into a sword, then into the Sun God. Then it became a curtain, temporarily hiding her face before she revealed one emotion after another. Joy. Sorrow. And hope.

De Jongh thought, Precious little hope for you, fan girl. Or for those sitting at your feet and gazing at you with such adoring eyes. They were *karayuki*, females sold abroad to military brothels in Japanese-occupied Manchuria, China, Southeast Asia, Korea, and the Pacific. The fan girl, a ravishing little thing with waist-length hair and an adorable mouth, appeared to be the oldest. Around fifteen, de Jongh guessed. A few of the others couldn't have been more than eight or nine. Most had been sold to a broker by parents too poor to feed them. The rest had probably been snatched off Tokyo streets by a pimp and taken on board the *Ukai* against their will.

All were bound for the port of Samchok in Korea, to be sold on the dock to the highest bidder. Nothing for them to look forward to but a lifetime of whoring for some callous, stonyhearted brothel keeper until they became too old or too disease-ridden to service customers. Last night, first night out at sea, the girls had been raped by Captain Pukhan and his

crew. It had been a foretaste of what the girls could expect
when the ship docked.

Over breakfast this morning, de Jongh had been forced to
listen to Captain Pukhan tell of throwing one twelve-year-old
overboard last night because she had resisted a bit too stren-
uously. But not before removing her clothes, which he planned
to sell.

De Jongh had refused Pukhan's invitation to join in last
night's goings-on. Nor would de Jongh allow the two *yakuza*
with him to indulge. The three of them were on Baron
Kanamori's business and had no time for diversions. De
Jongh, the *gaijin*, known to be an effective intelligence agent
and no one to argue with, was obeyed without question.
When challenged, he had the reputation of responding with
prompt and inflexible savagery.

Since the start of the war with China, Japan had flooded
that country's northern provinces with heroin and morphine in
an attempt to weaken the huge population and destroy their
will to resist. But today drug dealing had become merely a
way of making money. Some used Koreans to handle this for
them. Baron Kanamori, impoverished by the demands of
Japan's war machine on his fortune, used the *yakuza*. And the
gaijin.

De Jongh was in charge of getting four suitcases of heroin to
Samchok. Here the drugs would be exchanged for gold bul-
lion and a cargo of black market rice. Captain Pukhan, who
had made these trips before, would then take de Jongh to
Hong Kong, where he planned to exchange the gold and rice
for diamonds. Unlike others, who used their drug dealing for
personal profit, Baron Kanamori planned to use his profits in
a war Japan was losing. Honor demanded he do no less.

And because he loved the baron like a father, getting the
diamonds back to Japan was as important as anything de
Jongh had done in six years of serving Japan.

Guided by Kanamori, de Jongh had become one of Japan's
top agents and cipher experts. Even the most xenophobic
Japanese had been forced to admit how good he was. He was
also an expert at judo, archery, and knife fighting. As a
result, the *gaijin*'s spirit was strong. He was mentally respon-
sive and perceptive, traits enabling him to survive the hazardous infighting found in Japanese military and political circles.

And because he was as merciless as any feudal warrior, he

had made the word *gaijin* a term of respect, a word to be
feared. Baron Kanamori called de Jongh the knife used to
scrape the bones of the enemies.

De Jongh prided himself on seeing what he saw, then
acting on it.

De Jongh was resourceful, fearless, and in love with war.
A man was never as free as he was in war, he learned. One
came to war minus the distractions of moral considerations.

It was an attitude he'd observed in the *yakuza* over the
years and approved of. God knows it simplified life and
allowed one to give vent to instinctive social actions.

The *yakuza* traveling with him jokingly called de Jongh
their *oyabun*. Definitely a bit of truth in that. They belonged
to a small house, less than ten men, and had made themselves
available to the baron for tasks ranging from blackmail to
murder. Recently, however, their *oyabun* and his subchief
had been killed. Victims of what the Japanese called "Lord
B." or the "honorable visitors." Victims of American B-29
bombers striking from bases in China.

No one else in this *yakuza* group had shown any leadership
qualities, so all were now forced to turn to Baron Kanamori.
He fed them, gave them clothing, a place to sleep, and a bit
of pocket money. He, in effect, was their *oyabun* and de
Jongh his subchief, charged with seeing that they obeyed
him. These days the baron was old and ailing. Should anything happen to him, the *yakuza* house would have no one to
turn to but the *gaijin*.

On the *Ukai*, de Jongh watched the fan girl lean over and
speak softly to a youngster who'd had handfuls of her hair
torn out in last night's mass sexual assault. Lovely fan girl. A
breath of fresh air on this floating *pissoir*. De Jongh caught
her eye. He touched his cap to her. His reward: a delightful
smile. For a few seconds he felt less isolated.

She flicked her wrist at him, opening the fan and revealing
a painting of a mountain temple. Another flick and the temple
disappeared into a closed fan. Sheer magic. One more smile,
then she turned her attention back to the children who needed
her. No, she hadn't been flirting with de Jongh. He'd had
enough experience with women to know when one of them
was fishing. This one had greeted him as a friend, he was
sure of it. As someone who warmed her heart as she did his.

For a moment he was reminded of how lonely he had been since his wife and child had died.

The ship's crew went about its business, sometimes making rude remarks to the girls, but going no further. Captain Pukhan had ordered no carousing during the day. Everyone must be alert for enemy planes. Nor did Pukhan want to accidentally crash into another ship simply because his randy crew were all running about flashing the one-eyed trouser snake.

De Jongh also had rules for his men. One was to remain in the cabin with the heroin at all times. Anyone other than de Jongh or the *yakuza* setting foot inside their quarters was to be shot on sight. The *gaijin* believed, as did the Chinese, that there were only two honest men in the world: one was dead and the other unborn.

He watched the teenager's fan become a turbulent sea. As the fan undulated in her fingers she said, "The sea in spring/ all day long it rises and falls/just rises and falls."

De Jongh pushed himself away from the derrick mast. Had he heard correctly? He dropped the cigarette underfoot, ground it to ashes, and walked over to the fan girl. Women, as a rule, received little education in Japan. Yet this child had just recited a seventeenth-century haiku by Yosa Buson, one of his favorite poets. De Jongh had to talk to her.

At the sight of him, the youngsters at her feet edged away. Couldn't blame them, not after last night. The fan girl, however, didn't move. She smiled sweetly and bowed her head. The folded fan was in one slim hand, its tip touching her cheek. Her vulnerability was appealing, but ultimately it would have no effect on de Jongh. He didn't give a tinker's damn about her fate or that of the others. His advice to her would be to pray for divine dispensation. Pray hard.

Still, he was curious about her knowledge of Buson.

Her name was Kasumi and she was from the far north, from Sendai, where there was a terrible famine. People there had been forced into eating acorns, weeds, cats, tree bark. To feed themselves and two smaller children, her parents had sold her to a broker touring the country on behalf of Tokyo pimps. No, she did not hate her parents. It was her duty to serve them at all costs.

She had been attending a missionary school until the war broke out and the English Protestant missionaries had been interned by military authorities. The school had been burned. Kasumi and others had poked about in the ashes and that's where she'd found the book of Buson's poems, the only book she'd ever owned.

As for the fan, she'd learned to use it by watching her mother.

Kasumi told de Jongh that she might be able to endure what awaited her in Korea, if she knew she would eventually return one day to Japan. Her voice dropped to a whisper as she told him she had already been informed that her death in a foreign land was a certainty. The man she had been with last night had told her so.

"The captain?" de Jongh asked.

She shook her head. "A colonel."

De Jongh smiled, refusing to correct her. Of course the captain had kept this one for himself. She was the prettiest of the lot, wasn't she?

Kasumi said that the colonel had told her that neither her family nor the government would come to her aid. He was an important man in the government and knew of such things. Someone else would own her for the rest of her life and would do with her as he pleased. Kasumi was lucky, the colonel had said. He would show her what she would have to do to please men.

She dropped to her knees in front of de Jongh and tearfully begged his forgiveness for what she was about to ask. She was unworthy, but she would do anything he wanted, *anything*, if only he would be kind enough to carry a letter back to Japan and mail it to her parents. She loved them very much and bore them no ill will for what they had done to her. She wanted them to know they would always be in her heart.

A rare one, de Jongh thought. Despite not wanting to be moved by her, he was. And in thinking about her he thought of the colonel. On a whim de Jongh asked if the colonel was Japanese or Korean.

"Japanese," she said.

De Jongh's eyes hardened. He looked over his shoulder at the cabins, then turned back to Kasumi. He helped her to her feet, taking care to do it gently. An intelligent girl. Intelligent enough to memorize a seventeenth-century haiku. Definitely intelligent enough to know the difference between a Japanese and a Korean. Or between a captain and a colonel.

De Jongh was on the *Ukai* because the baron had ordered it, because the *Ukai* was the only ship available for this type of mission. And because Captain Pukhan could be bought and intimidated for a reasonable price. No ranking military officer would set foot on this tub if he didn't have to. If the baron hadn't mentioned another passenger it was because he hadn't known there was one. Baron Kanamori was ailing, a man in the winter of his life. But his mind remained razor sharp and he was exact in all things, a trait he had instilled in de Jongh.

The heroin.

A temptation of the first order. And temptation inevitably overcame any virtue.

De Jongh took a faded chrysanthemum from his jacket lapel and tucked it in Kasumi's hair near the right ear. She smiled, touched it, and looked at him with a gratitude that was embarrassing. De Jongh was the one who should be grateful. She had just saved his life.

Karma.

It had placed her onboard the *Ukai* to warn him.

It had killed his wife, young Kanamori's sister, and their small son, when the two had fled Tokyo's bombing raids for safety in Kanazawa, only to be buried alive in an avalanche.

It had caused de Jongh's mother to lock herself in the family garage, switch on a Rolls-Royce motor, and sit in the back seat until she died from carbon monoxide poisoning.

It had killed young Kanamori in England and brought de Jongh to Japan.

Karma had made him the *gaijin*.

De Jongh looked toward the bridge, at the wheelhouse. Captain, my captain. Any conniving aboard this tub has to include you, old fellow. Just the sort of thing you would have done, sucking up to the colonel last night by presenting him with pretty Kasumi for a bed partner.

A grinning Captain Pukhan waved down to de Jongh from a wheelhouse window. De Jongh smiled back, fluttering his fingers in reply. We shall see, dear boy, we shall see. Make a lamb of yourself and the wolf will eat you. To avoid becoming mutton, de Jongh would now fall back on the only safety and security he had ever known as an agent: suspicion and violence.

He drew Kasumi aside, away from the other children, and spoke to her privately. This, perhaps, was the most dicey part of his plan. He was now forced to trust this girl, whom he had met only moments ago. Once or twice he looked over his shoulder at the wheelhouse and caught Captain Pukhan and the first mate watching him. Hoping they were thinking naughty thoughts about him and Kasumi, de Jongh put an arm around her thin shoulders and softly kissed her hair. He watched Pukhan whisper to the first mate and the two of them leer. The *gaijin* was a man, after all.

De Jongh talked to the young girl for another ten minutes, then tipped his cap and began walking about the deck. Just your average seagoing Englishman out for his morning constitutional. The constitutional, however, was soon turned into a complete tour of the ship.

He strolled topside, speaking briefly with men scraping rust from a derrick boom and others repairing a cargo hatch cover. A few words with a hand lashing oil drums to a derrick mast, who told de Jongh about the ship's one antiaircraft gun, then it was off to spend a few minutes with a Korean who was answering the call of nature by standing at the railing and pissing in the ship's wake.

An hour later de Jongh returned to his cabin and ordered both *yakuza* to stay inside until he returned. Neither of them were to leave under any circumstances, nor were they to accept any food or drink brought to them. Guns were to be kept at the ready. De Jongh would explain later. He slipped his one bottle of scotch in a side pocket of his tweed jacket and left.

The engine room was diabolically hot and so noisy one had to shout to be heard. Pistons, valves, engines, and hissing boilers going all at once. All being attended by a trio of filthy, half-naked Koreans.

De Jongh was ordered out of the steam room in no uncertain terms. It was off limits. He removed the bottle of scotch from his pocket and held it high.

Twenty minutes later de Jongh left the engine room drenched in his own perspiration, but with the final bits of information he needed. On deck he leaned against a cargo crane and gulped air like a drowning man just out of water. The sun had climbed higher and the sea around the ship was still calm and empty. He was running out of time.

Kasumi. He shaded his eyes, looked for her and found her leading the girls in *janken*, the child's game. De Jongh and his wife had played it often. You used the right hand and extended or curled the fingers to represent scissors, paper, or stone. Scissors cut paper. Stone broke scissors. Paper covered stone. Japanese believed the game developed mental quickness. De Jongh hoped this was true, because unless Kasumi followed his instructions, he and his *yakuza* were dead men.

In their cabin, de Jongh told his *yakuza* of the danger now facing them. The two, Toki and Okesa, asked no questions. A good sign. It meant that de Jongh's spirit was strong and that they acknowledged him as their leader, their *oyabun*.

He told them what he had learned about the ship, then he told them of his plan and what they would be expected to do. The crew, he said, had no firearms. Captain Pukhan didn't trust them with guns, a wise move since his crew was composed of military deserters, criminals, and the human dregs who hung about any harbor. There was a supply of small arms in the captain's cabin under lock and key.

De Jongh said there was always the possibility that a crew member might have smuggled a gun on board. Some of the crew carried knives, but not to worry. Surprise was the best weapon of all.

Regarding the single deck gun, it was HA—high-angle, medium-caliber, and built for use on both surface and air targets. It was not, however, in working order. The gun had been allowed to rust and was missing at least two important parts. From what de Jongh could gather, none of the crew had been trained to use it.

De Jongh's conclusion: Captain Pukhan was a poor leader and his crew more than a bit lax.

The *Ukai* was scheduled to reach Korea in three days. De Jongh said during this time an attempt would certainly be made to kill him and the *yakuza*. There was no other way to get control of the heroin.

The colonel was obviously the brains behind any plot. Captain Pukhan was a craven, unimaginative cretin and lacked the intelligence to mount any intrigue on this level. It would be wise to assume that the colonel was armed. And because he was traveling alone he had undoubtedly enrolled a few or all of the crew in his scheme. Count the girls' pimp as one of the crew. Assume that all onboard were the enemy, save those in this cabin. And the girls, of course. One of them would be working with de Jongh.

De Jongh said, "I have been taught to seize the opportunity, avoid mistakes, and destroy the enemy at all costs. This I intend to do."

Both *yakuza* rose to their feet, heads bowed in respect. Toki, the older, spoke for them both. He said they had never faced such peril before, not even in Tokyo's many gang wars. But they had confidence in the *gaijin* and would obey his every command. His words had given them strength. They could now understand how he had come to be so highly regarded by many of Japan's most important men. They knew of no other leader to whom they would so freely entrust their lives as the *gaijin*.

De Jongh, who had changed to a fresh shirt as he talked, now stepped in front of a dirty, cracked mirror and began knotting his Etonian tie.

Toki said, "I respectfully ask, *gaijin,* when do we move against those who would kill us?"

De Jongh leaned forward and when his cold blue eyes met Toki's in the mirror, the Englishman smiled. "Now."

The engine room. In the sweltering semidarkness de Jongh and Kasumi stood with their backs to a metal staircase leading up on deck. His left hand rested on her shoulder. His right hand, held belt high, was hidden under a folded tweed jacket. The three-man Korean crew was too busy to take any notice of them. In the clamor of noisy engines and hissing boilers, de Jongh had to yell to get their attention.

The Koreans' eyes went to Kasumi. They were men of a hundred desires and few choices and could not stop staring at her. De Jongh spoke to them, knowing the Koreans were more interested in Kasumi than in anything he had to say. They couldn't tear their eyes from her.

De Jongh thanked them for showing him around the engine room earlier, but now he had another request. Would they kindly allow him to hide something down here, say, behind the staircase or in an empty oil drum? Nothing much. Just some suitcases.

They were in his cabin at the moment, being guarded by people he didn't really trust. How could one trust the *yakuza,* who were gangsters after all? He would feel safer if the two

Japanese with him didn't know where the suitcases were. He would pay the Koreans handsomely for their trouble. And he was making them a present of the girl. The captain had given her to de Jongh, to be used for his pleasure until evening. She would then be taken away, to be used by someone else.

He watched two of the Koreans exchange looks. So they knew about the suitcases. And the colonel. And that de Jongh had been marked for extinction.

De Jongh said the best time to move the suitcases out of his cabin was after dark, when the *yakuza* would be having dinner in the ship's mess. The Korean crew chief wiped his oily hands on a dirty rag, smiled, and nodded. Agreed. De Jongh's response to the smile was to bare his teeth and take his hand from Kasumi's shoulder. For the moment the world now pulled in one direction.

The other two Koreans removed their filthy headbands and hand rags. One hollow-chested little man with pustules on his cheeks went so far as to squat beside a bucket of brackish water and splash his face and arms. De Jongh watched him use one wet paw to smooth down coarse black hair. Manners maketh the man.

The crew chief reached out to touch Kasumi's breast.

De Jongh fired from under the tweed jacket and shot him in the face and in the chest as the engines drowned out the sound of the snub-nosed Walther PPK and the crew chief fell backward into the rising and falling pistons. The second Korean watched wide-eyed as pistons pounded the crew chief's corpse, crushing the right leg and hip. De Jongh dropped the tweed jacket to the oil-stained floor and shot the second Korean in the jaw and left lung, knocking him back against a hissing boiler and sending him sliding down, smearing the rust-colored metal with his blood.

De Jongh stepped past a stunned Kasumi, the Walther aimed at the head of the little Korean who had splashed himself with water from the bucket. The Korean, weeping and shaking his head, backed away. De Jongh ordered him to stop all engines. *Quickly*.

When it was done, de Jongh slipped the Walther into his waistband and nodded toward the staircase. The Korean was to hide beneath it, cover himself with canvas, and keep quiet if he wanted to live. As the Korean walked toward him, de

Jongh snapped his fingers and pointed to the tweed jacket.
"Pick it up and hand it to me," he said.

The Korean bent down and de Jongh, hands behind his
back, worked fast. He unbuttoned his left cuff, pulled a
dagger from a wrist sheath and kept it hidden behind his right
thigh. The handle was covered in sharkskin and had a silver
pommel topped with a gold-embossed letter *Y*. The blade was
sharp enough to draw blood with a touch.

The Korean, eyes averted, rose to his feet, jacket held out
in his right hand. De Jongh thanked him politely and reached
out with his left hand. Suddenly he grabbed the Korean's
wrist and pulled hard, dragging him forward and off-balance.
Before the Korean could recover, de Jongh stepped behind
him and cut his throat from ear to ear. With the engines off, it
was foolish to chance a shot that might be heard.

He leaned down, wiped the blood-stained blade in the
Korean's hair, then looked at Kasumi. She stood as rigid as a
statue, her face tight with terror. Their eyes met. She pleaded
silently for an answer, but de Jongh had none to offer. He had
no time to indulge or deceive her.

He heard footsteps on a flight of metal stairs above and
heard a man cursing in Japanese and Korean. Captain Pukhan.
Kasumi looked toward the stairs, then at de Jongh, who
smiled. A true smile and not merely the baring of his teeth.

She gently placed the fan on the floor, then reached behind
her neck and began unbuttoning the cheap brown dress she
wore. When the buttons were undone she slipped the dress off
one shoulder, then the other and let it fall around her feet.
She wore nothing underneath. She was thin, small-breasted,
an alluring child-woman. De Jongh tore his eyes from her and
turned back to the Korean whose throat he'd just slit. He
began to pull off the dead man's trousers. Kasumi dropped to
her knees beside him and unlaced the Korean's shoes. De
Jongh gave her a quick glance. He saw her fear, but he also
saw the childlike faith she had in him. Something to make de
Jongh *answerable* if he weren't careful.

Yes, there was a quality about her that touched a hidden
chord in him.

Both of them looked overhead at the same time. Toward
footsteps passing through a narrow corridor in the crew's
quarters and heading toward the landing and staircase leading
down to the engine room.

*   *   *

Captain Pukhan's anger was uncontrollable. The ship wasn't moving. Only he could give the order to stop engines and he'd done no such thing. With a war on, it was wise to keep moving while on the open sea. The Japan Sea was still fairly safe, but it was only a matter of time before American bombing raids out of China increased. When that happened, no sea in Asia would be safe from those devils. Also, Pukhan wanted everything onboard the *Ukai* to appear normal. He didn't want the *gaijin* asking questions. The Englishman had a reputation as a very dangerous man. Pukhan wouldn't be happy until they'd killed him.

Now Pukhan was standing in an empty engine room and his crew was nowhere to be found. Where were those dogs who had brought shame upon their master? He tightened his grip on the studded leather belt and squinted into the semi-darkness for someone, anyone, to beat on. A sound near the staircase made him spin around.

The girl. Naked under the staircase. The pretty one, whom he'd taken away from the crew last night and given to the colonel, the man who'd promised to make Pukhan rich. What was going on down here? Hadn't the crew heard his order about staying away from the girls during the day? And this one was special, reserved for the colonel. The colonel had promised to make Pukhan rich by giving him a share of the *gaijin*'s heroin, and by using his connections with the Japanese occupation forces in Hong Kong to see that Pukhan got another ship. A larger ship.

In return, it was up to Pukhan to do what he could for the colonel while he was on the *Ukai,* which meant seeing to it that this little whore was available whenever he wanted her. But she wouldn't be available if she were dead and that could happen if these stupid monkeys down here started fighting over her. He was going to make them pay dearly for using her. Quick punishment was long remembered.

Pukhan saw him. Naked legs and buttocks beside the girl. One of the crew was relaxing after having had his pleasure. Pukhan licked his lips and raised the studded belt high. He tiptoed toward the girl and the naked man. He was going to have some fun of his own.

Behind Pukhan, a shadow detached itself from the darkness and reached out for him.

*   *   *

De Jongh stepped from the deck and walked up the short staircase leading to the bridge. At the top of the staircase, he ducked his head and entered the wheelhouse. Bloody annoying these low ceilings and cramped rooms. Not to mention the foul air emanating from an unwashed, hard-drinking crew. Blame these maggoty surroundings on Captain Pukhan. One more reminder why anything Korean could only be looked upon as odious.

De Jongh now wore his tweed jacket and carried a battered bucket from the engine room. The bucket's contents were hidden by a bit of torn canvas covering the top. He nodded to Toki, a silent signal indicating that all was proceeding according to plan. Toki, with a Russian Nagant pistol, and Okesa, with a German Luger, had seized control of the wheelhouse. Their guns were trained on the first mate, helmsman, and radio operator. Both *yakuza* had positioned themselves as de Jongh ordered: just inside the wheelhouse entrance and out of sight of anyone on deck.

The first mate, a sullen, muscular Korean with crooked teeth and a low hairline, kept his back to a window that looked down on the deck and the six cabins. His arms were folded across his chest, and when de Jongh entered the wheelhouse the mate fixed his gaze on him and kept it there. De Jongh pegged him as a troublemaker. The helmsman, a stoop-shouldered, gray Japanese, stood behind a now slack wheel. He was an alcoholic and the passive type. No problem there. The radio operator, a small, baby-faced Japanese still in his teens, lay facedown in the middle of the floor, head facing the door. When de Jongh entered the wheelhouse he looked up with tears in his eyes and asked if he was going to be shot. Question ignored.

Since only the first mate appeared to be the pesky sort, de Jongh considered whether to kill him or not. He decided, no. He needed the bastard. Captain Pukhan had signed on the mate to keep order among the crew, which he did through nothing short of barbarism. Beyond this particular skill, the mate was little more than a malevolent simpleton. A wolf born to destroy. And with a mind unflawed by philosophical introspection. De Jongh thought, now's a good time to take the wind out of Wolfie's sails.

De Jongh placed the bucket on the cabin floor and removed a thin silver flask from a side jacket pocket. He uncapped it, poured brandy into his mouth, but did not swallow. Instead he rolled his tongue around in the fiery liquid and stared across the room at the first mate, who looked as if he wanted to pull out de Jongh's eyes. Without glancing down, de Jongh touched the bucket with his right instep, then violently shoved it at the first mate. Bucket, canvas, and a round object contained in the bucket sped across the floor. The bucket, trailing the bit of canvas, veered left but the round object rolled until it hit the mate's feet. The round object was Captain Pukhan's bloodied head. The mouth had been cut at the corners, giving it a grisly smirk. Nose and ears had been sliced off. Carved into the forehead were the Japanese characters for *Judas*.

The first mate, mouth open, stumbled backward. He pawed the wall to keep from falling and looked at de Jongh as though seeing him for the first time. The radio man whimpered and the helmsman turned away, head down and an arm hooked around the wheel to keep from collasping. Both *yakuza* fought to hide their shock. Toki, the older, forced himself to stare at the head until he began blinking so rapidly that he had to look up at the ceiling. De Jongh swallowed the brandy and ordered the first mate to pick up the head, put it back in the bucket, and hang the bucket from the wheel. The burly Korean obeyed, averting his eyes from the head the entire time. When he quickly glanced at de Jongh before dropping his gaze to the floor, his eyes were spiritless. Almost as lifeless as those of Captain Pukhan, whose disembodied head should be enough to give intelligence even to fools such as the first mate.

With certain people in the wheelhouse now sufficiently demoralized, de Jongh swallowed another mouthful of brandy, capped the flask, and sat down at the radio operator's table. Reaching inside his jacket, he took out a little black book, opened it to the back, and removed a folded sheet of paper covered in Japanese characters. The paper was a highly classified list of all Japanese military vessels operating in the Japan Sea for the next five days. He looked at a desk calendar, at his list, then set the list aside. He opened the black book, his code book.

Watched by the five Japanese and Koreans behind him, de Jongh studied the black book in silence. Minutes later he laid the book facedown on the desk, put on the earphones, and switched on the set. He loosened his tie, giving the set time to warm up. Then after selecting the correct frequency, he began sending immediately. He tapped the key in a practiced rhythm, eyes straight ahead on the gray, empty sea.

Message acknowledged.

He switched to receive, and used the radio operator's pencil and scratch pad to write down the incoming message in Japanese characters. A quick scan of the message, then it was time to acknowledge and switch off.

He turned over his code book and began decoding what he'd received. After studying the decoded message, he slipped it and his code book back into his jacket. He'd contacted a submarine less than three miles away. He knew its commander and could expect quick action. But the commander would still have to get clearance for what de Jongh wanted, and that meant contacting Japan. From there someone would have to get in touch with Baron Kanamori to verify certain coded words sent by de Jongh. The whole process might take a long time or it might take less. All de Jongh could do was wait. And hope no one on the *Ukai* became suspicious.

The *Ukai* had come to a complete stop. Under the *yakuza* guns the first mate had remained in the wheelhouse and announced to the crew that there was engine trouble. Captain Pukhan and the engine room crew would handle it. Everyone was to remain at their stations. Up to this point even the mysterious colonel had bought this little fable. But since the colonel was a man with suspicion in his thoughts, he wouldn't be buying anything for long. De Jongh knew just how suspicious the colonel could be.

A touch or two of the knife and Captain Pukhan couldn't stop blabbing. The man in Number 2 cabin was Colonel Takeo, the coarse, brutish Kempei-Tai officer who'd met de Jongh on his first trip to Japan six years ago and been his enemy ever since. Takeo, who was insanely jealous of de Jongh's success as an intelligence agent. Who'd attempted to destroy him more than once and might have succeeded, had it not been for Baron Kanamori. Takeo, who refused to call him by his Japanese name, Yamaga Razan.

De Jongh left the radio and walked toward the window overlooking the deck and cabins. He kept to the right and out of sight from below. When de Jongh had been accepted in the Kempei-Tai, Takeo had all but foamed at the mouth. God in

heaven knew that de Jongh had earned the honor ten times
over. Takeo, however, was one of those Japanese with a
pathological hatred of all non-Japanese. On the day of de
Jongh's admission into the secret police Takeo had told him
to his face. "I have taken a blood oath to kill you before this
war ends." De Jongh would always be an outsider, nothing
more than filth from the wrong womb. He was a rat who had
crawled up Baron Kanamori's ass for protection and who
would one day lose his good luck. No *gaijin* in the world was
fit to be among Japanese.

De Jongh offered no reply. A reply was a warning and in
true Japanese fashion, he had no wish to alert his enemy. He
had unsheathed a sword in his heart long ago and aimed it at
Takeo. Besides, there was no medicine that would cure a
fool.

De Jongh's trip on the *Ukai* was just the opportunity Takeo
had been seeking, according to the late Captain Pukhan.
Better to eliminate the *gaijin* out of sight of his friends, rather
than do it in Japan and raise questions. Any assistance offered
by Pukhan and his crew would be rewarded with a share of
the heroin and the good graces of the secret police. And how
many in the crew were prepared to wade in de Jongh's blood?
All of them. To a man they all had itchy palms.

When was de Jongh to be eliminated? This very night,
Pukhan said. In the ship's mess. Drugged food, followed by
beheading. And there would be no investigation of the *gaijin*'s
death, according to Colonel Takeo. In Japan, Takeo's tale
would carry the day. The *gaijin* had deserted to the British
forces in China. With Baron Kanamori's heroin, of course.
To ease Pukhan's troubled mind, Takeo had promised to
liquidate the baron as soon as possible.

As for the *gaijin*, hadn't Takeo been on him for some time?
That's why he'd personally followed the foreigner across the
Japan Sea; the *gaijin* was his special quarry. Sad to say,
Takeo had been unable to prevent the Englishman's escape,
but may he burn in the hottest part of hell, the *gaijin*, and be
reborn a thousand times without eyes and tongue because of
his treachery.

Had it not been for Takeo's lust, his plan might have
succeeded.

De Jongh turned from the window and looked at the radio.
Kasumi was in Number 2 cabin with Takeo. And de Jongh

was troubled at having sent her there. Unfortunately, there'd been no other way to divert Takeo; he wasn't too intelligent, but he was shrewd and cunning. Any other approach might have failed.

As an agent, de Jongh had used women before and never thought twice about it. So why was he bothered by what Takeo might do to the young girl?

Love. A glandular activity, nothing more. Sex with a bit of sentiment. But like it or not, Kasumi had had an effect on him. She'd set him to wondering if he could ever be alone again after knowing her. He neither knew how it came about or why, but, yes, he did like her. His feelings for her were not ruled by reason, God knows. Drawn to her? Yes. Not by choice, but by karma. He had to get her out of Takeo's hands as soon as possible.

He sat down and absentmindedly began tapping the dead key on the radio, tapping out the message he'd sent minutes ago. He was chained here until he received an answer. And the longer he sat in this chair, the more Kasumi suffered at Takeo's hands. De Jongh stood up and started to pace.

Stop thinking about her. Stop seeing her knocking at Takeo's door, quickly wiping away a tear, and entering the cabin because de Jongh had promised to mail a letter to her parents.

He paced and looked toward the cabins. I am the wrath to come.

It was thirty-five minutes before the baron's reply came in. During the wait no one in the wheelhouse had spoken. The silence was a space surrounding the *gaijin*'s every thought and action.

De Jongh decoded the baron's message when it arrived via the submarine, read it silently, then spoke his first words in some time. He said, "Jolly good," and stood up. His *yakuza* became more alert and watched his every move.

He took Captain Pukhan's keys from the handkerchief pocket of the tweed jacket and underhanded them to the first mate. Amusing to watch the keys bounce off the Korean's chest, then off his fingers as he fumbled to catch them and failed and had to stoop and retrieve them from the floor. Not exactly shaking, but definitely ruffled by the sight of his captain's bodiless head. There was a flare gun hooked to the wall over the wheelhouse entrance. De Jongh took it down, made sure it was loaded, and slipped it into a jacket pocket.

Without turning around, he ordered the first mate to follow
him. He smiled when the burly Korean rushed to obey.

No answer. Again the first mate knocked on the door of
Number 2 cabin. This time there was an answer. From inside
Colonel Takeo cursed the interruption, adding he didn't want
to be disturbed at the moment. Come back later. The first
mate identified himself, saying the captain had ordered him to
bring two messages to the colonel's cabin. The messages
were for the *gaijin,* from a Baron Kanamori. They had been
relayed to the *Ukai* by a submarine.

Takeo said nothing, then asked if the messages were coded.
The first mate said they were, but they made no sense to him.
Just columns of numbers, nothing more. The captain thought
the colonel might want to see them before they were passed
on to the *gaijin.* Takeo agreed. Just slip the messages under
the door, he said. He asked about the *gaijin*'s whereabouts.

"He's in the mess having tea," the first mate said.

"He dies tonight," Takeo said. "And do a good job, all of
you. If not, you'll have me to answer to. Now slide the damn
messages under the door and go away."

The first mate squatted, shoved the messages de Jongh had
given him under the door, and looked up at the *gaijin.* The
gaijin stood to the left of the door, back against the cabin.
Now he held the first mate's gaze and aimed a forefinger at a
deck crane only yards away to the right. His cold blue eyes
followed the Korean as he shuffled over to it. The Korean had
been similarly accommodating when ordered to enter the
captain's cabin, carry out a footlocker of guns, and dump it
overboard.

De Jongh remained away from the door vents, which might
allow him to be seen from inside Takeo's cabin. He removed
the flare gun from a side jacket pocket, cocked it, then reached
over with his left hand and knocked on the door. Two quick
taps. Pause. One tap. Two quick. Pause. Then one. The
signal Kasumi had to remember. And act on.

A quick glance over his shoulder at the deck crane. Christ
all bleeding mighty. Gone. The stupid cunt of a first mate had
vanished into thin air. Now de Jongh caught sight of him,
waddling toward the stern, toward three crew members who'd
gathered near the girls. Nothing to do but let him go and hope

the businss here was cleared up before he returned with his friends.

De Jongh stepped in front of the cabin door, backed up three steps, and waited.

The cabin door flew open, swinging out on deck and banging into the wall where de Jongh had been standing. At the same time a naked Kasumi ran from the cabin. There was blood on her thighs. Her face was wet with tears. She ran behind de Jongh and dropped to the deck. The fan was clutched in her hands.

A naked Takeo, shaven-headed, and potbellied, wearing only rimless glasses and holding de Jongh's messages, stood a few feet from the open door. De Jongh watched Takeo slowly lower his hands to his sides, watched him frown as his mind raced to connect the *gaijin* and the girl. When Takeo's mind said, "Trap," he spun and raced for a small table near a bunk bed, one arm reaching for the Mauser pistol lying beside a tray of foodstained dishes. De Jongh brought up his right hand, pointed the flare gun at a point several inches above Takeo's bare buttocks, and pulled the trigger. He heard the *pop* as the gun went off. Takeo shrieked as he was lifted off his feet and hurled across the room into a closet door and dropped to the floor, writhing there a few seconds before flipping over on his stomach, a hand reaching behind his bleeding back to pull out the smoking flare. De Jongh stepped forward, kicked the cabin door shut, then yanked the naked girl to her feet. They'd reached the staircase leading to the bridge when the flare exploded in Takeo's cabin. De Jongh turned in time to see the cabin door blow off its hinges and sail across the deck until it smashed into the crane where the first mate had been standing. A second later he watched a fireball fill the cabin and send roaring flames out onto the deck.

The first mate and three of the crew caught his eye. They stood near the crane and watched the fire. The first mate pointed to de Jongh, who drew his Walther, pushed Kasumi behind him, and waited. He heard the two *yakuza* on the stairs behind him, but did not turn around. Something else had caught his eye: the submarine surfacing on the starboard side of the *Ukai*. He saw its conning tower and hull number clear the water, then its forward deck, and he smiled, seeing

the submarine as a cathedral providing sanctuary against a
pursuing mob.

De Jongh wasn't the only one staring at the submarine. The
entire crew and the young girls were at the railing, watching
the sub's tower open and a well-trained crew scramble on
deck. De Jongh knew the commander, a close friend of his
named Shiba, with whom he practiced judo. Shiba, not yet
twenty-five, enjoyed running his crew through combat exercises so strenuous that many collapsed and had to be beaten
and kicked to get them moving again. Three men ran to each
of two deck guns. Others dropped a pair of inflatable rafts in
the water, then stepped aside as armed sailors jumped into the
rafts and began paddling toward the *Ukai*.

De Jongh slipped the Walther back into his waistband, took
off his jacket, and put it around a trembling and silently
weeping Kasumi. Pulling a handkerchief from the jacket, he
dried her tears, realizing that he wanted her forgiveness for
what he had just put her through. He took her into his arms
and stroked her hair and was still clinging to the girl when the
armed sailors boarded the *Ukai* and pointed their rifles at the
crew.

Six

Alexis Bendor bit into a pear and watched Simon punch and kick the heavy bag in his Manhattan health club. Mother's pride aside, the boy was good. Smooth and strong from start to finish. Nothing forced. He went after the bag with a cold fury, no surprise to Alexis, who knew there were times when Simon could, as he put it, "get down."

She watched her son with pleasure, forgetting for a few minutes that she was angry with him. Angry because Simon would not believe Rupert de Jongh was alive and would try to kill her. Angry because Erica and Molly were staying in the apartment, forcing Alexis to check into a hotel.

The one drawback to watching Simon's workout was its location. The heavy bag was near the eucalyptus sauna, which emitted an odor like pungent cough medicine. Each time the door to the room opened and closed, Alexis got a snootful.

Simon had insisted on calling the club the FitnessCenter, as if there wasn't another one in the world. It was in a high-rise on West Seventy-fourth Street, an area hit hard by real estate developers and ravenous landlords. Say goodbye to the neighborhood's character, its delicatessens, bakeries, Hispanics, shoe repair shops, Irish bars, jumble shops. Say hello to Korean-owned fruit stands, pricey card "shoppes," one-bedroom condominiums at $300,000, gay clothing stores (heavy on studded leather and fishnet underwear), and dozens of side-walk cafés.

The FitnessCenter was strictly high-tech, two floors of metal and chrome, with matching gray walls and carpeting. Wide windows offered a clear view of a gray Hudson River. All very fashionable, very depressing. The equipment was state of the art, the latest Nautilus and Universal weight-training machines, treadmills, stationary bicycles, and aerobic pieces. Alexis preferred the Honolulu club, with its sun deck, health food restaurant, and proximity to Waikiki Beach.

Alexis watched Simon work the heavy bag with a combination of karate and boxing techniques. His kicks had power. They sent the leather bag flying on its chain. When the bag swung back in his direction, Simon used his gloved hands. Left jabs, left hooks to set up the right. Alexis nodded in approval. There was, however, room for improvement.

"Circle more," she said. "Lateral movements. And double up."

Simon obeyed. A strong kick and the bag flew away. When it swung back, he sidestepped left out of its path and went to his left hand. Just the left. Hook twice to the body, then a left cross to the face. Alexis smiled. Beautiful.

It began with exercise. A top thief had to be able to climb like a mountaineer, run like an Olympic sprinter, and squeeze himself into very narrow places. Meaning he had to be agile, slim, and a hell of a lot more physically fit than the average man. The heavy hitters, Simon told Alexis, the guys who walked away with millions, all had medium builds like he did. None weighed over 170 pounds. Simon kept his weight at 160 exactly.

Speed bag. He kept it moving, kept it *clackety-clacking* like a machine gun. Or as a boxer once told Alexis, "You gotta make it sound like a cow pissing on a flat rock." Left, right, left, right. Then one hand for a minute at a time. Simon did it all. The girls watching from the Nautilus were positively salivating.

Simon's perseverance, admirable though it was, could be irritating at times. Such as his refusal to take Alexis seriously about Rupert de Jongh.

*   *   *

"Simon, I saw him clearly as I see you," she said. They were now in the cafeteria of the FitnessCenter. "And don't tell me I didn't."

"You saw *somebody*, okay? You saw an old man, some old dude catching the rays in Kapiolani Park with the rest of the tourists, and you freaked out. You're pushing yourself getting ready for this water run. What're you up to now, seven, eight miles a day? And two of them in knee-high water. That's enough to leave anybody exhausted and bleary-eyed."

"Mother has the DT's, does she? Like hell, sport. He wasn't just 'some old dude.' After what that son of a bitch did to me, you think I'd ever forget the way he sends code? I heard him tapping a ring against his cane."

"Hey, what did you just tell me?"

"About what?"

"About what happened when you started making telephone calls. About what happened when you started telling people de Jongh was alive and kicking."

Alexis threw up her hands in frustration and looked around the half-empty cafeteria.

Simon said, "Half of them didn't believe you. The other half didn't give a rat's ass. Isn't that what you said? So why put yourself through all this? Which reminds me. Why are you going to Washington, seeing as how all you've gotten from those people is a hard time?"

"Because I still have friends down there. Because I'm owed a few favors and intend to collect. When it comes to Rupert de Jongh, nobody's brushing me off over the phone and getting away with it. Bet on it, buster. This thing between him and me isn't finished. Someone's got to put an end to it. Either he will or I will."

Closing his eyes, Simon held his head between his hands. "Here we go again. More letters to the editor?"

"Times like these mother could use a little drink. Why don't you serve alcohol here?"

Simon said, "Two letters to the London Sunday *Times* about misprints in some chess game—"

"Kasparov and Korchnoi. More than just *some* chess game."

"Whatever. *Times* writes back, 'Wrong, lady. Your assumptions are unsound, groundless, imprudent, and unwise.' "

"You left out erroneous, inaccurate, and unseemly. Always liked that word, *unseemly*.'' One eyebrow rose like a curtain. ''You're saying being wrong about a chess game means being wrong about de Jongh? No, no, let me finish. One has nothing to do with the other. In any case I'm about to fire off one more letter to the *Times*—''

''Jesus.''

''Four mistakes in a second Kasparov and Korchnoi game. And this time, bozo, your mother knows what she's talking about.''

He grinned. ''Gonna hang in there, right? If I remember correctly, this isn't the first time you went scurrying off to check out a rumor concerning Mr. de Jongh.''

She gave him a look of mock innocence, wide eyes and all. *''Me?''*

''You. Whatever gave you the idea that de Jongh's mixed up with the *yakuza*? Sure you didn't confuse what happened to me and Molly in Japan with that old man in the park?''

''Not in this life, señor. There were two Japanese with de Jongh, his own goon squad, and one was missing a little finger.''

''So he caught his hand in a car door,'' Simon said. ''Or maybe he's a nearsighted butcher, who knows. What if somebody put the guy's hand between two pieces of bread and bit down hard?''

''Simon, *please*. They were bodyguards, I'm telling you. Thick necks, beady little eyes. The kind who look like they catch rats with their teeth. Another thing: I recognized the Korean with them, Kim Doo Kangnang.''

Simon scratched his head. ''Where have I heard that name before?''

''Seven years ago. You and I were in Washington at the same time.''

''Ah, yes. I hit two houses in Georgetown the same night. Didn't I pick you up for lunch just outside the Koreagate hearings? You pointed out some guy, a little Korean with big ears and a gold watch on each wrist.''

''That was Kangnang. One watch is on South Korean time, the other's on U.S. time. He was with the Korean CIA then, probably still is. He was one of the Koreans accused of bribing congressmen to keep the foreign aid flowing to his country.''

''Old Kim the Candyman,'' Simon said. ''Steady passing

out those goodies. All those envelopes full of hundred-dollar bills. If the investigation had been allowed to continue half of Congress would have ended up in the slammer. As it was, Jaworski quit. Said he wasn't getting any cooperation from Congress and the State Deaprtment.''

"Coverup, coverup, coverup," Alexis said. "Congress protected itself. Meanwhile, our Mr. Kim survived, with the help of the South Korean embassy. There was talk at the time about him being involved with the *yakuza*, but that got buried along with everything else. Ran into that evil little troll at a couple of Washington parties.''

"What happened?''

"We nodded and let it go at that. I'm sure he knew I was a player. Why else would I be at parties given by people in intelligence. One thing for sure: our Mr. Kim did not want to be seen with de Jongh. Turned his back to me and tried to pretend I wasn't there.''

She saw it in Simon's face. *Our Mr. Kim wasn't the only one who wasn't there*.

He said, "Tried reaching you when I got back from Japan.''

"I was in Los Angeles.''

"How's the lady doing?''

"What lady?''

Simon sipped at his tea and said nothing.

After a while Alexis said, "I just wanted to check on her, that's all.''

Simon looked at her. "Know what I think? I think you're working on a little scenario that involves this old guy in the park and the lady you hopped a plane to see.''

"Mrs. Oscar Koehl, wife of a Dutch businessman.''

"Except he ain't Dutch. And his wife used to be de Jongh's girl friend. Do me a favor, no more games. Why'd you go to L.A.?''

"To see Kasumi, why do you think?''

"What's wrong with the telephone?''

"I wanted to see her face when I asked her.''

Simon finished his tea. "I'll bite. What did you ask her?''

"I asked her if she'd heard from de Jongh lately.''

"And she said . . .''

"She said it was a strange question to be asking, seeing as how we all knew he had been dead for a long time.''

"Imagine that. And you believe her?''

"Indeed I do. Nothing could keep her and de Jongh apart. She'd take off like a shot if she knew where to find him, and vice versa."

"I'll take your word for it."

Alexis reached into her shoulder bag, pulled it out, and held it aloft. Her *pièce de résistance*.

"Oh, God," Simon said. "I should have known." Alexis was holding Kasumi's diary, which he had seen and heard of more times than he cared to remember.

"Practically worn away the pages just reading it," she said. "All but memorized the damn thing."

"I know, I know."

"My Japanese isn't what it used to be. Then again, what is? Before I left Hawaii I checked out a few pages with Paul."

"Jesus, you dragging him into this?"

"He was glad to help, believe me. He confirmed my original interpretation. De Jongh did make a promise to Kasumi about carting a lock of her hair back to Japan if she died overseas. She had this thing about not wanting to be buried abroad. Want to hear the rest?"

Simon returned to his empty teacup. "Can't wait."

"Mrs. Oscar Koehl, Kasumi, is dying."

Simon looked up.

"Bad heart," Alexis said. "Could go any time. Weeks, couple months at the most. I've spoken to her doctor."

Simon's eyes were half closed; he was piecing it all together. "Let's see. First you plan to locate this guy you say is de Jongh. Then you let him know his girl friend's still alive. He goes, 'Wow, I made her this promise forty years ago,' and just like that he comes running to L.A. to cut off a lock of her hair and take it back to Japan. How am I doing so far?"

"Go on."

He pushed aside the cup in front of him. "And when he shows up you'll be waiting, right?"

"To kill him."

Simon looked away. "The revenge of the eternal patriot. Talk about off the wall."

That one hurt. You're not doing too well when your own son thinks you're missing a few beans from your jar. But the Englishman was a shadow that refused to disappear. Nor was

Alexis free of the guilt and bad dreams brought on by the killing of her spy team thirty-eight years ago. De Jongh had used Alexis to do it. Damn him. Not revenge, son of mine, but justice, the only hope of all who suffer.

She thought, He'll come for me. For sure that little shit will come for me. I saw it in his face. He'll come.

She could have forced an argument with Simon, but that would have led to her war versus his war, and they had gone around on that one too many times. Hers had been a necessary war, backed by peace on the home front and everybody pulling together on and off the battlefield.

Vietnam, Simon's war, had been a horse of a different color. Domestic turmoil at home and a confused, incompetent, uncommitted military on the battlefield. Not to mention corrupt South Vietnamese politicians. Simon, like others, had returned from Nam in no mood to talk about patriotism.

Alexis had gotten headaches arguing with Simon over God and country and, yes, John Wayne, whom she had met and admired. When the shouting died down neither had convinced the other and, worse, Simon remained disconnected. The word gave Alexis the shivers, but no other word made sense. *Disconnected,* cut off, withdrawn. The Vietnam veteran's syndrome. And for the first time in their relationship, Simon had been actually antagonistic toward her.

Maybe he was right. It was Alexis, after all, who had talked him into accepting the CIA's offer to join its special unit. And that's how he ended up in Nam, where the CIA betrayed him and tried to kill him. She had been hurt by his coolness and there were times when it had been so painful she had lain awake at night crying. But God was kind sometimes and eventually they had become close again.

Still it was up to Alexis to maintain the peace, which meant keeping her war and her patriotism to herself. And saying nothing about his stealing, about her fear that Simon might wind up in prison or dead. After what he had gone through in Vietnam, she owed him something.

She had told him about the Nazi officer who had become enchanted by Kasumi's beauty, shyness, and submissiveness. With de Jongh's death, Kasumi had no way of surviving the violent upheaval sweeping Europe with the end of the war. Together she and the Nazi had escaped Europe via the "rat line," an underground railroad for Nazis organized by the

Vatican. The American CIC, Counter Intelligence Corps, knew all about it. The Nazi and Kasumi couldn't have pulled off the escape without American money, false papers, and protection.

Lord knows, Alexis didn't want any Nazi to go free. She wanted him, and a lot of others, dead. But her opinion didn't count for spit. The war in Europe was over and a new one was waiting in the wings. This time the enemy was the Soviet Union, which had big plans for exporting communism worldwide. Kasumi's Nazi knew a lot about the Soviet espionage system.

And because America was interested in identifying Communist agents in Germany, France, Poland, Bulgaria, Greece, Italy, and even America, Kasumi's Nazi and hundreds like him had to be kept alive and free. Which is how one Mr. and Mrs. Oscar Koehl came to make their way first to South America, then to Los Angeles, where over the years Mr. Koehl served as an informant for several U.S. intelligence agencies. And meanwhile prospered in the textile business—automobile floor carpeting, bedspreads, various polyester blends. Koehl, an alias, wasn't the worst of the Nazis, but in Simon's opinion he should have been wasted, not protected.

That was Alexis's war. And it was a long time ago. Simon's war was too fresh in his mind and too absurd to ever be seen as necessary and worth wrapping yourself around the flagpole for. Simon's war sucked.

Simon stood up, touched the bandages under his sweatshirt, and said, "Do me a favor and stop this shit about killing people, okay? War's over. Yours, mine, they're both over. I'm meeting Erica and Molly here. When's your plane leaving for Washington?"

Alexis kept her head down. "Eight fifteen tonight."

She felt his arm around her. "How you fixed for money?" he asked.

She shrugged, head still down.

"Thought so." He kissed her hair, which made her feel better, as did the $2,000 in cash he gave her. Simon never used credit cards or signed for anything. This attention from him was welcome, but Alexis was still pissed at his asking her to give up, to back off. She hadn't backed off in her life and wasn't about to start now. That was no way to win a war.

WASHINGTON, D.C.
1942

The war. Cryptanalysts worked in the Temporary Naval
Building, a drab, factorylike structure on Constitution Avenue. It wasn't designed for comfort; there was a war going on
and comfort had to be put aside for the duration. You were
there to develop the ability to find and trace a pattern in the
enemy's code and not get too frustrated and discouraged by
the endless, endless work and concentration necessary to get
it done. No computers, no machines. Do it through acute
observation. And pray you're right.

You worked with sheets of newsprint three by four feet
covered with groups of numbers, five digits to a line because
that was as many as the eye could see instantly and remember. A word with more than five letters meant working with
two or more lines. The Germans and Japanese didn't make it
easy. Forget about the numbers on a single line matching the
number of letters in a given word.

First rule: what one man has written, another can read.
Second rule: let's pretend. Make assumptions, take chances.
Surmise and try conjecture. Give it a whack.

Go down each column first, then up. Next go across each
line left to right, then alternate columns or lines. Then go
diagonally backward and forward, always looking for a repetition of two or more digits together. Hope and pray that any
repetition you discover isn't just the law of probability.

Keep searching for more repetition and go on from there.
It sounded insane even to think about, but the work was
thrilling.

Be careful at the beginning. Column after column, page
after page, would be meaningless, just gobbledegook and
gibberish that enemy broadcasters would send out to get you
discouraged and make you stop trying before you got to the
real message, which might start two feet down the sheet. By
the time you got there, your eyes were crossed and you were
mighty tired and disheartened.

But one of the great helps in Alexis's career was that she
had been brought up to sit at her desk and stay there until she
finished her homework. Other code women fresh from college
were victims of progressive education. Teacher had to make

the work interesting or, God help us, meaningful. Teacher is at fault, so you really don't have to try.

Alexis got just as tired and discouraged as anyone else, but it never occurred to her to just down tools, which the others frequently did. A chief petty officer, marvelous little man, would come around and cajole them into going on with their work. That was no way to win a war. Nobody had to cajole Alexis. Nobody.

Simon kissed her cheek and looked past her. Alexis turned to follow his gaze. Picking a path between the snackers was Molly, all glitzy in newly frizzed hair, red silk blouse open to reveal a sequin-studded tank top, fashionably baggy jeans, and spiked heels, and a more subdued Erica. Alexis flashed her warmest smile. Not for Erica and Molly, but for the man walking just behind them.

Alexis extended her arms. "Come here, you ugly little ginzo."

They embraced. His head came just to her shoulder.

He was Joseph D'Agosta, Dag for short, a retired New York City detective turned coin dealer. He was Simon's close friend. He was also Simon's fence, the man who picked the places to be robbed. Alexis liked him because he stood up to Simon, never hesitating to turn thumbs down on a target that appeared too dicey. Dag could hold his own, never easy when Simon opposed you. D'Agosta insisted that Simon consider himself a professional and not some Puerto Rican filling up a plastic garbage bag on the sly at K-Mart. "Use your head," Dag said, "so that people will say 'There he goes' instead of 'The clown's buried over there someplace.' "

D'Agosta was in his late forties, a dumpy, heavy-jowled man with receding hair, greased widow's peak, and a speech pattern like that of a dog chewing a bone. Dag the cop had been capable of brutal heroics. He had more than his share of commendations for bravery, had taught himself the violin and French cooking, and knew how important it was to a woman that a man be a good listener.

His blind spot, a big one in Alexis's mind, was his devotion to the Catholic church. Because of the church, D'Agosta had stayed in a loveless marriage for more than half his life, refusing to leave a drunken and mentally unstable wife. And there was a child, a nineteen-year-old daughter doomed to an early death from multiple sclerosis.

His presence at the club tonight meant he and Simon had business to discuss.

Simon detached himself from Erica and gave Alexis a farewell hug, saying that a car was waiting downstairs to take her to La Guardia and the shuttle for Washington. Alexis said she'd telephone Simon from Washington and, after a quick look at D'Agosta, added that Simon should be careful. "Promise," he said. What Alexis kept to herself was a feeling that she'd be safer in Hawaii with Simon there.

At the elevator, Alexis turned to wave to Simon. But all she saw was his back, his and D'Agosta's, as they walked toward the club office, Dag doing the talking, Simon listening intently. Molly stood in front of a mirror, holding her stomach and admiring herself. Only Erica saw Alexis and she waved. Alexis thought about waving back, but decided no. Maybe next time. Erica may be the love of her son's life, but she wasn't the love of hers.

Seven

STATEN ISLAND
JULY 1983

On a night that threatened rain, Simon Bendor hung by his
arms from the branch of an elm tree in Von Briesen Park. The
park looked out on New York Harbor and the lights of
Manhattan five miles across the water. The elm, one of
several near Simon, was within one hundred yards of the
house he was about to rob. Only the chance to score three-
quarters of a million would have brought him to this island of
drab homes, steep hills, pizza joints, and dirt roads.

Thirty minutes ago the house had gone dark. Simon had
remained hidden in the elm, giving a live-in couple time to
fall asleep. Now he released his grip on the branch, dropped
gracefully to the ground, and crouched. Remaining motionless, he listened for any sound indicating he had been seen.
Nothing. Except sea gulls squealing in a cloudless sky, while
a buoy trumpeted sadly in the harbor.

He was dressed in black. Ski mask, long-sleeved shirt,
pants, sneakers, and leather gloves. A black waterproof bag
hung from his right shoulder. Two FM radios were clipped to
his belt. One was tuned to local police frequencies, allowing
Simon to monitor police calls and transmissions; the other
was used to communicate with his driver, now waiting in a
car on the north side of the park.

Using a driver was the only way to fly. An empty car
parked in the wrong place automatically drew police atten-

tion. They'd run the plates through a computer and if the car was hot or the cops felt like playing a hunch, they'd stake out the car and grab whoever showed up. Park in front of the job, Dag said, and it's hello Attica and ten years of stitching mail bags. Be a pro. Park some distance away, then walk to the job. Afterward, find your way back to the car.

From the shadow of the elm tree Simon looked across a grassy incline at the house. It stood alone on a cliff facing New York Harbor, an elaborate, three-story wooden structure built by a nineteenth-century stage line owner and brick maker. It sat just inside Von Briesen Park and also had a view of the Verrazzano Bridge and Battery Weed, the sprawling old Staten Island fortress now a military museum. In the darkness the house reminded Simon of the one in *Psycho*, with its turrets, open-air balconies, and veranda encircling the first floor. Norman Bates would have loved it.

Irwin Tuckerman owned it. He was a wealthy lawyer specializing in legitimate business deals and tax shelters for what Dag called OC's, organized crime people. Tonight, Tuckerman was off playing the big spender, celebrating his twenty-seventh wedding anniversary by taking his wife to Atlantic City for a weekend of shows and gambling. In addition to Mrs. Tuckerman's jewelry, Simon was also interested in twenty stolen airline ticket plates, which could be used to validate tickets anywhere in the world for twenty airlines. "We're talking twenty thou a plate," Dag said.

Irwin Tuckerman also collected baseball cards. Collect, hell. The man was a fanatic. He owned the pre-1900 Gypsy Queen and Old Judge cigarette series, many of the cards signed by the actual players. He owned sets put out by Bouchers Gold Coin Cigarettes, Cracker Jacks, the 1949 Bowman Pacific League, and the best the Fleer and Topps Gum people had produced since 1920. Until Dag clued him in, Simon had no idea these little pieces of pasteboard were worth so much.

"You're gonna hit him for six cards," Dag said. "Just six. We're talking the most valuable cards in the world. Honus Wagner, Pittsburgh Pirates shortstop, 1910. Cigarette company put out the card, but Wagner, he don't smoke, so he gets pissed. Tells the company to stop printing them or he sues. They stop. But not before a certain number hit the market. Not many, but that's why they're rare. Only nineteen of these babies still around. Tuckerman, he owns six. They're worth twenty thousand apiece. Got a guy, a collector, he's going full price. Half for me, half for you. Expenses I do out of my end."

Fair enough. Dag was entitled. The fence was the key element in stealing. Without him to dispose of stolen merchandise, the thief was stuck with stuff he couldn't get rid of. Stuff that meant prison if he was caught holding it. A fence like Dag, who could line up a job and a buyer, who knew police procedures, security arrangements, who still had police connections, a guy like that was worth every penny.

On every job Simon did, Dag lined up the car and driver. Tonight's driver called herself Marsha, no last name, and she drove in silence, accompanied by a slavering Doberman who stared ominously over the front seat at Simon. Marsha was a tall, quiet, black girl in her twenties, who Dag said played classical cello and sold handmade leather belts to lunchtime crowds on Park Avenue. She drove confidently, knew where she was going, and didn't bother introducing the Doberman.

The biggest expense on this job was the Tuckermans' maid. She had told Dag about Mrs. Tuckerman's jewelry and the baseball cards. Her name was Secora Elizondro and she was a short, dark, cheerful Dominican of nineteen, with three illegitimate children in Santo Domingo to support. Three days ago she had returned to the Dominican Republic, telling the Tuckermans she had to see her children. The Tuckermans had no idea Secora would not be returning.

It had been Dag's suggestion that she leave and not come back. Irwin Tuckerman was not stupid. After he had been hit he would sit down, do a little thinking, and eventually connect Secora to the robbery.

Dag saw to it that she didn't leave emptyhanded. She had flown out of Kennedy with a color Sony, a microwave oven, a suitcase full of new shoes and videogames, and $8,000 in cash hidden in her girdle. For what it was worth, she also had Dag's promise to look her up if he was ever in Santo Domingo.

Dag had met Secora in a Queens bar near his in-laws. The bar was a hangout for Hispanics, night school students at nearby Queens College. Dag ignored the male students, the short-order cooks, messengers, building superintendents, guys who pushed racks of dresses in the garment center. He was interested in the women, maids who were in night school to improve their English. Maids who worked for people who owned stuff Simon could boost. Dominicans, Puerto Ricans, Colombians, Mexicans, Cubans, Salvadorans. Low-paid women who were always in need of money, and who knew where the main alarm was.

Simon had to admire the way Dag had gone about it. No hanging around the Hispanic bar getting saturated and feeding quarters into the jukebox. Instead, Dag had followed the women to Queens College, signing up for night courses in ballroom dancing, art appreciation, and Spanish for beginners. After that he was home free. All he had to do was take his time and choose the right woman. Choose, he told Simon, was something Puerto Ricans wore on their feet.

Simon knew Irwin Tuckerman only by reputation. A bastard. Vain, money-hungry, with a rotten temper. Mean as a snake, but with more brains before breakfast than ten college professors had all day. A shyster who had made his pile because he took his fee in anything—cash, stock, real estate, helicopters, jewelry, oil paintings, and cars. Horny, too, Dag had said. Secora picked up an extra fifty each time she and Tuckerman played hide the wienie.

"Ten minutes after Tuckerman dies," Dag said, "they'll have to beat his dick to death with a baseball bat."

Tuckerman had gotten his start with Meyer Lansky and other Jewish hoods before moving on. He still remained strong with Lansky's people, who were in Las Vegas and Atlantic City casinos, and associated with the wise guys as loan sharks. Tuckerman's connection with the Italians went back to the forties, when Frank Costello had taken over during Lucky Luciano's imprisonment and Vito Genovese's exile in Italy. In all that time the lawyer had never served a day behind bars. No wonder they called him "Mr. Teflon." Nothing ever stuck to the man.

At the elm tree, Simon rose to his feet, eyes on the darkened house. The live-in couple who did the cooking were definitely not midnight ramblers, Dag had said. Come ten o'clock it's warm milk, dentures in a glass, and beddy bye.

Simon looked up at the sky. No moon, not even a single star. Nice. The moon could be a problem. When it was shining there was no place you could hide.

He held out his gloved hand. Steady Eddie. Everything

under control. He felt alive. Shit, he could do anything. Any
fucking thing. He took a deep breath of damp, salty air.
Better here than on the western part of the island, where ten
thousand tons of garbage a day found its way to a dump that
was the biggest in the city. And better anywhere than near the
four-foot blacksnakes Dag said were on the island someplace.

A final radio check before hitting the house. The police
calls came in loud and clear and not a word about anything
wrong at the Tuckerman home. Beautiful. Tuckerman took
care of the local cops, so a squad car would be driving up to
the house before the night was over. If they didn't find
anything out of place they wouldn't even bother leaving the
car.

Marsha was next. She came in without a hint of static.
"No problem," she said. "Everything's cool." Simon said,
"Stay loose," then switched off. One more look around the
park, at the dark, quiet house, at the route he had chosen to
get there.

Show time.

He sprinted from shadow to shadow, using trees, stumps,
and bushes for cover, keeping low and running in a crouch
until he reached a low stone wall behind the house. He
dropped to his stomach in short, wet grass and listened. There
was the smell of the sea, mimosa, and rhododendrons, but no
sound from the house.

Simon rose to his knees, unzipped his black bag, and took
out his night vision goggles. When he had them strapped on,
he stood up. Unreal. Almost like daylight, thanks to infrared.

Everything around Simon was vivid and well defined. A
small garden between the stone wall and the house. A flagstone walk leading from the wall to the house. Wheelbarrow,
hose, and rake left on the walk. The NV's were worth the
$8,000 Simon had paid for them.

He moved along the flagstone walk, carefully avoiding the
wheelbarrow and tools left behind by the gardener, then
stepped off onto soft ground and walked to a cellar window.
Fucking unbelievable. With all the crime around people still
had bad security. Dag had told him a long time ago that 90
percent of all security was either ineffective or at a minimum.
Tuckerman's cellar window, for example, had no bars because Mrs. Tuckerman thought they were ugly and unnecessary in a quiet community like theirs. No alarm tapes on the

window either, and no suction cups on the inside, which might have picked up vibrations. Not even an alarm sticker to force a burglar to stop and think. Dumb.

Inside, Tuckerman had installed a few things for protection: alarms, motion detectors, electric eyes. Naturally, he had problems with all of it. Anybody who owned this high-tech crap had problems. The alarms had gone off a few times without a break-in. Twice Secora had set them off while vacuuming and once a frightened mouse had done the honors. Another time Tuckerman had been tapping golf balls across the carpet when one had rolled under the couch, touched a wire and it was sorry, officer.

Tuckerman's two Dalmatians had often set off a couple of the motion-sensitive detectors. The dogs were also responsible for the electric eyes in the house being raised from ground level to a higher height. High enough for the animals to walk under without breaking the beams. More than high enough for a burglar to crawl under without breaking the beams. Nice doggy.

Three false alarms meant a fine or an order to disconnect all security wires. Tuckerman had had his three and more, but smooth talker that he was, nothing had been disconnected. He had paid the fines, contributed to a couple of police charities, and all was forgiven.

His Dalmatians were named Truman and Roosevelt. Roosevelt had swallowed a needle and was at the vet's recovering from a throat operation. Truman now roamed the house alone, but usually ended up sleeping outside the Tuckermans' bedroom or near the kitchen stove for warmth. According to Secora, the dogs were nice most of the time, not vicious, but they were also ten years old and getting cranky. Simon would have to play it by ear with Truman.

Simon tapped on the cellar window. That was for Truman's benefit, just in case the dog had wandered down into the cellar. No response. Unzipping his bag, Simon removed a roll of black tape and tore off two six-inch strips. He dropped the roll back into his bag, zipped it, then attached the strips to a pane to form an *X*. With his clenched fist he struck the pane, cracking it. The tape held the broken glass in place.

Pulling at the tape, Simon freed bits of jagged glass, then dropped to one knee and used a hand to scoop at the soft earth. The glass went into the newly dug shallow hole. He carefully removed all of the broken pane and buried it, leaving an empty frame. Without glass a frame could pass a swift inspection and appear to be a clear pane.

Reaching in, he opened the window's single lock, then pulled out two long nails that had been inserted in holes connecting the top and bottom halves of the window. The nails were to prevent the closed window from being opened from the outside and weren't a bad idea; they just weren't enough. After he had buried the nails, Simon lifted up the bottom half of the window, pushed open shutters, and dropped inside to the concrete floor.

He closed the window and the shutters, then looked around. It was pitch black inside, but for Simon it was one o'clock in the afternoon, thanks to the night vision goggles. Because it was darker inside the house than out, he had to adjust the separate viewer on each eye. Otherwise, no problem.

Straight ahead was a staircase leading up to the kitchen and to the left of the staircase was the door to Tuckerman's wine cellar. The lawyer had made the newspapers when he paid $19,000 for a bottle of Chateau Lafite Rothschild 1929.

Simon tiptoed up the single flight of wooden stairs, keeping close to the wall, where the boards squeaked less. At the top he lay down on his stomach, crawled through an open doorway, under the pale beam of an electric eye, and into the kitchen. Here he stood up and looked around.

Big. Big enough for two refrigerators, a freezer, two stoves, several racks of dangling pots and utensils, and three nice-sized butcher block tables. Simon walked to the nearest fridge, opened the door, blinked at the sudden light and poked around among the vegetables until he found a particular head of lettuce. He closed the door, waited until his eyes again became accustomed to the infrared light, then turned the head of lettuce around in his gloved hands several times before finding what he wanted. An opening. The lettuce was made of vinyl, with a hollow core for hiding jewelry.

Simon shook the jewelry out of the fake lettuce head and into one hand. Well now. Diamond pendants, a diamond-encrusted bracelet, and one very special ring. All of it worth big bucks. Especially the ring. Simon hadn't seen one this beautiful in a long time. Platinum and gold and dotted with blue sapphires and rubies. First-class workmanship. He doubted if Dag would break up this baby. No wonder Mrs. Tuckerman wanted it around her all the time instead of locked away in some safety deposit box. Got some good news and some bad news for you, Mr. T. The good news is lettuce is low in calories and contains vitamin A. The bad news concerns the ring that you like so much.

Simon put the jewelry in his shoulder bag, then closed up the hole in the fake lettuce and replaced it among the rest of the vegetables. The frost chest was next. No more jewelry. No cash or drugs either. Just plastic trays of ice cubes, two packets of frozen corn and a half-eaten pint of diet strawberry ice cream. After removing a plate of sliced tongue and liverwurst from the refrigerator he closed the door, walked to the kitchen entrance, and stopped. He stared into a short passageway leading to the living room. It was narrow, dark. Both walls were lined with framed examples of Mrs. Tuckerman's needlepoint. There was something else in the passageway: an electric eye at either end. Here we go again. Simon lay down on his back.

He inched under the beams and along the passageway floor, which smelled of lemon-scented wax. One hand held the plate of sliced cold meat on his chest. Better the smell of the wax than the meat; Simon was a vegetarian and couldn't stand meat. No complaints about the electric eyes, though. They were between two and three feet off the ground. A waste of money. Let's hear it for Truman and Roosevelt.

Seconds later Simon was in the living room and on his feet. His eyes went up under the goggles. Impressive. He stood in a large room with high ceilings and the Victorian clutter of mahogany and leather furniture. There was a trio of Venetian chandeliers with shafts hidden under elaborate swags of pendants, portraits of bewhiskered nineteenth-century gentlemen with hands tucked inside frock coats, and a huge fireplace topped by a gilded mantlepiece.

Simon wondered if Tuckerman ever went near his shelves of gold-embossed books. He also wondered about the lawyer's collection of porcelain clowns and small enamel boxes spread out on tables near the front window. Probably worth a few thou. Forget it. Just grab the *A* stuff and do a low crawl out of here.

To Simon's left was a grand piano covered with expensively framed photographs. One was of Tuckerman and his wife in color and had been taken on a tennis court. She was fiftyish, a small, pretty woman in a sun hat, white pants suit, and sunglasses. She had the smile of someone who had once been happy. Tuckerman was to her right, a big, red-faced man in tennis whites, with a long head, long nose, and receding hair. An arrogant-looking bastard. He held his racquet shoulder high, gripping it as though he were about to pole-axe a steer. No smile on his wire-thin mouth. Definitely nobody you'd want to fuck with.

To work. Simon found the telephone where Secora had said it would be, on a small table under a wall aquarium. He picked up the receiver and listened for an alarm going out. Tuckerman paid extra for a leased line, something banks and jewelry stores usually included as part of their security system. Cut the line and an alarm went off at police headquarters or a security company. Simon wasn't about to cut the line. He just wanted to make sure he hadn't tripped a silent alarm, which might have triggered a warning tape over the phone. So far he hadn't. All he heard was a dial tone.

Forget the main alarm panel. It was outside over the front door and therefore no problem. No problem with the rest of the downstairs either. Gone were the motion detectors and the pressure-sensitive mats Tuckerman used to have under the living room rugs. Pets like Truman and Roosevelt made those kind of security devices totally useless. The next alarm Simon had to deal with was upstairs. Second floor. Where more jewelry and the stolen ticket plates were hidden.

But first the baseball cards. Tuckerman kept them in scrapbooks and metal boxes on the shelves of a walled bookcase near French doors leading to the veranda. He insisted that twice a week the boxes and scrapbooks be taken down from the shelves and the outsides be wiped with a sponge slightly dampened with a mild solution of warm water and alcohol. The job took a few hours and none of the help liked doing it. But Tuckerman was a freak for cleanliness. The man couldn't stand dirt or dust and the sight of a single cockroach, Secora said, was enough to drive him crazy.

At the bookcase Simon stood on tiptoe and pulled down a black scrapbook from the top shelf. First one from the right, Dag had said. A guy like Tuckerman, one who likes everything in its place, this kind of guy makes things easy for you.

Simon opened the book and turned the pages slowly. All of them were mounted on black paper and placed between cellophane for protection. You didn't need to be an expert to know Tuckerman had some good stuff here. Players from the American League Boston team and the National League Pittsburgh teams who in 1903 played the first World Series. Cy Young of the Boston Red Sox, who in 1904 pitched the first perfect game—nine innings, twenty-seven batters, and nobody reached first. Unbelievable.

Ty Cobb as an eighteen-year-old, his first year with the Detroit Tigers. Another Cobb card gave his lifetime batting average: .367. *Lifetime.* There were cards from 1912, the first year the Boston Braves played under that name, and on the back of that same page were cards when the Boston team played under the names the Beaneaters, the Doves, and the Rustlers. And lo and behold, a page with the six Honus Wagner cards. John Peter "Honus" Wagner. "The Flying Dutchman." Simon carefully tore out the entire page, put it in his bag, then set the scrapbook back on the shelf.

With the plate of sliced meat still in one hand, he tiptoed up a wide staircase to the second floor. Last door on the right. The master bedroom. He snorted in disgust. The meat stank. How the hell could people eat this stuff?

But he was glad he'd brought the meat along with him. Truman had been lying in front of the master bedroom door. Now he was up and staring at Simon, who froze, keeping his breathing as shallow as possible. No sudden moves. Stay cool. His face was hot and itchy under the ski mask and his shirt was drenched with perspiration. But he didn't lift a finger to scratch himself or wipe away a drop of sweat.

Thieves were antsy about dogs, any size dog. Man's best friend could chew you up or bark his guts out until someone came to see what all the noise was about. Truman's presence had been the one dicey thing about this job, but Simon had decided to go ahead anyway. The dog wasn't vicious, Secora had said. Testy and long in the tooth maybe, but not vicious. For $750,000 it was worth trying to get past him.

Simon crouched slowly, again no quick moves, and held the plate out to the Dalmatian. Truman loped forward, sniffed. Sniffed some more. Simon stopped breathing. The moment of truth. Three-quarters of a million dollars and maybe Simon's freedom riding on what a dog does in the next two seconds. A hell of a gamble. Simon loved it. It was living by choice and being in charge. It was saying fuck it to a life built on rules written by someone else.

Truman dug into the meat. Simon exhaled. His heartbeat started to level off. He set the plate down on the red-carpeted floor, then patted the Dalmatian's head. The waiter will bring you the wine list shortly. Truman wagged his tail and never looked up.

Simon rose and walked to a mirror on the wall to the left of the master bedroom door. Like everything else in the house the mirror was overdone and richly wrought. It was large, half Simon's size, with a thick, gilded frame ornately carved with swans, satyrs, and cherubs. It also hid an alarm wired to a wall safe directly behind it in the master bedroom.

Simon flexed his fingers, took a deep breath, and slowly lifted the mirror from the wall. Drop this sucker and he could expect a lot more than seven years of bad luck. More like ten to twenty. The alarm didn't go off.

This one was definitely on. A small red light said so. The key was still in it. Simon set the mirror on the floor and turned the key. Off went the red light. On came a white light. The alarm was off. And nothing on the police radio. Meaning he had not tripped a silent alarm. Let the good times roll. He looked down at Truman who, head at an angle, chewed slowly on the left side of his mouth as though having trouble with his teeth. Can't hide old age, bro'.

At the bedroom door, Simon turned the knob and inched the door open. He didn't expect anyone to be in the room, but it didn't hurt to be cautious. At five o'clock this afternoon Dag had telephoned Atlantic City and learned that the Tuckermans had checked into a leading hotel casino on the Boardwalk and would not be leaving until Monday morning.

Simon left the door ajar behind him. Let Truman come in if he wanted to. Keep him out and he might end up barking and scratching at the closed door because he couldn't get to his newfound buddy.

The bedroom was attractive and spacious. Very New England. Beamed ceilings, fireplace, spinning wheel, rocking chair, twin four-posters with frilly bedspreads. Watercolors and pewter mugs on the walls. Polished floor with throw rugs here and there. Bay windows overlooking the shoreline. Simon could easily imagine this room as a hiding place for ghosts and things that went bump in the night.

He stepped left to stare at a watercolor of children in wool caps and knickers skating on a frozen New England pond. Simon set the painting on the floor, removed a small crowbar from his shoulder bag, and with the gloved fingers of one hand traced the outline of the safe hidden behind the painting. Nothing special. He'd run into this type before and never had a problem. Small, less than a foot long, around six inches high. Roughly the size of a loaf of bread.

In minutes he had pried the safe loose from the wooden wall. He put it into his shoulder bag, along with the bits of wood he had gouged loose. He placed the bag near the door and returned the watercolor to its original position. Neatness counts.

Safe number two. This one was hidden in a walk-in closet near the windows, a closet that contained nothing but Tuckerman's monogrammed shirts and dozens of pairs of two-toned shoes. All of the shirts were expensive, hand-made, and monogramed. Each was ironed and on a wooden hanger. Dozens upon dozens of shoes, with an emphasis on two-tones, were neatly arranged on shiny metal racks. Vain to the bone, our Mr. Tuckerman. Simon wondered just how much closet space, if any, Mrs. Tuckerman was allowed.

Although the closet was big, Simon still had to shift some things around to give himself room. He moved two shoe racks into the bedroom, carefully laid a dozen shirts on one of the beds, and rolled the rug back on the closet floor to reveal a buried safe. Same type as the one in the wall. Tuckerman had planted it in the floor as though it were a land mine. A slight adjustment of the night vision goggles to allow for the added darkness in the closet and it was hi-ho, hi-ho, it's off to work we go.

Digging this one out was a bitch. Blame it on the rock-hard floor. Sweat poured into Simon's NV's and twice he had to take them off and shake out the moisture. But after ten minutes, he had the safe in his hands. It joined the other in the shoulder bag. That was half of the job. The other half was opening the safes.

Shoe racks, shirts, and rug were returned to their proper place in the closet. Closet wood chips went into the shoulder bag. As far as Simon could see the bedroom now looked untouched. Outside in the hall he turned the alarm back on, returned the mirror to the wall, and closed the bedroom door.

Truman's empty plate, licked clean, was added to the shoulder bag, which weighed a ton. Simon didn't want the robbery discovered until he was out of the house and far away.

He began tiptoeing along the hallway, toward the staircase, then stopped and looked back. Truman was following him. Simon grinned. Why not?

In the wine cellar, Simon worked on the safes while Truman lay on the cool concrete floor and watched, his black-and-white head resting on crossed front paws. Both safes were locked. Simon wasted no time going to the crowbar, pounding the bottom of one safe until he had made a hole. Then it was crowbar into the hole and twist. Pull. Use his foot. And then the hole was enlarged. Good part coming up.

He reached into the safe, got a grip on something, and pulled it out. Well now. A necklace, yes, but the kind Simon saw only rarely. Large stones in gold settings, with a white gold clasp. Talking six figures for this baby, whether Dag sold it as is or broke it up and sold the stones individually. Losing this necklace alone would be enough to drive up Tuckerman's insurance rates.

Simon's hand went back into the hole and came out. Two bracelets. No paste, no cut glass. One had forty, maybe fifty small stones set in gold. He went into the safe again. This time he came out with an envelope. Holy shit. Cash. All hundreds. Simon's heart did high-jumps in his chest. Dag hadn't mentioned anything about cash.

Human nature being what it was, Simon thought about holding out on Dag. But he eighty-sixed the idea immediately. Maybe Dag already knew and was testing Simon. Playing his little games. You could never tell about people, cops especially. And Dag did have a sense of humor. In any case, it didn't make sense to blow a relationship worth millions for the sake of a few thousand dollars.

Knowing Tuckerman, the money might be hot or the bills could be in sequence and the numbers recorded somewhere. Smart thing to do was turn the cash over to Dag and let him wash it at some track on Long Island or over in Jersey. Pay a ticket clerk two percent for handling it, no questions asked, and get back clean bills. Untraceable bills.

The second safe. Maybe Simon was getting tired or the safe was stronger than it looked, but it took fifteen minutes of very hard work before there was a hole big enough for his hand. All of the work was worth it when he touched the plates. Twenty thin pieces of metal approximately the size of an airline ticket. Simon brought them out a few at a time and dumped them in the shoulder bag.

He had to smile when he thought about Tuckerman. The lawyer would freak out when he learned his house had been hit: the man had a short fuse on the best of days. Having his privacy invaded would turn him into a raving animal. And while the jewelry was insured, he would have to make good on the plates, plus spend a fortune on new security. He was probably getting comped in Atlantic City, but this was still going to be one of the most expensive weekends of his life. Hey, Tuckerman, if you can't take a joke, fuck you.

Simon hid the damaged safes behind a pile of chopped wood, closed the door to the wine cellar, and looked around. That should do it. His visit to the Tuckermans was now history. He couldn't wait to get outside, to breathe fresh air and take off the NV's. One last radio check before going outside. He unclipped the police radio from his belt and squatted down beside Truman. Aloha, my friend. Couldn't have done it without you.

It happened without warning.

Thunder boomed, rattling the cellar windows and causing vibrations strong enough to be felt through the cement floor. A beating rain started immediately. The noises were sudden and terrified Truman. Simon had a hand on the Dalmatian's head when the old dog started to whine, then bark, and when the thunder cracked again he spun around in terror. His bony flanks struck Simon's hand, the hand holding the radio, and sent it flying across the cellar. The radio smashed into a steelplated boiler, bounced off and dropped to the stone floor. Son of a bitch.

Simon scurried across the floor, picked up the radio, and held it to his ear. Nothing. He turned up the volume as far as it would go. Forget it. Truman, you fucking dork. The cops could be heading to the house and Simon would never know it.

Which is exactly what Marsha had to say when she got through on the other radio. The transmission was bad; it crackled with static and echoes caused by the thunderstorm, but Marsha managed to communicate her bad news.

"Cops coming your way," she said. "Just thought I'd

doublecheck to make sure you'd heard. We got a lot of storm out here.''

" 'Preciate it. My police radio's broken. What's coming in on yours?''

"I'm guessing, but I'd say you hit a silent alarm somewhere. Either that, or they got some very suspicious cops out here. Could be nothing's up. Like maybe it's just their thing to have a look-see around the neighborhood. Heading your way, that's for sure.''

More thunder. A whining Truman cowered near the freezer.

Static. Echoes. Simon couldn't hear a word Marsha was saying. He asked her to repeat. "I said it's a bitch out here,'' she said. "Raining like you wouldn't believe. Look, let me drive over to the house. You won't have to come so far—''

"No way. Stay put. If the cops haven't made you, let's keep it that way. If they pick you up for any reason, we have two problems. How well do you know the roads 'round here?''

"Man, I was born on this shit island. How do you think I got to drive you around? Look, you sure 'bout me coming over? You got some running to do in this rain before you can reach me from where you are. Ain't but one way you can get here and that's the way you came in, along the road the cops are going to be traveling.'' Her voice said she wasn't sure about Simon being able to get past a squad car in darkness and bad weather.

He remembered something his mother once said: confidence is what you have before you know better. Shit, he didn't want to know better. The more you knew, the more you worried about what you stood to lose. So you ended up being frightened like Truman or so paralyzed you couldn't pick your nose. Simon was nobody's airhead; he knew exactly what he was doing. While the next few minutes were going to be a tough titty to chew, he had been there a few times before. More than a few times.

"Stay put,'' he said to Marsha. "I'm on my way.''

He switched off, put both radios in his bag and watched Truman slink up the stairs, tail between his legs. Simon felt a little pity for the dog. Old age was a bitch.

He climbed through the window and into the rain. Holy shit. He hadn't been ready for this. It was like a tropical rainstorm, a deluge that soaked him in seconds and pounded his body with the force of small rocks.

He took off the NV's and dropped them in the bag; they were no good in the rain. He shaded his eyes, then carefully picked his way out of the yard and into the park.

He jogged toward the road, the bag's strap cutting into his shoulder. No need to crouch or do a low crawl or do much hiding. With the storm raging someone would have to be close enough to touch him to see him. Simon ran under trees, then stepped into the road. He ran in the middle of the dirt road, in mud up to his ankles. Maybe he could reach Marsha before the squad car got this far. The rain had to be slowing the cops down.

Oh, shit. He saw the light down the road and directly ahead of him, small but getting bigger and definitely coming his way. He stood in the mud, shading his eyes with both hands to keep out the rain. Something was wrong. He sensed it, but couldn't put his finger on it. Suddenly he knew. *The light.* Simon wasn't looking at a set of headlights. The light moving toward him was too strong, too white for that. What the hell was going on here?

He looked around for somewhere to hide. He had to get away from that light. It was no ordinary light. It was some kind of searchlight, something probably designed for night prowling in this kind of shitty weather, a new weapon, as they say, in the never-ending war on crime.

The squad car crept along relentlessly, rising and falling with each dip in the road, splashing water as it hit puddles and the light, that damned light, sweeping left and right, turning the whole fucking world into sunshine. Jesus, it was like being back in Nam when slicks and hogs, gunships dripping with rockets, 40mm grenade launchers, and everything you could think of came swooping down out of the night, turning on their searchlights, powerful, powerful beams, and greasing everything and everyone in sight. Shooting the hell out of trees, dogs, huts, rice paddies, and Vietnamese, ours and theirs, and always with those fucking lights that had the brightness you'd see if you stood in front of hell and the gates swung open. Simon hated those lights.

If he didn't get out of the road, he was dead. The light on the squad car would blind him and he wouldn't know which way to turn. He'd lose all sense of direction. Simon and that police light. Time for a little one on one. The challenge was everything in life. What it came down to, he knew, was the animal instinct to survive, to do what you were afraid to do, to know and believe that the only way to overcome danger was to take risks.

Simon took a deep breath and did what he had done all his life. He ran toward the danger. He ran toward the light.

Eight

HAWAII
1965

In winter the offshore storms between Alaska and Siberia send strong waves racing thousands of miles across the Pacific until they hit Hawaii. Here the waves grow in ferocity, deepening into winter swells that crash on Oahu's northern shore with a force powerful enough to make the earth tremble underfoot. Salt spray reaches as far as the highway and strollers are often picked up off the white sandy beaches by high waves and washed out to sea. Thirty- and forty-foot waves are not uncommon. Fifty-foot waves appeared in 1969 to pound the coastline like an aerial bombing, killing Hawaiians and reducing homes to kindling. These were not tidal waves, but winter swells normal for November and December, rising like glistening black holes from a blue-gray sea.

Winter, however, is the surfing season, when bold wave riders rocket across the glassy front of a fast-breaking wave on surfboards called knee machines, bungie cords, stinger fins, and elephant guns. It is an exhilarating and dangerous feat, performed on waves speeding over jagged coral at 25 miles per hour. Surfing contests are held all over the world, but the professional meets in Hawaii's thunderous winter seas remain the most challenging and hazardous.

Oahu's Banzai Pipeline, say surfers, is the perfect wave. But even the most skilled find it terrifying. *Banzai* refers to the courage needed to ride the monstrous wave, and *pipeline* describes its tubelike shape as it breaks on shore.

Surfers racing through this roaring, saltwater tube report that they see nothing ahead of them except a dash of diminishing sunlight. The light is both a beacon and a warning. It signals that the tube is swiftly closing in on the surfer, making the race through it a frightening one. A surfer has fifteen seconds or less to escape before the tube plants him, buries him underwater in whirling sand or guillotines him, breaks his neck or back with the mighty wave's falling edge.

Though a surfer thrown from his board may survive the underwater sand storm and falling wave, he still faces the pipeline's most horrifying feature: long seconds of an airless blackness beneath the sea.

Finally, when the water recedes, there is an ocean floor covered with flesh-slicing coral heads and poison-spiked sea urchins.

Surviving such a ride, said the ancient Hawaiians, was to be reborn, to escape from a roaring saltwater tomb. Their word for surfing was *he'enalu. He:* to flow, to glide along, to flee out of fear. *Nalu:* the motion of a wave gliding onto the beach, the slimy liquid found on a newborn baby.

Simon Bendor found his rebirth within the deadly Banzai Pipeline. When he challenged the wave, it had answered by trapping and nearly killing him. But in staying alive he had learned to live fully, to demand the most from himself. The seconds within the pipeline had been a cleansing fire, washing away fear and uncertainty. The pipeline had taught him that life was jeopardy or nothing.

He was born in Venice, California, the Los Angeles beachfront developed by a turn-of-the-century businessman who wanted a Southern California Venice modeled on the one in Italy, complete with canals and gondolas. The area prospered for a time as tourists flocked to gondola rides, amusements parks, and seaside hotels lining a three-mile stretch of beach. But by the sixties Venice had deteriorated. Drawn by low rents, hippies flocked to the peaceful community, followed by gurus, poets, motorcycle gangs, actors, and old people with no place else to go. Simon grew up watching Venice turn into a ratty, down-at-the-heels community; but there was a lesson in its fate. Everything had to die; get the most out of life while you can.

His father was Shea Bendor, an airline pilot and one of the few Americans to fly with the British RAF during World War II. His mother, Alexis, taught English literature at Santa Monica College and because she spoke several languages also served as a substitute language teacher. Later he learned that as civilians both parents continued to work for American intelligence. Shea Bendor, with his blond, square-jawed good looks and slight limp, looked the hero he was. But away from the war his air medals for valor and his boyish charm were of little use and in the end the only thing he did heroically was lie to himself. He gambled and was a naive businessman. Eventually a modest trust fund and an interest in a Pasadena vineyard had to be disposed of to cover debts. If you were a girl, Alexis said to him, you'd always be pregnant because you don't know how to say no. Hell, he said, it's the gullible who get the most out of life.

When Simon was ten, the family was forced to take a cheaper house, in a neighborhood where Mexicans celebrated their holidays with midnight songfests and by firing guns in the air. Alexis kept the family afloat with a tight budget, loans from the college, and by insisting that Shea stop gambling and make no more business deals. She also made him apply for the veterans benefits he'd ignored, which the family now needed. She accepted more teaching hours and found extra work as a translator. To save money she cut Simon's hair, doing it in the moon's last quarter so the hair would grow back more vigorously.

Shea Bendor's luck had been good during the war. After that, Alexis said, his bread always fell to the floor buttered side down. Yet their love for one another wavered. Alexis felt responsible for seeing to it that this love never became mere habit. And she made Simon understand the truth about his father, that in peacetime there were men who remained at war with themselves, who needed a replacement for the absorbing adventure of combat. Drawn to excitement himself, Simon understood. Later he came to see how much he, like his father, drew on his mother's strength.

Occasionally Alexis Bendor would join her husband on his Far Eastern flights. They would bring Simon presents from Tokyo, Jakarta, Manila, Hong Kong, Singapore, and Hawaii.

Hawaii was the place Simon enjoyed hearing about the most. Hawaii, with its deep and mysterious past. Hawaii, the islands the gods had pulled from the depths of the ocean. Hawaii, where volcanos still rumbled and where the surfing was the best in the world. Paradise. Nothing else but.

On a few of their trips together one parent would come back first. Usually it was Simon's father. A day or two later Alexis would show up, give Simon his presents, and say nothing about being late.

Simon had only to look at Alexis to know there would be no discussion concerning her whereabouts while alone and out of the country. As for Shea Bendor, he treated his wife's delay as if it were routine. Simon, however, sensed there was something out of the ordinary about it. He told himself it had to do with the spy business, with collecting information for the men who came to the house from time to time, jarheads in bow ties and button-down shirts, who took his mother's elbow and guided her into the garden to talk in whispers, but who raised their voices and laughed out loud when they spoke of the old days.

But despite Alexis's regular absences, she was always there when Simon needed her. Like when two Chicano teenagers trashed him after he caught them stealing six-packs and Hershey Kisses from the supermarket he worked in after school. The greasers did a number on him, breaking his nose and closing one eye. Simon took it with a chilly calm and a hint of a smile, as though it was nothing more than a learning experience and he'd do better next time. Alexis made sure he would. A week later he was in a downtown L.A. gym having the gloves laced on by Lawrence van Gant, a chunky black man with the broadest nose Simon had ever seen. Van Gant, now a trainer, had been in the ring with Graziano, Bobo Olson, and Kid Gavilan.

Simon was a gifted athlete and learned fast, showing exceptional speed, balance, and a talent for putting together combinations. "Sunny Jim's got the goods," van Gant said to Alexis after fourteen-year-old Simon, with less than two years' experience, went three rounds with a seventeen-year-old Mexican lightweight from the Pan-Am games, and made the Mex look bad. The trainer gave Simon technique and something else, a philosophy. You want to win a fight, you turn ugly. Use what you got, to get what you want. Which is why it

made more sense to Simon, when threatened by a hulking,
stoned hippie caught urinating in the supermarket's dairy
case, to back off, put three egg-size *D* batteries in a sock,
then cold cock the bastard from behind.

Let Simon be the fire-eater of the family, the one to put his
head in the lion's mouth. It floored her sometimes, the way
he could do crazy things and be so relaxed, so at ease with
himself. He wasn't a bad boy if you overlooked the occasional school disorder, class clown nonsense showing off for
girls, cutting classes to go surfing. Take away his daredevil
streak and you'd have a rather quiet, well-mannered young
man. You wouldn't have Simon, however. The truth is Alexis
was having fun living vicariously through her son's antics.
Yet there were times when she wondered if she really knew
him, especially when his composure was all but inpenetrable.
*A boy's will is the wind's will/And the thoughts of youth are
long, long thoughts.*

Alexis wondered about those thoughts when Simon went
out for gymnastics. This was a sport calling for strength,
balance, flexibility. And nerves, above all. Simon had it all,
especially nerve; as he had with boxing, he pursued gymnastics boldly, certain of his own courage. Black students especially admired his cool as an athlete; they nicknamed him
"Hawk" because he flew and was out for blood. At one high
school meet the blacks started the chant "Hawk, Hawk,
Hawk," and the rest of the students picked it up as Simon
spun around on the high bar, then let go and hung upside
down in midair with nothing between him and the floor,
before doing two back flips and landing on his feet to cheers,
screams, feet pounding the floor. Alexis, in the audience,
almost passed out. It was an evening she never forgot because
a day later he presented her with the first-place medal he'd
won. Her name was engraved on the back.

Simon was sixteen when his dream came true. His family
moved to Hawaii, where his father had gotten a job with a
small airline flying to Manila, Singapore, Taipei, and Hong
Kong. Shea Bendor had run out of opportunities on the
mainland. Too many missed flights because of three-day
poker games and too many layovers spent in foreign casinos.
And there had been a scandal. His name had been used in an
Arizona land development deal that cost investors millions of

dollars and triggered several investigations. Honolulu became his last chance; it had come down to flying retread planes for a dragtail airline with grass and wild pigs on the runway.

Simon couldn't figure it out. His father gave his mother little and took away more, yet she stood by him. You'd think there'd be a limit to endless forgiveness, especially since everybody knew his father would never change. Did Alexis think Hawaii would make a difference? "When you're in love," she said to Simon, "it's not that easy to break off. Besides, I like to finish everything I start. Running away just isn't my style, you know that. He could change. Give him a chance."

Hawaii. Simon thought, You believe this place? How the hell could anybody ask more from life than to live here? Perfect weather, flowering trees, volcanic mountains, forests of sugarcane fields, and coral reefs that were home to millions of birds. And the beaches. Unreal. Jet-black beaches of crushed lava rock. Beaches of pink coral sand. Beaches of snow-white sand. Just looking at the girls drove you out of your gourd. Chinese, Japanese, Polynesian, and *haole,* white. A rainbow of foxy ladies in outrageous bikinis, dresses slit to the hip and cutoffs that showed more ass than he'd ever seen in California. Paradise for goddam sure.

Something else about Hawaii. Because of its location, a meeting place of East and West in the middle of the Pacific, the islands were wall to wall with spy operations and hush-hush military ventures. Spooks were all over the place, eavesdropping, bugging, prying. Alexis loved it. She'd walk Simon down to the Honolulu ports and beaches and point out Russian trawlers tied up or floating offshore. She said every government building, consulate, or trade commission was bugged or bugging someone else. Hawaii was Berlin with palm trees, a playground for operatives, agents, informants, and anyone else in tradecraft. What helped the game along was that Hawaii was a popular retirement community for ex-CIA people and military officers, many of whom, like Simon's parents, took a government assignment now and then. Players trying to hold onto a small piece of the franchise.

Simon thought about that when he found the large brown envelope in his room. He found it the day his family moved into their modest, two-story stucco on Merchant Street, Honolulu's Wall Street. A Chinese moving man had dumped a box of Alexis's books on Simon's bed, where it didn't belong. The envelope had fallen out of the box and Simon picked it up and, without thinking, looked inside. Yellowed press clippings, receipts for airplane tickets, Honolulu to L.A., one way, and some letters addressed to his mother. The letters were postmarked Hawaii. No return address.

He unfolded one clipping. It was from a San Francisco newspaper, dated December 15, 1943, and told of the murder of William Linder, a local lawyer and city council member. Linder's bloodied corpse had been found with a broken neck, broken collarbone, and cracked ribs. Police were certain the "heinous crime" had been the work of "John Kanna, an American-hating Jap who had escaped from the camp for Jap internees at Tule Lake, California." Kanna was still at large but police and FBI were determined to capture "this sadistic son of Nippon who had so fiendishly dispatched the decent white man who had befriended him over the years."

Sadistic son of Nippon. Were they fucking kidding or what. Alexis had told him about the country's treatment of Japanese-Americans during the war. She had to fight back the tears; it was one of the few times Simon ever heard her admit America had done something shitty. She had grown up with Japanese in her hometown of San Francisco; the idea that they might be saboteurs and foreign agents was imbecilic. Yet 120,000 Japanese-Americans had been taken from the West Coast and Hawaii and thrown into concentration camps in California, Texas, Wisconsin, and half a dozen other states. Why?

"Race prejudice and war hysteria," Alexis said. "After Pearl Harbor the country panicked. It wanted revenge against Japan and didn't care how it got it."

Simon read more of the clip. John Kanna, said police captain Swanson Baptiste, had been a leader of the November disturbances by Japs at the Tule Lake Segregation Center in California, disturbances inspired by the Japanese government for purposes of making America look bad. In the camp Kanna had hidden a shortwave radio that allowed him direct contact with Tokyo. Kanna was a fiend, a bloodthirsty subhuman, who in escaping had killed two MP's with his bare hands. Captain Baptiste said this was an affront to brave white Christian servicemen everywhere. Captain Baptiste offered to personally strap Kanna to the chair in the gas chamber and drop the pellet that would send this Jap to his ancestors.

Simon returned the clipping to the envelope. Even if Kanna had zapped three people, it was hard not to sympathize with him. If he hadn't been thrown into the internment camp in the first place, none of this would have happened. Simon wondered why his mother had been interested in the guy, and decided it had something to do with her OSS days.

Simon took a postcard-size black-and-white photograph from the envelope. Brown with age, it showed his mother and some Japanese guy standing close together on the front stairs of what looked to be a college library. The photo was from the thirties, around the time his mother had been attending the University of San Francisco. She looked like a skinny June Allyson, with her saddle shoes, ankle socks, and sweater with the sleeves pushed back to the elbows. She was squinting against the sun. The camera had caught her with an armful of books and with one hand on the Japanese guy's shoulder.

The Japanese guy could have been his mother's age. He came off more formal, in a jacket, tie, and a cap held in both hands. He stared straight ahead, no smile, no frown, just nothing on his face. You could read into his expression whatever the hell you wanted. But the man was like the sea. Take as many soundings in him as you wanted, there was no way you'd ever know his depth. He was standing there with Simon's mother, but he was really somewhere else. Funny thing is, Alexis seemed to understand that and not be bothered by it. The guy had good shoulders and stood with his feet apart, like a man on top of the situation. There was something between him and Simon's mother.

"Simon!"

Holy shit. Alexis. Standing in the doorway to Simon's room and looking angry. White-hot and freaked out. She ran into the room and snatched the photograph from him. "Don't you ever, ever do that again. Don't ever let me catch you prowling through my things again!"

Prowling through her things. Jesus. He wouldn't prowl through her things if he was paid by the hour, and she knew it. If some chink nerd hadn't dumped the box in the wrong room, Simon would never have seen the envelope. Maybe the heat or the strain of moving had turned his mother *bizarro*. Getting worked up over nothing wasn't Simon's style. Besides, it was dumb to worry. Every day you were above ground was a good day. He preferred to be in control of himself because it was the only way to call the shots. Self-control allowed him to do crazy things without getting hurt. Self-control is why he was one hell of a good athlete.

He propped himself up on one elbow and watched his mother give him the evil eye. Way she was carrying on, you'd think he'd nailed a dead baby to a tree. Wait her out. That's all, just wait her out.

Eventually she did something. Raised her shoulders, dropped them, and exhaled for a long time. She turned from him to stare through the window at the Chinese moving men two floors below on the front lawn. "If those gooks drop one more lamp, I'm going down there and pull somebody's heart out from the back." She walked to the doorway dragging her feet, subdued now, emotions reined in. She stopped at the doorway, back to Simon. "Your mother's having a nicotine fit, which happens when she hasn't had a cigarette for two days. Trying to quit for the umpteenth time. I'm sorry about what just happened."

"No sweat. You want to talk, we talk. You don't, we don't. Question: they ever catch that guy Kanna?"

He saw her head snap up and one hand get a white-knuckle grip on the doorjamb. Simon didn't need to look at her face to know the tension had returned. Her every gesture screamed that any mention of John Kanna made her uptight. Very. "No," she said. "They never caught him." And then she was gone. No further explanation, nothing about what did happen to Kanna. Just "No, they never caught him," and goodbye.

Simon sat up on the bed. Now what was that all about? Ask a question and watch your mother get an attitude and start crying, because that's what she'd been doing when she'd left his room. He wondered if she shouldn't wear a hat if she was going to be out in the sun so much.

By the time Simon was ready to graduate high school he had become Hawaii's golden boy, a well-known schoolboy athlete with offers of gymnastic and track scholarships to local and mainland colleges. All he had to do was pick one, then it was four more happy years as a jock, with partying on the side. Whether as competition or kicks, sports were indispensable to him. At any point in his life sports allowed Simon to know how good he was, how much he had achieved. And there was beauty in sports. Beauty in the way body and mind extended themselves to their limits.

His mother understood this better than his father. Better than his friends and some of his coaches. Years of following boxing had made her aware of the sensuality athletes felt in what they did. But though she took pride in Simon's achievements, she drew the line at his wanting to ride the Banzai Pipeline. The pipeline had killed and crippled surfers. So what if a few had ridden it and lived to tell the tale. Alexis had a bad feeling about that wave. Under no circumstances was Simon to even think about it. She insisted on his promise that he'd never surf the pipeline. He said what she wanted to hear.

But he had found freedom by taking risks. Risk taking was a drug. Once he had experienced it he was unable to do without it.

Simon was eighteen when he tried the Banzai Pipeline. One December dawn he packed his heaviest board in his jeep and drove north to Sunset Beach, home of the pipeline, home of the baddest wave around. He could surf rings around most of the guys on Waikiki and he had the balls, so why put it off? His father was flying drilling equipment to Jakarta for a group of Dutch oil men; his mother, who taught at the University of Hawaii, would be overseeing finals for the next five days. That meant she would be working eighteen hours at a stretch, so count on her to sleep on campus three nights a week rather than drive home exhausted. Simon had accepted a dual gymnastic-track scholarship to the University of Hawaii and was looking forward to a campus where you could show up for class in shorts, T-shirt, and bare feet. Very laid-back over there.

But first get the pipeline out of his system.

It was scary.

From a cliff overlooking Sunset Beach, Simon and dozens of people watched the winter waves maul the shoreline. The pipeline was powerful and wild. It crashed onto the beach with a roar; the strength of the water made the ground underfoot tremble slightly. None of the spectators spoke. All stared in silence at giant waves that formed themselves into an awesome curl before crashing onto the reef. No picnics on the beach today. No lovers strolling hand-in-hand on the shell-covered white sands. City and county fire engines were in place, parked on a red dirt road behind the cliffs, yellow and red lights revolving, while their crews watched the violent sea for anyone needing rescue. As always, warnings had been posted, but they were meaningless. Nothing could stop anyone determined to go out. And nobody was more determined than surfers.

In the past Simon had come north for winter surfing and to watch professional surfouts like World Cup Hawaii and the Duke Kahanomoku Classic. Each time the pipeline had drawn him like a magnet, but strictly as a spectator. Once he'd watched a girl try it and get really wiped out. Firemen had pulled her out of the water bleeding and unconscious. What stuck in Simon's mind most was her surfboard; it had been washed up on the beach with deep, ugly gouges in it from the razor-sharp coral hidden below the water.

And today the pipeline looked a lot meaner than it had when the girl had gotten zapped.

Fuck it and press. Don't worry. Just press on with the business at hand. Simon, his stomach starting to tighten, walked through the crowd and returned to his jeep. He pulled the "elephant gun" from the back seat. It was a ten-footer made of balsa-covered fiber glass, with a scooped nose to keep it above the water's surface and in the rear, a skeg, a fin to act as a vertical stabilizer. Weight: thirty-five pounds. No problem carrying it under one arm as he followed a dirt trail down the left side of the cliff.

At the base of the cliff he came to a low foothill, which served as a ramp leading down to the beach. Five or six people stood on the hill getting drenched for a closer look at the pipeline. Two had surfboards, but Simon could tell by looking at them that they weren't about to go into the water. Back in their neighborhoods these guys were probably hot dogs, really good surfers. But today they had come against something that definitely brought on an uneasiness of the mind.

For a few seconds Simon had that same feeling. Up close the pipeline looked overpowering. Unbeatable. And the roar. Some of the people on the ramp held their hands over their ears. Stood there with wet hair plastered to their heads and faces slick with saltwater and hands over their ears like monkeys hearing no evil.

He entered a dream. He waded farther into the sea, climbed on his board, and lay stomachdown, paddling with his arms, guiding his board toward "the line-up," the position in the water that would allow him to enter the pipeline. The anger of the ocean shocked him. He had to fight it from the beginning, fight to keep from being dragged out to sea. But he did it, stopped his board from being pulled in the wrong direction. He was in control now. Ready.

He stood up with perfect balance, guided the board with his feet as he'd done hundreds of times, and then he was in the line-up, gliding smoothly into the pipeline, elated beyond words, feeling the rush like never before. A quick glance to his left. The pipeline was climbing, rising out of sight, a frightening wall of water, tons of it over his head and closing in on him, a terrifying sight. Too late now to do anything but go forward, toward the danger.

The sun faded, shrank, and suddenly Simon was in darkness; he was inside a tube of water, surrounded by it, racing along a watery passage that was closing in on him by the second. *Enclosed by water with only seconds to flee along a shrinking escape route.* Simon screamed with joy. He was inside the pipeline and had never been so happy in his life.

He bent his knees, stretched his arms to the side. Fought for balance. The race to daylight was on. He concentrated on the patch of sun ahead of him. Unbelievable how fast the pipeline was closing in on him. He had to get more speed. Getting darker in here. Panic time.

The wave collapsed on him with a terrible swiftness, knocking him off his board and with great power pushed him down into the suffocating, gritty harshness of an underwater sandstorm. He twisted, kicked hard against the water, and tried to clear his eyes. And saw a blackness that robbed him of all sense of direction. Sick with dread he fought to escape the roaring water and deadly sand, using all of his strength in an attempt to reach the surface, *what he hoped, prayed, and begged God was the surface.* But the pipeline was ruthless and relentless; it crucified Simon but would not free him. It pulled, pushed, and spun him in so many directions and denied him air. He swallowed seawater and sand and knew he was going to die, knew he was heading into a permanent and terrible unknown. Should have listened to his mother and stayed away from here. Dumbshit. That's what he was and that's why he was going to die.

And then he was moving underwater with bullet speed, screaming as the razor-sharp coral shredded his body and broke both legs. In his remaining seconds of consciousness he realized a frightening truth—that he was no longer in control of his life. He had failed for the first time and knowing this Simon now gave himself up to the howling sea around him, to the tumultuous saltwater horror that was the Banzai Pipeline.

July of the following year. Simon sat in a koa wood chair on the sun deck of a house atop Mount Tantalus. A pair of metal crutches rested on a table near him. Second day in the house and he had yet to meet the man who owned it. A friend of his mother's, he knew that much, and by the looks of things the friend had a few bucks. The house was ranch style, one story, but beautifully constructed out of brick, redwood, and glass. Japanese and Western-style rooms, with teak temple carvings, lacquered tables, silk scrolls, Picasso line drawings, and a harpsichord. Matted floors and sliding doors made of rice paper.

But not one photograph or painting of the owner. Absolutely nothing around to indicate what he might look like. No wife, children, or relatives. Just one old Japanese manservant who seemed to come and go as he pleased. Alexis finally admitted to Simon that the owner was Japanese, but that's all she'd say. Simon would meet him soon enough and then everything would be explained.

Mount Tantalus was Honolulu's highest residential district and one of its most exclusive. Land of the well-heeled, Alexis said. Sanctuary for those who owned Hawaii. The kind, she said, who sat back and whispered because they knew you'd lean forward and listen to their every word. Tantalus was an hour from downtown Honolulu, but until yesterday Simon had never set foot here. Tantalus was only a fun place to be if you were into boredom.

Good old Tantalus. Lots of four-car garages, manicured lawns, and NO TRESPASSING signs, all hidden in a tropical forest of giant philodendrons and ferns. But no stores, movie houses, dry cleaners, or newsstands. Dull. Alexis said don't knock it; Tantalus was cool and damp enough to grow roses, the only place on Oahu you could do that. And you could walk along the forest trails and pick guava and passion fruit. Simon said that's great if you can walk, but since I can't it ain't so great. He now needed crutches, wheelchair, and braces. His legs might get a little stronger, doctors said, but not much. He'd have to wear the braces for the rest of his life.

The pipeline hadn't killed him. Yet it had. It had taken away his legs, his wheels, forever finishing him as a jock. There had been other injuries: broken arm, cracked ribs, severe cuts from coral, infection from poisonous sea urchins. None of this matched the damage done to his legs. Both had been broken and mangled. Simon had worn casts for months and when they'd come off he'd looked at his legs and cried. They shrunk down to sticks, legs that had once been eagle's wings, legs that had once let him fly and do it all. The scars alone were sickening to look at. Everything else had healed except his legs and, according to doctors, they never would.

Fucking doctors. He'd gotten the usual crap from them. "You have a lot to be thankful for, son, because you're alive. Accept what's happened and look to the future. It could have been worse, you know." No it couldn't be worse, doctor, and the only reason you think like you do is because you've got shit for brains. When he'd been rushed to the hospital from Sunset Beach the doctors had wanted to cut off his legs. "Only way to save his life," they said. "Bone breaks, nerve and cartilage damage. And the infection. It's a life-threatening situation, Mrs. Bendor, and we need your permission for immediate amputation."

"Never," Alexis said. "You don't know my son. He'll kill himself rather than live as a cripple and who in hell are you people to tell me I have to do this to him? *I have to?* No, I don't. And I won't." The doctors lowered their voices and talked reason to this hysterical woman. Alexis, however, wasn't buying it. "You'll have to kill me first," she said. Then she stopped talking to them entirely. She started talking to Washington, which brought in naval surgeons from Pearl Harbor, heavy hitters to join the operating team that worked on Simon for seventy-two hours. The hospital called her the Iron Cunt behind her back. But she saved Simon's legs.

And she'd done it alone. Shea Bendor had died in Indonesia, his body found in a paddy field in Bogor, a town forty miles south of Jakarta, the face so badly battered that identification could only be made through dental records. No suspects to date and Jakarta police reported little hope of finding any. Alexis said he'd been killed because of his cargo, which hadn't been drilling equipment. Shea Bendor had been carrying small arms: automatic rifles, mortars, .45 automatics, grenades. The new international currency.

His previous intelligence missions had been simple ones. All any airline pilot had to do was talk to foreigners, to businessmen, journalists, union leaders, then report back to American intelligence. Simple. Except that the world was becoming less simple every day. Alexis thought Shea's death might have been a warning for America to butt out of Indonesian affairs, or maybe certain people over there thought Shea knew more than he did. Maybe somebody tried to make a deal for the guns and Shea was in the way. Simon thought American intelligence and their Indonesian friends had changed the game plan at the last minute and his father had gotten caught in the middle. And become one more example of just how hard it was to be a hero in the new cruel world.

From the sun deck Simon had an incredible view of greater Honolulu from Diamond Head to Pearl Harbor. It wasn't nine o'clock in the morning, yet people were already out in the water. Surfers. Swimmers. Wind surfers standing on surfboards, clinging to multicolored sails and letting the wind take them anywhere. Simon blinked away tears.

He had gotten up early to avoid having anyone in the house see him drag himself from room to room on crutches. The humiliation of being viewed as a cripple almost matched the humiliation of actually being one. He wanted no more pitying visits from friends. Sympathy didn't strengthen Simon. It goddam unnerved him because he knew the truth, that people looking at him saw only what could happen to them. Which is why they felt more sorry for themselves than they did for Simon Bendor. His new function in life? Sit in his wheelchair and let others know there's always something worse.

He didn't mind his mother being around. She'd taken an unpaid leave from the university to nurse him, massage his legs, cook, and read to him. In the hospital she'd slept in his room to protect him, she said, to make sure the doctors didn't try any funny business. She'd been there through the worst of it, those days right after the pipeline wipeout, when the pain and depression had been so bad he fucking wanted to die. Only the endless moments of her love had kept him alive.

Simon had taken an occasional telephone call from Paul Anami, the Japanese kid who'd been the first to pull him out of the water at Sunset Beach. But that was it for condolence calls.

On the sun deck Simon looked around to see his mother and a Japanese man walking toward him. Both wore kimonos and clogs. His-and-her outfits. Just looking at them told Simon the couple were more than friends. His mother looked more relaxed than she had in a while. She'd taken time to put on lipstick, and her hair was combed and had a ribbon in it. Well now. He wondered if she and the Japanese guy were horsing around, then decided if they were she was entitled. He could see signs of the stress she'd been under for the past six months. She chain-smoked, had a nervous tic near the left eye. And there were lines in her face. For the first time Simon realized his mother was growing old and he worried about losing her.

The Japanese owned the house, no question about it. Now he hung back, allowing Alexis to walk forward and speak to Simon alone. The man could have been thirty-five or fifty, and looked familiar. Simon couldn't place him, not yet, but he'd stay with it until he did. The man was well built, with graying temples and the air of someone who depended only on himself. Simon thought, The man doesn't think he has any limitations. Like I used to be. He also thought, I recognize him. It was the man in the photograph with Alexis, the one taken in front of the library at the University of San Francisco, twenty-five, twenty-six years ago. Definitely the same man.

Alexis stood in front of Simon for almost a full minute, working up the courage to speak. When she did speak she looked out at the rain forest. "I've known him for a long time. We've been *involved*, I guess is how you'd put it, ever since we were students at the University of San Francisco. It would kill me if you thought less of me for what I've done, but the truth is I'm not ashamed. Your father knew and he accepted it. It made my life a lot easier because, you see, I wanted them both.''

She waited for Simon's reaction and when there was none she continued: ''Not easy for me to talk about this part of my life. I mean, how does a woman explain being in love with two men at once? Men do it all the time and it doesn't seem to bother them. Bothered the hell out of me, though. God, did it ever.''

Simon touched her. ''Look, it's your business, you and this guy.''

''I always took care of you, you know that.''

''Hey, you hear me complaining? Wasn't for you I'd be some kind of freak with stumps instead of what I got here.'' He jerked his head toward the Japanese. ''You don't have to go into it if you don't want to. You know me, I don't get upset about anything. Except . . .'' He looked down at his legs.

Alexis sat in a chair opposite Simon, an unlit Lucky Strike in one hand, a slim gold lighter in the other. ''That's why I've brought you here. Simon, you have to promise me something. Promise me you'll do whatever this man says, no questions asked. Trust me. Please, please trust me.''

Simon said he did, because it was true and because he had nothing to lose. Should have trusted her on the pipeline.

Alexis lit the Lucky, took one drag, then screwed the cigarette into a black coral ashtray. Her eyes went to the silent Japanese, then back to Simon. ''People here in Hawaii know him as Victor Yashima. But that's not his real name.''

Simon said, ''I know. His real name is John Kanna.''

Alexis's jaw dropped. ''Oh my God.'' She looked at the man and shook her head violently. Her denial. The man understood and nodded once; then his eyes went to Simon and stayed there. Simon, who was enjoying himself, held the Japanese's gaze and didn't look away until he felt Alexis grab his wrist. Hard. ''How on earth did you know?'' she demanded.

''The pipeline screwed up my legs. It didn't mess up my head. You mentioned the university just now. It reminded me of that photograph, the one you didn't want me to see. The one of you two together. It was taken in front of the university library. That's how I recognized Mr. Kanna just now. That, and the clipping about him escaping from the internment camp and wasting three guys.''

"Anything else?" Sarcasm and pride in her voice.

"Anything else," he said. "Let me see. Ah, yes. You got real uptight when I asked you if they'd caught Mr. Kanna. And there were some other things in that envelope of yours. Letters postmarked from Hawaii, with no return address. Receipts for airline tickets, Honolulu to L.A. one way—"

"Tell him everything." Kanna, speaking for the first time. And in the voice of a strong man who could afford to be gentle.

Alexis lit up, inhaled deeply, and blew smoke toward the sea. Her eyes went to Kanna. "Everything."

California, 1943. For Japanese-Americans facing wartime incarceration, the U.S. Army's rules were ironclad. Surrender voluntarily on an appointed date; bring no more baggage than can be carried by hand; one week to ten days to settle personal affairs, including the liquidation of businesses and the disposal or safeguarding of property. Under pressure to speedily get rid of all they owned, evacuees were easily victimized. They were preyed upon by greedy real estate agents, bargain hunters, swindlers, and other Caucasians who saw the chance to steal what they had long coveted. What the Japanese failed to sell was confiscated by the state and divided among local counties.

To protect their land John Kanna's family signed it over to William Linder, a San Francisco lawyer who handled their legal work. Linder promised to hold the valuable acreage in trust until the Kannas were released. But shortly after the Kannas were sent to California's Tule Lake internment camp, Linder sold the land and pocketed the money. Linder now feared the Kannas' vengeance, for he knew they were descendants of *ninja*, medieval spy-assassins, and belonged to the Mikkyo sect of Buddhism. Outwardly the family showed no signs of being different from other Japanese. They worked hard, kept to themselves, and caused no trouble. But like many martial artists who followed Mikkyo, they believed its magical practices and incantations strengthened their fighting skills. Mikkyo was a mysterious practice combining combat and the black arts with the supernatural healing of illnesses. The Japanese called this method of healing *Te-ate*, touching with hands. Although such powers were more likely to occur in ancient times, they could still be found in the present age.

John Kanna's father had cured Linder's only son of tuberculosis by touching the boy with his hands, by using Mikkyo, the power of Buddhist law, the metaphysical side of the Japanese warrior. The lawyer now feared that power and decided to strike first. He bribed two MP's from Tule Lake to murder the Kannas: John, his parents, and a twelve-year-old sister. Nothing to it, the MP's said. The camp had only one rule on attempted escapes: shoot to kill. You solve the problem by catching the Japs trying to break out.

On a cold December night the MP's herded the Kannas at gunpoint to a deserted part of the camp, site of the "attempted escape." With nothing to lose Kanna and his father fought back, using skills they had practiced in secret. They killed the MP's, but suffered casualties among their own. Kanna's mother was shot to death and his father mortally wounded. Dying, he asked that his son promise to kill William Linder.

"Wasn't easy," Alexis said. "John had to escape from that hell hole first. Past guard towers with machine guns aimed at eighteen thousand Japanese. Past barbed wire, armed guards, tanks, and a battalion of combat-equipped troops surrounding the camp. To this day I don't know how he did it. No food, no help from anyone, and in low winter temperatures. Goes without saying that he would have been shot on sight if anyone had caught him outside the camp."

"I read something about a short wave," Simon said. "About him communicating with Tokyo."

"They lied. For the record, no Japanese in this country committed a single act of sabotage or espionage, and Lord knows they had reason to after the way they were treated. John did not own a radio, shortwave or otherwise. The authorities knew the truth and tried to cover up."

"You said he didn't have any help. He had help from you, I would imagine."

"I meant help getting out of the camp. You're damn right he had help from me later on."

Simon eyed Kanna. Mr. Cool. Standing there like someone had pumped him full of sedatives. "What happened when you saw Linder?"

"I killed him." Matter of fact. And no regrets.

"Didn't you ask him why he'd done it, why he'd broken his word?"

"I had no interest in his reasons and nothing he said would have changed my mind."

Straight ahead like a compass pointing north. A one-track mind and a talent for taking care of business. Simon liked that.

These days John Kanna was a successful fish exporter who lived quietly, grew award-winning roses, and belonged to the Chamber of Commerce. He had never married. And because there was no statute of limitations on murder, he remained a fugitive facing execution for killing three men. But at Alexis's request he had agreed to do something about Simon's legs.

"Do what?" Simon asked. "Paint one red and one green, then use me as a traffic light for small cars?"

Whenever Alexis got angry, her nostrils flared and her nose turned red. Her nose was beet-red now.

Simon thought, shit, for a guy with bad legs I definitely put my foot in it this time. She was only trying to help. If he'd given up on his legs, his mother had not. On the other hand, he'd gone through this scene too many times, getting his hopes up with this specialist and that specialist, only to be disappointed. And who the hell was John Kanna anyway, except a man who'd croaked two MP's and a shyster lawyer? Simon's mother, Jesus, she didn't know when to quit. Next she'd be telling him he'd soon be tap dancing on a Charlotte Russe without denting the cherry.

He told his mother he'd do whatever she wanted. Then he looked at the sea, at two outrigger canoes racing each other toward Diamond Head. When he turned around, his mother was gone. John Kanna was sitting in her chair. Hadn't made a sound, Mr. Cool Kanna. On the table between Kanna and Simon was a color photograph of Alexis in a green-and-yellow muumuu taken here on the sun deck. Kanna tapped the photograph with a forefinger. "Spit on it."

Simon prided himself on being in control, but if he'd had his legs he'd have leaped across the table and punched out Kanna's lights.

Kanna picked up the photograph and stared at it. "Why did you refuse to do as I asked? It is nothing but a piece of paper."

"Not to me. And you know it."

Kanna's smile was thin. "So it is not merely a piece of paper to you. We are talking about a symbol of some importance, a symbol that arouses very strong emotions. Something that brings from you the power to fight the man who tells him to spit on it. Now let us see if you understand other symbols, if you can accept their power. The American flag is a symbol, is it not? It has meaning for you, perhaps. A medal won for your athletic ability is a symbol. And so is a keepsake from a pretty girl, maybe one of those girls whose telephone calls you refuse to answer. There are people who consider the sea and the sky to be symbols of God."

Kanna's voice was numbing. Spellbinding. Hypnotic. That was it. Hypnotic. Simon's eyes were drawn to Kanna's hands, now resting on the table but really not resting. The man was doing some strange things with his fingers. Simon heard him say, "a strong will can pierce stone. Your will must be made strong." Simon, who could barely keep his eyes open, thought, He can't be talking to me. Jesus, the man's fingers couldn't keep still. First, they were knitted together facing Kanna. Then knitted together, forefingers pointed at Simon. Then one fist on top of the other, a single thumb aimed at Simon. Fascinating to watch, but weird when you came down to it. Kanna didn't seem to be the nervous type. So why was he so antsy?

"Simon? Simon?" His mother. Standing beside his chair and shaking him. Pulling him out of a deep sleep. Would you believe this? One minute he's talking to Kanna and the next minute he's nodding out. And he was suddenly hungrier than he'd been in months.

"Brought you something to eat," Alexis said. "You could stand to gain a few pounds. Chicken sandwich on brown bread. Brown rice. Fruit. John says you have to be careful about what you eat."

"How long have I been asleep?"

"Over two hours."

"You're kidding."

She showed him her wristwatch. Going on twelve noon.

"Eat," she said. "When you've finished, John wants you to come inside. He'll be in the room just off the sun deck, the one with the altar."

Simon bit into a slice of mango. He'd only closed his eyes

for a second, a second that had turned out to be more than two hours long. Kanna had hypnotized him. Mikkyo. What else could it be? And the sleep was the best Simon had had since before the pipeline.

He said to his mother, "You knew what he was going to do, didn't you?"

"John said you were tense, that you had not slept properly in a long time."

"He's right about that."

"He's right about a lot of things. He's been watching you for—"

"Watching me?"

"He came to the hospital a few times."

"I never saw him. Did he come when I was asleep?"

"Only once. The rest of the times you were awake and never saw him."

"You're telling me I was awake and never saw him in my room? Wait a minute, I get it. He disguised himself as a doctor or something."

Alexis popped a grape into her mouth. "You recognized him when you saw him just now. Why didn't you recognize him when he was disguised as a doctor? If he was disguised as a doctor."

Simon stopped chewing and looked at the house.

Alexis, eyes on her son, reached for another grape. "John's waiting. Finish eating."

Kanna set the goal. The cultivation of mind and body, the development of mental and physical strength. The inner strength was more powerful. It calmed the mind, created self-confidence, and could even rejuvenate the body. Whether in combat or in daily life, a strong will made a man invincible. But first Simon had to believe in this power. He must work hard to bring it out in himself. Learn from his own experience that these mysteries did occur in life, that they were neither supernatural nor unexplainable. Neither words nor books could convey this knowledge. He would have to experience it for himself. If he did, the return of full strength to his legs would be just one of the rewards.

They trained together twice daily, at dawn and at night. Kanna, Simon learned, was a hard-nosed and icy teacher with flawless technique as a fighter, and that was the problem. He remained inflexible in his demands that Simon live up to his standards. How do you satisfy a man like that? You didn't. You just ran yourself ragged trying.

Kanna was perfection. A week of working with him and Simon understood how Kanna could break out of Tule Lake and send William Linder to that big courtroom in the sky. Whether throwing a punch, demonstrating flexibility exercises, showing Simon how to silently break in and out of a house, or showing him the ancient principles of Mikkyo, he was the complete warrior. Easy to respect, but difficult to like.

The training. The physical portion was karate and ninjitsu. Kanna forbade the wheelchair. Simon and he sat opposite each other on the sun deck and did stretching exercises, then punching, striking, blocking, and kicking techniques. Simon's kicks were pitiful. It took all he had to lift his legs an inch from the sun deck. But he got better with practice and muscle massages by Kanna's strong hands. Two weeks after the first session, Simon could raise both legs a couple of feet in the air and had no more use for the wheelchair.

Simon himself removed the braces when practicing ninjitsu. *Ninjas* were "stealers-in," commandos who could break into the most fortified castle or stronghold. Kanna devised his own way of teaching Simon to steal in. Simon had to crawl through the darkened house without making a sound, without bumping into furniture, knocking over lamps, or scaring the hell out of the cat. Whenever Simon made noise, Kanna, hidden in the darkness, would strike him about the head and shoulders with a bamboo stick.

Kanna's corrections were painful, but Simon enjoyed the game since it meant he was a competitor again. He became good at stealing in, so good that Kanna began leaving traps in his way—broken glass, tin cans, wind chimes. For the most part Simon got around them. But not always. John Kanna saw to that.

When Simon asked more questions about *ninjas* Kanna said they were superb escape artists, spies, and masters of deception who might disguise themselves as a soldier, a tree, a priest. *Ninjas* used darkness and rain to become invisible in the eyes of others. They could kill. A *ninja* would do anything to survive and held his own ability to be limitless. When Simon asked if there were other *ninjas* around, Kanna said yes but he would never point them out. A *ninja*'s life depended on secrecy. Most had enemies. Kanna said it was almost certain that Simon's *ninja* training would eventually bring him enemies. If it gives me back my legs, Simon said, it would be worth it.

Mikkyo. Kanna's teaching of the way to inner strength began with *kuji no in,* the inscribing of nine signs, the practice of knitting the fingers together to hypnotize an adversary or to increase self-confidence in times of danger. Twice daily Simon performed the hand movements in front of Kanna's small altar. He sat on the matted floor, back straight and eyes closed in an attempt to empty his mind and concentrate on the inner power. Then he pressed his index fingers at the base of his skull fifty times to stimulate his brain. Next, hands on thighs and twist his head to the right and left fifty times, then do the same with his upper body, loosening his neck and spinal cord. Then he rubbed his palms together to stimulate overall circulation. Breath control followed, deep, slow, and silent breathing.

All nine signs had individual finger positions and breathing exercises, as well as individual mental and physical goals. Each had separate symbols to be formed by using the fingers to draw nine horizontal and vertical lines in the air. Each dealt with a separate center of mental and physical power within the body. Each had different colors and assumed a different shape within the body. Simon had to commit all of this to memory. No mistakes. Some weeks he worked on a single sign; at other times he would perform one sign after another under Kanna's critical eye. A flick of Kanna's wrist and an error would be punished with a blow from the bamboo stick. In the end Simon came to believe, not because his mother or Kanna told him to but because his legs grew stronger. Because he saw for himself the power of Mikkyo.

Rin. *The first sign. Designed to train the mind and to tone all of the body's organs. Index fingers extended, all other fingers locked. Use index fingers to alternately trace five horizontal lines and four vertical lines in the air, creating a prescribed nine-line figure. Then, hands in lap, breath deeply, and exhale eighty-one times. On the final exhalation hold the breath and think of the inner power. Hold the air within for eighty-one heartbeats.*

To. *The second sign. Designed to flood the body with*

useful energy and to increase one's perception. Palms together, middle fingers over extended index fingers, other fingers locked. Again trace five horizontal and four vertical lines in the air, creating a second prescribed symbol sign.

Kai. *The third sign . . .*

The intense though distant relationship with John Kanna had turned Simon into an athlete again. He swam, went skin diving, and ran miles along the deserted trails of the Mount Tantalus rain forest. And he could fight with a savage skill beyond anything he had dreamed of as a boxer. He also surfed, but no more than twice a week and nothing dangerous. Simon didn't enjoy surfing anymore. He told himself he was older, in his twenties and past the beachboy scene. And that his workouts with Kanna, down to one a day, gave him enough to do.

And there was his job. Work, Kanna said, protected a man from boredom. It was his pleasure and reward. He hired Simon as a deckhand with one of his fishing fleets sailing out of Honolulu's Kewalo Basin. Simon found it neither pleasant nor rewarding. He only found it boring. Strictly bottom-rung stuff. Dull, blah work. Simon cooked for the crew, pulled in nets of fish until his hands were raw, then gutted the fish for hours back in Kanna's factory. To remove the smell, Simon showered three times a day and brought a change of clothing to work. His mother, back teaching at the University of Hawaii, agreed with Kanna. Since Simon had no interest in attending college, it was best he keep busy until he decided what to do with his future.

Simon had just come out of a long darkness; the rest of his life would have to be something created by him. The knowledge he'd gained from Kanna had put Simon beyond categorization and he had no idea what he wanted to do. But it would have to be exciting.

Over dinner one night Simon noticed a tension between his mother and Kanna. Usually they chattered away in Japanese as if he wasn't there; it was the only time he saw Kanna laugh or smile. Kanna wasn't the type to show emotion, but there was no doubt about his love for Alexis. With Simon fully recovered she'd talked about moving out, about finding another house she could afford. She'd sold the one on Merchant

Street to help pay Simon's medical bills. But when Kanna
had asked her to stay, she'd done so.

So what was tonight's uneasiness about? Simon watched
his mother pick at her food, toy with a glass of wine, and
finally light a cigarette.

"Are you afraid of the Banzai Pipeline?" Kanna suddenly
asked Simon.

The pipeline. No sense hiding it. Simon put down his knife
and fork and leaned back in his chair. "Yes," he said,
admitting what he'd known for some time. That's why he no
longer enjoyed surfing. It reminded him of when he'd lost his
confidence.

"Since you are afraid," Kanna said, "there is only one
thing you can do. You must ride it once more."

There it is, thought Simon. He wants me to do it and she
doesn't.

Kanna said, "Courage is doing what you are afraid to do.
Until you ride the pipeline, you will always be afraid."

To be indecisive, to be surprised, to be afraid. A warrior's
mind could suffer no greater sicknesses, according to Kanna.

Kanna looked at Alexis for a long time, then said to
Simon, "You are still trapped in the pipeline. You must free
yourself. You have practiced Mikkyo and now you are ready.
Faith in yourself is not mere belief. It is wanting to do a thing
and knowing you can. You have dreamed of defeating the
pipeline. It is time to take action."

"You think I can do it?" asked Simon.

Alexis looked away.

"What matters," said Kanna, "is what you think."

On a December morning, not unlike the one on which he
had been almost killed, Simon walked into the violent sea at
Sunset Beach carrying his surfboard. He paused to look over
his shoulder at his mother and John Kanna watching from the
low foothill, then he took a deep breath and did what he
would do all his life. He ran toward the danger. He ran
toward the pipeline.

Von Briesen Park, Staten Island. July 1983. Simon ran
toward the danger. He ran toward the squad car's blinding
light.

Slowed by the heavy downpour, the car could only creep
along the muddy road as its beam swept the park. Now the

beam stopped and began a sweep back in Simon's direction. He remembered what Kanna had taught him. Ninjas *can become invisible at will. It is done through subterfuge and guile. Through deception and deceit.* With the black canvas bag slapping his rib cage, Simon's mind and will drew on the *kuji no in* sign for the power to become unseeable.

He was just feet away from a pair of small boulders at roadside. He'd seen them during the first sweep of the police light. Not too big, and resting near each other at the base of a path leading into the park. Neither stone offered sufficient cover. Barely the size of a stereo speaker, but they were Simon's only chance. No trees or buildings nearby. Only the stones.

The light moved closer, passing over rain-slicked benches, a water fountain, a shuttered refreshment stand now badly battered by the storm. Seconds left before the light trapped Simon in the road.

He reached the rocks, dropped to the ground between them and lay on his right side. The canvas bag was against his chest, held there by his folded arms. Knees drawn up to his chin. Back to the road, to the squad car. Head down, eyes closed. His black garb blended with the night, with the dark rocks and mud. He froze. And willed that he be seen as a rock, as part of the night.

A second later he was bathed in a glare whose brilliance was blinding even through his closed eyelids. Simon concentrated. And remained motionless, fixed in the mud and rain, and then the squad car rolled up to him, splashing him with water, and from deep in his mind he faintly heard the steel guitars and fiddles of a country-and-western tune on the car radio, and then the light passed over him and the squad car advanced slowly up the road, toward the Tuckermans' home.

Simon remained immobile. A third rock barely visible in the rain and darkness. And only when the car was out of sight, its light a distant glow, did he stand up and race into the park, away from the road, a shadow speeding north, toward Marsha and his car.

PART TWO

Hyoshi.
Rhythm.

In combat, know the enemy's rhythm, use a rhythm
he cannot anticipate, upset his rhythm and win.

—MIYAMOTO MUSASHI,
Gorin no Sho

Nine

One A.M. In the room behind his small coin shop, Joe
D'Agosta pulled a worn sofa bed away from the wall. After
rolling back the threadbare brown carpeting, he knelt and
opened the floor safe. Leaving it open, he walked across the
room to a desk made from the hatch cover of a World War II
Liberty ship, took a .38 Smith & Wesson from his bathrobe
pocket, and placed it in front of a portable color Sony. The
Sony was tuned to wrestling from New Jersey.

He sat down in a director's chair with CECIL B. DE MILLE
stenciled in cracked gold lettering across the back. He was
about to reach into the damp canvas bag for the Tuckerman
loot, given him by Simon an hour ago, when a noise outside
the window made him freeze. One hand turned off the volume on the Sony. The other came to rest on the Smith &
Wesson. Only one window in the room and Dag had covered
it with an army blanket to hide the light. It was protected by
bars and a perimeter alarm, but why should that stop anybody
in this day and age? Both the window and a steel door opened
onto a back garden overgrown with weeds. Weeds wouldn't
stop a perpetrator either.

The Sony crackled with electrical interference. Dag relaxed. Nothing out there but rain and monster winds. The rain
might do the window some good. Twelve years in the shop
and Dag hadn't cleaned it once.

On the Sony, Sergeant Slaughter climbed through the ropes for the main bout of the night. The fans went bananas. They waved American flags and booed his elephantine opponent, the Iron Sheik, who was already in the ring. Slaughter received no respect from the Sheik, who was Iranian and bad to the bone. The Sheik denounced him, the fans, the referee, the world. Intimidating in dark glasses and marine drill hat, Slaughter brandished his swagger stick at his shaven-headed opponent and had to be restrained by his handlers. Here was one Iranian who could put his head between his legs and kiss his ass goodbye.

Joe D'Agosta's coin shop was fifteen minutes from Manhattan, in the Astoria section of Queens, called "Little Athens" because of its large Greek population. Italians had lived in the neat two-family homes until the 1950s, when immigration laws were relaxed and southern European immigrants were allowed into the country. Since then Astoria had become the largest Greek city outside of Greece, a place where a Greek could live his entire life without speaking English. Where shops sold gilt-edged icons, colorful head scarves from Crete, and pale-blue *koboli,* worry beads. Where restaurants had no menus, leaving customers to point to what they wanted on a steam table. Where window displays in meat markets featured rows of sheep's heads staring into the street.

D'Agosta's father, Carmine, had cursed the newcomers in English and Scidgie, his native Sicilian dialect, vowing no one was going to push him out of Astoria. To him, a Greek with class was one who took the dishes out of the sink before pissing in it. The D'Agostas remained in the red-brick house on Hoyt Avenue South and continued operating a wine supply shop on Ditmars Boulevard, selling oak kegs, grape presses, siphons, bottle corkers, and fruit extracts to Italians and Greeks, who made their own wine and liquors.

Now only Joe D'Agosta was left in the house with his wife and crippled daughter. The wine shop had become a clothing store selling caftans and hooded Greek shepherd capes made from rough boiled wool. His coin shop was around the corner from the clothing store; it faced the *bocci* courts in the park on Steinway Street, named for the nineteenth-century piano manufacturer who moved his workers to this isolated spot to keep them away from union organizers. Before Dag took over the small two-room shop it had been an Italian bakery with a reputation for excellent cannoli.

Once a week, local mob guys supposedly had used the bakery as a crematorium. Every Sunday, Dag's father said, they burned bodies in the oven. Sprinkled the corpse with sugar to hide the smell of charred flesh. Cooked everything to ashes except the skull, which just wouldn't burn no matter how long you left it in there. The skulls ended up being thrown in the East River only blocks away. Or buried under the bakery floor. Joe D'Agosta couldn't go near his floor safe in the back room without thinking, Today's the day I stick my hand down there and pull out a head covered in powdered sugar.

He'd installed the safe himself, a class E model that was fireproof and all but impossible to burglarize. After welding a two-foot-square steel plate to the bottom, he had dropped the safe in a hole drilled in the cement under the back room floorboards. Fresh cement was then packed around it and allowed to harden. Forget about anyone pulling that sucker out of the floor and walking off with it. The safe was in the floor to stay.

At his desk, Dag unzipped Simon's bag and dumped the contents in front of the Sony. Beautiful. Jewelry, baseball cards, airline ticket plates. All there, like Simon had said. Plus a little extra. An envelope full of hundreds. Simon hadn't taken the time to count it, he'd said, and Dag believed him. The guy was simply the best thief Dag had ever seen, and he'd seen them all. Simon had enough smarts to know you did your counting when the job was over and you were somewhere else.

Simon had a gift for stealing, a touch so good it was impossible to keep him out. Cops investigating his B&E's had given him a nickname: "the Magician." The burglar who could pull the sheet from under a sleeping man and not wake him.

At the beginning Dag had given Simon a few rules to follow. Wear gloves. Always work at night. Use a driver. Don't tell anyone you're a thief. And only steal the small stuff, things you'll have no trouble carrying. Jewelry, stamp and coin collections, antiques, paintings. And cash. Certain professionals—doctors, lawyers, accountants, bail bondsmen— had undeclared cash hanging around. Leave the big stuff—

cars, TVs, stereos, furniture—to junkies, collection agencies, and divorce lawyers. To know who's in or out of town read the gossip and society columns, *Town and Country* magazine, *People* magazine, the Social Register. If the schmucks are in the Hamptons, Palm Beach, or Europe, they can't be in their town houses. A thief who knows his business gets rich when people go on vacation.

Simon added a few rules of his own. Work alone when pulling the actual robbery. Stay in top physical shape. Avoid your fence's place of business. And never carry a gun, because sooner or later you'll use it. He hadn't become a thief to run up a body count. He was in it for the excitement and the money. Mustn't forget the money. Business without a profit was not a business any more than a pickle was a candy.

Dag screwed a loupe into his right eye, then picked up a bracelet and examined it for identification marks. He looked for initials, a Social Security number, for any electrically engraved marking that might help Mrs. Tuckerman identify her property. Not that she was ever going to get the chance. The Manhattan jeweler set to receive the bracelet planned to break up the setting and melt down the gold. Still, Dag had to let him know if the piece was clean or not. It was. Not a mark, not a dent. A second check, holding the bracelet under a black light, would tell Dag if it had been inscribed with invisible ink.

In the meantime, why put off counting the money?

Eyes glued to the television, he removed the wad of hundreds from the plain white envelope. Stewart Granger and James Mason were dueling with sabers on a winding staircase in a castle dungeon. A little slice and dice for a kingdom and a throne. Then the station switched to a commercial for a Motown's greatest hits album. No thanks. Dag liked the good colored music, the stuff he grew up with and you didn't hear on the radio anymore. Count Basie, Sarah Vaughan, and Mr. B., Billy Eckstine. These days the jungle bunny noise you heard on ghetto blasters in the street went right by him. At almost fifty, he couldn't understand it and wasn't about to try. Dag turned to the money. He wet his thumb, started to count, and stopped. A color photograph had fallen from the envelope and lay on top of Mrs. Tuckerman's earrings. He stared, not willing to touch it. Hairs rose on the back of his neck. The room was warm, the way Dag liked it because he couldn't stand air conditioning. A small fan was all the cool he needed. But now he felt *cold*. Stone cold.

The photograph was of a dead Japanese woman whose arms and legs were missing. Someone had cut them off with a power saw. Her torso lay in a bathtub red with her blood. Her name had been Teriko Ohta and once she had been very beautiful. She had been a partner in Liddell's, a Lincoln Center store that sold very expensive toys and clothing for children. The store had been named for Alice Liddell, the English child who'd been the inspiration for *Alice in Wonderland*. Last December a police launch out cruising the Hudson River for holiday suicides had found Teriko Ohta's torso floating among the ice chunks and garbage. For as long as he'd known her, Dag had been half in love with Teriko.

He picked up the photograph. Fifteen years on the cops meant seeing more than his share of dead meat. Experience said he wasn't supposed to feel anything when viewing a corpse. But Teriko's death had gotten to him. Didn't matter she'd brought it on herself by running with a fast crowd and hanging out with some very dangerous people. The photograph made Dag feel as sick as he'd felt seven months ago when he'd learned she was dead. One of these days he was going to get it through his thick dago head that there was nothing new about death.

Why would Tuckerman keep a photograph like this in his safe? Because he enjoyed looking at it. Because he'd had something to do with Teriko's death. He had to be one sick, unbalanced son of a bitch. Had he gotten his rocks off watching her die? Dag closed his eyes and shook his head. Should have listened to me, babe, when I told you to pull out. Pull out before the *yakuza* learn you're an informer.

He attached the scrambler to his phone, again looked at the photograph of Teriko, then dialed Simon's Columbus Avenue apartment. Simon was surprised to hear from him so soon. He asked Dag about the envelope.

"That's why I'm on the horn," Dag said. He told Simon about the photograph and why it was going to cost them both a few hundred thousand dollars.

Tuckerman, Dag said, would freak out over the missing photograph because whoever had it could end up owning him. The lawyer wasn't the type to let anybody hold something over his head, so count on him to lean on every fence between New York and Bora-Bora. He'd be using threats, influence, goon squads, anything to get out from under. Let Tuckerman locate one stone, one ring, and whoever had it was in deep shit until he revealed where it came from. And all because of the photograph on Dag's desk. The jewelry wasn't hot, Jack. It was red hot.

Simon chose his words carefully. "Okay, here's what I think. I see us with three choices. We can go to the cops, which is unlikely. We can squeeze Tuckerman, which is dumb. Or we can forget we ever saw the photograph. Besides, the cops already have Tuckerman down as a suspect in this case. Matter of public record."

"I say we be smart and dump the jewels in the East River. Like ten minutes ago."

"Am I really hearing this?"

"I think we can take a chance with the baseball cards and the plates. The cards are being laid off on a private collector, some clown who just wants to sit around looking at them by himself. The Cubans who get the plates, they keep to themselves. They run in altogether different circles from Tuckerman and spend a lotta time outta the country besides. Day after tomorrow, the plates should be in Miami. Maybe Bolivia or Peru."

Simon's voice was cool. Edgy. "Let's talk about the jewelry, for which I risked my ass tonight. What are the chances of finding another buyer? I mean somebody out of Manhattan."

"Hey, goombah, you ain't listening. I said Tuckerman's going to go looking everywhere for this shit. He has to. He don't know we can't make a move against him. Far as he's concerned, whoever's got this photograph has him by the onions."

"You're forgetting something," Simon said. "Back in December when they found what was left of Teriko the papers said Tuckerman and one of his clients were questioned by the D.A.'s office. So where's the mystery about Tuckerman being involved in this thing?"

"The other guy was Frankie Odori."

"I know the name. Japanese-American. Big bucks. Erica's played cards with him at a couple of big games. Has a Manhattan town house, a discothèque on East Sixty-third, and he's into real estate."

"Hollywood Frankie, they call him. Always partying, always getting his name in the columns. Likes to be seen with models and pretty girls like Teriko. You remember what else I told you about Frankie?''

''Not offhand.''

''I told you he was *yakuza* and that he probably had Teriko killed.''

Hollywood Frankie's image, Dag said, was the creation of an expensive press agent. But behind the glitz and big bucks, Hollywood Frankie was just another hood who blow-dried his hair and wore dark glasses at night. To be exact, he was more than just another hood; he was a front for Japan's biggest *yakuza* leader, a man said to be Frankie Odori's godfather. At precincts, funerals, cop bars, and retirement dinners, Dag had heard the same thing from DEA, FBI, vice and task force cops: Hollywood Frankie was so dirty he couldn't swim in a lake without leaving a ring around it. One interesting rumor, which not too many people took seriously: Frankie's godfather was *gaijin*, a white man. A foreigner who supposedly had made it big in the Tokyo underworld.

Teriko Ohta had partied with Odori and his crowd. She'd even been his lady for a while. A drug bust had left her with a tough choice. Go to prison or turn informant against Hollywood Frankie.

Dag had met her ten years ago, the same year he'd met Simon. At the time, thirty-eight-year-old Dag and his partner had been assigned as technical advisers on a cop movie being shot in Manhattan. The male star had something going with Teriko, a beautiful nineteen-year-old he'd brought with him from California. She and Dag hit it off from the beginning; he told her about New York, cops, Italians, and baroque music. She told him about film people, California, and her plans to be the first Japanese-American girl to become a Hollywood superstar.

Talking to Teriko was easy, relaxing, almost as good as talking to a shrink. He told her about his bad marriage, that he couldn't leave it because the Catholic church said marriage was forever. And the church mattered to Dag. It wasn't something he could tell everybody, but he told her. The church was his salvation.

In the last week of shooting, Dag and his partner made a drug bust on the set. They popped a production assistant holding a quarter kilo of cocaine. His name was Jesus Samuel and he was no virgin. He was a Rican with a very long rap sheet. Drugs, shoplifting, credit card thefts, passing bad checks, B&E, assault. A very busy boy. Teriko helped make the case against Señor Sam-well. By now the movie star who'd been her lover and protector had dumped her for the art director's wife, telling Teriko she was now on her own in the big city. So she was free to confirm what Dag knew, that the coke was for Marvin Movie Star, her ex-sweetie. As for Jesus Samuel, the Rican knew squat about film production and could barely write his name with a spray can. He was on the payroll as Marvin Movie Star's candyman, his drug connection. The case against Jesus and Marvin appeared airtight. Unfortunately, it wasn't.

Marvin Movie Star, his $200-an-hour lawyers, and a studio with a $14 million film to protect all got busy. It came down to Jesus agreeing to take the rap. In court he swore the drugs were his and had not been intended for sale. That made the charge possession, a lighter charge than dealing. He got six months.

Before being wheeled off to the slammer Jesus had something else to say. When he'd been arrested he'd been holding a half kilo of cocaine. Not a quarter, but half. Asked if he was accusing Dag and his partner of stealing his drugs, Jesus said, "Shit yeah." Now instead of being credible witnesses the two cops became defendants. There was no way they could make trouble for Marvin Movie Star or his studio. Not after the gospel according to Jesus Samuel.

At a trial in civil court both cops were acquitted. But they faced a second trial, this one a police department hearing, where the rules of evidence did not apply, where rumors, guess work, and hearsay could be used against an accused officer. When the hearing ended Dag and his partner were forced to resign years short of a full pension. Jesus had fucked them good. Teriko offered Dag her savings, $1,800, a loan until he got a job. It would be five years before he was eligible for a partial police pension. He didn't take her money. But he never forgot the offer.

After that she drifted in and out of his life. She stayed in New York and tried modeling, acting, and hairdressing. She got married and divorced, was a call girl for several months, and through all of it told Dag she was happy, that everything that happened to her was an experience. Something to learn from. What Dag learned was that she loved the fast lane. The parties, clubs, opening nights, and being photographed with famous names. Dag tried talking to her a few times, but it never took. All Dag could do was wait. Wait for the blow to come, the blow that would turn her around.

It happened on a return flight from South America. She'd flown to Peru with a Swiss film producer and left him there. As a going-away present he gave Teriko several ounces of uncut Colombian cocaine. She decided to sell the coke to New York friends, for whom it was the recreational drug of choice. She cut the fingers from a surgical glove, filled them with cocaine, then tied them off and swallowed each one. But on the plane to New York she became ill and at Kennedy she was rushed to the hospital, where a stomach pump barely saved her life. After that, DEA owned her. She could spend the next few years in prison fighting off bull dykes, or she could turn informant.

Teriko, the feds pointed out, had once been Frankie Odori's lady. And Odori was *yakuza*, a member of a foreign criminal syndicate now expanding in the United States. If she wanted her freedom, Teriko would have to give them Hollywood Frankie. Dag told her to get herself a lawyer and take her chances in court. The arrest was only her first offense. With delays and plea bargaining maybe she would get lucky. Teriko smiled and said it might be fun going after Frankie. It was another experience she could tell her grandchildren about one day, and meanwhile she'd be getting paid by DEA.

"She told me she'd slept with Tuckerman," Dag said to Simon as he shifted the phone from one ear to another.

"What the hell for?"

"He's the man in the middle, Tuckerman. He represents the wise guys, the La Serra brothers in particular. And he's Frankie's lawyer as well. Tuckerman and Hollywood Frankie. Right there you got all you need to bring the *yakuza* and the wise guys together. The La Serras need heroin and the *yakuza*'s swimming in the shit. That ain't all they're doing together, but it's a good enough start."

Simon said, "Let's talk about the jewelry."

"Know something? I'm getting vibes here, like maybe you don't believe I'm giving it to you straight. Like maybe you think I'm fucking you outta what you got coming."

"I didn't say that," Simon said coldly.

"You're forgetting something, *muchacho*. I work with one guy and that's you. So why should I cut my own throat?—"

"Look, all I know is I'm coming up short on this deal. An hour ago I had a nice chunk of money due me. Now it keeps shrinking even as we speak. Not that I'm saying there's no honor among thieves."

Dag looked at the photograph of Teriko's mutilated body. And gave up trying to control his anger. With a sweep of his arm he sent the jewelry flying from his desk. He stood up, kicked the director's chair away, and spoke in the soft voice he used when he felt like making trouble and didn't care who got hurt. "Hey, goombah, you want the jewelry? Be my guest. You come right on over here and pick it up. I'll have it waiting for you in a neat little package. It's yours, buddy boy. From me to you. Every fucking stone. Go make any deal you want and keep every penny. How's that grab you?"

Silence.

Then Simon said, "Teriko Ohta must've been some kind of lady."

"I thought she was."

Silence.

Again Simon was the first to break it. "They say bad things come in threes. Three times in one week I've come up against the *yakuza* and the last time costs me two hundred K."

"Want to run that by me slow?"

Simon told him about snatching Molly from the *yakuza* in Tokyo. And then there was the white-haired man Alexis had seen in Honolulu.

Dag chuckled. "Be funny if that guy was Frankie Odori's godfather and your mother had made him when DEA, the FBI, and cops haven't been able to."

"Yeah, hilarious. She's going crazy with this thing. That's why she's in Washington, to get help tracking down this guy."

Dag said, "I want you to see this photograph of Teriko. Want you to see for yourself what the *yakuza* does to people it doesn't like."

"I'm a believer. Do what you think best with the jewelry. You don't have to show me any photograph."

"Hey, slick, that's not why I want you to see the picture. You've got a nice payday coming from the plates and the baseball cards. Reason I want you to see this thing is I want you to start taking your mother seriously. What if she's right about this white-haired guy?''

"What if they start kicking midgets out of nudist colonies because they keep getting in people's hair? You want to be ridiculous? Then let's be ridiculous.''

"Listen, pal, you never argue with an Italian about mothers, 'cause he'll kick your fuckin' face in. If you don't want to worry about the *yakuza* coming for you, fine. But take care of your mother. I know what I see here in my hand, what them scumbags did to Teriko. You ever get a bullshit story from me?''

Simon said it was time to wrap up this conversation. He'd be at the club tomorrow around four in the afternoon to work out. Bring the picture over then. Dag agreed.

All Simon had to do was listen to his mother. Just listen. The both of them would feel better.

"It's almost midnight,'' Simon said. "She's asleep.''

Dag looked at the photograph. "Make the call, slick. While she's alive to appreciate it.''

Manhattan. Simon dialed his mother's hotel in Washington. After several rings the desk clerk cut in to say there was no answer in Mrs. Bendor's room and would Simon care to leave a message. He left his name and hung up. Alexis usually went to bed early, rarely later than ten. Simon walked to the kitchen, brewed some herbal tea, ate a light snack of sliced bananas and plain yogurt, then popped two potassium tablets and a vitamin E capsule. He debated whether or not to look in on Molly, decided he couldn't be bothered, then took a cup of tea into the living room. After finishing the tea and watching most of "Nightline,'' he telephoned his mother again. Twelve twenty-five and she still hadn't returned.

He hung up, then played with the automatic changer, switching from channel to channel, finally stopping at TBS in Atlanta. He watched the Mets score one run in the top of the ninth to tie the Braves, then he reached for the phone and dialed Washington again.

Twelve fifty-five. No answer from Alexis's room.

Well, he could worry or not worry. While trying to decide, he did the only thing left to him at the moment.

He dialed his mother once more.

Ten

Because she had come to Washington at just the right time, Alexis Bendor met the one man who believed her story that Rupert de Jongh was still alive.

Sir Michael Kingdom Marwood, of Britain's Foreign Office, was here from London on a two-day mission seeking American support for his country's position regarding Hong Kong. England's lease on Hong Kong expired in 1997. After that the People's Republic of China would take control of the colony, which had become quite a golden goose. Hong Kong provided China with a third of its foreign exchange. For months Marwood and other British diplomats had shuttled between Peking and London, attempting to cut a deal giving China what it insisted on, namely total authority. They hoped such an arrangement would keep England's finger in the pie as well.

It was quite a trying task, Marwood told Alexis. The Chinese possessed, in Bacon's words, a sinister wisdom. Nor were they prone to keeping promises. What ticked Marwood off was their insistence on getting the fine print right. Britain, meanwhile, could jolly well play dirty when it had to. And did. Results: drawn-out negotiations and a crisis of confidence among Hong Kong's freewheeling businessmen. The Hong Kong dollar had slumped to a new low, stock and property markets had dropped like a stone, and money was fleeing the colony in record amounts. Until recently the Bank of Thailand had been getting only $43,000 a month in funds from Hong Kong. Last September alone it received $17 million. It had now stopped giving out figures.

Over a late-night supper in an Afghanistan resturant on Pennsylvania Avenue, Marwood said to Alexis, "Southern Chinese. When they begin to age they buy a coffin and place it under the bed. The point, you see, is to get used to the idea of death. Every so often they pull the coffin out a bit at a time. No more, no less. Eventually the entire coffin is out in plain sight. Now, they're not anxious to die by any means. But by the time the coffin is completely in view, the entire family is adjusted to the idea of the coffin owner breathing his or her last. That's how the people in Hong Kong feel. They're getting ready."

Sir Michael Kingdom Marwood was in his mid-sixties, a tall, thin man with a delicate handsomeness and fine white hair parted in the middle. He came from a wealthy family and still managed to live well in an England with high taxes, high inflation, and with what he described as the blackmail that was socialism. He and his wife lived on an estate in Buckinghamshire and kept flats in London, Miami, and Gstaad. His clothing was made by Gieves and Hawkes, proud possessors of the address 1 Saville Row and once tailors to the Duke of Wellington and Lord Nelson. He collected handcrafted shotguns, seventeenth-century art, and smoked pre-Castro cigars stored in his private vault on London's Duke Street.

Alexis had known him almost forty years. Both had been in Allied intelligence during the war, meeting just before her ill-fated mission in Switzerland. After the war Marwood had followed a life mapped out for him by his family, which traced its ancestry back to Alice Perrers, the fourteenth-century mistress of King Edward III. Marwood, with sly humor, was fond of noting that Alice had been a rather cheesy sort. At Edward's deathbed she'd stolen the rings from his fingers, then fled the court.

Marwood's father pushed him into the foreign service. The Oxbridge old-boy network, to which father and son belonged, guided Marwood's professional footsteps until he eventually achieved the status of Whitehall mandarin. This was a guarantee against political fallout of any kind. Prime ministers and

Parliaments could come and go, but mandarins went on forever. They controlled civil service and civil service ran England.

Marwood, Alexis thought, seemed more amused than depressed by the compromises necessary in diplomacy. Behind
horn-rimmed glasses his pale blue eyes appeared to be on the
verge of winking. She'd always found him charming, though
a tad too genteel for the coarse world around him. He'd
introduced her to Shea Bendor at a London V-E party, de-
scribing him as "no one special, just someone who had
managed to be braver a minute or two longer than the rest of
us." The remark held its own meaning for Marwood, who,
on the night of Alexis's capture by de Jongh, had been in
Switzerland serving as her courier. On the road between
Geneva and Nyon he himself had been captured by the SS
and wounded in the left leg. Marwood escaped, but the leg
had to be amputated at the knee. He got around fairly well
with a wooden leg, often referring to himself as "Long John
Marwood, the only pirate with a top-security clearance."

In the Afghanistan restaurant he told Alexis that his two
days in Washington would be hectic ones. Just one meeting
after another. And he was, after all, getting rather long in the
tooth for this sort of exertion. Today his meetings with the
State Department had lasted until ten-thirty at night and would
start again at eight tomorrow morning. He was penciled in for
a quiet lunch with the vice-president at the White House, but
that could well be canceled if the trouble in Lebanon between
the Israelis and Palestinians became more heated. Bloody
Jews, Marwood said. One of them probably dropped a coin in
a Beirut café, which was why they were tearing up the city.

Tonight was the first Alexis had seen of Michael since he'd
received his knighthood eight years ago. Had eight years gone
by so fast? The mark of their passing was on Michael Marwood,
as they must be on Alexis. He looked tired and worn out.
Old. There were deep frown lines in his forehead and his
handsome face was pouchy. He was drinking too much. But
Alexis had never met a better raconteur. Whether it was
gossip about the royals or the tale of a Brazilian journalist
who caused a flap at a Paris party by mistaking an important
Middle Eastern king for Sammy Davis, Jr., Marwood told a
story with skill and wit.

Marwood and Alexis dined under the steely gaze of his

"minder," or bodyguard, a narrow-eyed Scot named Alan Bruce, who sat alone at the next table.

Marwood's telephone call telling Alexis he was in Washington had been a pleasant surprise. He'd had no trouble finding her. By badgering one official after another, she'd left a trail all over town. And why had he believed her story about de Jongh when others hadn't? Because he respected her intelligence. And because de Jongh's body had never been found. The *gaijin* had been an extremely clever man and his disappearance had been so unequivocal and unbounded. Marwood said it smacked of being well planned and highly organized. Yes, it made sense that the *gaijin* would still be involved with Japan in some fashion. De Jongh didn't give a bugger about anything in the universe save the Japanese.

The subject of Rupert de Jongh was temporarily put aside as waiters in harem pants, black boots, and blue turbans arrived at the table with trays of noodles stuffed with meat and scallions. Marwood, ever the diplomat, made small talk while the dishes were being set in front of them. He told Alexis about his collection of falcons, which he'd bred in captivity from imported stock and used to hunt grouse on the Scottish and Yorkshire moors. Because falcons hunted over long distances, Marwood attached tiny brass bells to their legs to make them easier to locate when the hunt was over. Today by a pleasant coincidence he'd been given several brass bells as a gift by an American State Department official, who'd brought them back from a tour of duty in Saudi Arabia. Marwood took one of the tiny bells from his pocket and presented it to a delighted Alexis, a souvenir of a marvelous evening.

"Well," Marwood said, "back to the subject of Mr. de Jongh. You did mention something about the *yakuza*."

"Sounds off the wall, as my son might say. But if any man could pull that off, de Jongh could. Unfortunately, I'm not having much luck convincing anyone other than you."

"You will, you will. In the fullness of time your legendary persistence will carry the day. You're not one to let the side down. Have you come up with anything besides the indifference of your countrymen?"

"Learned a few things about the *yakuza* that I didn't know. Until now they'd confined themselves in this country to Hawaii and the West Coast."

"Where most Japanese-Americans live."

She nodded. "But that's changing. The *yakuza*'s expanding in America for two reasons: more Japanese are here on business. And the *yakuza* are trying to make some sort of an arrangement with American organized crime. As someone in DEA told me, *yakuza* follow the money."

Marwood poured himself more red wine. "Don't we all."

Alexis said, "This DEA agent told me that Japanese businesses are allowed to deduct fifty percent of all profits as entertainment expenses. They don't have to account for it or explain how it's spent. And you can bet the *yakuza* finds ways to get its share. Twenty-five hundred *yakuza* gangs in Japan, with 110,000 members. That's a lot of sleazos, my friend."

"How does this compare to your American Mafia?"

"From what I'm told, the five New York crime families have around thirteen hundred members."

"Appears as though the Japanese have a numerical edge in the criminal department. We keep a file of sorts on the *yakuza* ourselves."

"Oh?"

"Strictly political reasons, oddly enough. We're interested in all Far Eastern groups who might influence their governments in one way or another. In Hong Kong and China you have underworld organizations called Triads and Tongs. Turns out China controls, or let's say heavily influences, these criminal elements and hasn't hesitated in the past to use them as it sees fit. By the same token we learned that the *yakuza* play a role in Japanese politics. They serve as goon squads for ultraconservative politicians. A bit of maiming and leg breaking on behalf of various fascist loonies. Back in the thirties the military seized control of Japan with the help of such thugs, who did their dirty work. Beating up newspapermen, blackmailing those who wanted peace, killing liberal politicians. It was as if your Al Capone applied his unique skills to put Herbert Hoover into office."

When Alexis asked if *yakuza* currently were involved with Japanese politicians, Marwood said yes. And at the highest level. It was a reciprocal arrangement; *yakuza* got a man into office and in turn received his political protection. In prestige-conscious Japan, the low status of gangsters demanded that they seek respectability, recognition, and fame. Consequently they encouraged a certain romantic mystique that had grown up around them, a romanticizing of their lives as Robin Hood figures who protected the weak against tyrants. They saw themselves as the last of the samurai, the only men in Japan who still believed in *bushido*. The gangs, Marwood said, were organized as corporations and engaged in legitimate businesses as well as illegitimate ones. The major groups had their own building in Tokyo and other cities, proudly flew their own flag from the masthead, and all members wore the gang's pin or badge.

"Excrementum cerebellum vincit," Alexis said. Bullshit baffles the brain.

"Agreed," Marwood said. "By the by, this finger-cutting ritual of theirs. Any idea how it came about? One of our chaps told me about it recently. Seems it began hundreds of years ago when Tokyo prostitutes sliced off a finger as a symbol of devotion to their pimps and lovers. *Yakuza* now do the same as an apology to their leader for having fouled up or for failing to discharge an order faithfully. Some cut off a finger to show how tough they are, how special and unpredictable they can be in a conformist society like Japan's. Bloody show-offs. Showing off is the reason many get themselves tattooed from head to toe as well."

Yakuza, he told Alexis, literally meant loser. The word stood for three numbers—*ya* (eight), *ku* (nine), *za* (three). The total, twenty, equaled the losing number in *Hanafuda,* a variation of a card game introduced to Japan in the sixteenth century by Dutch sailors. Around that time feudal Japan's losers—peasants, the homeless, clerks—banded together to resist those samurai who, lacking steady employment with a warlord, roamed the country taking advantage of anyone weaker than they. Joining these medieval losers were the *buraku-min*, those who performed what were considered sub-human tasks. They were butchers, leather tanners, handlers of dead bodies, and those who cleaned the filth and dead animals from temples. They were untouchables, among the most despised people in Japan. True losers or *yakuza*.

Alexis said, "We're talking about pimps, drug pushers, murderers. Real slime. Why shouldn't they be despised? De Jongh should feel right at home."

"So, is there anything I can do for you regarding the

elusive Mr. de Jongh? His form comes to mind each time I attach my wooden leg to my aging carcass.''

Alexis put down her fork. The moment of truth. ''You mentioned M16, that you had contacts here.''

''Not a thing I'm supposed to bandy about, but, yes, we do keep in touch with our intelligence services. Not that they always acquit themselves in an intelligent fashion, but that's another story.''

Alexis leaned forward. ''Have them track him down in Japan for me.''

''Just that? Nothing else?'' He smiled. ''And supposing we turn over that particular rock and dear Mr. de Jongh comes crawling out. Then what?''

Alexis leaned back and stared down into her unfinished food. ''I intend to kill him.''

Marwood puckered up his small mouth and studied her face. ''You have some sort of a plan, I assume. At least I get the impression you do.''

Alexis didn't look up. ''A friend once said to know and not act is not to know. I know de Jongh's alive. And when I have him in front of me I intend to act. I have to.''

''Your friend sounds quite wise.''

''He was.''

''Was?''

Alexis shook her head, indicating there was nothing else she wanted to say on the subject. To talk about John Kanna was to limit him. And relive the pain of his death. He'd been among four Japanese who'd died ten years ago when two American Vietnam veterans attacked a Buddhist shrine in Honolulu. Mentally disturbed and on drugs, the vets had hated the shrine because it reminded them of a Vietnamese temple. John would have been the first to appreciate the irony of his death, thought Alexis. He'd fled the U.S. Army and hid from them for years. But in the end it was the army that had killed him.

Alexis and Marwood spent another hour talking, with the churlish bodyguard Alan Bruce looking on. Marwood promised to give whatever help he could, though it was unlikely she'd hear from him until he returned to London. For Alexis, the fact that he'd listened was enough. She'd make sure to keep in touch.

Marwood smiled. ''Something tells me I'll definitely be

hearing from you. Patience concentrated. That's you, I'm afraid.''

"You might say I'm out to bite the dog that bit me."

On that they touched wineglasses.

Eleven

ENGLAND
1937

Once, at Eton, Michael Marwood performed an act of kindness for which he would suffer the rest of his life.

He and his fellow schoolboys often taunted barges passing them on the river at Windsor by shouting, "Who ate puppy pie under Marlow Bridge?" A century ago an Eton cook had discovered that food was being stolen from her kitchen. Determined to discourage future thefts, she collected a litter of unwanted puppies that had been drowned in the house, put them in a large pie dish and covered it with an appealing baked crust. She then left the pie in the kitchen and went away. Hours later it had disappeared. The next day what was left of the pie was discovered beneath Marlow Bridge, abandoned by thieves who had found it less appetizing than the usual plunder.

In his final Eton year, Marwood attained a status denied his father and grandfather, both of whom had attended the public school that educated the sons of Britain's ruling classes. He was elected a member of Pop, the exclusive club of some two dozen senior boys. All were entitled to wear white bow ties, wing collars, checkered trousers, and flowers in their buttonholes. Marwood now had rank and privilege, to be gloriously discharged to the exclusion and detriment of others. Since he was also an upperclassman this gave him unlimited power to oppress or do good to lower grades. Naturally, he felt a need to use that power, to experience the pleasure of having students give way to him. Thus one rainy afternoon he stopped several upperclass boys from forcing a frightened new student to eat the raw flesh of a strangled mongrel pup.

The new boy, a Hertfordshire lad, was being punished for his insolence. Marwood knew him as a stubborn little shit with a growing reputation for not bowing to anybody. Presumptuous and insulting in speech and manner. Obstinate in his refusal to accept the judgment of his betters. He was a slight, blond little thing with a proper father, a lord. But his mother? God help us all. She was a musical comedy actress. Placing her on the lower rung with Jews and dancing apes. Eton's upperclassmen had taken it upon themselves to punish the Hertfordshire lad for his common mother as well as for his arrogance. The bugger simply had to show more respect for his superiors and that's all there was to it.

Sad to say, no amount of insults and knocking about could dent the new boy's thick skull. So now the game had heated up and this afternoon a group of the lads had the Hertfordshire bloke on the loo floor and were shoving the raw, bleeding puppy meat into his mouth. Marwood stopped it. Not because he cared. He put an end to it because he wanted to test his power. And a right good feeling it was, too.

Whenever Marwood wanted to enjoy that feeling again he would step in and save this new boy from the sadistic behavior of upperclassmen. The new lad was grateful, in a chilly, aloof sort of way. Marwood found him standoffish, the sort who didn't belong. Worse, the bugger didn't want to belong. Not to anything English. The English lower classes were cretins, he told Marwood. And the upper classes, as evidenced by Eton, were happiest when inflicting cruelty on others. England could crumble and fall into the sea for all he cared.

Although good at sports, the new boy was not a true team player. Too self-contained, Marwood thought. Preferred his own company to that of others. Practically feline in his comings and goings. And when the occasion presented itself the Hertfordshire lad could fend for himself. Used a cricket bat to thrash one upperclass twit and dealt with another by gouging his arm in three places with a fountain pen. The more the school—students and teachers—mistreated him, the more he fought back. Marwood found himself admiring the bugger at times.

On the other hand, when the Hertfordshire lad vowed to kill everyone at Eton, Marwood excepted, the senior dismissed the threat as coming from someone whose intelligence was in the lowest measurable range. Mark this down as poor judgment on Marwood's part. The Hertfordshire lad would turn out to have superior powers of mind, along with a suicidal courage. And as Marwood was to learn, the lad's threat to put an end to a certain portion of the English race was no idle one.

The Hertfordshire youngster was Rupert de Jongh.

Years later, on a snowy Swiss road within sight of the Alps, de Jongh repaid Marwood's schoolboy kindness by shooting him in the left leg. The pain had been horrific. Making the adjustment to the loss of a limb had been even worse. But on balance Marwood had to admit he'd been lucky. Alexis Bendor and the others had fared much worse at the hands of de Jongh, whose pitiless nature had been unbounded. Two bullets in the left knee, therefore, could only be described as uncommon clemency. Said clemency, however, had turned Marwood into a cripple and sentenced him to a life of guilt and shame.

To live with what happened in Switzerland forty years ago, he relied on alcohol.

In recent years, with the memory becoming more unbearable, he often relied on heroin.

Washington, 1983. Minutes ago Marwood dropped Alexis Bendor at her hotel, thanked her for a marvelous evening, then left her with a chaste kiss on each cheek and with the feeling, by George, that things could be accomplished. But wasn't that a diplomat's job, to charm the world into adopting a positive attitude toward the future? Now Marwood and his minder, Alan Bruce, were in the presidential suite atop a hotel that looked out onto the White House and the Jefferson Memorial. Marwood had not slept overnight in the British embassy for years. Didn't like the place. No privacy. Difficult to relax in the midst of dinner parties, cocktail parties, and assorted press briefings. Nor was it the place to enjoy such illicit pleasures as heroin.

In a large beige bedroom decorated with ghastly prints of

Dutch cavaliers cavorting in a tavern, Marwood lay back on one of two twin beds and waited for his bodyguard to prepare the heroin for him. Nice to have someone around to do the dirty work for you when need be. Alan had no interest in the drug himself. His vices were marijuana in moderate amounts, starchy foods, and very young male prostitutes, whom he would often batter about after enjoying their favors.

Marwood would have preferred that his minder be more prudent in affairs of the heart, but one had to come to terms with human imperfection. Small sins aside, Alan Bruce had his good points. He was loyal, prided himself on obeying orders—fulfilling a contract, he called it—and had a padlock on his mouth, thank God. Furthermore, his capacity for wanton destruction would have awed a Goth. Some of the things he had done to blacks in Africa were so off-putting and repugnant that it was no mystery why certain emerging nations had taken a strong dislike to him.

Alan, working in shirtsleeves, went to the bathroom, used a penknife to unscrew the small grate covering the vent, reached into the opening, and removed a rolled towel. Next, he went to the kitchen, picked up a box of tin foil and a roll of paper towels, then returned to the bedroom where Marwood waited. As the diplomat propped himself up on an elbow to watch, the Scot used the second twin bed as his worktable. He pulled the cardboard tube from inside the roll of paper towels and set it aside. A section of tin foil was torn from the box and placed near the cardboard tube. Then Alan unrolled the towel uncovering a small cellophane bag of White Dragon Pearl, the chalky-white heroin that had been cut with a barbiturate called "barbitone."

He sprinkled some of the heroin on the piece of tin foil, placed the foil on the night table, and used an ashtray to grind the heroin chunks into powder. *White Dragon Pearl,* which Marwood had obtained in Hong Kong, was fifty percent pure. Far superior to the two percent pure found in America, which is why the American addict had to shoot it into his veins to get any kick at all. The strength of White Dragon Pearl made it possible to achieve euphoria in other ways.

Alan added a second sheet of tin foil beneath the first, then held a burning cigarette lighter beneath both. Marwood sat up. He licked his lips. My relief, my reward. The white powder melted, began to bubble. Seconds later, it darkened and became a black oily liquid.

Alan put down the lighter, then held the tin foil out to Marwood. The diplomat took the cardboard tube from beside his bodyguard, placed one end within an inch of the black liquid and took the other end in his mouth. He sucked in deeply. Chasing the dragon, the Chinese called it. Inhaling the sweetish smoke, which assumed a dragonlike shape as it rose in the air. For a time, Marwood thought, I can enjoy the absence of pain in the body and trouble in the soul. For a time.

Later a drowsy, relaxed Marwood lay on his bed in the darkened room and through half-closed eyes stared at a patch of ceiling made silver by moonlight. Alan had left him alone and was in the living room, eating baked beans and toast and watching American television, which apparently went on non-stop around the clock. Salt of the earth, Alan. Coarse and tasteless at times, but steadfast in his allegiance to whoever had purchased his services. Steadfast was an apt description of Alexis Bendor as well, and therein lay the problem. What to do about this woman who posed such a danger to Marwood. What to do indeed. But he already knew the answer to that, didn't he?

In this world, it was every man for himself and God against us all.

Marwood believed that money could achieve anything.

It guaranteed a contented mind, Lord knows, and insured that the fools around him did not become his equal. Money made it possible for him to labor with his brain, thereby governing those who labored with their hands. Money guaranteed that he want for nothing, that no desire go unsatisfied. Marwood regarded it as evidence of culture, a device to confirm his position in society. Milton was right. Money brought honor, friends, conquests, and realms.

Marwood required massive amounts of it, having chosen to live in a style described by a Fleet Street gossip columnist as too-too and la-di-da. His greatest expense was his country home. It was a residence that some regarded as unessential, but that Marwood looked upon as indispensable to his pleasure and comfort. The home, a magnificent manor house on 2,500 acres, was in Buckinghamshire, northwest of London.

The area was one of beechwoods—dense, green-gladed forests dotted with running streams, ancient paths, nightingales, and cherry blossoms. The villages had kept their traditional character, with Georgian houses, thatched cottages, cobbled courtyards, and old gabled and timbered inns. One inn, Mill House Stream, had a stream flowing through it. Edmund Burke was buried in Buckinghamshire and William Penn, founder of Pennsylvania, had lived in one of its villages. The notorious Hell Fire Club, the eighteenth-century group of gamblers and rakes, held orgies and black magic rituals in Buckinghamshire caves.

Marwood had closed off the western half of the centuries-old manor house called Burnham Hall. He'd been forced to do so by enormous operating expenses, heavy death duties, and high taxes. With his three children living away from him, there'd been even less reason to keep the great house as it had been in his father's day. Marwood and his wife now lived in the eastern half. Their apartments, which faced landscaped gardens and a private lake, included ten bedrooms. There were also three drawing rooms, a dining hall whose arching roof timbers looked down from a height of thirty-four feet, and a kitchen with separate pantry and buttery for making jams and ale. One drawing room, a favorite of his wife, Verity, contained Gobelin tapestries and a Virginal once played by Queen Elizabeth I. The pine- and walnut-paneled library contained over 10,000 books and several rare Gainsborough landscapes. Marwood's private study had a painted ceiling by Verrio and carved and gilded tables designed by William Kent.

His politics and wife—she was a distant Churchill relative— were both correct. And through his father he had inherited memberships in the right clubs: the Carlton, traditional for Tory party members; the Athenaeum, the mandarin stronghold, which still had the Duke of Wellington's mounting block preserved outside on the sidewalk; and White's, London's oldest and best-known club, "an oasis of civilization in a desert of democracy."

Only a fool would want to give up any of this. In fact, the idea of losing what he had filled him with revulsion and fear. Such a loss would make his existence seem empty and wasted. Marwood, however, needed help to survive. He was, as he knew, a man with severe limitations. He was a snob, paranoid, and self-pitying. He was also implacable in small things and lacked courage. He disliked confrontation of any sort and in difficult matters always sought the easy way out.

But he had a way of life worth preserving. At any price. How far would he go to keep all he had? As far as he'd gone that night in Switzerland forty years ago. When he had been indifferent to the survival of everyone except Michael Kingdom Marwood.

In his Washington hotel suite he sat up in bed. A guilty conscience needed no accuser. What Marwood needed was more heroin. He called out for Alan.

In another part of Washington, Alexis turned off the lamp and slid down into bed, crawling deeper beneath the covers. No need for the lamp now. It was almost 7:00 A.M., and the sun was coming into her hotel room, rising from behind the White House. For all the sleep she'd managed to get she could have spent the night reading or watching Garbo on the tube in *Anna Karenina*. No sense blaming the hotel. In Washington you couldn't do better than the Hay-Adams. Alexis was red-eyed, irritable, and sleepless because Rupert de Jongh was too much with her.

How the hell had de Jongh broken her code? Almost forty years later it still bothered her, because she had been the best, in a class by herself when it came to ciphers. Wounded pride after all this time? Goddam right. That and what he'd done to her and the others.

Alexis closed her eyes. It was as if de Jongh were near, somewhere in the city. Maybe in her room. Close enough for her to reach out and touch him. That's when she got out of bed and walked to the bathroom, sick to her stomach with an expectation of evil.

Twelve

When Kim Doo Kangnang first asked Michael Marwood to smuggle unspecified items from the Far East to Europe and America, via diplomatic pouch, Marwood said, "Are you mad? Why on earth have you come to me with this?"

Kangnang said, "A mutual acquaintance suggested I talk to you. He is aware of your financial difficulties. In fact, he knows a great deal about you, Mr. Marwood. He knows you have a lovely country home, one you could lose because of back taxes. You have other debts as well. Our friend says if these things are not settled, you could be toppled from your lofty perch. Those were his words, lofty perch. I speak English, but I do not understand lofty perch. You enjoy expensive things, Mr. Marwood, but you cannot afford them on your salary."

"You bastard."

"I think you mean slant-eyed, wily, Oriental bastard."

"Inform this so-called mutual acquaintance to keep his damn nose out of my affairs. And as for you, I strongly suggest you confine yourself to whoremongering on behalf of your pathetic little country. Do I make myself clear?"

Kangnang took his hand from his pocket and gave something to Marwood. It was the bow tie the diplomat had worn in his senior year at Eton as a member of Pop. In the grand manner of a monarch dispensing gold sovereigns to a crowd,

Marwood had celebrated graduation day by giving the bow tie to Rupert de Jongh. Now, more than thirty years later, Marwood stared at the bow tie as though it were a hissing cobra with a flared hood. De Jongh could not possibly be alive. He simply could not be alive.

The bow tie that binds, Marwood thought. He said, "All this time he has been presumed dead. Damn him, why contact me now?"

Kangnang said, "Makes a wonderful story, don't you think? What you English call heartwarming. Two schoolboys reach out to each other over the years. He's offering you his help, Mr. Marwood. Naturally, he expects something from you in return. Benefits received must be repaid. I can tell you he is a most generous man. For example, he has asked me to give you this. Please take it. It is yours merely for listening."

The Korean handed Marwood an envelope. The diplomat lifted the flap an inch or two and peeked in at the wad of fifty-pound notes. A fortune. Money Marwood needed badly. His eyes went to Kangnang, then returned to the money.

"There's a note inside," Kangnang said.

Marwood put on his bifocals, adjusted them to the end of his nose, and removed a folded piece of paper from the envelope. No signature on the note. Just a single typed sentence: *A secret is something you give to others to keep for you.* Anyone could have written it, but only one man had.

Suddenly Marwood was forced to remember things best forgotten.

On a February morning in 1945 he had been driving alone on a snow-covered road between Geneva and Nyon, congratulating himself on having put one over on a Nyon shopkeeper re a collection of beautiful chinaware now locked in the boot of Marwood's car. Marwood was at peace with the world, looking forward to lunch at the Beau Rivage, Geneva's finest hotel, where the omelettes were made with real eggs. Bugger Britain's rationing and the ghastly powdered eggs that went with it.

Two miles outside of Geneva a gray Citroën fell in behind Marwood. He ignored it; his mind was on a possible second luncheon course, veal kidneys, perhaps, or pig's feet, a Geneva specialty. The Citroën, however, jolted him out of his culinary reverie. It bumped him from behind and when he looked over his shoulder to see what the bloody hell was going on, the Citroën gathered speed, pulled alongside of Marwood, swerved left in front of him, and forced his car off the road. Dizzy with panic, Marwood wrestled with the steering wheel and fought like a mad man to control the bucking Opel. By the grace of God he missed several trees, though not by much, and finally skidded to a halt in a snowbank.

He slumped over the wheel, out of breath and on the verge of fainting—he just wasn't cut out for this sort of thing. And then he was being pulled from the Opel by two men in black leather coats, German by the torrent of curses and obscenities they unleashed at Marwood. A rough search of his person for weapons and, after finding none, they hurled him to the ground. Then they grabbed Marwood by the ankles and dragged him through knee-high snow, dragged him past a third man, who stayed behind with the cars. Marwood the upended turtle, soon to be victimized by mischievous schoolboys and powerless to prevent it. The snow covered his face and his head took a couple of severe bumps; he demanded an explanation. The Germans ignored him. They dragged him farther from the road, down a small hill and under an abandoned Roman amphitheater.

Beneath the tiers of stone seats, two Japanese in sheepskin jackets awaited them. A third man was present, but he stood hidden in long shadows cast by a cold sun shining down on the oval-shaped arena. A terror-stricken Marwood saw the third man's rubber boots and the bottom portion of his fur-lined Burberry coat, nothing more. Marwood tried to push himself off the ground, but one of the Japanese kicked him in the ribs, knocking him back.

Marwood was ordered to strip. When he hesitated, a German slapped him in the face with a gloved hand. Weeping silently, Marwood did as he was ordered. When he was naked and shivering and feeling thoroughly ashamed, the Germans and Japanese removed their belts and beat him with the buckled ends. His screams echoed beneath the stone arena and still the man in the shadows did not move.

A command from the man in German stopped the beating. On his second command, both the Japanese and Germans opened their pants and urinated on the sobbing, bleeding Marwood. The Germans laughed. When it was done the man in the shadows stepped forward. Marwood, wishing for death, looked up at a man in a plaid Burberry topcoat and Panama hat.

"It has been a while," the man said in English. "Forgive me if I don't shake hands."

Rupert de Jongh.

Marwood's heart leaped. Saved.

Dear Rupert. His old school chum was older, more filled out in face and body. No longer the put-upon schoolboy. Definitely in command of himself and of others. You could see it in the way the Japs and Jerries deferred to him.

"Marwood," de Jongh said, as though the two had just met at the entrance to a St. James club. "Been donkey's years, hasn't it?"

De Jongh removed doeskin gloves, fitted a cigarette into an ivory holder, and lit it. Player's tobacco by the smell of it. Not one of Marwood's favorites.

De Jongh said, "You appear to be at a disadvantage. Perhaps I can be of service. The way you were to me some years ago."

Confused and frightened, Marwood remained on the stone floor, where he somehow felt less exposed. Whatever was going on here would not have happened had he listened to Alexis. She had warned him not to be too impressed with Switzerland's neutrality. There are 200,000 Swiss Germans in the country, she said, and a good number of them are ardent Nazis. Watch your step, especially when traveling alone in the countryside. The countryside was a picture postcard but sparsely populated. Her advice: stick to Geneva. And above all, check in twice daily with either the British or American legations.

Marwood, however, saw no reason to take her seriously. He knew as much about Switzerland and geopolitics as she did and resented being told what to do by Americans who were Johnny-come-latelies to the war.

Earlier in the week he had driven around Lake Geneva, sightseeing and relaxing and finding it hard to believe that the war existed. No air-raid warnings, no bombed-out churches, no sandbags piled in front of your home. God bless the Swiss banking system, which the Germans had decided to use rather than destroy. From Lake Geneva, Marwood had continued on to Morges to see its famed thirteenth-century castle and statue of Paderewski. Lovely.

Yesterday he had driven forty miles to Lausanne, where Voltaire and Gibbon had lived, and where Marwood had spent delightful summer holidays with his parents when he was a lad. How had he explained this trip to Miss Waycross? Simple. He had lied, telling her it had been necessary in order to make contact with a Swiss businessman who might be of use to British espionage. Marwood was only on loan to Miss Waycross and the Americans. He was still a British subject and let no one forget it.

But now Marwood was alone, naked, covered in welts, piss, and blood, and ready to plead for his life, to do anything that would keep him alive.

De Jongh said, "Do you know I was not supposed to be in Lausanne the day I spotted you. Oh, you have changed, dear boy. So have we all. But I had no trouble recognizing you. Still striding about as though you own the earth. Absurd, really. Wasn't it Shaw who said an Englishman thinks he is moral when he is only uncomfortable. At the moment you must be convinced you're quite moral."

De Jongh stepped over a small puddle of urine, made a face, then leaned close to Marwood. "You have been followed for the past twenty-four hours, but I suppose you haven't noticed. You are a British agent, am I correct?"

Marwood nodded.

"Here in Switzerland to do what?" de Jongh asked.

"To spy on you. And take you prisoner or kill you."

De Jongh raised one eyebrow. "Fancy that," he said. Then he asked how Marwood came to know de Jongh would be in Geneva.

Marwood mentioned Richard Wagner and told de Jongh his real name. Then he told him about Alexis Waycross and how she had followed de Jongh's career over the years. And broken his Miami spy ring. De Jongh seemed very interested in her. The two Etonians talked for almost an hour, a great deal of that time about Alexis Waycross. When they finished, a relaxed de Jongh smiled and offered Marwood a cigarette. He helped Marwood into his torn clothes, attempted to put him at his ease, and said that war was a nasty business and sometimes one had to do things that were not always proper.

But make no mistake. De Jongh had not forgotten what Marwood had done for him at Eton and that's why Marwood was being allowed to live. He could return to Geneva, provid-

ing he gave his word not to mention what happened beneath
the arena today. Marwood gave his word. He would say
nothing to anyone. De Jongh could count on him.

They left the amphitheater together, Japs walking ahead, de
Jongh and Marwood bringing up the rear and reminiscing
about their school days together. The Germans had left for
Geneva a half hour ago to pick up Alexis Waycross and the
others. At Marwood's car de Jongh said, "Silly me, we can't
let you go back like this. Must make it look convincing, dear
fellow. Make it appear as though you have been dicing with
death and somehow pulled off a hair-raising escape."

De Jongh took a Luger from the pocket of his Burberry and
put two bullets through the boot, damaging the chinaware,
but under the circumstances Marwood decided not to complain. One more bullet in the back window and de Jongh said,
"There, that should do it." He shook Marwood's hand and
told him to drive carefully and perhaps they'd meet again.

A relieved Marwood slid behind the wheel and was about
to close the door when de Jongh said, "One more thing, dear
boy," and shot him twice in the left knee. Marwood screamed
and fell from the car into the snow.

Half crazed with pain, he watched de Jongh use Marwood's
own belt to tie a tourniquet above the wound. As he worked
de Jongh spoke to Marwood, calling him spineless and a
coward, something de Jongh would keep secret. In return
Marwood was to keep silent about his own collaboration here
today. A secret was something you give to others to keep for
you. Both were now keeping secrets for each other.

De Jongh finished, stood up, and brushed snow from his
Burberry. "Validates your forthcoming heroic pose, wouldn't
you say? I don't think I need caution you about watching your
words regarding this incident. It could mean prison for having
betrayed your comrades. By now I'm sure you've guessed I
intend to do unto them before they do unto me. Don't ever
forget the part you've played in this little tableau, for which
you have my undying thanks. I am so looking forward to
meeting your Miss Waycross. One can only hope she'll confirm Richard Wagner's true identity."

When a semiconscious Marwood had been placed in his
car, de Jongh slammed the door and leaned in. "Do drive
carefully. Road's a bit icy the nearer you get to Geneva.
Secrets, dear fellow. Secrets."

*   *   *

Washington. At exactly 7:14 in the morning Sir Michael Marwood selected the suit he would wear for his State Department meetings and White House luncheon. It was black with chalk stripes. Dignified and somber. The twentieth century's Roman toga, though at 700 pounds somewhat more expensive. And it had Savile Row touches that pleased Marwood. The sleeves had three buttons each, with buttonholes that could be unbuttoned if so desired. Since it was bad form to show more than half an inch of shirt sleeve, Marwood's sleeves measured precisely five inches from the thumbnail. Marwood had selected a double vent to cover what his cheeky tailor described as a spreading assterior.

Custom-made shirt to go with the somber suit, hand stitched from ten separate measurements and made of 100 percent Egyptian cotton. Eighty quid each and ordered a dozen at a time from an individual paper pattern kept on file until the customer died or went bankrupt. But so long as he remained a diplomat empowered to travel the world and walk through customs without being searched, Marwood would not go bankrupt. He was paid quite handsomely to smuggle certain commodities under diplomatic cover for Rupert de Jongh and his *yakuza* associates. Marwood had brought some of those commodities with him to Washington. Two suitcases, one containing several plastic bags of uncut heroin, the other with almost eight million American dollars.

Waiting for Marwood at Dulles Airport had been the Limousine he always insisted upon. It was from a car service he praised lavishly to the embassy, which was not allowed to use its regular service to pick up Marwood. He praised the service of his choice for its clean vehicles, skilled drivers, lavish interiors, which included a bar, television, two telephones, and tinted, bulletproof glass. What could the embassy do but order the limo and foot the bill?

At the airport the two special suitcases were placed in the front seat of the limousine between Alan Bruce and the driver, a Japanese with dark glasses and a scarred right cheek. Marwood and whoever the embassy had sent to greet him sat in the back talking about one thing and another. At the hotel, Marwood and the embassy people went on ahead, leaving Alan Bruce to see to the luggage. He did, ignoring the two suitcases in the front seat, which were beside the driver when he pulled away. It was that simple. Six hours later the suit-cases were in New York with Frankie Odori, de Jongh's godson.

Marwood's agreement called for him to deal only with de Jongh and Kangnang. When this was not possible, Alan Bruce would pick up the drugs and/or cash. And as Kangnang had said, de Jongh was a generous man. But that generosity would come to an end if de Jongh was arrested or killed. And Alexis Bendor was just the lady who could bring this about if left to her own devices. She had been the only member of her team to survive the confrontation with the *gaijin*. In fact, she was the only agent ever to get the better of him and live to tell about it. Could she cause trouble for de Jongh and Marwood? Most assuredly.

Marwood thought, All I've ever wanted out of life was not to get hurt. That's all. Ironic that he should be decorated for his daring wartime escape. Losing the leg had indeed lent credence to the occasion, as de Jongh had said it would.

Marwood finished dressing, then sat on the edge of his bed and drank tea and brandy. He was about to betray Alexis for the second time and his conscience made a small attempt to point out the distinction between right and wrong. But for the most part his conscience had ceased to speak to him years ago and had in effect become his accomplice. Marwood no longer judged himself in the light of moral laws. Money was his passbook into a life and society of his own choosing, money that came from de Jongh. Nothing must happen to de Jongh.

Marwood found a piece of hotel stationery and carefully printed several sentences in block letters. Then he set a cassette recorder on the night table, saw that he was running late, and began to work faster. He checked what he'd written once more, then called Alan Bruce into the bedroom. Alan was ordered to study the message, ask questions, and read it back to Marwood. Then it was time for Alan to read it into a blank tape on the cassette.

"The woman seen in the Honolulu park is Alexis Bendor, Bendor being her married name. That's spelled *B-E-N-D-O-R*. She is a widow and lives in Honolulu with her son, an only child and the owner of a private health club also in Honolulu. They share a home together in a suburb called Mount Tanta-lus. Mrs. Bendor owns a bookstore located in a Waikiki shopping mall. The store is called Cantos, after the epic poem by Ezra Pound.''

Marwood played the cassette twice, congratulated Alan Bruce on an excellent reading, then placed the cassette in a sealed envelope. He handed it to Alan Bruce, who slipped it inside his jacket.

In the limousine taking Marwood to the State Department Alan Bruce sat beside the Japanese driver who had picked them up at Dulles Airport. After the car pulled away from the hotel Bruce handed the envelope to the driver and said it must be taken to New York immediately and handed to Frankie Odori, no one else. The driver accepted it without a word, never taking his eyes off the road.

In the back seat Marwood remembered that the driver wore a bow tie, a black one and completely unlike the one Marwood had given de Jongh. But the bow tie reminded the diplomat of his old school chum and of the chains that bound them together, chains once too slight to be felt and now too strong to be broken.

Thirteen

Detective Lieutenant Raymond Manoa, chocolate milk shake in hand, sat in his parked Datsun staring at the all-male crowd. Opening night for Hotel Street's newest gay bar. The place didn't look like much, but Manoa had never seen a fag joint that belonged in *Better Homes and Gardens*. This one called itself the Address Book and didn't appear to be anything special. Just another hole in the wall in crummy downtown, squeezed between a Chinese herb shop and a run-down Vietnamese restaurant. Whoever owned the bar had popped for a few bucks to install a classy-looking front door. Beautifully polished koa wood, complete with a sliding metal peephole. The front window was the same as it was in gay bars all over the world, darkly tinted glass designed to stop people from peering inside and pointing a finger.

Two hulking Samoans in black silk shirts and white pants stood outside checking invitations, small address books with the bar's address and telephone number stamped on the front. Raymond Manoa thought the invitation was the kind of pussy smart you'd expect from a fruit. Cutesy shit. Being around people who could think of stuff like that made the detective feel uncomfortable. There was such a thing as being too fucking clever. Honolulu rarely had more than two or three gay bars at any given time. If Manoa had his way, they'd all be shut down. Fags were weak and he couldn't stomach weak men.

He glanced at his watch, saw it was just after 10:00 P.M., and leaned forward to punch a button on the car radio. He played with the tuner until the reception was clear. On Fridays a local station played an hour of *himeni*, the old Christian hymns brought to Hawaii from New England by nineteenth-century missionaries. Manoa, a good baritone, hummed along with the choir on "Now Praise My Soul the King of Heaven." The Christian religion meant nothing to him. He had never set foot in a church and had never touched a Bible. But goddamn, he loved those old hymns. Forget the words. He sang them, sure, but he didn't know what they meant. Didn't fucking care, either. What mattered was the music. It excited him as it had his ancestors, who had never heard melody and harmony in music until the Christians' arrival 160 years ago.

Manoa would be the first to admit that Hotel Street and hymns didn't exactly go together. Hotel Street was Honolulu's red light district, six blocks of raunch and sleaze in the middle of Chinatown. Flop houses, pimps, porn movie theaters, and dirty bookstores. Filipino pool halls, chop suey joints, GI's on the prowl, and boy prostitutes hanging out in doorways.

Down here you could have your dick tattooed, score cocaine and angel dust, sell stolen tourist cameras and car radios to pawnshops that didn't give a rat's ass how you got them. You could watch a live sex show, dance with a transvestite, and eat Mongolian cuisine if that shit turned you on. Forget the nightly police patrols or the cruising cop cars with their whirling blue lights. Come sundown, bruddah, Hotel Street was no place for amateurs.

Raymond Manoa was here because he had followed Paul Anami to the Address Book and following this dinge queen—Anami had a thing for pretty black boys—was step one in Manoa's plan to kill Alexis Bendor.

Using a matchbook cover, Manoa dug bits of food from between his teeth. He'd eaten dinner in the car, paper plates heaped with beef teriyaki, sashimi, and rice. And kalua pork, pig stuffed with hissing hot rocks, rubbed with salt, and cooked in an earthen pit lined with banana stumps, lava rocks, and kiawe wood. Kalua pig was authentic island food,

the kind Manoa would eat until it came out of his ears. These
days, unfortunately, it was almost impossible to find it in
Hawaii. Like other ancient Polynesian customs, it was fucking hard to come by.

Blame it on the new Hawaii, the one Manoa could do
without. The Hawaii with too many newcomers and too many
changes. Manoa was *keiki aina*, child of the soil, a pure-
blooded Hawaiian and proud of it, bruddah. He didn't like the
idea of Hawaii becoming a foreign country. The only people
doing anything about it were the young Hawaiians and mixed
bloods. They were not about to sit still while their beaches
and land were being taken away and they were being screwed
out of the good jobs. No way, brah. They were becoming
violent. Doing some ass kicking. Taking out their anger on
tourists, whites, and anybody who wasn't Hawaiian. Shit,
why not?

Raymond Manoa was in his early forties, a chunky, round-
faced, brown-skinned man with graying kinky hair and a
pleasant smile. In more than twenty years as a cop he'd
averaged six commendations a year for valor. During that
time he'd been shot three times and knifed twice in the line of
duty. Proud of his scars, Manoa referred to them as his
jewelry. He was currently assigned to Honolulu Airport, where
he worked with customs, airport security, and the agricultural
units that sprayed incoming and outgoing planes.

Manoa was a man of contradictions. On one hand he was
soft-spoken and polite, with a reserved, correct friendliness.
But there was a dark side to him that few knew about, one
rooted in ancient island superstitions and past violent confrontations between his family and whites. He admitted to no
one how gratifying and biologically necessary he found such
savagery.

His ancestors had been *kahunas*, priests and advisers to
Kamehameha I, greatest of all Hawaiian kings. Even Manoa
had to admit that Kamehameha's conquest of the Hawaiian
chain's populated islands had been bloody. Under his rule
tribal wars and human sacrifices had wiped out over half the
population. But it was Kamehameha who had created the
kingdom of Hawaii. If whites thought he was barbaric, well,
that was their problem. Manoa wasn't interested in what
whites thought. What mattered was that Kamehameha's Ha-

waii had belonged to children of the soil. Not to white businessmen or Japanese businessmen.

The *mana* always told Manoa what to do and now it told him that Hawaiians must take back their land. Only children of the soil understood *mana,* a supernormal power possessed by a person or things. *Mana* belonged to the ancient Polynesian religion, to the old, sacred customs. To get that power, said the *kahunas,* you must kill your enemy and eat his heart, the center of his power and forcefulness. Manoa had been eighteen when he'd killed the *haole* responsible for his father's death and eaten the man's heart. After that the *mana* had belonged to the detective. After that he'd had the strength and vitality to do whatever he wished.

Manoa listened carefully each time the *mana* spoke to him. These days it spoke to him of the beast with many heads, the tourists and permanent residents flooding into Hawaii. Mainland whites by the thousands. And boatloads of Koreans, Chinese, Thais, and Vietnamese to go along with the Japanese, the real political power in Hawaii. A tidal wave of whites and gooks. Messengers bearing bad news.

What could Manoa do about it? Two months ago he had gone to Japan at the *gaijin's* invitation and in the quiet of the *yakuza* leader's Yokohama home the detective was given an answer. He was to run in next year's Hawaii State Senate election. Manoa thought, Holy shit, but he kept quiet and listened. The *gaijin* did not like to be interrupted. Still, this election business was the last thing the detective expected, and if part of him said the idea was crazy, the rest of him listened closely to the *gaijin's* every word.

Yes, Japanese-Americans were the power people in Hawaii, in control of the governorship, important judgeships, the state's congressional delegation and major businesses. AJA's—Americans of Japanese Ancestry—were barely a fourth of the state's population, but they ran Hawaii. The *gaijin,* however, saw that changing.

Whites, he predicted, would soon be the largest group and Manoa agreed. But they were years away from effectively organizing their voting power. Meanwhile they were perceived by island residents as greedy and destructive. And in the *gaijin's* opinion the Japanese were due to suffer from an inevitable backlash against the many Orientals pouring into the state. It was right that a pure-blood like Raymond Manoa now step forward and speak for his kind. Close behind the *gaijin*'s words came the voice of the *mana* saying, yes, this was the detective's destiny. Be a true child of the soil, said the power. Take what is yours.

Manoa, the *gaijin* pointed out, had advantages over other potential candidates. He was a local boy who'd made good, the son of impoverished native Hawaiians who'd worked his way up from pineapple field hand, cane cutter, and dock walloper to become a heroic officer of the law, one popular with press and public alike. Manoa was against the coddling of criminals, an issue cutting across racial and party lines. And he revered the land. Native Hawaiians would admire him for this, of course, but so would ecology-minded voters of other races.

All Manoa needed was financial backing and the correct publicity campaign and he would be a most attractive candidate. The *gaijin* was certain Detective Lieutenant Manoa would appeal to the growing number of Hawaiian voters who felt Hawaii had too many white and Japanese faces in high places.

Manoa had more going for him than just his Hawaiian heritage and the *gaijin*'s money. "You are owed favors by certain prominent Hawaiians," the Englishman said. "Next year's Senate race would be an appropriate time to collect, I should think."

Manoa nodded. There was the seventeen-year-old white girl who was being gang raped on the Waianae Coast one night by four Hawaiian males until Manoa stepped in and started kicking ass and taking names. He'd put two of her assailants in the hospital. The girl's father was a heavy-duty newspaper owner and he had vowed he wouldn't forget what the detective had done for his daughter. And there was the banker whose fag son had posed for some dirty pictures, which an interior decorator had come across while decorating the son's Waikiki condo. The decorator copped the photographs, then attempted a little blackmail. Manoa had paid the decorator a visit, then walked away with the photographs, the negatives, and the decorator's promise that he wouldn't be doing anything so stupid any time soon.

And don't forget the Japanese-American wife of Hawaii's most powerful senator. Caught her ass trying to smuggle several Paris designer gowns past customs without paying duty. The lady had gone into hysterics until Manoa calmed her down, then called the senator, who'd come running and used his clout to put a lid on things. You've got a friend when you need one, he'd said to Manoa.

The detective also had favors owed him by others who carried a lot of weight in the islands. Why hadn't he collected? Because he hadn't known what to ask for. Now he did.

Call in your IOU's next year, the *gaijin* said. There'll be an experienced campaign manager to advise you on how best to go about it. You'll win, the Englishman told him, because I want you to. Nor would Manoa's political career stop with the Hawaiian Senate. When the *gaijin* decided it was time to reach out for more, the detective would do just that. The U.S. Congress. Perhaps the governorship. There was so much to be done for the Hawaiian people, the real Hawaiian people. And there was much to be done for the *gaijin*. The detective understood.

Manoa thought, this is what I was born for. He was so elated that he could have burst into song, cut loose with one of the hymns he liked. He wouldn't have traded this moment for anything on earth. He left Japan determined to win next year's election even if he had to waste a few people to do it. Winning was going to turn his life around. Shit, winning was going to turn Hawaii around. Believe it, bruddah.

But some old broad named Alexis Bendor was in the picture and now the situation was hairy, because if she brought down the *gaijin*, Manoa could kiss that Senate seat goodbye. Where the fuck would he get the money to run for office unless he got it from the Englishman? Take away the *gaijin* and you know what Manoa had to look forward to? A skimpy pension and some half-assed security job in a beachfront hotel or in a Chinatown noodle factory. Which was as much fun as beating his meat with a hammer.

With the *gaijin* calling the shots, Manoa would become a man everybody called "Mister." Wasn't a soul on this earth as smart as the *gaijin*. No way Manoa could win the election without him. And there was no way the Bendor woman was going to be allowed to make trouble. The sooner she got whacked, the better.

What kind of trouble could Alexis Bendor lay on the *gaijin?* All the lady had to do was get one newspaperman on her side, just one. Or get a single congressman to see it her way and start an investigation, and the publicity would send the Italians in New York running for cover. The only thing the *gaijin* would get out of New York was *no mas, no mas.* Mob guys didn't like their names in the paper.

The *gaijin* didn't want his name in the paper either, not with a $200 million luxury hotel under construction on Oahu's western shore. Not with investments in two shopping malls, including a new one going up in St. Louis Heights. Not with money in new condos being built in Hanauma Bay, near the beach where they filmed *From Here to Eternity.* Not with the kind of money the *gaijin* was moving through Hawaii these days, heavy bread out of Hong Kong belonging to some very important people.

The *yakuza* leader also controlled a pair of tour companies catering to Japanese tourists here and on the mainland, a gold mine because the Japs were big spenders. These tour companies were also tied into prostitution and drug and gambling interests, since Jap tourists, the men especially, loved to party. Not even competition from another *yakuza* group trying to expand in Hawaii could stop the *gaijin* from walking off with a big piece of the Japanese tourist trade. And nobody, not local mobs or rival *yakuza*, were dealing as much heroin as the Englishman. Fucking unbelievable the number of keys he was bringing into Hawaii from the "Golden Triangle" before moving them on to Japan.

Yesterday, the La Serra brothers had sent the *gaijin* something more valuable than money, something the *yakuza* leader needed very badly if he wanted to come out on top in Japan's gang war. Guns. Better than anything Honolulu police were carrying around. The weapons had been hidden on an air freighter flying out of Newark and were strictly state of the art, every one a perfect ten. Manoa had been at the airport when they landed, which is what the *gaijin* was paying him for.

At the airport the police lieutenant had purposely kept the plane waiting on the tarmac until dark, until there was only him, a few other officials, and a spray crew that was on the *gaijin*'s payroll. With Manoa checking the plane himself, all the remaining customs and security people could think was everything's cool, no problems.

When he saw the guns, Manoa's eyebrows went up. Very,

very nice. Three Uzis, a half dozen Smith & Wesson Model 60s, four Colt Pythons, and three Smith & Wesson .44 magnums, the *Dirty Harry* special. Manoa would have given his left ball to own one of these, but he wasn't about to rip off the *gaijin*. All the stuff was new and came with ammunition. The La Serras had even thrown in a half dozen bulletproof vests. Score one for the pizza eaters.

A cheap Saturday Night Special, .22 caliber and worth ten bucks in Hawaii or the mainland, sold for $10,000 in Japan, where guns were hard to come by. The Smith & Wessons and Colt Pythons would go for twice that, if the *gaijin* wanted to sell, and Manoa was pretty sure he wouldn't. As for the Uzis, they were worth at least forty grand each. The *yakuza* leader was going to be one happy dude.

Under Manoa's direction, the spray crew hid the guns under their equipment, then carted them off the plane and loaded everything onto a green panel truck. A minute later the spray crew drove off into the night, carrying enough fire power to wipe out an army. Manoa was no brain surgeon, but he knew this much: the *gaijin* did not want to lose a mainland contact like the La Serras. And bruddah, that's what would go down if the Bendor woman got lucky.

But the lady was not dumb. She knew somebody was after her because she'd checked out of her D.C. hotel, then disappeared. Just like that. The *gaijin*'s people in Washington had traced her to Philadelphia, where she'd purchased tickets on two flights, one to Toronto and one to Atlanta. Which city did she fly to? Neither one. But she'd kept the *gaijin*'s people busy checking out both reservations. Meanwhile, she was nowhere to be found. Yes, sir, Mrs. Bendor was one smart *wahine*, one smart woman.

She wasn't in New York City, that's for sure. Her son was there, hanging out in a health club he owned when he wasn't spending his time with a lady gambler. She was another smart *wahine*. Frankie Odori, the *gaijin*'s godson, had lost money to her more than once. He'd also hit on her a couple of times, Manoa had heard, and got nowhere. Miss Erica didn't believe in mixing business with pleasure.

How much time had the *gaijin* given Manoa to snuff the Bendor woman? A week, no more. And no excuses. In the next month the *yakuza* leader would be moving a lot of heroin to the mainland and a ton of money out of Hong Kong.

Nothing had better go wrong. But with the Bendor woman poking around, anything was possible.

Two days ago the detective had dropped into a Waikiki hotel and used a computer belonging to the ex-FBI guy in charge of hotel security. Manoa asked him for help in running a credit check on some locals. Just a little bit of moonlighting Manoa didn't want the department to know about. The feeb said I won't tell if you won't, then punched in the names handed him by Manoa.

Alexis Bendor. Squeaky clean, the computer said. Member of ecology and civic groups, author of two books, one on codes and ciphers, the other on World War II espionage. Former college literature and language teacher. A jogger. Has ties to American intelligence. Big deal, Manoa thought. So do half the people in Hawaii and it don't amount to much. No debts, no police record. A model citizen.

Simon Bendor. His life on the computer screen started out impressively. One of Hawaii's most publicized schoolboy athletes until a serious surfing accident, from which he staged a miraculous recovery. Now he lives a quiet life, the computer said. He was a businessman with an excellent credit rating. Owner of two successful health clubs, one in Honolulu, one in Manhattan. Shares a Mount Tantalus home with his mother. Put him down as a mama's boy, Manoa thought. Ain't cut the cord yet. No outstanding debts, no police record. No wife, no children. Yes, sir, he's mama's little darling.

No personal credit cards or charge accounts. Now what kind of businessman is that, the feeb said. Ain't he ever heard of three-martini lunches? Why does our boy Simon insist on paying in cash? Health club bills were paid by check and corporate credit cards, but our boy Simon never signed them. A manager did. Health club bills conducted through a couple of corporations. Nothing from the computer on them. A crafty little cuss, Mr. Simon. The feeb said, I think the operative word here is *shifty*.

And then there was the Vietnam service. The computer came up with *nada*. Zero. "Shit," said the feeb, "now I got to know what the fuck's shaking here." He made two long-distance calls to Washington and after that Manoa decided he'd been too quick to call Mr. Simon a mama's boy.

Last days of the Vietnam War. Mr. Simon had gone to

work for the CIA, setting up and training a special operations unit. The unit's job: covert actions. Dirty tricks. The unit, the feeb said, rescued a few Americans, zapped some people, stole documents, and collected intelligence. It operated under extraordinary secrecy and was on the order of the Green Berets, Navy SEAL teams, and other commando units. Since the Iranian hostage crisis a lot of Washington departments had similar units. "Get this," the feeb said. "Congress doesn't know most of these units exist."

Brother Simon, the feeb said, did good work, meaning he was one bad dude. He might look as harmless as a Twinkie, but the man had ice water in his veins. Maybe not a fag. Sad to say, Brother Bendor and the CIA had not parted on good terms, but these things happen. The feeb lacked the necessary security clearance to obtain all the details, but in any case it wasn't the sort of thing people in Washington wanted to go into.

Time for Manoa to back off. He'd learned something important, which was don't underestimate Mr. Simon. So what if he lived with his mother. The dude was still a hard case, the kind who took his gloves off one finger at a time.

In any case, Manoa couldn't very well fly to the Big Apple and do a number on Mr. Simon to make him tell where mama was hiding. New York wasn't Manoa's town; he'd stand out like a sore thumb. And the *gaijin* wanted the *yakuza* kept out of it, so no use bringing in Frankie and his people. Besides, Mr. Simon might be on his way back to Honolulu or he could very well decide to follow his lady around for a while. Manoa didn't have the time to play games.

That left just one other person who might know where Mrs. Bendor was, a person Manoa could reach out and touch right here in Honolulu. A certain Mr. Paul Anami. Mr. Paul was a friend of the Bendors, the man who was keeping an eye on Mrs. Bendor's book shop while she was away, the man who popped in and out of the Bendors' Mount Tantalus home while they were gone, maybe to water the plants or to see that the housekeeper went easy on the booze. Mr. Paul had even shown up at Simon Bendor's Honolulu health club, not only to improve his body but to talk to the manager, maybe to make sure the customers had enough clean towels while Simon Bendor was away. Mr. Paul was a good friend. Trustworthy and dependable.

Interesting medical history he had, too. High-strung, on
medication for his nerves, and currently being treated for
same by a private physician. Hospitalized twice for emotional
disorders. A respected antique dealer. Not the kind to deal in
stolen goods, according to Manoa's informants. But Mr. Paul
was a coal miner, a gay with a taste for blacks.

Homosexual and Japanese. Two reasons why Manoa was
going to enjoy doing a number on Mr. Paul. The detective
was going to break him down. Turn him into a basket case.
Which was much smarter than beating him up and having him
complain. Or killing him and having someone else complain.
Mr. Paul was going to have a nervous breakdown and when
his head was malfunctioning, then he'd be ready to help
Manoa kill Mrs. Bendor.

The *mana* told the detective how to go about it.

Raymond Manoa followed the yellow Jaguar down Queen
Emma Street, then along Pali highway. On Nuuanu Avenue
Paul Anami slowed the Jaguar down and pointed out places of
interest to the handsome young black man beside him.

Manoa wanted to speed things up. He'd put in a long day
and was anxious to get started on Mr. Paul. But the detective
could do nothing until Mr. Paul got onto the four-lane highway leading to his home in the Nuuanu Valley. Mr. Paul had
to be making good money; he drove a Jag and valley homes
were not cheap. This was where the early ruling whites and
Christian missionaries had built grand estates for themselves
and where today many Asian consul generals preferred to
live. Manoa sometimes drove out there during the rainy season and sat in his car with the windshield wipers going
clack-clack, clack-clack, while he smoked Maui Wowee and
stared at the waterfalls plunging over the cliff faces, knowing
the water would never reach bottom because the valley winds
would whip them skyward once more in the form of spray.
The detective would smile because he had seen Lono, god of
wind and thunder, at play.

In the Datsun he watched the Jag creep past the Soto Zen
Temple and stop, motor running, at the Royal Mausoleum six
blocks farther on, where Hawaii's kings and queens lay buried. Mr. Paul must have said something to get the black guy's
attention because the spade leaned across the antique dealer
to get a better look at the burial ground. Manoa braked and

cut his lights. Great. Maybe we'll get home in time for Christmas.

The detective watched the Jag pull away from the Royal Mausoleum, pick up speed, and tool on down the avenue, toward the four-lane highway leading to the Nuuanu Valley. About time Mr. Paul got his ass in gear and headed home. Manoa reached down for the two-way radio on the seat between his legs, brought it up to his mouth, and flicked the sending switch. He spoke briefly to the two *yakuza* in a maroon Buick behind him, then put the radio down. No mistakes, he'd told them. Manoa had to account to the *gaijin* if this thing went down wrong. The guys in the Buick would have it worse. They would have to account to Manoa and the *gaijin*.

The Jag turned onto the four-lane highway. Well, all right. Manoa put his foot down on the accelerator, sending the Datsun leaping forward. Only after he was on the highway and gaining on the Jag did he take his eyes off the road and look at the items on the seat beside him. A doctor's bag. Two pairs of thick workman's gloves. A gourd mask made from the dried, hollowed-out shell of a large squash, the type worn by Hawaiian warriors hundreds of years ago. Manoa had waited long enough for his pleasure. In a couple of minutes he was going to start enjoying it.

Traffic this time of night was extremely slight in both directions. Only one vehicle passed Manoa and Anami, a van full of white kids laughing and drinking and probably doing a little grass as well. Manoa figured them for campers heading for the Koolau Mountains near the valley. Not too smart, if that's what they were planning to do. White kids camping out these days, particularly at night, were asking for it. Native Hawaiians and mixed bloods would give it to them for sure.

Manoa felt the temperature drop as the highway climbed higher along cool, tree-covered slopes. He inhaled the pleasant odor of tall eucalyptus trees lining both sides of the highway. To his left razor-edged mountains were silhouetted against a star-filled sky. Getting nearer the valley now. Two hundred years ago his ancestors had fought beside Kamehameha the Great in this valley, driving the natives of Oahu before them, killing thousands and forcing thousands more over the Pali precipice and onto jagged rocks a thousand feet below.

The valley. The closer Manoa came to it, the more psyched he became.

Ahead of him, the Jag slowed down. No sweat. Mr. Paul was just shifting gears for the climb up the highway and through a mountain tunnel, then into the Nuuanu Valley. Manoa, eyes unnaturally bright, picked up the hand radio. "Do it now," he said to the Buick following him.

The Buick's souped-up motor roared as the car switched lanes. In seconds it blew by Manoa and caught the Jag. Then forced the Jag off the road, into the dark red dirt, horn blaring, headlights aimed at the vines dangling from the eucalyptus trees. Manoa pushed the Datsun for all it was worth, closing the gap between himself and the two cars. How *do* you *do*, Mr. Paul.

The detective turned off the highway and into the dirt. Hit the brakes hard. Blocked the Jag from the rear. Mr. Paul was boxed in tight.

The *mana* took over. Carried along by its power, Manoa moved swiftly. He yanked off the dark glasses and denim cap he'd worn to hide his face and tossed them over his shoulder into the back seat. Off with his sweat-stained red T-shirt. Then he put on the gourd mask, which had a space cut out in front for his eyes and nose. Thin strips of white cloth dangled from the front and back of the mask. Manoa now had the frightening, skull-like appearance of an eighteenth-century Hawaiian warrior.

Next, the work gloves. Wasn't easy putting on both pair, one over the other, but it had to be done. Manoa had to protect his hands from the contents of the bag.

The two *yakuza* were out of the Buick. Following Manoa's orders they stood on either side of the Jag with flashlights trained on Paul Anami and the black. No guns. Guns sometimes went off. Besides Mr. Paul and his friend were pussies, not fighters. But the *yakuza* wore ski masks, dark glasses, long-sleeve shirts, and gloves. Manoa's idea. Make it hard for Mr. Paul to identify anybody's race.

Inside the Jag, Anami and the black covered their faces with their arms and shrank in their seats. Anami said, "What's this all about?" Jesus, did he really expect an answer? The black, scared shitless, kept quiet.

Manoa started running. Ran right at the Jag, screaming as warriors of old had done on the battlefield. Manoa's shouts

echoed in the night-shrouded forest and along the empty
highway and he goddam knew what he looked like in that
mask, coming out of the darkness and into a thin shaft of
light. Paul Anami knew, too. And so did the little swish with
him. Anami went rigid. Mouth open, eyes wide. Face drained
of all color. The spade came apart a lot faster. He found his
tongue, but all he could do was say "Oh, no" over and over
and cry his little heart out.

Manoa felt as strong as any *kahuna* on the eve of battle,
felt himself strong enough to reach up and pull stars down
from the sky. He unzipped the doctor's bag, took care not to
put his hands inside and then he howled with the force of the
mana, a sound that made one masked *yakuza* drop his flashlight and as Manoa howled he threw the bag's contents into
the Jag's front seat.

Heaved the ugliest fucking rat you ever saw right at Mr.
Paul and Midnight.

A Hawaiian waterfront rat, two feet long and hungry, rust
colored, with plenty of tail and plenty of meat.

The rat brushed Anami's chest, bounced off his right thigh
and scrambled across the screaming black's legs. What happened next was no surprise. The two tore out of the Jag
squealing, ending up in the dirt, Mr. Paul in white silk and
beige and the black, a skinny, little thing, with stringy Michael Jackson hair, in turquoise tank top and baggy yellow
jeans with lots of snaps and zippers.

Manoa leaped over the prone Anami, yelling and waving
the doctor's bag to drive the rat out of the Jag. Then the
detective was behind the wheel, driving off with the front
doors still open and flapping. Both *yakuza* started running,
one to the Buick, the other to Manoa's Datsun. In seconds
their cars were turning around, spraying dirt, then straighten-
ing out to speed toward the highway.

Tires squealing, the Buick chased after the Jag. The Datsun,
with no traffic to worry about, U-turned across two lanes and
headed back to Honolulu.

Leaving a terrorized Paul Anami in almost total darkness
and with the weeping black in the dirt at his feet.

Dawn. A green Mercury circled a pond ringed by African
tulips and came to a halt in the graveled driveway in front of
Paul Anami's home. The driver and the man beside him were

Honolulu police detectives. Behind the driver sat Paul Anami, exhausted and still shaken. To his right was David LaPointe, a black dancer currently appearing in a revue at a Waikiki hotel. Both detectives eyed the house. They were in the presence of money, the thing you used to keep score in life. Paul Anami may have lost his car, but he sure as hell was winning elsewhere.

The two-story house was made of white clapboard, with a lanai and at least three acres of ground. It came with a swimming pool, tennis court, and more than a few eucalyptus, pine, banyan, and golden trees. A white millionaire had built it in the nineteenth century with sugarcane profits and presented it to his bride, a member of the Hawaiian royal family. Both detectives could smell the sea and through the mist make out the sheer green walls of the Koolau Mountains, the green dotted with the silver of several waterfalls. Pretty view. Pretty house. The man who lived here should look a lot happier than he did at the moment.

Detective Sergeant George Amoy, a thickset Chinese-Portuguese still depressed over having turned fifty yesterday, swiveled around in the driver's seat and said to Paul Anami, "You're home." Anami said nothing. Didn't move either. Amoy thought, He's taken it hard, having his car ripped off. Didn't help either, when some of the guys at headquarters had laughed about the rat being tossed into Anami's lap. Amoy hadn't laughed. Not because he was a nice guy, but because all Amoy had on his mind was getting old. Like it or not, he was coming to the end of his life with shit to show for it.

The truck driver who'd dropped Anami and his friend at police headquarters hadn't come inside, but since he hadn't seen what happened, he wouldn't have been much of a witness. Two men dressed in black and carrying flashlights. A flying rat. And some bare-chested crazy in a gourd mask yelling his ass off. Amoy and his partner, a chain-smoking little Irishman named Jack Patrick Bury, had only Mr. Anami's and Mr. LaPointe's word that any of this had happened. And it didn't help matters that Mr. Anami and Mr. LaPointe couldn't agree on exactly where the incident had occurred. They picked spots off the highway that were twenty yards apart. Amoy had used a flashlight to check out the two "scenes of the crime" and had come up with nothing. Too dark to see clearly and Amoy wasn't sure if it would be worthwhile going back later today to look around some more. The department was short on manpower and the bottom line was neither queen knew exactly where the car had been snatched.

In the front of the Mercury, Jackie Pat froze in the act of lighting a Winston. "I see something," he said.

Amoy turned his back on Anami. "Where?"

Jackie Pat pointed a nicotine-stained forefinger. "Garage." He held the Winston between his teeth, reached into the glove compartment, and took out a flashlight. He opened the car door, shifted around in his seat, and aimed the flashlight beam to the left of the house.

Both Amoy and Jackie Pat stared in the direction of the garage for long seconds and then Amoy swiveled around again to look at Anami and said, "You want to tell me what's going on here?"

Anami lifted his chin. Glassy-eyed and still out of it. Amoy didn't care about Mr. Anami's condition anymore.

The detective said, "Look where I'm pointing, where Detective Bury is shining the flashlight. What do you see?"

Anami turned his head slowly and saw his Jaguar.

LaPointe saw it too and said, "I don't believe this shit," and hugging himself slid down in his seat.

Paul Anami placed a hand over his heart, felt the vial of pills in his shirt pocket and frowned at the Jaguar as if trying to remember who owned it.

Jackie Pat was out of the car now and so was Amoy and it was he who invited Anami out, opening the back door and taking the antique dealer's arm. Amoy said, "Let's go over and look at the car, Mr. Anami," and he kept his hand on the antique dealer's elbow because this whole thing was beginning to sound like wacko time.

At the Jaguar, Anami whispered the car was his and Jackie Pat said beautiful, because he'd been scheduled to go off duty hours ago and also had an 8:00 A.M. court appearance this morning. And at the moment Jackie Pat was being jerked around by a queen and didn't like it. Jackie Pat had a short fuse and Amoy knew it. So the Chinese-Protuguese stepped between his partner and Anami and said, "I think we ought to talk."

Amoy, thinking of his high blood pressure and about turning fifty, forced himself to speak calmly, telling Anami that if he had anything to say the cops were willing to listen. But the Jaguar reported as being stolen apparently wasn't. And the truth was that Anami now had a credibility problem. A very large credibility problem.

PART THREE

Ma.
Distancing.

Ma is the key to victory. *Ma* is not just the difference between near and far. Seeing through all condi-
tions of change, not letting the opponent take the
initiative, always holding the advantage and advancing the fight are the cardinal points of *ma* in life.

—KOTODA YAHEI,
Ittōsai sensei kempō sho

Fourteen

LOS ANGELES
JULY 1983

Alexis Bendor landed at Los Angeles International Airport
and rented a Chevy shortly before noon. She took the freeway
downtown, congratulating herself on having missed the morning rush hour. The day was hot and windless. The smog, one
of Southern California's least desirable features, was eye-
stinging. Alexis rolled up the windows and turned on the air
conditioning. L.A., bless it, had as many cars as New York
and Texas combined. Add heavy industrial pollution to ex-
haust fumes, and breathing became an adventure. No classical
music or Sinatra on the radio, unfortunately, so Alexis settled
for Mantovani, singing along with his syrupy strings on "These
Foolish Things Remind Me of You."

She had come here to steal, a fact she had trouble admitting
to herself, let alone anyone else. Alexis had almost telephoned Simon to tell him about it, but in the end she decided
to say nothing of her plan to steal a photograph of Mr. and
Mrs. Oscar Koehl and get it into the hands of Rupert de
Jongh. Simon would think she was out of her mind. I'm not
hearing this, he'd say. Mother or no mother. I'm really not
hearing this.

Oscar Koehl, a.k.a. Arthur Kuby, wouldn't like it either,
particularly when he learned that the photograph was to be
used as bait to lure Rupert de Jongh to California. Lure him
to a dying Kasumi, where Alexis would be waiting to kill

him. The smart thing, Alexis decided, was to keep quiet about her plans. Just steal the photograph, then tell Simon about it when the deed was done. Very tough to steal and explain why at the same time.

Nearing the city, she settled on Santa Monica Boulevard as the best route to Oscar Koehl's Beverly Hills home. Sunset Boulevard was quicker, but that meant driving along Sunset Strip, an area she could not abide. Years ago, when Alexis lived in California, the Strip, a two-mile stretch of Sunset Boulevard, had been nothing less than magic. It had been glamor and glitter, sparkling with nightclubs that were enchanted kingdoms, clubs like Ciro's, the Mocambo, and the Trocadero. On Alexis's third wedding anniversary Shea had splurged, taking her to see Judy Garland at the Trocadero. What a night that had been. First Garland. Then later waiting in the coat-check line behind Clark Gable. The king himself. Garland and Gable. *Praising what is lost/Makes the remembrance dear.*

Today Sunset Strip was run-down and faded, the site of liquor stores, country-and-western clubs, teenage whores in hot pants, garish billboards promoting heavy-metal rock groups. Just thinking about the place depressed Alexis. Sunset Strip made her afraid of the future. Life, alas, was an irreversible process.

This time Alexis had not telephoned Koehl to say she was coming. No sense warning him since there was always the chance he might refuse to see her. Mr. Koehl did not enjoy being reminded of Rupert de Jongh, something that happened whenever he heard from Alexis. The former Nazi intelligence officer wanted as much distance between his wife and the *gaijin* as possible, which Alexis could understand. Dead or alive, de Jongh had a hold on Kasumi Koehl.

Alexis turned onto a quiet street of Georgian and Spanish-style mansions. She was wondering how she was going to steal a photograph of the Koehls with them looking on, when she saw the ambulance. It raced by on the cross street in front of her, siren wailing. Christ almighty. Of course it had to be Kasumi. And without Kasumi there was no chance of luring Rupert de Jongh closer.

At the bottom of an incline a security guard opened a pair of wrought-iron gates and let the ambulance pass through. It sped along a pebbled driveway lined on either side by jew hedges. The gate and guard were part of security expenses Koehl had complained about to Alexis. Crime in Los Angeles, he said, was being committed by Mexican illegals, the sort of people who weren't ready to walk on their hind legs.

Alexis was just seconds behind the ambulance, but the guard was already shoving the gates closed. She braked in front of the gates. And lied.

She pressed the button that opened the window on the driver's side. "I'm with the hospital," she said.

The guard, a large man with mirrored sunglasses and pointed sideburns, took one hand from the gates and let it fall to an oiled black leather holster on his right hip. He stared at Alexis for a long time. She shivered and forced herself to hold his gaze, concentrating on his uniform, on the yellow epaulettes, shirt zippers, silver whistle dangling from a breast pocket, American flag patch on his right shoulder. She was about to say, "Don't shoot, just let me leave quietly," when the guard straightened up and pulled back on the gates. Alexis drove through, promising God she'd never again do anything like this as long as she lived.

She arrived at a two-story Tudor mansion in time to see a pair of paramedics leap from the ambulance and race around to the back of the vehicle. One was a light-skinned black man with receding reddish hair. The other was a stumpy Chicano woman who appeared to be in charge. Working fast, they removed a stretcher and portable oxygen tank, then raced along a flagstone walk leading to the mansion. The Chicano woman, Alexis noticed, carried the rolled-up stretcher under one arm as easily as if it were a place mat.

Waiting for them at the door was Nurse Leticia Stones, who was not one of Alexis's favorite people. They'd met here on Alexis's last visit and taken an instant dislike to one another. Nurse Stones was a dwarfish middle-aged woman with spaces between her teeth, a bumpy nose, and an air of discreet hysteria. She had abnormal energy and a need to oppress. Definitely a woman who insisted on being taken seriously.

She directed the paramedics upstairs, urging them on in a tiresome nasal whine. Then she turned to block Alexis's way into the mansion. Alexis smiled and imagined herself sticking a fork in Nurse Stones's eye. She asked the nurse who the ambulance was for.

"Emergency," Nurse Stones said. One small, blue-veined hand was on the beeper clipped to her waist. A slightly paranoid Alexis visualized the nurse summoning the guard at the gate and ordering him to kill. The woman was excitable, the type who mistook raisins for rat turds and got carried away.

Alexis asked if the ambulance was for Mrs. Koehl. Nurse Stones said she wasn't aware that Alexis was expected.

Alexis said, "Not too surprising, since I'm not here to see you."

Nurse Stones cleared her throat. "I'm afraid the Koehls can't see anyone at the moment. Mrs. Koehl's being taken to the hospital. She was having lunch when she started complaining of chest pains and some sort of numbness in her left arm. She was also having trouble breathing."

Alexis's fist tightened around the strap on her shoulder bag. "But she is alive."

"Look Miss—"

"Mrs. Mrs. Bendor."

"Bendor. I really don't have time to go into all this right now. We're rather busy around here. Why don't you just give me a message and I'll see that it's passed on."

Nurse Stones took a step backward, one hand reaching out for the door. The gleam in her eyes said, I can't wait to slam it in your face.

Oscar Koehl came to Alexis's rescue. He called down from the second floor for Nurse Stones to come upstairs. "Right now." His voice was almost a shriek. Panic.

Nurse Stones spun around and ran across a foyer covered in red tiles. She left the front door open. Alexis exhaled. As the goldfish said, If there's no God who changes the water?

From the foyer she walked into a large entrance hall in time to see Nurse Stones jog up a marble staircase and turn right on the second-floor landing. Alexis looked left, at a long sunken living room where she'd last seen the photograph. Nobody here. Change that. A Filipino houseboy in a white jacket and black bow tie was supposedly dusting the room. But instead he stood near a huge console television set and flicked a feather duster at the top, eyes on the screen, where three half-naked and shapely aerobics dancers bent over with behinds facing the camera. When the dancers turned, sat

down on the floor, and lay back with pelvises arched in the
air, the feather duster came to a halt.

The sight of someone else doing what he shouldn't be
doing cheered up Alexis. She grinned and cleared her throat.
The houseboy came to life. He kept his back to her, turned
off the television set and flicked the duster at the screen.
Seconds later he hurried out of the room, leaving Alexis
alone. And the photograph was right where it should be, in an
Art Deco frame on a coffee table beside a Queen Anne wing
chair. Alexis's heart began to pound as it did in the last mile
of a marathon. She looked behind her, saw no one, then
walked down three stairs into the living room. You're not a
thief if they don't catch you.

Oscar Koehl was well off and then some. The living room
had half-timbered walls, beamed ceilings, and sliding glass
doors looking out onto a pool, guest bungalow, patio, and
cactus garden. The paintings on the walls were Flemish,
nineteenth-century English watercolors, and a Degas pastel
that stopped Alexis in her tracks. Not because it was beautiful, which it was, but because she had some idea of its value.
Last year she had helped Paul Anami find a buyer for a Degas
owned by the widow of a South Vietnamese general. The
buyer had been a retired defense contactor living on Maui.
Price: $750,000. And the widow's Degas had been smaller
than Oscar Koehl's.

Alexis sat down in the Queen Anne wing chair and crossed
her legs. She had a clear view of the living room, marble
staircase in the entrance hall and, of course, the photograph.
Something else caught her eye. A Japanese doll. It rested
within reach on a 1920s brown tea cart. Kasumi Koehl still
collected dolls, as many Japanese women did all their lives.
This one was a *daruma,* named for the Indian priest credited
with founding Zen Buddhism. It was six inches high and a
cute little thing. Made from rubber. No arms or legs. Woman's face and red robe painted on and the rounded bottom
weighted so that it always returned to an upright position
when knocked over.

Alexis reached out and touched it with a forefinger. She
smiled as it wobbled. John Kanna had told her about the
daruma. The Japanese kept them as a reminder that the only
way to succeed at anything was to persevere. Never give up.

Seven times pushed over, eight times it rises, went a proverb about the *daruma*.

Alexis leaned forward to look at it. Only one eye painted in. Interesting. The custom was to paint in a single eye, then make a wish. When the wish was granted you painted in the other eye. Alexis thought, Now wouldn't it be something if that missing eye had to do with Kasumi's long-lost love, one Rupert de Jongh. Anything was possible.

Alexis watched a male servant enter the entrance hall, probably from the kitchen, then hurry upstairs. The sound of a power tool came from the cactus garden. Sooner or later someone would turn their attention to Alexis and what then? Best not to think about it. Just do what she came here to do and get out. She stood up and walked toward the photograph. Christ, she'd be glad when this tacky little part of her life was history.

The coffee table containing the photograph was very California, green-tinted glass resting on polished driftwood. The photograph, according to an ashtray in the picture, had been taken at the Biltmore, a hotel that had been a favorite of Mary Pickford, Eleanor Roosevelt, J. Paul Getty, and Ronald Reagan. Koehl wore a tuxedo and had one arm around the bare shoulders of Kasumi, who was dressed in a dark, strapless gown. Both sat at a dining room or nightclub table and had apparently been celebrating. The label on a champagne bottle read MOET. Only the best for Mr. and Mrs. Oscar Koehl.

The photograph, Alexis guessed, had to be over ten years old. Koehl was slimmer and had more hair than he did now. He and Kasumi were smiling, unaware of the tragedy just months away. A bit of irony there, thought Alexis. A German and a Japanese, past enemies of the United States, producing a son who graduates West Point with honors and dies in Vietnam.

What effect would this photograph have on Rupert de Jongh? Based on what Alexis knew about him, it should turn the man upside down and inside out and, Lord, what she wouldn't give to be there when that happened. The *gaijin* caught off guard. Definitely worth seeing. Not only is his beloved Kasumi alive, but she's married to none other than Arthur Kuby, his old comrade in arms. De Jongh's loyalties were few, but strong. He had adored Kasumi and now that she was dying it was time to remind him of the sacred vow he had made, the one Kasumi had written in her diary and underlined. The diary Alexis had read so often that she had memorized sections of it by heart: *I am happy, happy, happy. Today Rupert-san said that should I die away from Japan he will carry a lock of my hair back to the deep north, to Sendai, where I was born. He has promised that a part of me will be buried in my beloved Japan. He says that this is a sacred vow, a samurai's oath, which must be fulfilled.*

He'll come, Alexis thought. He'll come and I'll kill him and I'll live again.

In Koehl's living room, she reached out for the photograph. Now or never.

"May I help you?" A woman's voice. Coming from behind Alexis.

Alexis froze with her hand on the frame. After a few seconds she turned and smiled as though she meant it. Smiled at a young Chicano maid standing at the edge of the sunken living room. Probably sent by the aerobics-loving houseboy to see to the guest. A small, dark girl still in her teens, wearing a white cap and apron, items Alexis thought had gone out with slavery. Attractive, but someone should tell her that in America women shaved their legs. Alexis recognized the maid from last week, but had trouble remembering her name. For some reason she kept wanting to call the girl Pedro. Definitely not her name.

Alexis kept a hand over her heart, one way of stopping it from jumping out of her chest. Larceny was hard on the old pump. After this job she was definitely withdrawing from theft as a way of life. Let Simon carry the torch alone. What in hell was the maid's name? The maid recognized Alexis because she was studying her.

Alexis was about to ask her for a glass of water, anything to get her out of the room, when she heard a noise coming from the top of the marble staircase. They were bringing Kasumi down on the stretcher. Nurse Stones had taken charge, telling the paramedics to be careful, telling Oscar Koehl to stay out of the way. Koehl kept repeating, "Don't drop her." In seconds they would be at the bottom of the staircase and in the entrance hall. Where they would have a clear view of Alexis's every move.

Pilar. That was the maid's name.

Alexis said, "Pilar, may I trouble you for a glass of water?" And don't hurry back.

"I get it for you," the maid said. And walked toward the kitchen.

Too late.

They were at the bottom of the stairs, Kasumi Koehl wrapped in a pink blanket and strapped to a stretcher gripped by the two paramedics, and Nurse Stones on the bottom steps, arms in the air and giving orders, saying stop, go, stop. And Oscar Koehl on the staircase behind the stretcher, anxiously staring down at his unconscious wife. He was still a tall, imposing figure, but now he was bald and overweight, with horn-rimmed glasses and a hearing aid.

Five people on the staircase. And two, Oscar Koehl and Nurse Stones, now staring at Alexis. They know, she thought. They know and they're going to stop me.

Then Pilar walked into the entrance hall, one hand carrying a glass of water on a small silver tray. Nurse Stones looked at the glass of water, then at Alexis, and finally at Pilar, whom she told to carry the water back to the kitchen. This instant. Pilar had better things to do than wait on uninvited guests. Mrs. Bendor, Nurse Stones said, would be leaving immediately.

Pilar hesitated. Her eyes darted from Alexis to Nurse Stones to Oscar Koehl. Alexis thought, the girl's probably been taught a certain amount of manners, but Stones, the poison dwarf, could care less. Which was true. The nurse raised her nasal whine to a higher pitch and said that if Pilar didn't understand English, perhaps it might be a good idea if she returned to Juarez on the next Greyhound. It could be arranged, you know. Koehl, taking care not to look at Alexis, said nothing.

While Nurse Stones, back to Alexis, was the center of all eyes, Alexis did what she'd come to the Koehl home to do. She snatched the photograph from the table and shoved it into her shoulder bag. Jammed it down hard on top of a pair of Yves St. Laurent sunglasses and heard them crack. She felt terrified.

Not a minute too soon. The poison dwarf turned to face her. "Your car's blocking the ambulance, Mrs. Bendor. Would you please move it?"

"Glad to. Oscar."

Koehl heard her, but he kept his eyes on his wife. She

watched him lean down, stroke Kasumi's hair, and whisper to her, and for the first time it occurred to Alexis that Koehl loved his wife, perhaps as much as de Jongh did.

Heart pounding, Alexis left the house without speaking to Koehl. She would move her car, drive away from the poison dwarf, and stop off at the nearest bar for a stiff drink. Some tiger piss to calm her nerves.

Then she would call Simon and tell him what she'd done and why. Tell him how well she'd done it, too. Hell, when you're over the hill, you pick up speed.

Fifteen

In a windowless basement room of his headquarters, Rupert de Jongh watched one of his *yakuza*, a gangling middle-aged man named Takara, place his left hand on a clean square of cloth on a low table between them. Both men knelt on a floor that was covered in rectangular straw mats. De Jongh wore a dark blue kimono, headband, and split-toed socks fastened on the inner sides of his feet by small metal clasps. In his right hand he carried a folding fan made from bamboo slats and strong Japanese paper. The fan was old. Its slats were loose and the paintings on either side—a Kyoto temple garden and a mountain lake in winter—were cracked and faded. To throw the fan away, however, was unthinkable. It had once belonged to Kasumi.

Takara wore a flowered kimono. His large head was close cropped and an ugly scar ran down the left side of his face, a reminder of a past sword fight in the service of his *oyabun*, de Jongh. A dozen *yakuza* lieutenants and soldiers stood behind him, ready to witness his punishment.

Taller than anyone else in the room, Takara had been made touchy and vitriolic by an anal fistula. He was also highly sexed and had fathered thirteen children by two wives and several mistresses. The secret of his potency, he bragged, was eating toasted seaweed and pickled cabbage twice daily. De Jongh wondered if this diet wasn't the factor in the tall man's foul disposition, though the *gaijin* had to admit that Takara's odiousness had its uses. It insured obedience from employees in the bathhouses and gay bars he managed for de Jongh. And it made him effective in collecting protection money. Takara was a thorn to be used in drawing out other thorns.

He'd recently taken another mistress, a chubby seventeen-year-old with dyed red hair, front teeth capped in jade and gold, and a sex drive to match his. Her name was Tomiko and she worked at one of de Jongh's clubs, where nude women strolled a huge circular bar and offered dildoes to customers to do with them whatever they wanted. Sometimes drunken or daring customers were enticed onto the bar for sex.

The club was within blocks of de Jongh's headquarters, a dark and bulky building in Asakusa, the square mile that was Tokyo's oldest and most traditional entertainment district. In the past the building had been a Portuguese bank, a training school for sumo wrestlers, and an office building for American occupation forces. Asakusa's crowded alleys, streets stalls, covered passageways, and open-air markets still carried the sounds and smells of ancient Japan. And it remained a shopper's delight, offering the cheapest priced goods in Tokyo, causing thousands of bargain hunters to flood the area daily.

Asakusa, however, stood for one thing: pleasure. It was to be found in the district's nude shows, beer halls, nightclubs, and famed Kokusai Theater, where lavish stage shows featured three hundred beautiful young girls. Today Asakusa was what it had been for fifteen hundred years, the living embodiment of *ukiyo*, the floating world. A life of sensual gratification accepted without a thought to the future. A world where one lived for the moment, enjoying the moon and autumn leaves, women and music, and drifting on the current of life like a gourd floating downstream.

Twice a week, Takara interrupted his payoff collections to visit the club where Tomiko happily performed on the bar. He then took her into the manager's office for an enthusiastic sex session on a green leather couch. Two bodyguards were stationed in front of the door to prevent interruptions.

Yesterday, however, three masked men with knives had been waiting in the office for Takara and his teenage paramour. Somehow the intruders had entered the rear of the club unseen, then made their way to the office undetected by employees, customers, and hostesses. Takara was threatened with castration if he did not turn over the money he was carrying. Money that belonged to the *gaijin*.

The belligerent bagman fought back, aided by bodyguards armed with guns from America. Two of the thieves escaped. But a third suffered a thigh wound and was captured.

An enraged de Jongh soon learned that his hated rival Uraga was behind the bungled holdup. It was Uraga's way of saying that Kisen's murder had gone unavenged, and therefore the *gaijin*'s house was weak.

De Jongh lost no time in reacting. Three hours after the incident an old man on a bicycle handed a shopping bag to a guard in front of Uraga's Tokyo headquarters in the Shinjuku district. A gift for the *oyabun*, the old man said before peddling away.

The bag was filled with dark, moist earth. And hidden inside the dirt was a pair of freshly amputated human hands. One belonged to the club manager, who had betrayed the *gaijin* by hiding Uraga's men in his office. The other belonged to the captured *yakuza*. A severed hand was the age-old punishment for thieves.

Also in the bag was a glass vial containing several human teeth. The teeth were covered in jade and edged in gold. The *gaijin*'s instincts had told him, correctly, that Tomiko had been working for Uraga and had helped set the trap for Takara. As for the bag of dark earth, it said that the club manager, Uraga's man, and Tomiko had been buried alive. The debt owed Uraga had been promptly paid.

And for thinking of his own pleasure, for nearly causing the *gaijin* to lose face, Takara would also have to be punished.

In the basement room of the *gaijin*'s headquarters, the tall man picked up a long knife lying on the low table in front of him and placed the cutting edge on the first knuckle of the little finger of his left hand. The dull edge of the blade rested beneath the hand's other three fingers. The thumb was pulled back, out of danger.

The absolute obedience demanded by an *oyabun* created a bond so deep that it often allowed him to communicate his wishes to his *yakuza* without words. A *kobun* was trained to feel his leader's commands simply by looking at him and sensing what had to be done. An *oyabun* could remain silent, yet still give orders. One could not be a *yakuza* and wait for the *oyabun* to dictate his every move. A true *yakuza* looked at his leader's eyes and knew when to take action.

Takara stared at an expressionless de Jongh.

And when he knew, he acted.

He took a deep breath, made a fist with his right hand, and lifted it high overhead. Then he brought it down hard on top of the three fingers of his left hand, severing the tip of the little finger. He shivered, but did not cry out.

Keeping his bloodied left hand in place, he used his right to reach into a sleeve of his kimono, take out a red silk handkerchief and lay it on the table. Then he picked up the severed finger tip, wrapped it in the handkerchief, bowed his head, and held the handkerchief out to de Jongh.

The *gaijin* said nothing. Nor did he move for a long time. And when the wait had become almost unbearable for those watching, de Jongh took the handkerchief and slipped it into his kimono at the breast.

Takara, perspiring heavily, exhaled.

His apology, his self-mutilation, had been accepted. Had it been rejected he would have been killed instantly.

Ii kao. A good face. Something an *oyabun* had to maintain at all costs. Power, prestige, and influence all depended on *ii kao*. Insults, an attack on himself or his men, even an error in performing *yakuza* ritual, could leave an *oyabun*'s face "crushed" or "smeared with mud." De Jongh dare not appear indecisive or irresolute in anything. Among *yakuza*, tripping with the feet or the tongue could both prove costly. Deliberate, yes, but decide at once.

In the almost bare basement room de Jongh rose from the floor and walked to where a small Shinto shrine rested on a wall shelf. The shelf also contained gifts of food and clothing—boiled noodles, rice cakes and sake, warm rice wine in an earthernware jug. There were clogs, an umbrella made from coarse oil paper and bamboo, and a neatly folded hemp kimono for summer wear. Attached to one of the kimono's lapels was the black-and-silver pin of the *Shinanui-kai*, de Jongh's *yakuza* group.

The gifts were offerings for the dead. For Kisen.

Keeping his back to his men, de Jongh knelt in front of the shrine and considered whether to tell them that he knew the identity of Kisen's murderer. Final confirmation was lacking, but it could and would be obtained shortly. Meanwhile, the *gaijin's* intuition and instincts told him he was on target. Spot on. Kisen had been killed by Alexis Waycross's son.

Reports on the pursuit of Kisen's murderer were being submitted to de Jongh daily. They came in from his people all over the world: rumors, half-truths, unconscious ignorance, and false hopes. He read them all, dismissing most as imbecilic and a form of sewage. Reports from Hawaii and the American mainland, however, had drawn his attention, and when combined with information from Raymond Manoa, Nora Bart, and other Westerners, they had assumed new value.

Simon Bendor's name had appeared several times, always in connection with others under surveillance. It was de Jongh alone who had connected him to Kisen. Only the *gaijin* had examined and carefully compared all reports, doing it alone so as to prevent an ambitious lieutenant from using the information to advance his own career at de Jongh's expense. Thus the *gaijin* had determined that it was Simon Bendor who had executed Kisen.

With the picture of an expiring Victor Pascal quite fresh in her mind, Nora Bart had been only too glad to join forces with the *gaijin's* people in Los Angeles. She'd been among the first to learn that Molly January had a sister, one familiar to *yakuza* who sent gambling junkets to America and the Caribbean. The sister's name was Erica Styler and she was a professional gambler.

Nora Bart had confirmed the relationship between the two women by contacting the Los Angeles chapter of three theatrical unions. Molly January was indeed a member of all three and on forms listing next of kin she had entered the name Erica Styler. Her sister. Bills incurred in Los Angeles by the January woman had been paid for by Miss Styler, which showed a certain concern. Nora Bart added something she'd been too frightened to think of when she was in Tokyo watching Victor Pascal die. At Los Angeles Airport, just prior to the Tokyo flight, Molly January had taken out an insurance policy. Beneficiary: her sister, Miss Styler.

The *gaijin's* Los Angeles people added more. Miss Styler had contacted the Japanese consulate there regarding her sister's disappearance in Tokyo. From the loyal Miss Styler the trail had quickly led to Simon Bendor. They had been seen together in Honolulu, Atlantic City, Las Vegas, and New

York. The same Simon Bendor uncovered by Raymond Manoa
in probing the background of Alexis Waycross.

Mr. Bendor, Raymond Manoa had said, was an accomplished athlete, with boxing and karate skills. And he had
worked for the CIA in Southeast Asia, in a capacity so secret
that even Manoa's FBI contact could not learn specific details. Covert intelligence operations, most likely. Making Alexis
Waycross's son a highly skilled practitioner of dirty tricks.

Definitely a combative character, our Mr. Bendor. A man
quite capable of being the blind wild-beast, as Tennyson
might say. The son of Alexis Waycross had grown up to be a
master of the science of destruction. One with more than a
passing resemblance to the Westerner who had trounced Victor Pascal with little difficulty, then sent Kisen to dwell
among the gods.

Truth needed no further proof than truth itself. Fact number
one: Simon Bendor was a trained assassin. Fact number two:
he was a close friend of Erica Styler and the most likely
candidate to play the role of knight errant if she needed one.

One must see what one sees. And what de Jongh saw was
the one man in Erica Styler's life who could have entered
Japan unnoticed and walked out with Erica Styler's sister.

Fate ruled the affairs of mankind with no recognizable
order. How else to explain the chance encounter with Alexis
in Hawaii, one so potentially damaging that it might have
toppled de Jongh from power? Yet it was this same encounter
that had made it necessary for him to dig into her life, thus
learning the name of the man who had dispatched Kisen. Once
again the *gaijin* possessed the luck of having talent and a
talent for having luck.

Of course, he had no qualms about killing mother and son.
She was a lioness whose cub had grown into a leopard.

But there were whispers of doubt that said de Jongh might
be wrong at a time when he could ill afford to be. The
whispers said that the reappearance of Alexis Waycross Bendor
could be pushing him into a conclusion of an irrational nature. The whispers said that the *gaijin* could well be on the
verge of making the one mistake that could not be rectified in
a hundred lifetimes.

Should the *gaijin*'s wisdom fail in this matter he could
expect future evil. From his own men. From Uraga. From
Kisen's spirit, now in the netherworld. All were watching de

Jongh to see if he did more than merely hide behind his tongue. He had stumbled against this particular rock and must pick himself up.

In front of the shrine he closed his eyes, inhaled sharply, then exhaled for long seconds, pushing down hard on the muscles just below his navel. He sat on his heels, neck and back straight, wrists on his thighs, palms up. Zen breathing. The single most important technique in the martial arts. The key to total concentration and control of all situations, martial or otherwise.

He felt the air travel up the back of his head, down his spine, and into the lower abdomen. From here he pushed it out through his nostrils in long, inaudible breaths, in extraordinarily long exhalations. The significance of this practice could not be exaggerated, for a man was weakest when breathing in and strongest when breathing out. Strong in body, mind, and spirit. Of the three, the spirit strength mattered most of all, for in the end it was the spirit that decided.

One attack could determine life or death. An attack delivered in the space of one breath and guided by the warrior's spirit.

De Jongh exhaled, seeing clearly in his mind what he must do. Three enemies to kill. The mother. Her son. And the American woman Kisen had lusted after. But nothing must go wrong. He must, at all times, avoid the unlikely and the unpleasant. For all of the power and money that was his, de Jongh sometimes found that serving the *yakuza* was like sleeping with a tiger. His own house, the Japanese underworld, and his rival, Uraga, would all be watching and waiting for the mistake that could not be rectified in a hundred lifetimes.

He had already made one mistake by not killing Alexis Bendor in Switzerland when he had the chance. That mistake had cost Kasumi's life, leaving de Jongh with a sense of loss and longing that acted as a permanent accuser within his own soul. He had not made that mistake with the *Ukai*. On board the submarine he had seen to Kasumi's comfort, left his *yakuza* to watch her, then gone forward, where he'd found Shiba and ordered him to torpedo the *Ukai*. Sink the freighter with everyone aboard. For the girls, it had been an act of mercy; they had nothing to look forward to but a very slow death. For the crew, it had been payment in kind.

Kasumi. She and de Jongh had grown to love one another
with an intensity found only in war, with death hovering over
them each day, knowing their love ended their loneliness and
made them part of human existence once more. De Jongh
could never love or trust anyone as he had Kasumi.

But for now he pushed her memory aside, remembering he
was an *oyabun*, the master who must make his house respected, remembering that his authority could no longer survive in the face of doubt, remembering that he had held
power too long to give up its pleasures now.

Meditating at the shrine had given him an answer. He
turned to his *yakuza* and said, "I have located the man who
murdered Kisen. I have also located the woman who was the
cause of our brother's death. Within three days both shall be
dead."

Sixteen

Erica Styler arrived from New York shortly after dark. She ordered the driver of her rented Chrysler to bypass the Boardwalk casinos and take her directly to the marina, a mile or so from the glitzy tourist area. Some other time she might have called on the casino owners and gamblers she knew here. Maybe talked shop, exchanged gossip, told a few lies. It was good business to get out and about. Let people see the lady gambler, the high roller and poker superstar who was comped in Atlantic City and Las Vegas like any male gambler. But tonight she was late for a high-stake game, late because her darling little sister, Molly, had embarrassed the hell out of her by bringing drugs into Simon's apartment. Talk about the shit hitting the fan.

Simon, let us say, had gotten just a wee bit testy. There'd been an argument: Erica and Simon versus Molly, with Molly defending her right to get high, then demanding to be moved somewhere else and the sooner the better. Simon said that could be arranged, which is what he did. Erica had gotten involved in moving Molly out, leaving her drained when it was over. Not the right frame of mind to be in when you're taking on the people eaters, the pros and hard-nosed amateurs who played poker with a total disregard for money.

The game was being held in the Caribbean, Atlantic City's newest hotel-casino and the biggest in the marina area. Erica thought the hotel, with its tall, gray, glassy towers and enclosed skywalks, looked more "Star Wars" than steel band. Inside, however, the Caribbean more than lived up to its name. Her driver let Erica out at the entrance, in front of a black doorman. She hurried past him and into a lobby alive with cages of multicolored birds, actual palm and fruit trees, Jamaican reggae bands, and limbo dancers writhing under a low horizontal bar that was on fire. She wondered if authenticity also included eating the hotel's food and getting the trots.

A uniformed security guard stopped her at a private elevator. She watched him unbutton his holster and keep one hand on the gun butt while examining her I.D. A very heads-up dude. He also made two telephone calls to check her out with casino personnel before allowing Erica upstairs.

As usual, she was the only woman in the game. And looking drop-dead gorgeous, if she did say so herself. She wore a wide-shouldered cream silk dress, thin-heeled electric-blue shoes, round metal earrings to match, and topping it off, a dynamite Waikiki tan, courtesy of Simon. The reaction from the men was: who cares? She was among poker players; sex wasn't the reason they'd gathered around a leather-edged, felt-covered table. The highest compliment she'd get tonight is she's one of the boys. Given a choice, Erica preferred their money over their goodwill.

She greeted the four players she knew; two professional gamblers, plus a Chinese trader from Hong Kong, and a Japanese who was big in Hawaiian real estate. The Japanese, Mickey Kosugi, introduced her to the two players she hadn't come up against until tonight. One was a dark-haired Colombian named Betancourt, a fortyish, squared-shaped man wearing a ruby stud in one ear, a beige leisure suit, gold chains and white perforated shoes. He'd already let it be known that he was in import-exports. Erica didn't buy it. She read him as a drug dealer. Big-time, if he was in a game like this. Someone with money to burn. An action player, who could afford to take chances. Which made him dangerous, Erica knew, because that style of play would force everyone else to bet heavily whether they could afford to or not.

The Colombian's line of work wasn't Erica's concern. She'd played cards with drug dealers before. Who hadn't, in the big money games? She'd also played against wise guys, crooked union officials, crooked cops, crooked judges, investment brokers who robbed their clients blind for poker money, embezzlers who juggled the books to get a stake, con men who got their stake by selling land they didn't own, and others of questionable morality. Gambling attracted people who liked action. Aggressive people. People who didn't always show sensitive discernment. To Erica they were card players, nothing more.

The other new player, new to her, was Ox Clifford, a 300-pound, middle-aged, pointy-headed Oklahoman, who chewed tobacco and who Erica had been told owned more nuclear power plants than anybody else in America. The Colombian had actually looked at her before turning his attention back to his hand. At least his hot Latin blood had bubbled briefly. Ox Clifford, however, never acknowledged her presence. He never looked up from his cards. Didn't bother Erica. If Man Mountain had come to play, so had she.

She made her initial chip buy-in of a big dime. Ten thousand dollars. It was a $1,000–$2,000 game, making the first buy-in ten times the minimum. The game, her second since Molly had been brought back from Japan a week ago, was by invitation only, strictly private, a courtesy to the high rollers who gambled regularly in the Caribbean's casino. And to management's delight, often lost big. Erica had once watched the Hong Kong trader, a dapper and ageless little man named Kwok, drop $2 million at craps in one evening and never bat an eye.

This year she'd been staying at the hotel with Simon when the chunky, laid-back Mickey Kosugi had dropped $500,000 playing golf on the Caribbean's course. When you talked about Kwok and Kosugi, you were talking about players. And when players wanted anything in Atlantic City or Las Vegas, they got it. Both had asked that Erica be invited to the game; she'd played against them before and done well. The total she'd taken from the two probably came to over $200,000.

In a game this big the players didn't deal the cards. The hotel furnished a house dealer who shuffled, cut, and dealt, preventing any player from cutting the cards to benefit himself. Before each round a silver dollar was placed in front of a player to the dealer's left. This was the "button" and identified the imaginary dealer; the first card was always dealt to his left. With each round the button was moved clockwise, from player to player, giving everyone a shot at "dealing the cards." The game had no "rake," no house cut from every pot. But each player paid $50 an hour for his seat, the money covering expenses for the dealer, plus a cook, bartender, and waitress who served food and drinks from the penthouse kitchen and bar.

Erica had been a professional gambler since she was seventeen. She'd played poker all over America, in Europe, England, South America, and places in between. Since starting out with her father, also a gambler, she'd sat in games held in the best of places and the worst of places. But she'd never seen anything like this penthouse. It was a five-bedroom duplex facing the ocean, with handcrafted marble floors, Baccarat chandeliers, a small video arcade, twenty-four-hour butler service, three terraces, telex, redwood sauna, six bathrooms, and a mammoth living room with a waterfall and rock garden. Talk about mind-blowing. Colley Styler, her dad, had never played anywhere like this. It was the kind of joint he'd have described as an enticing pleasure, a joyous excess.

But by 12:30 A.M., Erica found nothing joyous about being here. She'd lost over $30,000, most of it to Ox Clifford, O.C. for short, who twice drew three cards to a pair and made four of a kind each time. He'd used the SWAG system. Scientific Wild Ass Guess. Seven players and only one, Kwok, was in her class. So why was Erica losing? Because she'd forgotten the first rule of poker: be alert. Watch to see if you're being cheated or intimidated. Watch to see if you're giving your opponents clues they need to beat you. Erica could kill Molly. Baby sister had fucked up big sister's concentration. Big sister wasn't evaluating the players or their moves. Big sister wasn't coming up with the strategy needed to win. How did Colley put it? "Molly's as pretty as whipped cream on pie, but lordy, that girl can truly find a way to make you serious mad."

Molly's motto was: if you're going to do it, you might as well overdo it. Take the amount of drugs she'd scored and brought back to Simon's place. Angel dust, Thai sticks, Benzedrine, Dexedrine, cocaine. Plus she'd laid out money, Erica's money, for some forged doctor's prescriptions allowing her to get her hot little hands on straight codeine from drug stores. No, Erica hadn't given her the money. Baby sister had ripped off big sister. Stolen $3,500 from Erica's bag. Then waited until Simon had gone to his health club and Erica had left, to have tonight's game money, fifty thou, wired from Las Vegas, where she lived. With no one between her and the door, Molly had toodled on out to find a candy man, some total sleaze she'd known before moving to L.A. in April.

In the past when Molly had needed certain drugs, Erica had paid for them. But those drugs had been Equanil, Compazine, Thorazine, all tranquilizers prescribed by doctors to ease Molly's excitable behavior. What little sister had brought back to Simon's apartment qualified only as substance abuse. Erica couldn't blame him for going berserk. He'd returned home to find Molly in the living room with some Puerto Rican fag and a skinny black guy with a pink headband and nose ring, the three of them stoned out of their minds and dancing to the Psychedelic Furs on MTV, volume up to the max.

Friends, Molly'd said to Simon. Outasight dancers from a jazz class she used to attend on Seventh Avenue. Simon turned off the TV and told the two friends to dance the fuck out of his apartment. Simon didn't raise his voice, Erica knew, but she could imagine his tone. Molly told her the two guys left shivering, pretending they felt a sudden chill.

Simon reminded Molly about the no-drugs rule in his home, that scoring drugs meant dealing with the underworld and maybe getting cheated or killed. It could also attract the attention of the cops. Molly didn't know he was a thief; she knew him as the owner of a couple of health clubs, who invested his money wisely. Erica took his side. Molly's next move was totally desperate; she heaved an ashtray at Erica, missing her but hitting a new compact disk player and gouging it good. Welcome to Molly's rules of argument.

Simon said, "That tears it." He took Erica into the bedroom, closed the door, and told her Molly's out as of this minute.

Simon had problems of his own. Joe D'Agosta had lined up a job for him tonight. Erica had the game in Atlantic City, which could last five hours or five days. Neither of them would be around to baby-sit Molly. Someone would have to do it. Someone like Dag. Let's see if he'll put her up for a few days. After that, maybe it'll be safe for her to go bopping around on her own.

Simon walked over to a night table, picked up a silver-framed photograph, and stared at it. Erica had seen it earlier. It was a picture of the Japanese woman called Kasumi and her husband, an ex-Nazi now getting rich in L.A. Simon's mother Alexis had air-expressed the picture from California, along with an unusual request. She wanted Simon to break into Frankie Odori's Manhattan town house and leave the photograph where Frankie would find it. Leave it with a note saying Kasumi was alive, but dying. And giving the address where she could be found.

Erica listened to Simon relate the scenario concocted around the photograph by his mother. Hollywood Frankie would see the photograph, get excited, and send it to his godfather in Tokyo, a big man in the Japanese underworld. The godfather had also been a top World War II spy for Japan, killing a few of Alexis's friends and damn near killing her, something she'd never been able to forget. Weirdest part of the tale: the godfather was an Englishman, and he'd loved Kasumi deeply, promising her during the war that if she died outside Japan he'd carry a lock of her hair back there and bury it.

It was Alexis's belief that if this Englishman knew Kasumi was alive he'd come running to L.A. And when he did, Alexis would be waiting to kill him.

Erica loved it. No, she and Alexis didn't get along, because Simon's mother would always resent any woman in his life. That was Alexis's privilege. But it didn't stop Erica from admiring the old gal's moxie. You had to admire anyone who wanted to get even badly enough to lure a man to his beloved's deathbed, then blow him away when he showed up.

She watched Simon leave the bed and return the photograph to the night table. She asked him how he planned to handle the photograph.

He'd discussed it with Dag, protector of endangered women. Joe's opinion: she's your mother and you owe her, so do it. Joe then mentioned Teriko, the Japanese girl Frankie had chopped up with electric saws. Alexis could end up that way if she was telling the truth about the *gaijin*.

Simon said to Erica, "Joe played me like a violin. He knows how I feel about my mother, so he says hit two places in one night. The job he's got for me tonight is here in Manhattan, just blocks from Frankie's town house. Won't even need a driver. I can walk from one to the other."

Erica was frightened and excited at the same time. Simon could do that to a woman. She said, "That's asking a lot of you. *Two*. Twice the problems, twice the risks. Christ." Look at him, she thought. Everything under control and master of the situation. Cool Hand Bendor.

"Just remembered something, Simon," Erica warned, "Frankie tapes his telephone calls. Some of them, anyway. I've seen him do it. He always spoke in Japanese, not that it told me anything, since I don't speak Japanese. But suppose you could get your hands on some of those tapes?"

"I'll bite. Why would I want to do that?"

"Because it might be one way of learning whether or not he's got this English godfather, this *gaijin* character Joe mentioned. Alexis speaks Japanese. So does Paul. Let them listen to the tapes and translate. Might be a way of getting Alexis off your back once and for all."

"I like it. Wouldn't mind learning myself whether the guy's for real or if my mother's going tapioca in her old age. Yeah, I like it. It's going to be a long night."

"You love it."

He smiled. "Let's talk about Molly, now."

Over the phone, Joe D'Agosta agreed to take Molly for a few days. She could stay at his coin shop, in the back room. He'd sleep on a cot in the front room. Reason he wasn't taking Molly home to his wife, he told Erica, is because he didn't have a death wish. His wife, Rita, had her little ways, some of which would inspire fear in Charles Manson. He'd pick up Molly outside the health club, even though he himself wasn't too keen on exercise. He told Erica he was Italian and if God had wanted him to bend over there'd be ravioli on the ground.

Molly told Erica to forget it, she wasn't going to Queens. Nothing to do there but file your nails and lose contact with the universe. No way, no how, and that was final. Simon asked if she wanted a second opinion.

They met Joe D'Agosta in front of the West End Avenue building housing Simon's health club. By now Molly had cooled out and was actually talking to Erica without raising her voice. And there were no more dirty looks for Simon, who'd flushed Molly's entire stash down the toilet. Now Erica and Molly were weeping in each other's arms and talking about being family and sticking together. Erica said

Molly ought to go back to hairdressing, something she did well. Molly replied hairdressing sucked. She wanted to be somebody, not stand on her feet with a blow dryer in one hand and a dye pot in the other, which was a great way to end up with varicose veins and age spots and nothing else.

Erica looked into her sister's eyes and saw what she really wanted: confirmation that she should go on living. Molly was scared. Name and fame, all she'd pinned her hopes on, hadn't come her way and the ground under her feet was getting shaky. When that happened, it was easy for ambition to turn nasty. Everything on God's green earth seemed to be standing between Molly and celebrity. Erica wondered if her little sister would ever admit that she didn't have the talent to take her to the top of the mountain.

Dag, bless his heart, seemed to know what was going on. Before driving off he took Erica aside like some Dutch uncle and promised to keep an eye on Molly, who he said was really a good kid. Unfortunately, she'd sold herself a line of bullshit and now believed it. Molly had to forget about *People* magazine, forget about appearing on the "Merv Griffin Show," forget about having her face on some cruddy T-shirt, forget about appearing in *Time* and *Newsweek*. Molly had to listen to her true self, her real self, and be blessed. Give her time.

But in the Caribbean's penthouse Erica couldn't stop worrying about Molly. Worry, however, was interfering with her ability to play poker, a luxury she couldn't afford. You didn't survive in a game of this size without confidence, not when you were looking at pots worth over $150,000. Forget any ideas concerning benevolence, which you might have picked up from family, church, or state. A successful poker player went for the jugular every time. Her father would say, "If a rattlesnake ever bit a poker player, the snake would die."

Confidence. Betting courage. Heart. Call it what you will, but for a gambler it came down to the same thing: nerve. Lose it and you were through. When her father lost his, it had cost him his life. In thirty years of gambling he'd won and lost $30 million, dying broke, as he'd expected to. Gambling, he told Erica, was more exciting than being caught in a storm at sea. It was when he'd lost his nerve that the storm came to frighten him. A large bet of any kind eventually held terror for Collison Styler and he even played good hands poorly. He was murdered, Erica knew, because he'd lost his nerve.

Toward the end he'd fallen in with a card mob, a group of poker cheats working as a team. Erica tried to get him to leave them, but failed. He now felt he couldn't win any other way and he wasn't about to stop playing. During one California racing season the card mob broke into a warehouse and substituted three cartons of marked cards for legitimate ones. They had removed the glassine wrappings and box stickers, marked every card with special ink, then replaced the wrappings, adhesive, and box stickers. When the marked cards hit the stores, hotels, and private games, Erica's father and his fellow cheats cleaned up. But word of the marked cards got out and a New Orleans Mafia don, who'd been taken for plenty, had each member of the card mob tracked down and executed.

Erica's father had been last on the hit list. Six years ago he'd turned the ignition key in a Plymouth parked in the driveway of a stucco house in Trenton, exploding several sticks of dynamite wired to the motor. Erica's mother, a passenger in the car, had died with her husband. Leaving the high-strung Molly Noel Styler in her sister's care.

Nerve.

Erica'd had it from the beginning. Her father, a warm, soft-spoken man with a degree in anthropology and a talent for playing stride piano, had taught her everything about the game from how to play five-card draw to ways of spotting a mechanic, a card cheat. But he didn't have to teach her how to have nerve. You had it or you didn't. She was an aggressive player, one who couldn't be intimidated or leaned on, who bet the numbers, the big money; who took her losses calmly, but when the game got down and dirty, could be as hard-nosed as a Texas highway patrolman.

Nerve.

Erica had shown it at twenty-two, when she'd decided to get out on her own as a professional gambler, breaking up her partnership with her father, getting away from his slower, more conservative style of play and moving to Las Vegas, where the action was fast and lasted twenty-four hours a day. She'd shown nerve when she'd divorced Claudio, the Spanish flamenco dancer from the Desert Inn, who'd left their second-anniversary party in the company of an Australian show girl to get more ice and hadn't returned until three weeks later. And she'd shown it when she'd twice used the magnum: to gut-shoot one of three black kids who'd come at her with knives in a Chicago parking lot and to blow away the jaw of a Mexican waiting in a Phoenix motel room to rape her.

If it hadn't been for nerve, Simon's nerve, he and Erica would never have met. Simon Bendor, the green-eyed wild man. Gutsy, ballsy, and the last of the free spirits. If that didn't make him erotic in her eyes, nothing would. Thank God he didn't play cards, because no gambler alive could match his icy-nerved cool. Playing poker with him would be like holding a wolf by the ears. Simon was at his best when he had to put it all on the line, and that included his life. Erica took chances, too. But not like Simon did. She'd fallen in love with him at first sight. Fallen in love with the man the police called the "Magician." Fallen in love with his nerve.

Last October in New York she'd taken a break from a poker game and gone to the bathroom to freshen up, review her strategy and think on what she'd learned about the other five players. The game was in a luxury condo just off Fifth Avenue, across from the Plaza Hotel and Central Park. Erica loved this part of Manhattan, especially in autumn, when park leaves were turning gold and Fifth Avenue stores had one clearance sale after another.

In the second-floor bathroom Erica looked at her watch: 2:15 A.M. She was up twenty thou and change, not bad for six hours' work. But she was dog tired, wiped out by the game, the flight from Vegas, by too many cigarettes and not enough protein, and, for sure, not enough sleep. There were some ferocious players downstairs, particularly the condo owner, a fiftyish ex-show girl who was the wealthy widow of a taxicab magnate. The widow was as smart as a tree full of owls and on a rush, a winning streak that was leaving everyone for dead except Erica.

Erica was freshening her lipstick when she heard a noise outside the bathroom window. No sweat. The window was thick safety glass and locked from the inside. A brick might crack it but not penetrate it. And the bathroom was eight stories above the street, twelve stories from the roof. No fire escapes, no ledges to speak of. Impossible for anyone to climb up or down. Erica was as safe as you could be in this town. But when she heard someone rap on the glass, holy shit. She jumped, almost lost her balance, dropped her lipstick in the basin.

She looked at the window, saw the outline of a man's head and shoulders, saw him bang on the window with his fist, then try to push it up with the flat of his hand and get nowhere. Erica took her magnum from her purse, walked to the window, and opened it. She aimed the magnum at the masked figure hanging below her from a narrow ledge. She asked what the hell he was doing out there. He said hanging by his fingertips eight stories above Fifty-eighth Street and he'd sure appreciate it if she'd let him climb inside.

Cupping the butt of the magnum in both hands, Erica backed up, gun sight picking up the largest target, his chest, as the intruder came through the window. At this range she couldn't miss; a bullet from the magnum would leave a hole in him the size of an orange. He was masked and dressed in black from head to toe, a midnight-creeping Zorro. Erica ordered him to sit on the toilet and not move. He obeyed; she noticed his hands were bleeding. She watched him look around the bathroom, taking in everything from a heated towel rack to a sunken bathtub to a small bamboo makeup table with a lighted mirror. He took in Erica, too. Behind his ski mask she sensed Zorro was extremely alert, concentrating, focused, and wide awake. She backed up until she felt the bathroom door behind her.

Talk about calm. She watched him casually pull several sheets of toilet paper from a roll, blot his bloody hands, then drop the stained tissue into a black canvas bag hanging from his shoulder. A radio on his right hip squawked with police calls about an intruder in the area. Guess who. Erica watched him lower the volume, cross his ankles, and eye her through the ski mask slits. The bastard was the essence of tranquility. She, on the other hand, was scared shitless. Meanwhile, he was checking her out, eyes moving up and down, missing nothing. Oddly enough, he gave off no hostile vibes. Erica had the feeling he simply wanted to walk away, no muss, no fuss, no bother.

She thought of something to say. "You're a thief."

"And you?" Nice voice.

"I play cards for a living." Maybe he'd think she was tough. Tough guys played cards didn't they?

"Professional gambler," he said. "And doing all right."

Erica's jaw dropped.

He aimed a forefinger at her. "The gun. High rollers often

pack heat. Self-defense. And your watch doesn't come cheap.
It's an Ademars Piquet, Royal Oak model. Octagon shape,
very thin. Nice design. Comes with diamonds, so it must
have set you back, say, fifteen thousand. The dress looks like
Ted Lapidus and the shoes . . . don't know about the shoes.
Italian?''

"Galvani.''

He nodded, impressed. "How about that. Handmade right
here in Manhattan. Had to run you eight, nine hundred dollars
a pair.''

She thought, On target. Son of a bitch, you didn't miss
once. She cleared her throat and asked him who was he
climbing up the face of this building at two in the morning?

He reached for more toilet paper and told Erica that was a
good question. What happened was, he'd run into a little
problem next door at the Augustus Club, one of the oldest
private clubs in New York City. Some heavy-duty people in
politics and business made the club their home away from
home. Zorro, as Erica called the man in black, liked the
place; it dated back to Lincoln's time, had big leather chairs,
wonderful old bird-cage elevators, a portrait gallery of past
club presidents. No sense boring Erica with specifics, but
he'd completed his business at the club and was about to
leave when—ready for this?—someone broke in. A competitor, Zorro said.

Erica couldn't help herself. She laughed out loud. "You
mean a second thief tried to rob the club while you were
there?''

Zorro turned up bloody palms. "That's America at its
best.''

The competitor wasn't very good, he told Erica, seeing as
how he tripped off a silent alarm, alerting a security guard,
who then put three bullets in his chest. The guard worked for
a firm with a reputation for wasting prowlers, the firm's way
of saying go play somewhere else. For the most part, the
firm's policy worked. "Most people in the business,'' Zorro
said, "avoided buildings under contract to the firm.''

"Not you,'' Erica said.

Zorro shrugged. Anyway, the shots woke up sleeping club
members, who panicked. And because the club members
were movers and shakers, it didn't take the cops long to
respond in force, with shotguns, flak vests, smoke grenades,

long flashlights with beams powerful enough to melt your
eyeballs. First thing they did was hit the back of the club in
force. And if Erica looked out the bathroom window she'd
see at least four squad cars in the front, along with a SWAT
van. Meanwhile, security guards and cops were searching the
inside of the club inch by inch. It was time to improvise,
Zorro told Erica. So he'd gone to the roof of the Augustus
Club and from there began climbing up the front of Erica's
high-rise.

Erica said, "There's nothing to hold on to. Nothing. How
did you do it?"

"Clean living and the power of prayer," he said. All that
was missing was him flicking his eyebrows à la Groucho
Marx. He said he'd run into locked windows or occupied
apartments on his climb and had to keep going, since he
avoided confrontation. He wasn't even armed. Desperation
made him knock on her bathroom window. His hands were
too bloody, too slippery. If he continued climbing he'd have
lost his grip and fallen.

Erica thought, This guy is really off the wall. He could
have been killed by a security guard, by cops, by an eight-
story fall, and he doesn't seem worried about any of it. The
excitement she felt made her hands tremble.

That's when he asked her the number of people in the
apartment. Without thinking Erica said five card players, plus
two servants. And there was the daughter of the woman who
owned the apartment, plus the daughter's two small children.

How many rooms?

Ten, twelve. The apartment was a duplex. Why did he
want to know?

"There has to be a kitchen," he said.

"First floor," Erica said. "Where they're playing cards."
What was all this leading to, she wanted to know. The gun
was getting heavy, but she didn't tell him that.

He stood up, put the second batch of bloodied tissue in the
black canvas bag and said, "I don't think you want to shoot
me. Anyway, I'll make you a bet. Something right up your
alley. Twenty thousand dollars says I can walk out of this
apartment without being seen."

Erica rolled her eyes toward the ceiling. "Give me a
break." Eyes back to him. "Let me get this straight. You
want me to let you go. And you want me to pay you twenty

thousand dollars when you get away. Mister, you're a head case, you know that?''

"Didn't say you had to put up any money."

"Oh? And what do I put up? Don't answer."

"If you lose, you have dinner with me. I'll accept your word as a gambler."

"Mind telling me how I collect if you get caught?"

He patted the black canvas bag. "My money's here. I'll see that you get it."

"Your money. You mean the Augustus Club's money, don't you?"

"Do we have a bet? Yes or no?"

Talk about nerve. Her heart shook at the thought of what this man must really be like. He'd just offered her the kind of action any gambler would kill for. The money involved meant nothing; the action was everything. Damn right she was interested. The player in her would bet on anything—flies circling around a sugar cube, two raindrops racing down a windowpane. When would she ever get a chance to bet on something like this, something like Zorro? Seeing's believing, her dad had said, but feeling is God's own truth. Erica felt something for this man.

She dropped her arms, magnum in her left hand. She said, "It's a bet. But on one condition. The mask comes off."

He thought about it for a few seconds, then removed the mask.

He was gorgeous. Blond hair streaked by the sun. Green eyes. Tanned. Stone gorgeous. And he might as well have had the words *dangerous as hell* written across his forehead. They stared at each other, two contending powers, a man who took more chances than anyone she'd ever known, and a woman who risked all each time she sat down to play cards. Jesus, she thought. Something's happening between us, happening here and now and we both know it. He was a find, a fire, and would offer her more rewards and punishments than any man she'd been involved with. She was totally unaware of the game downstairs, which said it all.

She said, "Can you really do it, get out of here without being seen?"

"It's gonna cost me twenty K if I don't. And maybe a lot more."

She turned her back to him, put the magnum in her purse,

then took a washcloth from the towel rack. She wet it with
warm water and gently wiped the blood from his hands. She
watched him take a pair of surgeon's gloves from the black
canvas bag and pulled them gingerly on his hands. When he
finished she handed him the bloodied washcloth and he put
that in the bag. Erica didn't trust herself to speak. She looked
down at the tile floor.

He touched her hair. "I owe you one."

He put on the ski mask, stepped past her, then stopped at
the door and looked over his shoulder. Erica's back was to
him. She said, "Erica Styler. I'm staying across the street at
the Plaza."

He turned, cracked the door, looked left and right, then
entered the hallway. The door closed behind Erica, but she
never heard it. She walked to the mirror, brushed tears from
her eyes with her fingertips, and told herself the whole thing
was crazy, that he was going to get caught and she'd never
see him again. She looked at the open window, at the toilet
where he'd sat, and realized there was nothing in the bathroom to indicate he'd ever been here. And she didn't even
know his name. She stared at her reflection in the mirror and
said aloud, "What the hell's going on here?" and that's when
the bathroom light went out. In the pitch-blackness, Erica
laughed and wept because she knew. *Knew.* Zorro was going
to win their bet.

She made her way to the bathroom door, arms stretched out
before her, opened the door, and heard card players downstairs cursing and making bad jokes and heard the widow say
in her Kentucky drawl that it was probably some kind of short
or maybe the fuse. The widow said she'd have it fixed in two
shakes of a lamb's tail. Everybody just sit tight, stay cool,
and keep away from the discards in the center of the table
because she had eyes like a cat. She asked where the hell was
the Third World when she needed it, meaning the West
Indian who was one of two sleep-in help and rumored to be
her lover.

Upstairs in the darkness, Erica leaned against the bathroom
doorjamb and said, "He did it, he did it, he did it. The
goddam fuse box in the kitchen, is how. Zorro you are
something."

The next day he telephoned her just before 11:00 A.M. Erica
picked up on the first ring, hoping it was him, and if it wasn't

she was going to hang up, because she didn't want to tie up the line. But it was him and he said, I owe you one. Was she ready to go out to dinner, ready to go now?

Now? Dinner? She said, "You're kidding." Then she said, "I take that back. You're not kidding."

He told her to check out of her room immediately and meet him downstairs with her luggage.

She asked him where were they going and, by the way, what was his name?

"My name's Simon," he said, "and we're going to Hawaii."

In the Caribbean's penthouse, Erica watched the new player, Ox Clifford, use remarkably small pink hands to rake in a pile of chips worth over $112,000. The corpulent Oklahoman's victory ritual followed; he spat tobacco juice into a Styrofoam cup, mumbled "Lordy, I do love to play this game," then began stacking his chips with his left hand according to color—white on the left side, blue on the right. Erica didn't feel like sitting through this time-honored practice again, not when she was losing, so she excused herself, saying she had to powder her nose. She left the table and walked across the huge living room to a circular metal staircase leading to the duplex's second floor. When the going gets tough, the tough disappear.

During the last hour she'd won back her losses and gone up ten thousand. Then they'd played Ox's game, Hold 'Em, and he'd drawn a third queen to beat her three jacks, costing Erica $40,000. Ox was like the guy who'd been shot at and missed; he was the luckiest man alive.

In the second-floor bathroom, Erica looked through a window at the ocean and a star-filled sky, reminding herself that no one could win 100 percent of the time. She prayed she wasn't running bad, losing money *and* her composure at the same time. She'd seen card players have one disastrous game, hell, drop one big hand, and never play well again. Maybe taking a break right now was a good idea. Give her a chance to clear her head and fall back on the gambler's standby, superstition. Gamblers had more superstitions than a Stone Age tribe. They believed in lucky seats, lucky clothes, changing apartments when losing, avoiding unlucky foods, arriving at the game by a certain route, stacking their chips in a particular way. Erica's solution to her current losing night was to visit the second-floor bathroom of a duplex. That's where she'd been the night she'd left a poker game, met Simon, then returned to the game and won $97,000.

Like everything else in the penthouse, when you talked about the bathroom you were talking totally awesome. A large marble tub and two marble basins all had gold faucets. There were ten-foot potted palms, thick gold carpeting, two slot machines, a cordless telephone, a couch covered in blue silk, and for makeup tables, a pair of imitation eighteenth-century French commodes with rococo mounts of dragons, shells, sprays, and scrolls on top of kingwood veneer. A color television set was decorated across the top and sides with casino chips worth $100,000 each.

Until recently the highest value of any Atlantic City chip had been $1,000. But the town was doing such incredible business, almost $1.8 billion yearly from only ten casinos, that the New Jersey Casino Control Commission now authorized $25,000, $50,000, and $100,000 chips. The $100,000 chips attached to the bathroom television set, however, had been put in to stay. Erica doubted if they could be pried loose with a crowbar.

Her mind went to Simon, who was gambling with his life tonight, not once but twice. She loved him because of his daring, which didn't stop her from feeling uneasy about what he was doing. She knew she was in love with Simon when she had stopped comparing him to other men she knew, when she saw nothing in him to criticize, when she realized that she found almost as much pleasure in loving as in being loved. Before Simon, Erica had wanted the emotion and sex of love but never for long, since long relationships deteriorated into a mutual dependence interrupted by boredom and betrayal. This marked the first time she'd considered love's responsibility, something new for a woman who'd spent her life keeping all she had and trying for all she could. How long would it last? For as long as they both remained generous in their passions, and no longer.

She looked at her watch, saw it was almost 2:30 A.M. and was struck by a wild idea. She was going to telephone Molly at Joe D'Agosta's place in Queens. Do it right now. Why not? It was something she wished she'd done when dad was alive. Just get on the horn, wake him up, and say, "Hi, I love you." There'd been a period when she'd blamed herself for his death because she'd been the one to end their partnership. That's why she'd put up with Molly's willful, mule-headed behavior rather than walk away and have her end up as their father had. Talking to Molly might allow Erica to cool out, get on top of her game, and send her charging downstairs ready to hang Ox Clifford's fat ass on a fence. Molly was probably wide awake anyway. She was a freak for Mary Tyler Moore reruns and would stay up all hours to watch them.

Erica took an address book from her purse, found Joe D'Agosta's number and dialed. There was no answer.

She decided on professional help, so she dialed the New Jersey operator and asked him to get the number. Three minutes later the operator told Erica that the Joseph D'Agosta line in Astoria appeared dead. The operator said the problem might be mechanical, a damaged line or a local power failure. No, the line wasn't busy, nor was it off the hook. He was trying to find a supervisor, maybe get him to send a maintenance truck to check that area. But it wasn't easy finding anyone in authority this hour of the morning. Erica could either try the number later or contact him and he'd give her whatever information he had.

She asked him to check the Queens directory for any D'Agosta listing, home or business. He did and found only a business number, the one Joe'd given her. Erica thought, There's always the chance he's taken Molly home, but that would be dumb since, to hear him tell it, his wife barks at the moon. In any case, Erica didn't have Joe's home number.

She hung up and chewed her thumbnail. Erica didn't want to worry about Molly because worry led to fear. What the hell was she worrying about anyway? Joe D'Agosta was an ex-cop, one of the few people Simon trusted in this world, and that was saying a lot. Don't blame him for the phone company's inefficiency. Blame Ma Bell.

Erica walked over to a bathroom mirror, remembering that losing meant believing the worst about everything. A diminished income usually brought on pessimism. What Erica needed was a rush, a winning streak, three or four nice pots in a row. She had to go downstairs and play cards like she was capable of doing. Don't let this thing with Molly hang around like a bad smell. Put it aside and take care of business.

But before returning to the game, Erica telephoned Simon's answering service at his Manhattan apartment and left a message: "Check out Molly as soon as you come in. Make sure she's all right, then call me at this number in Atlantic City. I don't think there's a problem, just want to know if Molly is okay. You know how sisters are."

Erica also dialed Joe's coin shop again. She took her time, making certain she got all the numbers correct, area code included. An operator cut in, saying there appeared to be some difficulty with the number, that for some reason the line had gone dead.

Seventeen

MANHATTAN
JULY 1983

Near sundown, in a limousine parked near a Ukrainian church on quiet West End Avenue, Nora Bart leaned forward and pointed across the street at Molly January and Simon Bendor.

She identified them by name, then slumped down in the back seat, glad she was sitting alone and not up front with Frankie Odori's two boys. She watched the pair of *yakuza* converse briefly in Japanese, then the one she considered the more hostile, a young weight lifter with mirrored sunglasses and a discolored front tooth, spoke to her, saying she'd better know what she was talking about. The *gaijin* didn't want any mistakes.

Nora Bart wanted to say, Would you like me to get out of the car, walk over there, and ask them if they've been in Tokyo recently? But she remembered Yokohama and a bleeding Victor Pascal hanging naked in the *gaijin*'s walled garden, and decided it wasn't smart to provoke these people. Her therapist had said to avoid negative feedback, the kind you got from bad vibes, because it left you uncentered. Not in control of your space and energies.

So she pushed her Ray-Bans into her newly dyed platinum hair and again looked through the darkened window glass at the four people—two women, two men—standing on the sidewalk in front of a high-rise built of hard gray granite and embellished with iron balconies. The blonde in the blue jumpsuit was definitely Molly January, the girl Nora Bart and Victor had sent to Tokyo a few weeks ago. The blond-haired guy in the white jeans and green shirt, standing with his back to her, was Simon Bendor. Nora Bart had never met him, but she knew what he looked like. His picture was in a health club brochure sent to her from Honolulu by Sergeant Manoa. When Nora and Victor had carried guns, money, and drugs to Hawaii from California, Manoa was one of the people they turned the stuff over to.

She said Simon Bendor was the same size as the army captain she'd seen in Tokyo, the one who'd destroyed Victor and greased Kisen. The hair was different and there was no mustache, but both men were the same size. No way of telling if Simon Bendor was actually the same man, she was only sure about Molly January.

Nora Bart watched the weight lifter take a Polaroid camera off the dashboard, remove his sunglasses, and begin to snap photographs of the four people in front of the high-rise. Molly January was talking to her sister, Erica Styler, who Nora recognized from a photograph given her by the *yakuza* in L.A. Simon Bendor, a hunk with a great ass, was off to the side talking to a dumpy guy in a baseball cap, space shoes, Bermuda shorts, and a bowling shirt. Nora Bart didn't know who the guy was, but she knew a walking hemorrhoid when she saw one. I mean we're talking nerd here and no style at all.

Style was Nora Bart sitting in the air-conditioned limo wearing black lace stockings, red stiletto heels, black leather miniskirt, and a Levi's jeans jacket with sleeves pushed back to the elbows. Style was the black studded dog collar around her neck, three gold studs in each ear, a red snakeskin shoulder bag from Ann Taylor. Style was Nora Bart taking herself down to Melrose Avenue the day after she returned from Japan and getting herself a short haircut with "attitude."

Unfortunately, style cost money, something she had very little of at the moment. Without Victor to run the agency, Nora Bart, to put it mildly, was in deep shit. She had no business sense; she couldn't balance a checkbook, make out a payroll, handle quarterly tax payments, deal with salesmen. Victor had said she was a great piece of ass, but if you put her brain on the end of a fork it would look like a BB on a four-lane highway.

What Nora Bart did well was talk to the girls who answered ads Victor placed in the trades and West Coast newspapers. She had this little act where she'd pretend to have gone to Japan as a performer and she'd tell the girls how great it was over there, how she'd made good money dancing in clubs, appearing on TV, and doing some modeling on the side. By the time she finished the girls were drooling, ready to flap their arms and fly directly from the office to Tokyo. If a bitch hears it from another bitch, Victor told her, she'll buy the whole scam.

Technically, the agency was still in business. Some of the old trade ads were still bringing in telephone calls from girls who wanted to work in the Far East as "well-paid singers, dancers, models." Nora Bart, however, wasn't interviewing anymore. The *gaijin*'s orders. She'd finally gotten to meet the white-haired Englishman who led the Jacuzzi boys, and he'd told her not to send any more American girls to Japan. Nor would she be making any courier runs until the *gaijin* had dealt with the man who'd murdered Kisen and taken away Molly January. The man who'd somehow learned of Victor Pascal and Nora Bart's connection to the *yakuza*.

She was willing to do whatever she was told. Anything was better than winding up like Victor. She didn't need a college degree to know that in Yokohama she'd been on the roof, maybe an inch away from being snuffed. The *gaijin* had blamed her and Victor for Kisen's death, which is why he'd wasted Victor. But for some reason the white-haired Englishman, who impressed Nora Bart as cold-blooded and unfeeling, had given her a second chance, warning her to make the most of it. Better believe she would.

Back in L.A. she'd worked her buns off checking out Molly January, coming up with bits and pieces from theatrical guilds, shops, hotels, and Las Vegas, turning it all over to the Jacuzzi boys, who then passed it on to the *gaijin*. That's how she'd learned about Erica Styler and Simon Bendor. None of the *gaijin*'s L.A. or New York people told Nora any more than she absolutely had to know, but she was picking up vibes that said somebody thought Simon Bendor just might be the mysterious "army captain."

She'd been ordered to fly to New York and work with Frankie Odori in making a positive identification on Molly January and Simon Bendor. This was one thing the *gaijin*

didn't want handled in a slipshod or half-assed way, and in
any case, Nora Bart wasn't in a position to refuse. It was her
first trip east without Victor and she was a little antsy about
it. In the past, when they'd worked as mules between L.A.
and New York, he'd been the one to deal with Frankie Odori,
a guy who gave Nora Bart the creeps. She just didn't like
being around him now, after hearing what he'd done to that
Japanese girl Teriko Ohta. You got to watch Frankie, Victor
had said. Hollywood Frankie will smile and tell you everything's all right, then he'll tie your asshole in a knot.

Victor. Nora Bart would miss him. For sure. But he was
gone and she had to get used to him not being there for her
anymore. She knew how to do that. Move into a mellow
space where she owned her own feelings. And program herself to be free, the way she'd been taught in group therapy.
That's what she'd done at fifteen, when she'd run away from
her Vancouver home and a depressingly dull existence. And
at nineteen, when she'd dumped a boring hockey player and
their six-month-old son and left Toronto for what Victor
called the planet Hollywood. A change of scenery, some
good times, some good dope, and pretty soon it was as
though the past had never happened. She had the game plan
for turning Victor into history. All she had to do was put it
into practice.

Money was an immediate problem. She had $1,500 in the
bank and there was a little over $2,200 in the agency account.
None of this would last very long, not the way she spent
money. Lately she'd been pissing it away on clothes, payments on a Ferrari Spyder, drugs, a new VCR, dance classes,
a heart operation for her Yorkshire terrier. Plus she'd kept her
West Hollywood apartment, even though she spent most of
her time at Victor's Malibu beach house. Money poured in
from the Jacuzzi boys, but Nora Bart just couldn't hold on to
it.

Victor had two bank accounts and two insurance policies,
adding up to a nice piece of change. One night when they
were both wired from free-basing cocaine, he'd told her how
much he really cared for her, that the other women didn't
mean shit and she had to believe he was telling it from the
heart. To prove he wasn't just talking trash, he had signed
over one of the insurance policies to her, one worth $90,000.
At the moment Nora Bart could definitely use the money, but

to get it she'd have to tell the insurance company why Victor wasn't around anymore. Which was one way to get the Jacuzzi boys to pull the plug on her. For sure. Face it, she couldn't go near the insurance money or Victor's bank accounts. For all the good his money was doing her, it might as well be buried in China somewhere.

To support herself Nora had called a few people this week and told them she was interested in hustling again. Thank God she didn't have to work through pimps or the kind of sickos who whipped their girls with heated coat hangers. Her contacts were strictly top of the line, people who could deliver the big spenders. Nora Bart had no interest in anyone on food stamps, or who waited in line for free cheese.

She called two escort services, one of which guaranteed her $3,500 a week tax-free. A second promised nothing lower than $500 tricks. She called a wealthy German woman in Laurel Canyon, who refused to take on a girl until the girl's chart had been drawn up by an astrologer at a cost of $1,800. And she telephoned a former studio casting director, who specialized in parties for rich foreigners living in exile in L.A. Nora Bart was a good worker and everyone was glad to hear from her.

She had her rules to work by, however, and gave them up front. Champagne tricks preferred. Bring on the guys who could afford to pay. As Victor used to say, first the checks appeal, then the sex appeal. Freak tricks and threesomes cost extra. So did zoo numbers, anything with animals. Unnatural? Unnatural was anything that hurt. A lot.

Cocaine was a problem she'd have to live with. Nora did her share, but it didn't cause women the sexual problems it did men. A man with a heavy coke habit simply couldn't get it up. She knew girls who refused to trick with known cokeheads no matter how much money was involved. Nothing a girl did could bring on an erection. Even kamikazes did it one time, which is more than you could say for a guy really into nose candy.

Hollywood Frankie had some of the best dope around and was generous with it, but on this trip to New York Nora Bart wouldn't be getting any. She wouldn't be meeting him or going anywhere near his Manhattan town house. Yesterday two of his men had met her at Kennedy Airport, taken her to a Fifth Avenue hotel, and ordered her to stay put until they contacted her again. The room was comfortable and she could order room service, but she wasn't to leave or entertain visitors. With memories of Victor dying in the *gaijin*'s nice little garden and the *gaijin*'s icy blue eyes burning holes in her, Nora Bart got the message. But staying cooped up in a hotel room alone was a bummer because she loved to shop in this town. Her only hope was to pick up something at Kennedy on the way back.

She did receive a telephone call from Frankie, who confirmed what his people had told her. She was here to identify Molly January and Simon Bendor, nothing else. No partying, no shopping, no seeing old friends, not even a walk in the park. Just do what she came here for and, the minute she finished, clear out for L.A. Don't fuck up, such as getting seen by the wrong people while she was in New York, dig?

Nora Bart noticed that Frankie didn't kid around with her as he'd done in the past. No hitting on her, no invitation to one of his parties, no small talk about people they both knew in L.A. He was all business this time, letting Nora know her ass was on the line, and to understand that all she had to do was think of Teriko.

She spent yesterday and most of today in the hotel room, trying not to be scared, wishing Victor was here to stand between her and Frankie. To give herself something else to think about, Nora watched TV, danced to some Al Jarreau, Bob James, and Chaka Khan tapes she'd brought with her, and tried to finish a Danielle Steele novel she'd been working on for a month. And she ate because of nerves, pigging out on lobster tails, key lime pie, salads, filet mignon, club sandwiches, home fries, raspberries and cream. Eating made her feel better. It always did. And with her metabolism, there wasn't any way she'd gain weight. Victor always said he never kept a dog around because she'd eat it. Woman, you on a sea food diet, he told her. Every time you see food, you eat it.

Late this afternoon Nora Bart had received a telephone call in her hotel room from one of Frankie's boys who'd picked her up at the airport. She recognized his voice; he was the weight lifter with the discolored tooth and thick neck and he was calling from the lobby downstairs, which shook her up. Pack your things, he told her, then leave the hotel and get into a stretch limousine parked in front. No questions, just do it.

And forget about checking out. Somebody was taking care of that right now.

Nora Bart asked a question anyway: "Where are you taking me?"

"To do what you came here to do."

Click. End of questions and answers.

The stretch limousine, comfortable and air-conditioned against the muggy July heat, carried Nora Bart and two silent *yakuza* past luxury hotels on Central Park South to Columbus Circle. Here the car turned right on Broadway and in light traffic made its way north to West Seventy-third Street, where it turned left at a tiny park filled with Puerto Rican drag queens, drunks, and bag ladies. All that sleaze was enough to make Nora Bart puke. Hard to believe it belonged to the same city with the elegance of Fifth Avenue. But that was the beauty of the Big Apple, Victor used to say. You had shit and silk laid out side by side and plenty of both to choose from.

One block away from the park, on the corner of Seventy-third Street and West End Avenue, the limousine stopped at the side entrance of a red-brick-and-limestone Ukrainian church. The trip had taken fifteen minutes, with no one saying a word to Nora Bart. While that left her edgy, she decided she was better off minus any conversation, since she didn't want to hear about the Jacuzzi boys' plans for Molly January and Simon Bendor.

The limousine was in a quiet neighborhood of high-rises with doormen and awnings, and brownstones with polished front doors and burglar alarm decals in the front windows, all of it indicating that the people living around here had money. But Nora Bart saw no one who looked like Molly January and Simon Bendor. If she left the limousine and walked straight ahead, crossing West End Avenue and strolling down a slight hill, she'd come to a park and then to the bank of the Hudson River, where she could stand and stare across at New Jersey and some ugly factory buildings. Big fucking deal.

Other interesting sights? A Puerto Rican teenage boy, bare arms blue with heart-and-cross tattoos, walked by carrying a ghetto blaster bellowing out a rap record. A chubby red-headed woman in a sun dress, baby strapped to her chest, crossed in front of the limo to get to the other side of the street. A black woman in nurses' white and a thin, very old white man with a metal walker inched along the sidewalk behind the limousine. Boring, boring, boring.

Nora Bart saw them. She'd missed them at first because she was too busy bitching to herself about being here for no reason. Holy shit, there they were. Big as life, and just several yards away from the front of the limousine. A young Japanese couple in jeans, running shoes, and tank tops, the woman slim and pretty and holding two crash helmets by the straps as the man crouched over a sleek-looking Honda motorcycle that was all polished leather, chrome, and gleaming steel. Nora Bart watched the woman stare at the stretch limo for a few seconds, then tap the man on the shoulder. Without looking at her, he closed the door to the motor compartment and stood up. Both strapped on their helmets, then straddled the Honda. The man kick-started the bike and the engine roared into life immediately. Seconds later, the couple turned the corner and disappeared. Frankie's people. For sure.

The limo now slowly turned the same corner and stopped almost immediately, halting in front of the church, giving Nora Bart her first glimpse of Molly January since saying goodbye to her at Los Angeles International Airport a few weeks ago. Molly and three other people were across the street, in front of a high-rise in the middle of the block. It was also Nora Bart's first look at Erica Styler and Simon Bendor together. After a few seconds of staring she pointed across the street thinking, *Better you than me.*

The weightlifter swiveled around in the front seat and handed her one of the Polaroid shots he'd taken. She looked at it, thinking who gives a shit, and told him it was great. When she tried to hand it back, he shook his head and told her to keep it as a souvenir of her visit to New York. Son of a bitch was proud of his work. Nora Bart looked at it again, shrugged, and slipped it into her shoulder bag next to Victor's gun. He'd bought it a few months ago at an exclusive Rodeo Drive store, one of those places where you telephoned for an appointment before being allowed to shop there.

The gun was a .38 Smith & Wesson and had cost Victor $15,000. Nora Bart wasn't comfortable around guns, but she had to admit this one was a beauty. It was made of solid gold, with a black ivory and diamond studded handled, the sort of expensive toy Victor went for the minute he learned everyone

in Bel Air and Palm Springs went for it, too. He'd even had a
permit for the gun, surprising Nora Bart by doing something
legally for a change. She'd brought it with her to New York
because she wasn't going to let the *gaijin*'s people do to her
what they'd done to Victor or Teriko. Before that happened,
she'd kill somebody. Or herself.

None of the Jacuzzi boys had said or done anything to
make her feel she was in trouble. All she had to do, supposedly, was point out Molly January and Simon what's his
name, then she'd be off the hook. But a couple of things
about this whole business bothered her. One was the number
of people the *gaijin* was using to track down Simon and
Molly. He was using a hell of a lot, meaning it was very
important to him that Simon and Molly get wasted. If it was
that important, Nora Bart had to wonder if she'd be allowed
to walk around knowing what she did.

The second thing that bothered her was what she'd learned
about the Japanese from working with them, and that was you
never, never knew what they were thinking. A Japanese wore
a mask over his mask, keeping you at a distance and hiding
the truth about himself from everybody. Victor called them
actors, role players who blew smoke. If you think you know
them, he said, you don't. You can do business with them for
twenty years and they'll still cloud up and rain on you one
day.

Nora Bart looked through the limo's dark glass and watched
Molly January and the dumpy guy in the baseball cap get into
a beat-up blue van that needed a wash job in the worst way.
Molly and her sister were crying and Nora wondered what
that was all about. In the front seat of the limo, the two
yakuza were getting worked up, chattering away in Japanese
and pointing at the van and she prayed there wasn't going to
be any shooting. Jesus, she didn't need anything that radical.

The *yakuza* behind the wheel—Nora called him Elton
John because he had the same square shape, balding head, and
spaces between his front teeth—switched on the ignition, and
when the blue van pulled away the limo followed. Both
vehicles traveled one block to Seventy-second Street, then
turned left. Still not much traffic. A blue-and-silver bus going
the other way, a Coca-Cola truck behind the limo, a handful
of cars in either of two lanes.

A police car coming toward the limo made Nora Bart's

heart leap. There were two uniformed cops in the front seat, one of them a woman laughing at something her male partner said and slapping the dashboard with the palm of her hand. The squad car, a blue-and-white, was in the left hand lane and Nora Bart had a stong urge to go for it, just leap out of the limo, throw herself in front of the blue-and-white and take her chances. The Jacuzzi boys didn't need her anymore, not really. And it didn't leave her feeling too good. Jesus, she could use something to eat right now.

The squad car passed them and turned right on West End Avenue. Too late.

At Broadway and Seventy-second the van stopped for a red light. Two cars away, the limo did the same. Nora Bart looked around and saw plenty of people. People entering and leaving a subway stop, entering and leaving an off-track betting parlor, a fruit stand owned by Koreans, a dry cleaners, a dairy restaurant, jewelry store, a couple of delicatessens. All she had to do was get out and there was nothing the weight lifter and his buddy could do in front of so many witnesses.

She asked the weight lifter why were they following the van instead of staying with Simon Bendor, who had done the actual killing. Weight lifter said they knew where Bendor lived and where he worked, but they didn't know where the other guy was taking the Molly woman.

Nora Bart told herself that made sense. Nothing for her to act freaky-deaky over. Victor said she often came on dippy when she should be laid-back and mellow. That's why she was going broke paying her therapist, to try and find out why she acted spacy when she didn't want to.

She forced herself to sound friendly, positive, and in control. Not negative in any way. "Glad you guys got what you want," she said to the weight lifter and Elton. "Like, you don't need me anymore, right? Just drop me anywhere. I'll find my own way to the airport. Say hello to Frankie for me, okay?"

No answer. The limousine followed the blue van along Seventy-second Street and into Central Park. Both vehicles headed south.

Nora Bart had her mouth open to speak when someone up front pushed a button sending a plastic shield sliding up from behind the front seat, cutting her off from the two men in front of her. She saw them speaking to each other, but she couldn't hear a word. Not one word. Still she saw their faces, their body language, and they were acting as if she wasn't even there. As if she were dead.

Eighteen

MANHATTAN
JULY 1983

Twelve-ten A.M. Simon Bendor followed a middle-aged Indian couple to the front door of a luxury apartment house on the Upper East Side. His blond hair was hidden by a dark wig with a pony tail and he also wore blue granny glasses, a false mustache, and a green T-shirt that read DOM AND JIMMY B'S RESTAURANT. He carried a flat cardboard box with *large pepperoni pizza* scrawled in pencil on the top and a white shopping bag smelling of Italian sauces and garlic bread.

The identically tubby Indians, who'd just gotten out of a taxi, turned to look at him with a sudden overwhelming terror. They were, after all, living in Manhattan, where crime and fear were necessary evils along the journey of life. Wickedness and iniquity could be found even here, on a tree-shaded street of recycled Italian palazzos, neo-French Renaissance mansions, classical town houses, and spacious condominiums. The absence of a doorman only added to the Indians' misgivings. The building had a doorman, but he went off duty promptly at midnight, a recent economy measure instituted by management.

Simon grinned at the Indians and held out the food. "Delivery."

The tension was broken. Grateful for the reprieve, the Indians relaxed and gladly grinned back. The husband, jowly and perspiring in a blue-and-white striped seersucker, unlocked the double glass doors, pushed one aside, and said to Simon, "Please to go." Simon shook his head and in a Texas twang said, "After you ma'am," to the Indian's wife, a graying pretty woman in sandals, beige-and-yellow sari, and with a red caste mark in the center of her forehead. She clutched a *King and I* theater program and also carried a restaurant doggy bag. As Simon followed her into the building, she smiled and held up the doggy bag, saying, "We both have food, yes?" Simon said, "That we do, ma'am. That we most certainly do." He included her husband in his smile, which was as good a mask as any.

The three entered an empty lobby of white enameled brick walls, fern motifs, commodious armchairs, and sofas of red velour. The fifteen-story building had two elevators, and when the husband pushed the starter button one door slid open immediately. Simon preferred to ride alone, but that meant waiting, with the possibility of being seen by more people. Since he was about to break into Frankie Odori's town house next door, the fewer people who saw him, the better.

He did the smart thing: he followed the Indian couple into the empty car and watched the husband push a button for the eighth floor. Still smiling, probably because he was glad to be alive, the Indian asked Simon his floor. Simon, twanging it all the way, said, "Two, good buddy," and watched the Indian do the honors. The Indian also punched the close button and the door slid shut.

Simon got off on the second floor, said good night to the smiling Indians, and stood in the empty corridor until the elevator door closed and the car began to rise again. Then he looked around for an EXIT sign, saw one to his left and walked toward it, stepped onto a small landing, and after softly closing the door behind him, remained still for a full two minutes, counting off the seconds in his head and giving his eyes time to adjust to the dim light. When he'd finished counting and heard nothing, Simon began tiptoeing down the staircase.

He passed the lobby level and continued his descent for one more flight until he reached the basement. He stopped on the bottom step. All quiet. Simon sat down, placed the pizza on the concrete floor, and thought, It's too dark down here for tenant safety. Management could definitely do a better job.

One bulb, not too strong, over a tenant's bulletin board hanging on the wall directly in front of him. A handful of bulbs, also not too bright, scattered in the two passages left and right of the staircase. Not enough. Not nearly enough.

All management had to do was double the number of bulbs, 200-watt minimum, and it would make all the difference in the world. But don't expect any changes until the building had been hit a few times and tenants started bitching. People did only as much as they had to in this life, never as much as they should.

The back door would put Simon only a few feet from the rear of Frankie Odori's town house. What Simon knew about Frankie's town house and this apartment building next to it had been picked up in a hurry from Dag, who'd gotten it from Jake Otto, an ex-cop turned security guard. Nor had Otto bothered to ask Joe why he wanted to know, a courtesy cops and ex-cops extended to one another. The moody and emaciated-looking Double O, as Dag called him, had problems of his own. He was still bitter over being kicked off the force three years ago because of an affair with a woman informant in a major narcotics investigation. The defense waited until the trial to reveal that an investigating officer, Jake Otto, was enjoying what could only be termed an intimate and personal relationship with the woman whose testimony the prosecution hoped would send several men to prison. The defense called that collusion and the judge agreed. The case was thrown out and twelve major Cuban traffickers walked. A two-year investigation went down the toilet, taking Double O's career right along with it.

Jake Otto had also left his wife and five children, not a good idea, since the wife had a devoted father who was the third-ranking police official in New York City. He was also the kind of enemy quick to discover anyone's mistakes and he made certain that Jake Otto would never again work as a cop. As for the woman, a Cuban twenty years younger than Otto, she'd recently walked out on him. To escape the vengeance of the dealers she betrayed she had moved to Montreal, leaving Otto alone to drink straight vodka for a good part of the day. Much of that drinking was done in cop bars in Queens, where he and Joe kept in touch. Boozing, however, had cost Jake Otto two security jobs, currently leaving him, as he put it, free from confinement and forced labor.

He'd been working for Spears Security when the company had installed burglar alarms and locks in Frankie Odori's town house and in the two luxury apartment buildings on either side of it. Dag had gone to Otto, after Teriko Ohta's death, looking for something to tie Frankie to the killing. But all Otto could say was that Hollywood Frankie was a prick who would beat a crippled broad to death with her own crutches. Frankie probably smoked Teriko, Otto said, to discourage anyone else from fucking him over.

That was why Simon didn't like Erica involving herself in tonight's burglary without consulting him first. She had telephoned Frankie to ask if he had a game coming up soon. She wasn't interested in tonight because she had something going in Atlantic City. But she was thinking of hanging around New York for a few days instead of returning home to Vegas right away. Frankie mentioned that he'd heard about the Caribbean game and would give anything to sit in. He wished Erica good luck and said he had a game set for Friday. As usual, she had a standing invitation. Tonight all he had going was a small party. "Very, very private, if you know what I mean." Just him, one or two friends, and a couple of groovy ladies.

"Orgy time," Erica told Simon. "Wesson oil, some Bolivian marching powder, and let's break out the Polaroids. Tacky. It means he'll be there when you arrive. You still want to go ahead with it?"

"Got no choice. Alexis doesn't want the photograph put in the mail. She wants it done right away, while Kasumi is still alive. Besides, she thinks it'll shake Frankie up having strangers come and go in his home whenever they feel like it. She says it's the kind of mind game the *gaijin* likes to play, assuming there is a *gaijin*. Anyway, she wants Frankie to get a taste of it. By the by, before you do anything like this again, like going near Frankie, you check it out with me. The last thing I need is for something to go wrong tonight and have him connect you to it. Understand?" Later on, when Simon mentioned it to Dag, the ex-cop agreed that Frankie was a shit and enjoyed dumping on women. The bastard was low enough to walk under a snake's belly wearing a top hat, and you didn't fuck with those kind of people. Avoid him, period.

Then there was tonight's second job, the one worth $300,000. Joe Dag had met a maid in his ballroom dancing class at Queens College, a big-hipped Salvadorean. Her name was

Concepción and she worked for a wealthy Frenchman in Manhattan, a banker who lived in an East Seventy-fourth Street town house and who'd moved his family to New York to escape France's Socialist government. Concepción said the Frenchman loved collecting coins. He'd just gotten his hands on some old pennies and she knew they were valuable because the Frenchman acted silly each time he played with them.

Joe didn't tell Concepción what they were worth, but he did tell Simon. "Five thousand bucks a piece. Eighteen Fifty-nine Indian Heads. And he's got twenty of those suckers. Somebody I know, a rich kid with too much money and not enough to do, he wants them in the worst way. He's also an autograph collector, the Frenchman. Got two letters signed by Leonardo da Vinci. Got one signed by Johann Sebastian Bach and a piece of sheet music in Handel's own handwriting. All together those little slips of paper are worth more than two hundred thousand. A private collector's creaming in his pants to get his hands on the stuff, no questions asked."

Tonight the Frenchman and his wife were attending a Bastille Day celebration, a dinner dance at the Waldorf-Astoria. Their three children were in Swiss private schools, leaving only one servant in the house and he was usually in bed by ten. Concepción had the night off and planned to go dancing at a Washington Heights *merengue* club with some Dominicans until six or seven o'clock the next morning.

Who to hit first: Frankie or the Frenchman? "Frankie," Simon told Dag. "I want to do it and get it out of the way. Drop off the photograph then split. Also, I won't have to carry any of the Frenchman's stuff with me. Free and easy. That's the way I like it."

Joe said, "Here's something you won't like. I think you should use a driver. Sure, the jobs are only seven blocks apart, but you'd be surprised how many people will see you in the wrong place at the wrong time. There's less chance of that happening in a car."

Joe was right, of course, and Simon bowed to his own instincts, which said listen to the Italian. The only reliable driver Dag could get on such short notice was Marsha, the black woman Simon had used on the Tuckerman job last week. Marsha and her Doberman. Marsha turned out to be as good in Manhattan as she'd been on Staten Island. She'd

showed up with the Italian food Simon had requested. And
she'd cruised Frankie's neighborhood without drawing attention to herself. During that time they'd watched three women
and one man enter Frankie's town house at different times,
meaning the perimeter alarm system, the system guarding the
door and windows, was turned off. Simon received confirmation on this when he noticed a first-floor window being raised
without an alarm sounding.

Simon and Marsha had also waited in the car, away from
the TV monitors covering the front of Frankie's place, for
someone to show up at the apartment house on the right, the
one where the doorman left at midnight and where any tenant
could be used as a key by a delivery boy.

In the basement Simon removed his wig, false mustache,
glasses, and T-shirt, dropping them on top of the food in the
white shopping bag. Then he reached down to the bottom of
the bag, beneath the garlic bread and foil-wrapped plastic
dishes of lasagna, veal, and sausages, and pulled out a black
wool cap and long-sleeved black shirt. He put them on, then
reached in again and took out a ski mask, two radios, and his
black shoulder bag. He unzipped the shoulder bag, removed
the night vision goggles and put them on, adjusting the
infrared viewer on each eye.

Radios next. He tuned the police radio to the frequency
Joe'd given him, then turned it off and clipped it to his belt.
He picked up the CB radio and contacted Marsha, keeping his
voice low. How did things look from her end? She came in
strong, no static. She was a couple of blocks away, around
the corner on Madison Avenue, parked in front of an art
gallery. Wouldn't be there for long, though. A blue-and-
white had just cruised by. Hadn't stopped, but it had slowed
down as the cop behind the wheel gave her a long look.

There was always the chance, she said, that the heat might
take a notion to circle the block and check her out in greater
detail. She was the wrong color to be lurking in an expensive
part of town this hour of the night. She was going to try
another street, maybe hop over to Central Park, which wasn't
all that far away. In any case, she'd do her best to keep
within radio range. Simon told her to stay loose, then switched
off.

He hooked the CB radio to his belt, put on a pair of

surgeon's gloves, and looked at his hands. Steady Eddie. He could do anything. Anyfuckingthing.

Show time.

He picked up the food and walked along the corridor toward the laundry room. There was the faint sound of a car horn behind him, but Simon didn't turn around. It came from the garage. According to Jake Otto there were two locked doors between the basement and the garage. After a tenant parked his car, an attendant checked him out on a television monitor, then buzzed him through the first door. Entrance to the second door, leading into the basement and to the elevator, was gained through a coded identification card inserted in a reader, an electric lock. The card guard system also furnished a printout listing the time a tenant entered the building. Great if a wife wanted to know when her husband *really* came home.

Getting from the garage to the basement elevator would only take a couple of minutes, all the time Simon had to unlock the laundry room and get out of sight.

He jogged the last few steps to the laundry room door, set the food down and eyed the lock. Jake Otto was right. When it came to inside locks, management had played it cheap. This one was a joke. It was a springlatch, a key-in-the-knob lock. Easy as hell to open. You could knock if off with a hammer, put it out with a pair of pliers, depress the bolt with a credit card or a kitchen knife.

Simon did it his way. He took a six-inch piece of Venetian blind from his bag, inserted it between the door and doorjamb, and slipped the lock. Seconds later he was inside the pitch-black laundry room, seeing everything as though it were high noon, leaning against the closed door, and listening to the metal door open and close at the garage end of the corridor. When the elevator had come and gone, carrying the tenant upstairs, Simon exhaled. Alone at last.

He looked around the narrow laundry room. It was divided down the middle by wooden benches, with washing machines and dryers lining either wall. There was the smell of bleach and steam-dried clothes. A cigarette machine to the left of the entrance was partially blocked by pillowcases of laundry resting on a pair of stools. Simon walked over to the washer nearer the cigarette machine, shoved the food inside, and closed the door. He'd pick it up on the way back.

But first he had to go calling on Hollywood Frankie. Meaning get through the back door of the apartment building located at the opposite end of the laundry room. Well now. Management had gone for a bit more money this time. The door was made of steel and solidly mounted, with the hinges inside. Smart. It had a spider lock—four steel bolts reaching into metal sockets below, above, and on either side of the door. A good lock, professionally installed. It would certainly stop most intruders from getting inside. Simon, however, was already inside. To get out, all he had to do was turn a knob and push. After he'd dealt with the alarm.

Crouching in front of the door, he touched the wire. It ran across the top of the door, down to the floor, then left along the baseboard to a single barred window. A perimeter alarm guarding the entrances, complete with a bell or siren, detectors and a control box, all of it somewhere in the laundry room. He found the control box where Jake Otto said Spears Security had installed it, to the right of the door and near the ceiling, out of reach of animals, children, and puckish scamps like Simon.

He stood on a stool and examined the control box without touching it. He'd run across this model before and wouldn't recommend it. It had a toggle switch, allowing anyone to turn it off. A key-activating switch offered better protection, since only someone with a key could shut the system off. The model Simon was looking at also lacked a battery-backup power supply. Those control boxes with battery backup were the ones to watch out for. The second they were cut off, the battery backup activated the alarm and the whole world came running.

Simon turned off the toggle switch, stepped down from the stool, and placed it to one side. Must remember to turn the alarm on when he came through again. He opened the door slowly, cracking it just enough to slide out of the building and into the extremely hot night. It was a scorcher, close to 90 degrees with humidity to match. He pulled the door closed behind him, leaving it unlocked and apparently undisturbed.

He stood invisible in the darkness at the base of a narrow stairwell, listening to the whine of mosquitos and looking at a metal staircase leading up to a walled patio area belonging to the building. The patio was being redone because it was cracking and sinking, damage that building management didn't want spreading to the apartment house. Simon also heard a welcome noise: the subdued roar of dozens of air conditioners. Love it. Air conditioners meant closed windows and less chance of being seen or heard.

He turned toward the light bulb over the door. It had a photoelectric cell screwed directly into the socket, making the bulb light-sensitive and primed to go on automatically in the dark. Wire mesh protected the bulb from vandals. A good idea. Except the bulb was burned out and hadn't been replaced. Fucking unreal how careless people were about security. Some time back Simon had robbed the Connecticut home of a rich shoe manufacturer, who'd then gone out and spent a fortune on every security device you could think of. Recently the man had been told that every alarm he'd bought and installed at great cost hadn't been operating for over a year. How was that for being inattentive to the point of recklessness?

Simon tiptoed up the metal staircase, stopped at the top, and looked around at the backs of the buildings around him. Love those dark windows. They were everywhere. Front, back, left and right. Only a half dozen windows had lights and all but one had shades, shutters, or blinds. Frankie's town house had lighted windows on the first, third, and fifth floors. It was a five-story, red-brick neo-Georgian building with French balconies and casement windows. Above an eight-foot-tall brick wall separating the town house from the apartment building, Simon could see the glow of floodlights, which Jake Otto said were trained on a very nice backyard garden. Frankie loved his garden parties, but tonight's social ramble, complete with consenting adults and maritals aids, was taking place indoors.

Simon glanced at the sky. Plenty of stars, along with a half-moon drifting in and out of gray clouds. A single patch of moonlight could hurt him. He would have to move from shadow to shadow and blend in with the darkness near the buildings.

To work.

He adjusted the NV's for more light, then stepped onto the patio. He walked past bags of powdered cement and piles of bricks, a mortar tub, hoses, trowels, and brick layers' hammers, until he reached a dark corner formed by the apartment building and the wall. After looking at the wall to make sure it wasn't topped with broken glass, he leaped in the air, arms stretched overhead. He caught the top of the wall with both hands, then slowly pulled himself up until he could see into the garden. Empty. But well lit for security.

Simon kept his eyes away from the floodlights, attached above a pair of ground-floor windows that were protected by decorative iron grilling. He checked out the garden, however. Well-tended and very pretty, with roses, yellow irises, and sweet Williams. There was a metal table and two chairs in one corner, a barbecue grill in another, and just below Simon a pergola, a passageway with a roof of trelliswork on which climbing plants had been trained to grow. Frankie or someone who worked for him had a green thumb.

Simon easily pulled himself onto the wall, stood up, and inched left, an acrobat moving sideways along a tightrope. When his shoulder brushed the apartment building, he reached out and placed a hand on Frankie's town house, then looked up at a pair of French balconies. One was directly overhead, just three feet away and attached to the apartment house. It led to an arched door that was half stained glass and half wood. The other balcony was almost five feet away, in front of a casement window on the second floor of Frankie's town house. Both balconies were too high for intruders to reach, supposedly. Surprise, surprise.

Eyes on the apartment house balcony, Simon spread both arms to the side, crouched, and leaped straight up in the air. Catching the bottom of the balcony, he let his body swing back and forth, then pulled himself up to sit on the railing facing the town house. He looked over his shoulder at the darkened door, then back at Frankie's balcony. It was straight ahead and not that easy to reach. If he missed, it was a two-story fall. Shit, don't even think about it.

He brought his feet up and under him, then stood up with perfect balance, still facing Frankie's place and concentrating now, arms to the side. When he was ready he crouched and leaped as far as he could, arms extending in front as though reaching for the high bar, gliding through the darkness with perfect form, willing himself to make it. He felt a higher energy level take him over and then he was truly the hawk in flight, infatuated with the risk and the thrill, and then both hands caught the base of the balcony and he swung back and forth, his body forming an L-shape as it passed just above the garden lights. Jesus, was he psyched. But in control. Ready to call the plays and run the show.

Like most French balconies, this one had barely enough room for two people to stand side by side. Simon pulled himself up, then climbed over the knee-high railing and a flower box of tea roses and found himself staring into Frankie's dark office. Double O was right on the money. Second floor rear, he'd told Joe, and no alarms, no tapes on the window, no wires, no warning decals. The office window was clean because Frankie didn't think he needed protection there. It was two stories above ground level, with no fire escape, and he always had men around the house who could deal with break-ins. All Frankie had wanted from Spears was a TV monitor for the front, floodlights for the garden, and a perimeter alarm for the front and back doors and for all ground-floor windows. Anything else was a waste of money.

He argued that if he wired each window he'd go broke. Even Otto admitted there was some truth in this. Wiring all the windows in a building was incredibly expensive, which is why nobody ever did it. Frankie wasn't worried about getting hit; he had at least two armed men on the premises at all times, his own people, and that ought to be enough. If he needed more, he'd get more. Spears disagreed, but arguing with Frankie was a waste of time. When he didn't feel like arguing anymore, he'd start talking Japanese to one of his Japanese friends, leaving you feeling like you were wearing white socks and a blue suit.

Give Erica credit, too. She'd learned that Frankie would be fucking his brains out elsewhere in the house and wouldn't be working late in the office. Had somebody else been in the office, Simon had planned to leave the photograph and his mother's unsigned note on the balcony. Now he smiled at the thought of leaving it on Frankie's desk, propped up against the telephone.

Simon loved casement windows because there wasn't a way in the world to make them secure. They opened outside on hinges, so you couldn't protect them with bars or wires. There was a single latch, a locking device that secured this type of window to the center part of the frame. Which didn't stop it from being pried open easily. And if the window was partially open, like this one, burglars had even less work to do.

He stepped up to the window, again made sure the office was empty, then removed a screwdriver from his bag. Inserting it in the narrow space between the window and its frame, he worked it left, then right. When the opening was wide enough he stuck a hand through and turned the crank handle. The window parted, both halves swinging out toward him. Simon dropped the screwdriver into the bag, then brought the police radio to his ear, turning up the volume just loud enough to hear. No alarm going out. No security service or police response. Jake Otto was one righteous dude. Simon switched the volume off, clipped the radio to his belt, then climbed through the window and into Frankie's office.

First things first. Such as an escape route. He turned and pushed both halves of the window open as far as they would go, then picked up a rattan chair and crossed a parquet floor to the office door. Tilting the chair on its hind legs, he shoved the back under the doorknob. In the event of unwelcome visitors this should buy Simon enough time to make it to the window.

He was about to leave the door when he heard a woman moan. And she wasn't in pain, at least not the kind of pain you complained about. The moaning came from across the hall. A man's voice said, "You like that, huh? You really dig that shit, right?" The woman said, "Don't stop, please don't stop," and someone else, a second man, said something Simon couldn't make out. But he got the message. Hollywood Frankie and friends were indulging in a bit of merry-making and tomfoolery.

Simon heard a buzzing sound, which could have been an electric razor or a blender. Except he knew it was neither. Frankie, said Erica, tells people he's big on meat substitutes. Like dildoes and vibrators and those vaginal steel balls you buy in Japan. The man's a class act. Simon, ear to the door and thinking, The things a boy does for his mother, heard the buzzing speed up and a woman cry out, "Oh, God, oh, God," and a man say, "Give it up, baby, give it up." If a smoke alarm went off in that room, Simon wouldn't be surprised.

He turned to look at the office. Fucking enormous. And lavishly decorated with rattan furniture, Chinese mirror paintings, Japanese lacquered screens, fireplace, walnut-paneled walls, Japanese vases, and Chinese figurines. The honey-col-

ored parquet floor gleamed as though it had been waxed only
minutes ago. There was also room for two desks, a personal
computer, calculator, telex, a television set with a large square
screen, and some very expensive stereo components. An
exercycle and a punching bag were in a corner near several
file cabinets. And don't forget the three telephones: touchtone,
Snoopy phone, and a Mickey Mouse phone. Nothing but the
best for Frankie.

He was also big on having his picture taken. There were
framed photographs of him posing with celebrities in his
Manhattan discothèque; of him at the wheel of a motorboat,
which he raced professionally in America and in Japan; of
Frankie in Boston with a local beauty queen, the two cutting
the ribbon of his latest one hour photo shop. And there was
Frankie and the smiling mayor of New York at City Hall, the
two of them holding onto a check made out to a charity for
crippled children. Good-looking, baby-faced Frankie. A little
man who was too narrow between the eyes, but who at
thirty-five looked ten years younger and was partial to black
leather, suedes, aviator glasses, and lizard-skin cowboy boots.
Hollywood Frankie with enough chains around his neck to
tow his car out of the mud. He didn't look like a hood. He
looked like a small boy trying to appear tough, like someone
trying to fart higher than his ass.

Simon walked over to a black metal desk near the computer
and the telex. Frankie's desk. Complete with photographs of
the man himself and an unusual paperweight, a stone Chinese
turtle bearing the initials F.O. Reaching into his canvas bag,
Simon removed the photograph of Kasumi and her husband,
then tucked it between Snoopy's arm and the telephone receiver. He leaned his mother's note, in a plain white envelope, against Snoopy's knees. If you can't take a joke, Frankie,
fuck you.

Was Rupert de Jongh still alive? We'll either have the
answer soon, Simon thought, or we won't get any answer at
all. After tonight Simon would be free to ignore the subject of
Mr. de Jongh. After tonight Alexis could pursue truth, justice, and the American way on her own.

Simon checked out the top of Frankie's desk. Neat. Fold-
ers, typed pages, photographs, reference books. A place for
everything and everything in its place. The Japanese kept
detailed records on the damndest things. Didn't matter whether

it was important or not, just write it down. No other people on earth collected information so zealously. Even Paul Anami was that way. Joe D'Agosta had told Simon about *yakuza* who'd been arrested in California and Hawaii. All had been found carrying pages of itemized information on the drugs and cash in their possession, how much they were allotted in travel expenses, how to deal with business associates, and what to do in case of trouble with the authorities.

Speaking of details and itemizing, there was the matter of Frankie's telephone cassette tapes. Simon found them in a cassette case between Snoopy and the touchtone phone. Simon himself had a couple of cases just like it to store his fusion jazz and classical cassettes. The case held fifty tapes, with a lined sheet of paper inside the lid to list them in order. Time to pull a switcherooney. He reached into his bag and took out two packs of blank cassettes. Each pack held six blanks, which he'd bound together with masking tape to prevent them from rattling and making noise. Simon removed the masking tape, placed the blanks to one side, and lifted up the night vision goggles. When he'd shaken out the perspiration, he fitted them to his eyes again, pulled Frankie's case toward him, and opened it.

All of Frankie's tapes were in individual plastic boxes with a date marked on the spine in English. Simon looked at the list. Well, what have we here? Forty-three tapes with names written down in Japanese and English. Simon's eyebrows went up under the goggles. Good golly, Miss Molly. Three telphone calls in the past two days from none other than Hawaii's own Raymond Manoa. Simon knew him only by reputation, but what a reputation. Manoa the media darling, a self-proclaimed child of the soil, a heavy-handed enforcer of the law who'd blown away a few people in his time. A goddam fire eater. Someone who'd kick a hole in you if you looked at him the wrong way. If Hollywood Frankie was up to his eyebrows in Japanese criminal activities, what did that make Raymond Manoa? Chances are it made him a hired hand. Hawaii's hero cop had probably been bought and paid for by the *yakuza*. Maybe Manoa was calling to complain about the way Frankie had messed up some vacation photographs, but Simon doubted it. These tapes could probably send Hawaii's hero cop to the slammer.

Manoa's name on the list made Simon decide to take the

twelve most recent tapes. Numbers 31 through 43. He removed them from the case, took them out of their plastic
jackets, and replaced them with blanks. Blanks back in the
carrier case. Frankie's cassettes bound together with masking
tape and dropped into Simon's bag. If the gods were kind, it
might be weeks before Frankie noticed any of his cassettes
were missing.

Time to be running along. Th-th-that's all, folks.

Simon looked over the desk. Mustn't forget anything. He
was about to turn away when something caught his eye and
he froze. He'd been concentrating on the cassettes, working
fast so that he could get to the Frenchman's place before
madame et monsieur returned. His mind had been on the
cassettes and he hadn't really looked at the photographs.
Not just the ones of Frankie, but a particular eight-by-ten
glossy lying on top of a file folder. The glossy was of Molly
January. Looking at it suddenly gave Simon a bad feeling. A
very bad feeling.

He adjusted the NV's for more light, then picked up Molly's photograph. Definitely Erica's younger sister, with a
lion's mane of blond hair swirling around her head, her teeth
perfect, her lips parted and wet. A Marilyn Monroe clone.
The kind Japanese men went crazy over. Her name, resumé,
and clothes sizes were on the back. The resumé was all lies
from start to finish, but that was Molly. She'd conjured up a
background that presented her as the second coming of Liza
Minnelli. Frankie wasn't a casting agent and he wasn't a
producer, he was *yakuza* and there was only one reason why
he'd have a photograph of Molly January in his possession.
One reason only. Simon, growing increasingly tense, laid the
photograph down and picked up the file folder. He opened the
cover.

Christ, no.

He stared at a photograph of Erica taken in Las Vegas a
few months ago during the World Series of Poker. Erica
looking like a beautiful ice princess, oblivious to the camera,
to spectators, to everything but the cards on the table in front
of her. Simon lifted the photograph to look at the pages
underneath. It got worse. There was information on him.
Vietnam service, home and business addresses in Hawaii and
Manhattan. Very fucking thorough.

Information on Molly, Erica, and his mother. Alexis had

her own neatly typed page. Clipped to it was a dust jacket containing her photograph, the jacket taken from a book she'd written on codes and ciphers. A piece of memo paper fell from the folder to the floor. Simon crouched, picked it up, and flinched when he read the address of Joe D'Agosta's coin shop in Queens. Simon rose and continued going through the file. There was a brochure from his Honolulu health club with his photograph encircled in red pencil. Also written on the brochure in red was the name Nora Bart, a TWA flight number, and yesterday's date. For the first time in years, Simon felt nervous and uncomfortable.

He closed the folder, then placed it and Molly's photograph back where he'd found them. How in hell had they managed to find him and Molly? *How?* He knew why. The *yakuza* had come looking for them because of the man Simon had killed in Tokyo, which is exactly what Paul Anami had said would happen. They never forget, Paul had said. They'll dig in and they won't let go until it's settled and settled their way.

Molly's photograph and the file on Frankie's desk said it all. Frankie did have a godfather, a big man in the under-world, as Dag had pointed out. And in rescuing Molly, Simon had gone against that godfather without knowing it. Frankie's godfather was also the *gaijin*, the old man who after forty years still wanted to kill Alexis. The man only she believed was still alive.

Alexis had been right all along, but all Simon had done was pat her on the head and yawn in her face. He'd let her down when she needed him; he'd have to live with that the rest of his life. By taking that guy out in Tokyo, the one Molly had said was a major hood, Simon had led the *gaijin* to his mother. It was all there in Frankie's little folder.

Simon put Alexis's note and the photograph of Kasumi and her husband back in his bag. The *yakuza* already knew where to find his mother. No sense making it any easier for them. From here on he and Alexis would be working together on this thing. Wasting people is something he thought he'd left behind in Nam, but if that's what it took to keep his mother alive, then he'd start doing it again.

Alexis, Kasumi, and Rupert de Jongh. Two women and a man tied to the past by guilt, obligation, and hatred. Tied to a past they couldn't relive and couldn't put behind them. And like it or not, Simon was now a player.

To calm himself, he began breathing deeply and when he felt more relaxed he examined the top of Frankie's desk. What was he looking for? He'd know it when he found it. Three framed photographs near a slim vase of tea roses caught his eye. One was a young and pretty Japanese woman in a kimono, arms around the shoulders of two small boys. Could be Frankie's wife. Joe'd said there was a wife somewhere in Japan, not that Frankie took marriage seriously. Frankie's philosophy on that subject had always been, I'm not married, my wife's married.

Second photograph. The same two little boys, each wearing identical dark school uniforms, were seated by the side of an ornamental pool in a walled garden. A man in clogs and kimono stood over the boys and was handing them bits of bread to feed the fish, who'd come to the edge of the pool to take the bread from the boys' fingers. The man was small, white-haired, Caucasian.

Third photograph. This had been taken in a studio some years back, when Frankie was in his late teens. It was a black-and-white shot of Frankie in a baseball uniform, a bat over his shoulder. Flanking him on either side were two men, one Japanese, one white. Both men wore kimonos. More than likely the elder Japanese was Frankie's father. The white man, the same one helping the boys to feed the pool fish, was probably a close family friend. Meet Rupert de Jongh. The *gaijin*. Hollywood Frankie's mysterious godfather, who'd taken the time to pose for some rare family photographs. Simon picked up the photograph of de Jongh and Frankie's sons and dropped it in his bag. Alexis could confirm de Jongh's identity easier from this shot than from the one taken in Frankie's youth.

Alexis. He had to warn her in a hurry. And apologize. Had to warn Joe and Erica, too. But he couldn't do that from here. Using the phone in Frankie's office was suicide. He'd have to get to a public telephone and do it quickly.

He jogged to the office door, removed the chair, and put it back in its original position. Then he climbed through the window and onto the balcony, turned the crank handle and closed the window. That's when it hit him. He was being watched. Maybe not at this very minute, but he was definitely being watched. That's what Frankie's file was all about. Simon's home, his health clubs. They fucking knew where he was almost every minute of the day. Had they followed him here? He doubted it.

Earlier he'd walked eight blocks from his Columbus Avenue apartment to a crowded Broadway restaurant, going directly to the men's room. When he'd left he'd been wearing the wig, T-shirt, false mustache, and granny glasses of a slovenly-looking delivery man. Then he'd taken a cab downtown to the South Street Seaport, where he'd lost himself among the crowds flooding the shops, restaurants, and docked clipper ships. When it was time to meet Marsha he had walked six blocks to a deserted part of the pier and her car, making sure he hadn't been followed. This was his procedure with every job.

As for dropping in on the Frenchman tonight, that would have to wait. Nothing mattered now except getting to a phone.

On the balcony Simon took the CB radio from his belt, made contact with Marsha, and told her to be in front of the apartment building in ten minutes with the motor running. He didn't tell her the second job had been scratched. Time enough for that when he was in the car.

He looked from Frankie's balcony to the apartment house balcony. The distance between the two looked greater than it had earlier and he knew why. For the first time since he'd gotten wiped out in the Banzai Pipeline he felt threatened. Felt his energy disappearing. Something terrible was invading his mind. He dreaded making the jump.

The moon was out from behind the clouds. Its silver light fell softly on the darkened balcony of Frankie's town house. On Simon. He shivered.

He thought of his mother. And he remembered John Kanna.

That's when he closed his eyes and concentrated on the power of Mikkyo, on the strength to be found in *kuji no in,* the nine signs. He selected *To,* the second sign, the one that could flood his body with energy and increase his perception. He placed his palms together, middle fingers over extended index fingers, other fingers locked. Moving his clasped hands, he traced five horizontal and four vertical lines in the air, breathed deeply, then opened his eyes.

Leaping to the rail, he stood balanced and still, arms outstretched.

Seconds later he crouched and leaped toward the apartment building.

Nineteen

Joe D'Agosta finished playing the last note of Samuel Barber's Adagio for Strings, then looked down at Molly January, who'd fallen asleep on the sofa in back of his coin shop. He stood with his arms at his sides, violin in one hand, bow in the other, thinking she was clowning around, pretending his playing had made her nod out. A minute ago she'd said, "You play good," and there'd been tears in her eyes. As a cop, trained to analyze and observe, he knew she hadn't been bullshitting. She'd really enjoyed his music, leaving D'Agosta pretty pleased with himself.

He hadn't played for anyone since Lorraine and that was four years ago. Good old Lorraine. She'd sat on this same sofa, in this same room, and told him she was thirty-six years old, that her biological clock was ticking, and that she wanted children, along with a husband who wasn't on loan. Ultimatum delivered, she chain-smoked and listened to a frightened and confused D'Agosta play a Russian folk song, him with the crazy idea that the music would smooth things over and keep her in his life on his terms. But when the song was over, a tearful Lorraine walked out of the shop without saying goodbye. After that he was more afraid of the loneliness within himself than ever.

D'Agosta watched Molly's breathing become slower, watched her chest rise and fall, and knew she wasn't faking. She'd definitely nodded out. He checked his watch and saw it was after midnight. No wonder she'd crashed.

Simon might have had his problems with Miss January, but Dag wasn't having a bit of trouble. Under the false eyelashes, fashionable baggy clothes, and showbiz crap, Molly was a sweet kid. Tonight, before he'd started cooking dinner, she'd somehow talked him into letting her cut and blow dry his hair. She'd done a good job, surprising the hell out of him. He was nobody's Robert Redford, but when she finished it looked as though he had more hair up there than he actually did.

She'd also laughed at his jokes and listened to him tell about being on the cops and about coin collecting and maybe that's why he'd knocked himself out putting together a special dinner: chicken roasted in tarragon sauce, mashed potatoes and compote of apples, string beans, and for dessert, fruit mousse with sponge fingers. "Really neat," she said between mouthfuls. "This stuff's really neat." Truth was, her being here had given him one of the best days he could remember. And she was so goddam beautiful that it hurt to look at her. In this trash pile of a shop Molly January was the sun come down to earth, a reminder of the promise and hope D'Agosta had left behind. She was at the age where you spent most of your time in the future. Maybe that's why she reminded him of Teriko. Molly said D'Agosta reminded her of a penguin, but that was all right since she'd always liked penguins.

He returned the violin to its case, then carried it to a small closet near the bathroom. After placing the case on the shelf, he removed an overcoat and two sports jackets from the closet, leaving it empty. Coats and jackets were dumped on his desk with the rest of his clothes. That left the closet for Molly, who had yet to unpack. Her two suitcases and a shoulder bag were on the floor near Dag's Cecil B. De Mille chair. Right where he'd put them hours ago. Erica's little sister wasn't exactly organized.

D'Agosta took a blanket from the chair, unfolded it, and covered Molly. She was still wearing her blue jumpsuit, gold lamé Roman sandals, and torquoise necklace made of plastic balls the size of small rocks. No sense waking her. At his desk he turned the fan down to low and trained it on the sofa. This is it for air conditioning, kid. Sorry.

Unplugging the portable Sony, he carried it and the scrambler to the front of the shop, where he'd set up a cot for himself. After attaching the scrambler to the telephone near the cash register he placed the Sony on a glass-topped counter, connected its plug to an extension cord, and plugged the extension into a wall socket. He switched on the set, selected his channel, then played around with the antenna and fine tuner. Took a while, but he got a picture. A ''Columbo'' rerun. Peter Falk and his polluted raincoat. Something to kill time until Simon checked in. D'Agosta couldn't wait to get his hands on the Frenchman's pennies.

He turned down the volume of the Sony, tiptoed into the back room and into the bedroom, where he closed the door. He stripped down to his shorts, undershirt, and ankle socks, took a terry-cloth robe from the back of the door, and put it on. Then he cleaned his teeth and spent a few minutes admiring his new haircut in the mirror. He thought, Maybe I ought to put a plastic slipcover over my head to protect my good looks.

Unbelievable the way he and Molly had hit it off. D'Agosta was old enough to be her father. And she was supposed to be a basket case. Simon had led him to expect some bimbo tough enough to pick up hell and put it in her purse. Instead Molly had turned out to be a breath of fresh air, a kid who enjoyed clowning around and who wasn't all that stupid.

What was it she'd said to him in the van while they were driving across the Fifty-ninth Street Bridge?

''No offense, but I think there's more to your friend Simon Bendor than meets the eye. Like he's supposed to be an ordinary businessman, a guy running a couple of health clubs. But he goes to Japan and get's me out. Now that ain't no ordinary businessman, know what I'm saying? Like he's too cool sometimes, like maybe he's got something to hide. How'd you two meet anyway?''

''Through a mutual friend, guy named Matty, who was with Simon in Vietnam. They both served in a special combat unit connected to the CIA. Matty was a neighborhood kid I watched grow up. A little wild sometimes, but basically a good guy. Also, I guess you could say I helped Simon finance his health clubs.''

''Oh, you mean like you put him in touch with people who had money?''

D'Agosta found himself laughing and choking at the same

time. "Yeah. You got it. That's exactly what I did, all right. Put him in touch with people who had money."

Did the same for Matty too, Dag thought, until the night Matty slipped on a snow covered hotel catwalk and fell twenty-five stories to his death on Park Avenue, with six hundred thou in stolen jewelry hanging from his neck in a black canvas bag.

In the front room, D'Agosta sipped espresso with his eyes on the Sony. Lieutenant Columbo, cigar in hand, had hunkered down beside a Bel-Air swimming pool and was peering into the clear blue water, half-closed eyes hiding a crafty little mind. D'Agosta wore a pair of slippers Molly'd bought for him while they were shopping for food. She'd picked up cosmetics for herself, a blow-dryer, and a T-shirt reading "Life is hard and then you die." She'd forced D'Agosta to accept the slippers, explaining you could never have too many gloves or slippers because you were always losing them. He'd been too embarrassed to admit that he didn't own a single pair, that the ones she'd bought him were his first in years. Jesus, were they comfortable. His toes were so happy they were ready to throw a party for his feet.

Columbo's problems reminded D'Agosta of something Molly had said during dinner. Apparently Simon had wasted some guy in Japan. A guy who'd been big in the *yakuza*. Simon hadn't told D'Agosta about it, not that they told each other every little thing that went on in their lives. There were times when they'd go months without seeing or talking to each other. They were close in their own way, the way loners were close, meaning their relationship functioned best when conducted with distance between them.

If Molly was righteous about the killing, she wasn't the only one who had to be careful. D'Agosta wished Simon had told him about dusting the Jap. It was always nice to know these little things.

Tomorrow D'Agosta planned to close the shop early and take Molly for a drive along the Jersey shore, maybe stop and have some onion soup, stone crabs, and beaujolais. She was looking forward to it, complaining she'd been cooped up in Simon's apartment for over a week and had been going out of her mind. That dead *yakuza* left behind by Simon made D'Agosta decide to bring along his Smith & Wesson while out with Molly. Be alert. That's what the world needed. More lerts.

D'Agosta slid off the stool, walked from behind the counter, and looked into the back room. Molly, bless her, hadn't moved. Still dead to the world. He closed the door softly, leaving the light on as Erica had told him to. Be prepared, Erica'd said. Molly might have a nightmare; forgetting Tokyo wasn't easy, especially since she refused to see a shrink. Molly was tired of being told she wasn't happy, that she had to adapt to reality, that it was necessary for her to resolve her various inner conflicts. She'd heard the same shit from every shrink she'd ever seen and didn't want to hear it anymore. D'Agosta said, Do it your way and forget what anyone else tells you.

He was about to return to "Columbo" when he heard a light tapping at his front door. He stopped, looked at the door, and when he heard the tapping again he casually walked to the counter, reached beneath a copy of the *Daily News* lying near the Sony, and pulled out the .38 Smith & Wesson. Thumbing off the safety, he slipped the piece into a pocket of his robe and kept his hand on it.

More rapping on the door.

D'Agosta ran a hand through his hair and looked around the shop.

Front door and one display window covered by venetian blinds inside, iron gates outside. Anyone on the street could easily see the light he had in the front room, unfortunately. Maybe it was a drunk, some local booze hound, which had happened in the past. Or it could be a bunch of dipshit kids showing off, banging on his door like they'd done one morning at three in the A.M., asking "Mr. Coin Man" if he had change of a quarter. Over the years there'd been a few real emergencies, like a next-door neighbor, somebody's wife, who wanted D'Agosta's help in getting her husband to the hospital. The poor bastard had managed to get a piece of glass in one eye and was going crazy.

Regarding OPP, other people's property, there wasn't any on the premises. D'Agosta was a firm believer in the principle of fast turnover. Anything stolen by Simon was disposed of within twelve hours or dumped in the river. No exceptions. Sitting on hot items could mean a trip to the slammer, and at this point in his life D'Agosta had no wish to be sent away to college. He did have valuable coins in the shop, legitimate stuff, but each night he cleaned out the window and two display counters in the front room, hiding the expensive stock in the floor safe in back. The rest went into a box safe up front. All he had in the window now was the cloth that covered the empty shelves and four books on rare coins. Cash? Six hundred bucks in the register and that's it. He should have dropped that in the floor safe, but Molly's being here had made him forget.

Tap-tap-tap on the front door.

D'Agosta walked to the door, peeked through the blinds, and saw a lone woman on a dark, empty street. She was holding a handkerchief to her face, which didn't prevent him from seeing she'd been beaten up. Swollen lip, one eye practically closed, blood on the handkerchief. She'd definitely been smacked around. D'Agosta watched her dab at her nose, look at the handkerchief, and shiver. He looked past her again to make sure Steinway Street was empty. It was.

The woman was young. Lean. She wore punkish clothes and a short hairstyle, and there was a dog collar around her neck. A ditz who'd gotten herself in a bind.

She leaned toward the door and said in a husky voice, "Hello? I see some light. Anybody in there?"

D'Agosta said, "Yeah?"

"Oh, mister, would you please do me a favor? Would you call me a cab? I had some trouble with a couple of guys and I had to jump out of their car. Nobody around here will help me. I knocked on a couple of doors, but I didn't get any answer. Nothing's open on this block. Neither one of the phone booths around here works. I think there's something wrong with them. I saw your light. Please, would you just make that call for me? Those guys are still out here cruising the neighborhood for me. Please, I need your help."

D'Agosta shook his head. What the fuck could he do, walk away?

He took his hand out of his pocket, reached overhead, and turned off the alarm control box over the front door. Then he told the woman outside to wait a minute and walked over to the cash register, where he pulled his key ring from under the *Daily News*. He was about to return to the door when he looked at the telephone. After a second's hesitation D'Agosta picked up the receiver and put it to his ear. The line was dead. Which wasn't going to help things when Simon called, but that could wait.

D'Agosta unlocked the front door, opened it, and stared through the iron gate at the battered woman. Jesus, what a mess. Her eye was not only closed but becoming discolored. And with a mouth swollen that bad, you could bet a few loose teeth went along with it. She'd probably met a couple of guys at a party or some disco and they'd offered her a lift home or said let's go cop some good dope. In return, mama, all you gotta do is spread your legs.

D'Agosta unlocked the padlock, put it and the key ring in the empty pocket of his robe, then gripped the gates with both hands and pulled toward the doorjamb. The fuck's going on here? Halfway. That's as far as the gate would go and no farther. Earlier tonight, when he'd locked up, the gate had been running as smoothly as a Rolls-Royce engine. He oiled it once a week, twice a week in winter. Bought a new one every two years. Now all of a sudden it was acting up. It was as if there was an obstacle on the runner slowing the gate down.

D'Agosta said just a minute to the woman, then stepped between the gate and right doorjamb, pushing the gate with both hands, putting his back into it, determined to fold that sucker up if it killed him. Suddenly something popped out onto the sidewalk and the gate sped into the left doorjamb. D'Agosta almost lost his balance.

He looked down and saw a piece of wood, a twelve-inch ruler broken in half. Something shoved into the base of the gate to hold it in place. He bent down to pick it up with his left hand and at the same time shoved his right hand into his pocket for the Smith & Wesson.

Someone struck him on the back of the head. Hard. D'Agosta dropped to his knees in front of the gate, almost out, almost, and thinking it's the same kind of bitching pain as the last time, the week after he'd made detective and a nigger transvestite had slugged him behind the ear with a coffee thermos.

D'Agosta on his knees, thinking then, thinking now, Get your piece, dago, and smoke this fucker.

He clung to the gate with one hand and clawed at the pocket of his robe with the other and that's when the man behind him punched D'Agosta in the arm. Two shots from a stonelike fist. Right bicep. Right forearm. D'Agosta didn't

know anybody alive could hit that hard. The guy had probably punched him in the head to start with. D'Agosta caught a
quick glimpse of him. Not tall. But muscular. Built like a
weight lifter. A Japanese.

D'Agosta's arm went numb. It just wasn't there anymore.
He clutched it and suddenly it started to pain him so much
that he fell down, landing on his back inside the coin shop.
Screaming. He didn't scream long. Two men grabbed his
arms and dragged him toward the counter. After that it became a very, very bad dream, when one of the men, a
balding, stocky Japanese, sat on his chest, leaned down, and
pressed both thumbs against the sides of D'Agosta's neck.
The ex-cop stopped screaming. Then he found he was having
trouble breathing. After that everything went black.

On the sidewalk the weight lifter shoved Nora Bart into the
coin shop, followed her inside, and closed the door. She
looked down at a stilled D'Agosta, then turned toward the
television set. She was watching it and dabbing at her face
with a bloodstained handkerchief when the three *yakuza* walked
past her and into the back room.

Twenty

Raymond Manoa had no difficulty breaking into Paul Anami's Nuuanu Valley home. He began by parking a quarter of a mile away, leaving a borrowed Volkswagen hidden in a clump of eucalyptus trees off a curving dirt road. Then in the cool dawn he walked along the empty road to the white clapboard house, circling the property until he faced the swimming pool. To reach the house itself he kept to the shadows of two mammoth banyan trees, crossed a flagstone-covered patio, and stood in front of a pair of sliding glass doors.

The detective looked east at the dark mass that was the Koolau Mountains, where his ancestors had gone into battle behind feather and wicker sculptures of Ku, the god of war, the island snatcher. Where warriors had fought with stonehead clubs, strangling cords, eighteen-foot-long spears, wooden daggers lined with shark's teeth, slingshots, tree branches, and rocks. Where *kahunas*, the high priests from whom Manoa was descended, had performed human sacrifices to insure victory in battle.

He looked at his reflection in the glass doors. He was bare-chested and wore jeans, black leather gloves, and the gourd mask. A screwdriver was tucked in his belt and he carried a broom handle with two nails hammered in one end. He was dressed for his *kaua*, his war with Paul Anami and other enemies of the children of the soil. The dark, quiet house said Mr. Paul and his one servant were still catching some Z's, enjoying their sack time. Manoa wasn't here to rip off the place. All he wanted to do was get inside and mess with Mr. Paul's mind.

The detective had laid the ground for this little visit yesterday, when he'd showed up at the house personally to answer a complaint made by the antique dealer. Seems Mr. Paul had been receiving some weird telephone calls. Somebody had been calling him at his home and antique shop and threatening to dump more rats in his lap. Mr. Paul didn't think it was funny. In fact, he found it quite upsetting, especially on those occasions when the caller would ring him and say nothing at all. Now that was scary. Warnings about rats being left in his refrigerator and turned loose in the shop didn't add to Mr. Paul's peace of mind either.

The antique dealer had contacted the police, but had gotten nowhere. No one had seen the first rat, except Mr. Paul and his boyfriend. The feeling among police officers was that Mr. Paul wasn't wrapped too tight. *Pupule*. Crazy. Raymond Manoa knew for a fact that the complaint wasn't even written up. The detective had been hanging around precinct headquarters when the call had come in and the desk sergeant who'd taken it, the third he'd taken from Anami that day, simply listened, then hung up and went back to reading *Hustler* magazine. "Wacko," the desk sergeant said without looking up. "I'm getting tired of this fucking *mahu*, faggot, bugging me." That's all Manoa wanted to hear.

Manoa had then driven out to Anami's house and given the little queen some *hoomalimali*, sweet talk that didn't mean a goddam thing, telling him not to be discouraged by police indifference. Just hang in there, bruddah. Keep calling and let us know what's shakin'. This time Manoa was talking to Anami without a handkerchief over the receiver, not that Mr. Paul would have noticed the difference. The man was on the verge of tears and very down on the Honolulu Police Department. Manoa, of course, agreed that Anami wasn't getting a fair shake. So the detective offered him some suggestions. Tape the calls yourself. Or write down whatever you can remember. And note the time and date each call comes in.

"Meanwhile," Manoa said, "let's check out the house to see what security's like. This caller could be jerking you around or he could be serious." And so sweet Mr. Paul gave

Manoa a guided tour of the house and grounds and Manoa
lied through his teeth, saying security was okay. No sense
telling the man that the few locks he had protecting his place
really and truly sucked. On his own, Mr. Paul said that
maybe it might be a good idea not to go out at night for the
next few days. He was a little too nervous to be around
people right now. Manoa thought about it, then nodded. It
just might be the smart thing to do.

For Manoa, the smart thing was to attack the antique dealer
at dawn, when a man's sleep was deepest. Now he crouched
in front of the glass door on the right and used the point of the
screwdriver to pry it up and out of its track. Tucking the
screwdriver back into his belt, the detective stood up and with
gloved hands lifted the door from the top and bottom tracks,
then stepped right and carefully leaned the sheet of glass
against the white clapboard house. Sorry to tell you this,
bruddah, but glass doors ain't shit. Locks, steel pins, a
Charley bar—they might slow a perp down, but they can't
keep him out. No way. Not as long as there are screwdrivers
and crowbars in this world.

Manoa removed his shoes, left them on the patio, then
picked up the broom handle and stepped into a circular glass
dining room. Pretty, but too precious for his taste. He walked
across the carpeted floor, opened a burled walnut door, and
tiptoed along the mirrored hallway, passing a dining room
and a library and finally reaching a staircase leading to the
second floor. He tiptoed up the carpeted staircase, then along
the hall, following a thin path of light coming through a
stained-glass window at the far end of the corridor. Midway
in the corridor he stopped and placed an ear to a door on his
left. The master bedroom, Mr. Paul had said. Coming at you,
bruddah.

Manoa opened the door slowly, slipped through, taking
care not to hit the door or wall with his broomstick or to
scratch anything with the nails. Inside he closed the door
behind him, stopped and listened. And allowed his eyes to get
used to the dark. There was a tiny bit of light coming from a
crack in the drapes. It fell on the bed, on Mr. Paul's legs and
feet, which were covered by a blanket. No need for air
conditioning in the valley, brah. Rich people lived out here
because it was cool, quiet, and didn't have factory smoke or
poor Hawaiians living in tin shacks and eating out of garbage

cans. Just thinking about Mr. Paul and other Japs and whites having it so good made Manoa angry. Time for a little payback.

He walked over to the large, circular bed where Mr. Paul lay on his left side, back to Manoa. Placing the broom handle on the bed, the detective reached into his back pocket and took out a balled-up pair of socks. Next he removed a pair of handcuffs tucked into his pants at the small of his back. He stared down at the antique dealer and when he heard the voice of the *mana*, the spirit power that lived in all creatures and all things, he attacked.

He leaped on Anami, jammed the rolled socks in his mouth and cuffed both hands behind his back. Then Manoa removed his belt and tied the antique dealer's ankles together. A terrified Anami, cries muffled by the crude gag, kicked out with both legs, catching Manoa painfully in the thigh. Incensed, the detective punched him in the kidney. Payback, bruddah. Anami went rigid, back arched, then collapsed.

Manoa grabbed a fistful of Anami's hair, pulled his head off the bed, then leaned down so that the Japanese could see the gourd mask. Mr. Paul's eyes practically left their sockets. And when Manoa softly chanted an old Polynesian prayer used by *kahunas* during human sacrifices, Mr. Paul twisted and turned for all he was worth. Nowhere to run and nowhere to hide, my man.

And Anami was in the nude. Perfect.

Manoa pushed him over on his stomach, picked up the broom handle and sat on Anami's thighs. Right hand gripping the broom handle near the nail end, the detective shoved it, gently at first, then more firmly, into the antique dealer's anus. Anami, eyes all whites, tried to raise himself up and throw off Manoa. Forget it, brah. Manoa was too strong. With one hand he pressed down on Anami's buttocks, keeping him in place. With the other he shoved the broom handle and nails deeper into his ass.

Broom handle and nails. A punishment used by labor goons against farm workers trying to organize against wealthy, white landowners.

Now for a power play, to show who was boss. Manoa pulled the broom handle from Anami's body, then unzipped his fly, gripped his erect penis, and entered Anami, riding him viciously as the Japanese moaned in pain. When he was finished the detective used the blanket to wipe himself and wipe the blood from the broom handle. Then he zipped up his pants, untied Anami's ankles, and placed the belt around his own waist.

Picking up the screwdriver, he pressed its point against Anami's temple and said, "One sound, just one, and you're dead meat."

Screw driver and broom handle in one hand, Manoa backed away from the sobbing Anami, then opened the bedroom door, closed it, and ran lightly down the hallway, down the staircase, and back to the glass dining room. It took him less than two minutes to return the glass door to its tracks and pick up his shoes. Then he ran across the patio and around the pool and into the shadows of the banyan trees, feeling the power of the *mana* in him as he raced ahead of the dawn.

On the road, away from the house, he laughed out loud, the sound echoing among the trees. I mean, who's gonna believe you, Mr. Paul? I know the song you're singing, bruddah, but who's gonna listen? You ain't got nobody on your side, brah.

But you got me, 'cause I'll be listening, my man. I'll listen 'cause you're gonna tell me where I can find Alexis Bendor. And you're gonna help me whack her, bruddah. You and me, we're gonna waste that old lady together.

Twenty-One

In the living room of his Manhattan condominium, Simon Bendor sat in a black leather armchair and gave no sign that he heard the voice coming from a portable radio cassette recorder on the glass-topped coffee table in front of him.

Dressed in a bathrobe and briefs, he sipped herbal tea and used a ballpoint pen to make notes on a FitnessCenter memo pad. At 9:45 A.M., when an English bracket clock over the fireplace began striking the quarter hour, he stopped writing long enough to look in its direction. He listened to the chimes, then leaned forward, pressed the *stop* button on the cassette recorder, then pressed rewind. As he waited for the tape to reverse itself, he underlined three names on the memo pad. Rupert de Jongh. Sir Michael Marwood. Detective Lieutenant Raymond Manoa. When the tape finished rewinding, Simon pressed *play*, flopped back in his chair, and looked at Joe D'Agosta, who sat in a similar armchair to his left quietly chain-smoking and drinking black coffee.

From time to time D'Agosta rubbed his right bicep and forearm, trying to work the feeling back into his arm. His eyes were red-rimmed, his face puffy from lack of sleep, and he hadn't shaved. He sat slumped in his chair, looking old and defeated and staring straight ahead at nothing. An ashtray in front of him was close to overflowing.

Simon said, "Listen." D'Agosta nodded but didn't look at him.

The voice coming from the cassette recorder was male and spoke with a strong Scottish brogue.

"The woman seen in the Honolulu Park is Alexis Bendor, Bendor being her married name. That's spelled *B-E-N-D-O-R*. She is a widow and lives in Honolulu with her son, an only child and the owner of a private health club, also in Honolulu. They share a home together in a suburb called Mount Tantalus. Mrs. Bendor owns a bookstore located in a Waikiki shopping mall. The store is called—"

Simon leaned forward and pressed the stop button. Then he looked at D'Agosta and tapped the memo pad with his ballpoint pen. "It wasn't you and it wasn't me. Marwood gave my mother up. That's how they found us. This tape says so and so does the file on Frankie's desk. The guy on the tape is a Scotsman named Alan Bruce. He's Marwood's bodyguard. Alexis had dinner with them last week in Washington. Dag, listen. Marwood gave her up. He's the bastard who pointed the finger and there was no way in the world we could have stopped him. The man's been a *yakuza* mule for a long time. De Jongh got his hooks into Marwood a long time ago and hasn't let go."

D'Agosta said, "At first, I tired to lay it off on you. I told myself you never mentioned having smoked that guy in Tokyo. If you'd done that, I said, then maybe I'd have been more on guard and maybe they'd never gotten to Molly. But that's bullshit. Truth is, I have to take the weight. It's on me. She was handed over to me and I fucking blew it."

"No you didn't. I was the one who didn't take Alexis seriously, remember? You tried to tell me, she tried to tell me, but I didn't listen. I listened with my ears, but not with my head, with my heart. And now she's out there somewhere and they're trying to kill her and I don't know where she is. Try living with that."

"Where'd she call from last time?"

"L.A. Right after she copped the photograph. And just before she was off to the hospital to check on Kasumi. Looks like Mrs. Koehl's only got weeks, maybe days. My guess is Alexis will probably head for Honolulu. She's got friends who can at least hide her out for a few days or until I can get to her. I wish the hell she'd bothered to check in with Paul."

D'Agosta lit another Winston and took a deep drag. "No word from him either?"

Simon, who hadn't gone to bed since hitting Frankie's town house, yawned and shook his head. "Called his home twice. Nothing. Too early to try the shop, but I've left a message with his service. You want to try the cops again before Erica wakes up? Maybe they'll have something by now."

Simon thought: dumb. Shouldn't have reminded him. The pain on D'Agosta's face said thinking about Molly's disappearance was torture.

D'Agosta, eyes on the hallway leading to the guest bedroom, where Erica was sleeping, said, "They won't have anything to tell me. Like I told you, nothing happens on a missing-persons case for twenty-four hours. Ninety-nine percent of all missing persons turn up the next day. That's why the cops wait. We got at least another twelve hours before they'll even think about getting off their asses. Most we can hope for is that they start looking tomorrow or within the next couple of days. Which, as we both know, is going to be too late. She's dead. You know it. I know it. The kid's dead."

He turned his sad eyes toward Simon. "Bastards even grabbed her suitcases. I don't know if they planned it that way, or they just did it on the spur of the moment. But they took all her stuff and when the cops check out my place there isn't a fucking thing to say she'd ever been there. Not one fucking thing, unless you count my word, and believe me when I tell you that ain't enough when it comes to police regulations. The fact that I know guys down at the precinct don't mean shit. They don't make the rules."

He looked down at his cigarette. "One thing's for sure. I used to think I wasn't getting old, that I was only getting better. Used to say, I can still jump as high, I just can't stay up too long. Well, forget that. I ain't as smart as I used to be and it cost Molly her life. They followed us from Manhattan and I never picked up on it. Cut my fucking telephone wires, then used that broad to . . . Jesus."

"Nora Bart. According to Frankie, she's in town."

"That twat runs a game on me like you wouldn't believe and I fall for it. Gets me to open the door and I do everything but carry her over the threshold."

Simon said, "Tell me something. If you had it to do over again, same circumstances, would you do it any differently?"

D'Agosta refilled his coffee cup. "Maybe you ought to be asking Molly that. Ask her if she'd trust us with her life again." He looked at Simon. "You and me, we were supposed to keep her alive. Know what burns my ass? Tuckerman. Six to five he was there when the Japs wasted her. Just like he was there when they did Teriko."

He sipped coffee, then stared into the cup. "What did you tell Marsha?"

"She's cool, so I didn't have to tell her much. Told her I was skipping the second job, but she'd be paid for both. I also promised her five bills for taking me out to your place, no questions asked. Had to break our rule about that, especially when I saw your name in Frankie's file and I couldn't get you on the phone."

"I'll take care of Marsha. She knows I'm good for it. You understand why I had to bring in the cops."

"You said if a missing person turns up dead and you hadn't reported them missing, you might have a problem. Look, in your place I'd have done the same."

"In my place," D'Agosta said, "I'd blow my brains out if I had the balls."

For a few seconds Dag studied Simon as though seeing him for the first time. And not liking what he saw. "Man, nothing gets to you, does it? You're just sitting there, sipping tea as calm as you please. No tears, right? Shit, you could probably perform brain surgery with a rusty spoon in an earthquake and your hand wouldn't shake. You haven't been to bed all night but nobody could tell by looking at you. Tell me something: you feel anything 'bout what happened? 'Cause, man, I would really like to know."

Simon lifted up the top page on his memo pad, made a note, then placed the pad and ballpoint pen on the coffee table. He shifted in his chair until he was almost facing D'Agosta. "Okay, you got it out of your system. Now listen up, because I don't have time to wipe your nose or hold your hand. Any self-pity I felt, I got rid of it in Frankie's place when I looked at that file and saw our names. And in case you forget, my mother's name's at the top of that list."

He saw D'Agosta look away. "Right now, I'm trying to live with the fact that maybe she's already dead." He pointed to the tapes. "I know Raymond Manoa's been told to waste her. Now you want to look at me and tell me I don't feel anything?"

D'Agosta looked at the ceiling. "Hospital wants me to have a brain scan. They want to check the swelling in the back of my head. There goes five hundred bucks right there. This thing with Molly brought out a lot of shit I thought I'd forgotten about Teriko. I lose two women to the *yakuza*. Know what that feels like to a man who believes you should give your life for a woman if necessary?"

Simon's voice was soft. "Feeling bad isn't going to cut it. I don't like what happened to Molly and I don't like what it's doing to Erica. And for forty years, Rupert de Jongh's been a part of my mother's nightmares. Now all of a sudden the nightmare's come true for her and she's got to handle it alone. There's only one answer to all of this and that's to do something about it."

"Like what?"

Simon gripped his right wrist and began to rotate it, loosening the joint. "Like kill de Jongh. And Manoa. Marwood, too, if I have to."

D'Agosta sat up in his chair and looked at Simon for a long time. "You mean it, don't you."

Simon pointed to the cassette tapes. They'd been laid out on the coffee table in three verticle rows. "Frankie's tapes. First row: five tapes in English. Frankie talking to Raymond Manoa. Frankie talking to Nora Bart. Frankie in Hawaii talking to the La Serra brothers in New York, and wouldn't the feds like to hear that? Frankie talking to Manoa again. All long-distance calls, by the way. Erica was right."

Simon pointed to the second row of tapes. "These four are mixed. You got people speaking in English and Japanese. On all of them it's Frankie talking to a guy who has an English accent."

D'Agosta said, "The *gaijin*. Frankie's godfather."

"Rupert de Jongh. The little man who wasn't there. On these same tapes Frankie's talking to an Oriental who speaks piss-poor English. My guess is it's Kim Doo Kangnang, the Korean CIA guy my mother told me about. I've seen him once or twice. Very big on gold watches, Kim."

Simon pointed to the last three tapes. "All Japanese. Can't make heads or tails of them. Now, I know these tapes can't

be used in court. We're talking illegally obtained evidence,
no search warrants, no probable cause, shit like that. In any
case, I'd prefer to hand a couple of them over to a newspaper.
A newspaper that loves the good stuff, the real dirt."

D'Agosta snorted. "Your boy Manoa's dirty as they come.
Gun smuggling, narcotics trafficking, bagman on that new
luxury hotel going up on Oahu, the one that belongs to the
gaijin."

"The one Frankie says cost over $200 million. I thought
you missed that one." D'Agosta had fallen asleep in the chair
for an hour or so. Simon, rather than wake him, had continued listening to the tapes alone.

"I'm Italian. I got good ears. Let's back up a bit. You said
something about hitting three people."

"I'll get to that. First things first. You missed something
while you were asleep."

"Like what?"

"Like the tape that says that the *gaijin*'s bringing $50
million into Hawaii this weekend."

"You're kidding."

"One man," Simon said. "That's all they need to carry
it."

"One man bringing in fifty million? Hey, you're talking
about a lot of suitcases. One man?"

"One man with diplomatic cover."

"Marwood."

"Diplomatic cover and fifty million in rare stamps."

D'Agosta whistled.

Simon selected a tape from the first row and slipped it into
the recorder. "Listen up."

It was a conversation between Raymond Manoa and Frankie
Odori, one that started out friendly enough, with the detective
saying that he was closing in on Alexis Bendor and should
have that little matter taken care of in the next few days, as
the *gaijin* had ordered. And speaking of the *gaijin*, he had
something for Frankie to do.

MANOA: Marwood, the English guy? He's coming to Honolulu straight from Hong Kong.
FRANKIE: Hey, like tell me something I don't know.
MANOA: He's taking himself a little vacation and he's gonna
be carrying them stamps, which you know about. What you

don't know is the *gaijin* wants you to come here and pick'em up. Then he wants you to fly to the Cayman Islands and turn them over—

FRANKIE: Hey dude, you don't tell me what to do. Kim's supposed to take them stamps to the islands.

MANOA: Hey, bruddah, don't argue with me. I just work here. Your godfather feels this deal's too important to trust outsiders. You know how your people feel about Koreans. Marwood he's gotta trust and you, you're family.

FRANKIE: Jesus, man, I don't want to make no trip to Hawaii. I'm sick of that place. I'm always making trips there. I got a business to run, you know.

MANOA: Man, I don't wanna know. You got a complaint, you take it up with your godfather. All I know is your ass is supposed to be here this weekend to pick up them stamps. If I was you, I'd do it.

FRANKIE: I'm gonna call my godfather and straighten this shit out.

MANOA: Your privilege, brah. But I'm bettin' I see you in Hawaii and soon.

Simon removed the tape and replaced it with another from that same row. "In this one Manoa and Frankie get down a little bit. Probably made after Frankie talked to his godfather."

Simon pressed play.

Manoa did most of the talking, rubbing it in, saying Frankie'd been dumb to imagine he could get around his godfather. Fifty million dollars meant nothing had better go wrong, especially when you considered who owned those stamps. Some heavy-duty people, brah. Chinese politicians and generals in the Republic of China. Powerful people with secret bank accounts in Hong Kong banks. People who wanted their money out of the British Royal Crown Colony and in other countries long before their own system of government took over Hong Kong and made that money worthless. Or before the accounts were discovered and confiscated.

The *gaijin* had been smuggling their money out of Hong Kong for months, but never an amount as large as this. If anything went wrong, not even he could stand up to these people. They had more power in the Far East than any *yakuza* leader dreamed of. Their influence was everywhere. That's why Frankie could only obey his godfather, no matter how many bad meals he had to face in Honolulu. Frankie had better be at the Lauhala this Wednesday and no bullshit.

When the tape ended Simon said, "One problem. They never say exactly where or when the exchange will take place. I'm hoping that's on these Japanese tapes. Alexis and Paul will have to help me with that."

He rose from his chair, walked to the fireplace, then took a key from under the English bracket clock and began winding the timepiece. "I mentioned hitting Manoa, Marwood, and de Jongh."

D'Agosta stared at the lit end of a cigarette. "So you did, so you did. I was wondering when you'd get back to that. Even a proctologist takes on only one asshole at a time. But not you, goombah. You're going for three."

Simon said it was all tied in with the $50 million. Grabbing the money and killing the Hawaiian cop and the two Englishmen went together. D'Agosta said, "Sure it does. Anybody can see that." Except he didn't seem to be interested. Simon watched him toy with a disposable lighter, flicking it on and off, eyes on the flame. And the bitterness of a few minutes ago was now back in D'Agosta's voice.

The ex-cop said, "You always were a smartass. I bet you can sit on an ice cream cone and tell me what flavor it is. Excuse me, but right now I'm not in the mood for any off-the-wall shit. I just can't get used to losing women to the *yakuza*."

Placing the lighter on the arm of his chair, he held up an index finger. "You're talking about whacking a cop, Manoa. A cop you tell me is very popular in his hometown and may be going into politics."

"A cop who's very dirty. It's on tape. And he is going into politics, or so he tells Frankie. In any case, if he does anything to my mother he's dead. I don't give a shit if he's running for president."

"Okay, okay. Maybe, just maybe you might pull that one off." D'Agosta held up a second finger. "Marwood. A foreign diplomat. We're talking heavy-duty hit right here. Doing him ain't the same as running over a rabbit in the middle of the road."

"But it can be done. Fact is, he's the easiest of the three. I've already worked it out."

D'Agosta raised his eyebrows. "Try this one, señor. The

gaijin. Your friend and mine, Rupert de Jongh. You couldn't get near him if Jesus took you by the hand and led you every step of the way. He's on home ground, with no reason to leave. He's got ten thousand people guarding him, and he's got more political clout than the wise guys in this country ever dreamed of. Hey señor, know what your problem is? You just don't think big enough.''

The ex-cop looked down at the floor and shook his head. ''How the hell you gonna beat those fucking people? Tell me how. And why didn't they smoke me when they had the chance?''

Simon said, ''You haven't done anything to them. My guess is you and Erica have nothing to worry about.''

''Be still my heart.'' He looked up.

''Let's suppose by some miracle you get lucky and take out all three of them. What about de Jongh's people? In case you haven't noticed, they have very long memories.''

''I've noticed. That's where the fifty million comes in. It's going to get the *yakuza* off our backs, me and Alexis.''

''If I didn't know better, I'd swear you were engaging in the abuse of certain controlled substances. Killing ain't your style, goombah. Stealing's what you do best. Wanna tell me what makes you think you can change your game and win, especially against the *gaijin?*''

Simon turned his back to D'Agosta and stared at the hands on the English bracket clock, thinking that his secret side, those things he'd done in Nam and had tried to forget, hadn't really gone away. They were in hiding, buried in a corner of his mind, lurking there and waiting for a fitting time to reappear. His mother's past had just done the same thing to her. In Nam Simon had been ordered to kill, and that's what he'd done and done well. But after a while he'd caught himself enjoying it. Wasting people had taken the place of thrill seeking and that's when he knew he had to stop or go under. Stop or become less than a human being. Working for the CIA wasn't why his mother and John Kanna had rebuilt Simon's crippled body after the Banzai Pipeline wipeout.

He looked over his shoulder at D'Agosta. ''You asked me why I think I can win against the *gaijin*. You already know the answer. Matty told you why.''

He watched D'Agosta think, saw him remembering Matty saying that when it came to taking out guys in Nam, Simon was in a class by himself. "Thanks, but no thanks," D'Agosta had told Matty. "No way I'm working with some burnt-out looneytune. Never mind how good you think he is. I won't have anybody like that around me if I can help it."

"Check him out," Matty'd said. "The guy's not what you think. He can turn it off, the weird shit. I've seen him do it, seen him go days, weeks, acting normal, laid back, like he never even heard of Vietnam. But come time to get down, just point him in the right direction and get out of his way. You gotta remember, Dag, the man didn't act on his own. He did what he was told to do, no more, no less. But he did it with style. I tell you, just watching him was a trip."

Matty had told Dag about the CIA trouble, when the case officer had tried to waste them both. That little incident had been Simon's last killing in Vietnam. After that he'd had it. No more wasting anybody. He'd joined the special CIA combat intelligence unit because he and his mother needed the money. The Japanese guy she and Simon had been living with died, leaving behind tax problems that had wiped out his estate. To put bread on the table Simon's mother had gotten him a job. He was to help train a new and top secret CIA unit in *ninja* tactics. The military in certain foreign countries were going in for similar training and it was time the United States caught up. Simon took the job to please his mother, but it soon became boring. He didn't want to instruct. He wanted action.

Assigned to Saigon, he and Matty took to their work with enthusiasm. They stole documents, broke into safes, blackmailed politicians and businessmen, served as couriers and bodyguards, ran security checks, planted false information with newspapers, and terminated their share of Asians, not to mention non-Asians. Simon was the best, so at the request of the CIA he did a few jobs on his own. Some of those jobs involved terminations that had to appear as if the party involved had died a natural death. Matty said it was beautiful to watch Simon Bendor, Mr. B., in action.

But Mr. B. couldn't win the war alone. There came a time in the battle for hearts and minds when it was obvious that Charley was going to win and the only thing an American could do was get out with his ass in one piece. And engage in a bit of profitable thievery, if at all possible. A Vietnamese interpreter named Loan, who was attached to Simon's unit, told him about a scam being run by a CIA case officer. The officer had arranged for a mercy airlift to leave the country. Vietnamese orphans to be escorted out of Saigon and back to the States by women. Nice idea. Except that all of the women would be handpicked by the case officer and carrying contraband belonging to him and a couple of friends. Contraband like embezzled CIA funds, gold, narcotics, diamonds.

Loan's wife and two kids had been bumped off the flight, to be replaced by a woman obligated to the case officer. Loan was worried about his family's safety. He'd been promised help by the Americans and the Cong were tightening a noose around Saigon's neck. He didn't care about himself, but at least the Americans could take care of his wife and two sons. Could Simon help?

According to Matty, Simon, who didn't like the case officer, simply threatened to blow up the plane just before takeoff if Loan's family wasn't aboard. With his reputation, who wanted to find out if he was serious? Loan's wife and sons were given passage out of Saigon, but the case officer, with one more flight of contraband to go, thought he'd have more peace of mind if Simon were dead.

The case officer ordered Matty, Simon, and Loan to go to a safe house on the edge of the city and destroy important papers hidden there. The case officer said the CIA didn't want those papers falling into the hands of Charley. Loan was going along to check anything written in Vietnamese and see what might be worth saving.

It was Loan, with connections to the Saigon underworld, who learned that it was a trap. Four South Vietnamese carrying Viet Cong I.D. would be waiting in the house to kill Matty, Loan, and Simon. The hired guns were deserters, scumbags who survived by hooking up with people like the case officer, who was always in need of scumbags. Simon could have walked away from the trap, but that wasn't his style. Mr. B. always ran toward the danger.

On his own he went to the house, snuck in, and killed the four would-be assassins. But he did not consider the matter closed. Back in Saigon he went after the case officer. He snuck into the guy's hotel, past armed Montagnard tribesmen in the halls and on the roof, and got into the case officer's bedroom. Mr. B. didn't zap the dude, Matty said. All he did was cold cock the sucker while he slept, then cut the Achilles tendon of his right leg, crippling him for life. And when the case officer came to, he was wearing a necklace of fresh ears cut from the hired killers.

Matty said you had to look at it in the light of what was going down over there. It was a crazy time and there were no rules when it came to staying alive. The case officer had the CIA behind him. All Simon had was himself, and what he was saying to the guy was if you're gonna bring it to me, you better bring it good.

Believe it or not, Matty told D'Agosta, the whole thing ended right there. The CIA guy thought Simon was out of his mind, to be avoided at all costs, because if you tried to kill him and blew it, well, what could I tell you? D'Agosta understood the killings, but the ears and the crippling was something else again. It took a lot of talking by Matty to get D'Agosta to agree to even see Mr. B.

In Simon's living room, D'Agosta rubbed his sore arm and said, "You really think you can pull it off? Hit the three of them?"

"If I don't, I'm dead. Me and Alexis. It's all or nothing."

"What about the fifty million? How does that get you off the hook?"

"You heard Manoa and Frankie. Those stamps belong to some heavy people. Even the *gaijin* can't afford to have them as enemies. So if those stamps don't get to where they're going, who takes the blame?"

"De Jongh."

"And if he's dead?"

"Whoever takes over for him."

"Exactly. And the replacement's going to have his hands full just trying to survive. You heard Frankie mention the gang war going on in Japan, about how his godfather needed the guns they're getting from the La Serra brothers. When de Jongh goes down, the sharks in the underworld are going to smell blood and they're going to move in."

D'Agosta said, "You plan on giving de Jongh's replacement the stamps if he promises to leave you alone?"

"Shit no. He couldn't make a promise like that and live. Especially not to anybody who took out his leader. No, I've got something else in mind for those stamps. When I get my hands on them, that's the last de Jongh or his people will ever see of those little pieces of paper."

D'Agosta's smile was genuine. "You are a silver-tongued devil, let me tell you. You almost got me believing you can do it."

"There's a way." Simon walked to the coffee table and picked up the photograph of Kasumi and her husband. "There is definitely a way. This, plus Kasumi's diary, which is her voice come to life. I'd give anything to see the *gaijin*'s face when he's holding them both in his hands."

There was a long silence. Then D'Agosta said, "You think he'll come? If he does, oh, boy. Now that's going to be some kind of party. Tell you something: nobody in his right mind's going to bet the rent money on you, but still."

"I'm betting he can." It was Erica. She stood at the top of the sunken living room, barefoot and in one of Simon's robes. Her eyes were bloodshot and her face puffy from weeping. Simon had telephoned her in Atlantic City with the news of Molly's disappearance and Erica had left the game immediately, hiring a car and driver to take her to Queens. She'd been losing heavily. Molly's disappearance, however, was an even bigger loss.

"I couldn't sleep," she said. "Any word from the police?"

D'Agosta looked away and mumbled no. Erica came down into the living room, walked over to the ex-cop, and hugged him. Both wept. She said, "Wasn't your fault, Joe. Any man, any real man, would have opened that door. This thing with Molly didn't start with you, it started in L.A. weeks ago. They were determined to get her, just like they're determined to get Simon and his mother."

Simon told her about Marwood, about how he'd betrayed Alexis to Rupert de Jongh on two occasions, forty years apart.

Erica stood beside D'Agosta's chair and held his hand. "Unreal. Whatever you do to that sonofabitch, you ought to do it twice." She took one of D'Agosta's cigarettes, lit it, and dragged deeply. The coughing started almost immediately. Another drag and the coughing stopped. She sat down in Simon's chair. He came over to her and after they kissed she said, "Molly's dead. The sooner I face it, the better. Finding her corpse is only going to make it official."

She stopped, fought for control, and with tears rolling down her face, continued. "I intend to do whatever I can to help you and don't bother telling me I can't. It's the only thing that will keep me from coming apart."

Simon, on his knees beside her, said, "You're out of it as far as the *yakuza* is concerned. I want you to know that."

She blew smoke at the ceiling, then looked at him. "I'm in."

D'Agosta shrugged. "What the hell. One of these days I'm gonna run into Matty, wherever the hell he is, and we're gonna exchange war stories. This way I'll have one of my own that even he can't top. Let's go for it, goombah."

The telephone rang before Simon could answer. He said, "Alexis," leaped to his feet, and ran to an end table. He snatched up the receiver, listened, then put a hand over the receiver's mouth, grinned, and whispered "Alexis" to D'Agosta and Erica. To his mother he said, "Hey, ace, where've you been?"

"Around the world and back again, it feels like. I'm at the airport in Honolulu. Just landed. What about the photograph? Did you—"

"Listen. I didn't leave the picture with Frankie. Now, before you flip out, let me explain."

She didn't want to hear it. In a tired, sad voice she said, "Simon, I asked you to do one thing for me and you couldn't bring yourself to do it. You gave me your word." She sounded on the verge of tears.

"I know, I know. Just hear me out—"

He could feel her backing off before she even said a word. "Look, if you don't mind I'm too played out to argue. If you didn't want to do it, all you had to do was say so. Why get my hopes up? You have any idea what I'm going through? No, I suppose you don't. Your self-regard was always rather high and you haven't changed much over the years. I'm going to call Paul and see if I can stay out in the valley with him for a few days. I'm afraid to go back to the house or even to the shop, but I'm sure you think that's funny. Maybe I am some sort of joke to you in my declining years, but you did give me your word you'd leave that picture with Frankie Odori."

"Ma, please."

"Thanks for nothing." She hung up.

Simon almost pulled the phone from the wall in frustration. She could be pigheaded at times and this was damn sure one of those times. Self-regard. Maybe. But not now. He was a believer and he wanted her to know that. He began dialing again, ignoring Erica, who asked him if anything was wrong.

There was. He had a mother whose life was characterized by perseverence. A headstrong woman all the way, but if she hadn't been that way he'd still be in a wheelchair. Or dead.

When he finished dialing, he waiting, willing the phone to ring at the other end in a hurry. When Paul Anami answered, Simon didn't give him a chance to say much. He told him that Alexis would be calling and to take care of her as a personal favor. Tell her that Simon did believe her, believed everything she'd said. Alexis would understand. No time to go into it now, but it might be a good idea if Paul and Alexis both checked into some out-of-the-way hotel for the next few days. Find someone to take care of the shops. Simon couldn't explain, but it had to do with the *yakuza*, with that trip Simon had made to Tokyo. Something had gone wrong, seriously wrong. After Paul and Alexis had found a place he was to call here and leave a number on the service where he could be reached. And don't leave the hotel until Simon got there.

Paul sounded overwhelmed by it all. He hardly said a word, but then again Simon didn't give him much chance to talk.

When Simon hung up Erica came to him and he took her in his arms. "She didn't give me a chance to explain about the picture, about the file, the tapes," he said. "I'm leaving for Hawaii. Got to get to her as soon as possible. One of de Jongh's people in Hawaii might spot her. Shit."

Erica said, "We'd better get started."

He drew back to look at her, at the face he'd always thought of as both strong and beautiful, and he heard her say again, "We'd better get started."

In Honolulu Raymond Manoa sat in Paul Anami's living room, feet on a koa wood table, while he toyed with a crystal goblet and watched the antique dealer hang up the phone. Mr. Paul, bless his heart, couldn't have been more accommodating. He'd said all the right things to Simon Bendor and his mother. The old lady, especially, had been persuaded. Come on out to the valley, Mrs. Bendor, and make yourself to home. Be my guest for as long as you like. My house is your house. Beautiful, Mr. Paul. Fucking beautiful.

And her little boy, Simon, helped set it up. Ain't that a bitch.

Manoa put down the goblet, swung his feet to the floor,

and rose. After yawning and stretching he walked over to stand behind Anami's bamboo chair. The antique dealer, a nervous tic near his left eye, looked up at the detective submissively. The man's got no fight left in him, Manoa thought, but he does have a lot of gratitude. The detective began massaging Anami's shoulder muscles and the back of his neck, doing it gently, expertly, while humming "Rock of Ages." Eventually he used both thumbs to softly pressure the base of the skull, something he knew would cool out Mr. Paul. Anami was quiet, unresisting. He might still freak out, but not before Manoa got all possible use out of him. At the moment Manoa was being a good samaritan, here to help a man who was in trouble.

Leaning over the chair he put his mouth to Anami's ear and whispered, "I'm your friend, Mr. Paul, sir. With you all the way. See, the problem is nobody believes a word you're sayin'. Cops, people at the hospital who treated you, I mean nobody believes word one. You say you been raped, okay? They say you're gay and maybe what went down wasn't really a rape. Like it was just a party with some crazy friends that got out of hand, know what I'm sayin'? Believe me, I know what I'm talking about."

Manoa stood up while continuing the massage. "Me, I believe you. I'm on your side, but I'm the only one. Now you just do like I tell you and I see nobody bothers you no more. Trust me, bruddah. Trust 'Big Ray.' Hey, ain't it time for them pills you take?"

PART FOUR

Chi.
Concentration of total
strength through
meditation.

All things come into existence,
And thence we see them return.
Look at the things that have been flourishing:
Each goes back to its origin . . .
It means reversion to destiny.
Reversion to destiny is called eternity.

—LAO TZU,
TAO TE CHING

Twenty-Two

LOS ANGELES INTERNATIONAL AIRPORT
AUGUST 1983

Nora Bart stepped onto the C bus, found a window seat not
too far behind the driver, then took off her shoes and began
massaging her feet. She was still on remote, wiped out by jet
lag and the Percodan she'd taken to ease the pain of the
beating received from the *yakuza* in New York. The drug had
left her with a touch of nausea and dizziness, but at least she
was alive. Which was more than you could say for Molly
January.

Still, this was one bus ride Nora Bart was not looking
forward to, not at eight-thirty in the morning. And on an
empty stomach. She'd already spent an hour in the arrivals
terminal because the dipshits at the airline had lost the Louis
Vuitton bag she'd bought at Kennedy Airport before taking
off for L.A. What freaked her out was that the bag contained
two new pairs of shoes, an $800 sweater she'd gotten on sale
for $300, and a Sony Walkman with a bitching speaker. The
airline people had apologized, but that wasn't the same as
getting the bag back.

And there was the bus ride itself, a ride she'd taken with
Victor a few times. She was on her way to the airport garage,
where she'd left her car, but she wouldn't be getting there any
time soon. All of the terminal buildings were arranged in a
gigantic oval and the C bus would be stopping at each one,
picking up and discharging passengers before finally making

its way to a huge parking island of stacked garages. It was not the quickest ride in the world. Not by far.

Nora Bart would be lucky to get to her car by nine o'clock. After that it was another hour and a half north on the Pacific Coast Highway to Victor's Malibu Beach home, where she was going to pick up some clothes. And Victor's car. He wouldn't be using his Thunderbird anymore and she had plans for it. At Kennedy she'd bought a one-way ticket from L.A. to Toronto, leaving tonight. Between now and then she'd pack, sell the Ferrari, and use Victor's car to return to the airport.

How long would she stay in Canada? A month. Forever. Right now she had no way of knowing. All she knew for sure was that she'd gotten some bad vibes in New York, especially when she was being punched out. That's when she'd decided that if she lived through the Jacuzzi boys' little scenario, she would definitely split from L.A.

Getting beat up was necessary, she'd been told. If she didn't look or act like a woman in trouble, the man in the shop might become suspicious. What choice did she have? So she'd gone along with it, hoping to God they didn't kill her. She'd tried to protect her face, but the weight lifter with the rotten tooth had pushed her hands aside and laid into her, knocking her silly, telling her not to scream or it would get worse. She was sure the bastard was getting off on it.

Anything had to be better than being in Molly January's shoes. Nora Bart hadn't seen her die, but you didn't have to be there to know that the Jacuzzi boys would do a real gross-out on her as they'd done on Teriko Ohta and a few others. Nora Bart was at least on this side of the grave. Though for a minute or two back in New York she'd thought the weight lifter fully intended to clean her clock. But after they'd gotten their hands on Molly January, they'd dropped Nora near a taxi stand and said she was free to return to L.A. She wasn't needed anymore. Hallelujah.

On the C bus, she looked at her reflection in a compact mirror. Black eye almost hidden by the Ray-Bans. Bruised left cheek covered by makeup. Thank God the lip wasn't any worse. On the trip back a flight attendant had given her ice to hold against her mouth and that had stopped the swelling. Whether in L.A. or Toronto, she'd need time to heal if she planned on hustling. You couldn't count on getting much for damaged goods.

She was going to rest a couple of weeks, maybe do some group therapy while in Canada. Right now she felt uncentered, too tense and unbalanced after what she'd gone through in New York. Too much negative energy in that town. When she returned to group she'd be able to process it out, go over things in her head. From there she'd move on to creating her own reality, one without any obligation to the Jacuzzi boys. Chisel that thought in granite.

The C bus was slower than usual because of the construction going on at the airport. Some bus riders were fascinated by what was going on, by the building of a new five-story international terminal, a new domestic terminal, and additional parking space. Nora Bart, sorry to say, wasn't one of those who were fascinated.

To tart with, the fucking Percodan was making her sick. God, she wished she had some blow; she'd done the last of her coke on the plane, sitting in that tiny toilet and praying they didn't hit an air pocket and spill the shit. She could also use some Darvon, which she kept in her West Hollywood apartment. It helped with the pain she suffered as a dancer. All dancers had knee problems; choreographers were becoming more and more demanding, creating incredibly difficult and intricate steps to call attention to themselves. Bastards. They didn't have to dance, but they insisted on you ruining your body to make them look good. They could all fuck off and die.

The construction itself was driving her up the wall. The noise was unreal. Jackhammers, generators, concrete mixers, steel girders banging against one another. The racket, plus coming down from the Percodan, was turning her into a basket case. When she got this antsy she had to eat, stuff her face until her jaws ached. The breakfast they'd given her on the plane—orange juice, sweet roll, coffee—was a joke. On the way to Victor's she'd stop off at Fung's for chicken with pine nuts and minced squab on lettuce leaves. How about fried ice cream for dessert. Oh, yes.

She watched the bus pull up to the AeroMexico terminal. Christ, here it comes. Tons of Mexicans piled on carrying cheap suitcases, shopping bags, cassette recorders, guitars, children. Mucho children. Nora Bart wondered if any of the

Mexicans were carrying jumper cables, since they were the biggest car thieves in L.A., bar none. A small, dark woman in sandals and a red dress sat down beside Nora Bart. She looked like a teenager, but she was carrying a baby in her arms. Frankly, the kid was sort of cute. Dark eyes, pretty smile, and hair like his mother's. Last year Victor had used Mexican workmen to repair the sun deck on his beach house, but he wasn't at all happy with what they'd done. They were so stupid, he said, that you had to give them toilet paper with instructions printed on every sheet.

Maybe it was the lack of sleep or the end effect of the Percodan, but Nora Bart suddenly found herself nodding out. At the parking island she woke up to find the bus jammed, with people standing in the aisles and pushing against those who were seated. The cute Mexican baby had suddenly started crying and the mother had unbuttoned her dress to give him a breast. Great. And across the aisle some redneck with a voice that wouldn't quit was yelling at a skinny little Vietnamese who'd been looking over the redneck's shoulder at his newspaper. Nora Bart put her hands over her ears.

The driver opened the doors and the bus started to empty out. She decided to stay right where she was until there was room to move. Going up against this crowd was like running into a brick wall. When everybody else was off, then and only then would she get up. Talk about being jumpy. If she didn't get some food soon, she'd go bananas. The more she thought about it, the more pissed she became at the airline for losing her new bag. If she hadn't had to spend an hour chasing it down, she'd be at Victor's by now or at least somewhere taking in nourishment.

After what appeared to be the last passenger stepped off the bus, Nora Bart put on her shoes and stood up. Whoa. Dizzy. She gripped the seat, eyes closed, then opened her eyes to stare at the back of the bus, focused, and then her jaw dropped. There was one passenger remaining, a slim Japanese in sunglasses, a cream-colored silk shirt, gold chains, and shoulder-length black hair. His nose was flat, as though he'd been struck in it several times, and he cracked his knuckles while staring at Nora Bart.

She knew him, Jesus, did she know him. Jimmy Haito. A few years ago he'd been a lightweight boxer around L.A. and in Hawaii under the name Jimmy Hi-Ho. Now he was a *yakuza* enforcer. He'd killed two people that Nora Bart knew of.

Her mind tried to lie to her, but her fear rejected the untruth. She knew why Jimmy Hi-Ho was at the airport. Those bad vibes she'd had in New York were coming back stronger. The Jacuzzi boys never had any intention of letting her live. They'd been running a game on her all the time and they'd get her like they got Victor and Molly January and like they'd soon get the Bendor guy and his mother. Victor was right. They were all pricks. Frankie, Kisen, Jimmy Hi-Ho, and the *gaijin*. Especially the *gaijin*.

Jimmy Hi-Ho adjusted his dark glasses on his long face. "Hey, Nora, hey, mama. Why you go to Canada? Don't you know it gets cold up there?"

He leaned forward, arms on the seat in front of him. He puckered his lips and made kissing noises. "Come on back here with me so's we can talk."

Nora Bart stood rigid in the aisle, hearing the driver say, "You getting off or what?"

She thought of how Victor had died, then reached into her shoulder bag and pulled out his pretty gun. The bus driver, a plump black man, saw the piece and said, "Jesus," then leaped from his seat and through the open door, landing on the pavement and wincing in pain.

Nora Bart aimed the gun at Jimmy Hi-Ho and pulled the trigger three times. One bullet cobwebbed part of the back window, another hit the metal top of a seat and set off sparks, and the third buried itself in the aisle floor.

Jimmy Hi-Ho, scrunched down between the seats, yelled she was fucking crazy, that he wasn't carrying a piece, that all he wanted to do was talk. Nora Bart didn't believe him, so she fired again, hitting the overhead luggage rack. Jimmy Hi-Ho, down on the floor and hidden from her, yelled, "Knock it off, man, fucking knock it off and let's talk."

Nora Bart heard the sirens, heard people screaming as they ran to get away from the bus, and she felt sick to her stomach, felt it was all too much to handle by herself, especially with Victor not around to take care of things.

She sat down in the seat where a teenage Mexican mother had been, kicked off her red stiletto heels, looked down at her lap, then put the gun barrel in her mouth and pulled the trigger. At the crack of the .38, she fell back on the seat, landing on her side, the curled fingers of one small hand coming to rest on the studded dog collar around her neck.

Twenty-Three

Alexis Bendor loved the guest towels in Paul Anami's Nuuanu Valley home. Each of the ones laid out in her room was a different size and color, and smelled of a particular Hawaiian flower. What superb taste Paul had, along with a quality of imagination missing in most people. Since Alexis knew her flowers, it was a pleasant challenge to identify each towel according to scent. Gardenia, hibiscus, orchid, ginger, and allamanda, a Brazilian flower that had somehow found its way to the islands. Dear sweet Paul. She'd loved him ever since he'd pulled Simon from the water after the Banzai Pipeline had almost killed him.

Tonight, after covering her face with avocado paste, she wiped off the paste with tissues and rinsed in warm water. Then she patted her face dry with the gardenia towel, then the allamanda. Heaven. There'd been a time when she could afford to eat avocados at least twice a week, but that was before the 800 calories found in each one started going to her hips. Meanwhile, you couldn't beat avocado as a face cream, something known by every woman in Hawaii. As for cleansing the skin from within, lemon juice and water was all you needed. Unfortunately, nothing could remove the lines in her face. As Moms Mabley said of old age, you just woke up one morning and you got it.

Alexis's room was on the second floor and across from the

master bedroom. It was high-ceilinged and wallpapered, with
a Thai teak parquet floor and an overhead fan. With her hair
in curlers, she sat in a four-poster bed wearing one of Paul's
caftans and read Kasumi's diary. A crystal goblet of water
and lemon juice stood on a night table, separated from Alexis
by mosquito netting, which hung from the bed on all sides. A
small clock radio next to the goblet softly played a Bach
mass.

Was Kasumi only sixteen when she'd written most of this?
What a smart kid she'd been, one with a sense of humor and
a rare talent for self-analysis. True, she'd been hurt at being
sold by her parents, but she'd forgiven them and was determined to do her duty by acceding to their wishes. Alexis
found Kasumi's love for Rupert de Jongh both naive and
serious, not too surprising since the girl was, after all, a
teenager. De Jongh was her savior, the god who'd delivered
her from a disgusting life. He could do no wrong.

Nor did she fear him, as so many others did. She wrote
freely of the jokes she played on the *gaijin,* of the times she
disagreed with something he'd said, of the need to have her
heart and lips always be one. Better silence than a lie, she'd
written.

As wartime romances went, this one had its moments.
Despite whatever deprivations they may have encountered,
the two somehow managed to continue the eternal lovers'
custom of gift giving. Nothing elaborate. A comb. A fountain
pen. A book of poems. A fan. And in both cases each was
touched by the other's thoughtfulness. Neither seemed to consider gratitude a burden. Had Alexis not been victimized by
de Jongh, she might have found his affair with Kasumi
touching. But each time she felt a twinge of sympathy, she
touched the scar tissue where her right ear used to be.

The diary contained a few English phrases patiently copied
down by Kasumi at de Jongh's insistence. On the whole,
however, the young girl did not like the language, which she
thought too limiting and not very subtle. Once, when de
Jongh had been forced to briefly leave her alone, she'd
written, "I am afraid of losing what I have; I am afraid I will
not get what I most want." What she wanted and was afraid
of losing had been the *gaijin.*

And hadn't de Jongh killed for her?

Their love was real enough.

Alexis rubbed her eyes to keep awake, then checked the entries mentioning de Jongh's promise to carry a lock of Kasumi's hair back to Japan upon her death. He'd made that promise as a samurai and such an oath was never to be taken lightly. To keep it meant honor and glory in many lives to come. To break it meant dishonor and shame for equally as long. Rupert de Jongh had two reasons for living up to that vow: he was more Japanese than the Japanese. And Kasumi had once saved his life.

Alexis had seen him at the *Bon* festival in Honolulu, so there was no chance de Jongh had forgotten Kasumi. He'd shown up to honor her. The *gaijin* was not a man to forget. The Japanese revered their dead. *Bon* festivals were celebrated throughout July and into August, with singing, dancing, food, and lights—candles, lanterns, bonfires.

Alexis had tried discussing Kasumi and de Jongh with Paul, but he seemed more tense than usual, going to his medicine more frequently than he'd done in the past. He seemed depressed. His conversation didn't have its usual bite; the bitch wit was missing. Was he off his feed because a new lover was making him suffer the tortures of the damned? Alexis, who'd grown used to Paul's affairs, didn't press him. He might talk to her about it later and he might not. Let that be his decisioin.

Tense or not, Paul was still a good cook. He'd prepared dinner himself, whipping up a meal of *saimin,* clear noodle soup, thin-sliced raw fish wrapped around shredded white turnip, boiled spare ribs marinated in ginger, mango ice cream, and champagne. For some reason he'd sent his Filipino servant, Juan, away for a couple of days telling Alexis only that it was necessary. When he'd said that, Paul had looked toward the second floor of the house, as though someone was up there listening.

When Alexis had asked him if they were alone he'd hesitated, then said there wasn't anything to worry about. Everything was being taken care of and out came the pills again. She wondered if Paul had a loved one stashed upstairs, but if so that was his business. Alexis was just too tired to care.

She closed the diary. Talk about exhausted. This was how she used to feel before Simon had mapped out a diet and exercise program for her. Simon. Why hadn't he left the photograph with Frankie as promised? And what was this

business about believing everything she'd said? That was the
message she'd gotten from Paul. Did it mean he believed
Rupert de Jongh was alive and intended to kill her? She
wished she knew, because if Simon was going to help her it
would make all the difference in the world. De Jongh was a
dangerous man, but he wasn't as tough as Alexis's son.
Nobody was.

Something would have to be done soon about getting de
Jongh and Kasumi together, because Kasumi had only days to
live. If she died before Alexis could make use of her . . .
Damn unfair of Simon not to keep his word. That photograph
would have been just the bait to lure de Jongh within range.
The bait to lure the *gaijin* to his death.

Alexis was too tired to clean her teeth or take the curlers
out of her hair. Sleeping with curlers was something she
usually avoided, a habit left over from her marriage and from
living with John Kanna. No woman alive looked good in
curlers. Therefore she should never allow a man to see her in
them. But she was too beat to lift her arms.

She put the diary and her bifocals in a drawer of the night
table and turned off the clock radio and night light. She was
asleep within seconds.

Raymond Manoa sat alone in the darkness of a second-
floor veranda in Paul Anami's home. He stared east, past the
tennis court and at the Koolau Mountains in the distance,
where he often gained spiritual strength by walking alone
over old Polynesian battlefields. Where he'd sit for hours in
an abandoned *luakini heiau,* a war temple once kept spiritually alive with human sacrifices conducted by his *kahuna*
ancestors. For Manoa this was the real and eternal Hawaii.

He looked to his left, at the window of Alexis Bendor's
room, which was next to his. Her light had just gone out,
meaning she'd turned in for the night. No hurry. Give her
time to get into a deep sleep before paying a social call. He
leaned forward, reached into a shopping bag at his feet, and
took out two small packets of macadamia nuts. After eating
them he went to the shopping bag again, this time for three
bananas, a large bag of potato chips, and a quart of coconut
milk. He chewed slowly, sitting upright in a bamboo chair
and bringing the food to his mouth with alternating hands.
When he'd finished he wiped his mouth and hands on the tail

of the yellow-and-orange *aloha* shirt he wore, then left his chair to walk to the edge of the veranda and listen.

All quiet around the house and grounds. Except for crickets, mosquitos, and doves. From the woods just beyond the house came the sounds of Japanese quail and bamboo partridges, birds Manoa's family had once hunted for food. And somewhere on the veranda there were click beetles, the bug that when upside down would snap its body by using a tiny spring hinge, repeating the process until it righted itself.

Anyone could have heard those sounds, but there was something else in the night that Manoa alone could hear. It was the *mana* telling him to come to the Koolau Mountains. And bring the *haole* woman for sacrifice. Do it now.

He looked at Alexis Bendor's room and wondered if it might not be too soon to go to her. She could still be awake or just sleeping lightly. The *mana*, however, must be obeyed. It commanded and instructed him in all things. It was too powerful to be opposed. Had it not given him the perfect excuse to be in Paul Anami's home when Alexis Bendor arrived? Offer Anami your help, the *mana* had said, for he is a frightened man, one willing to reach out to anyone. Tell him you will spend the night with him, a precaution against another attack by the man in the gourd mask.

Say nothing about me being here, Manoa told the antique dealer. Keep it a secret even from Mrs. Bendor. Might alarm her and we wouldn't want that, now would we? Tomorrow Manoa might bring her into the picture. Tonight, however, she didn't have to be told anything.

Should the telephone ring Manoa would pick up the extension. Just let the gourd man try anything. Manoa would be ready for him. And if Anami spotted an intruder on the grounds or anywhere near the house, just holler. Manoa would come running and, bruddah, would he take care of business. Might be a good idea, Mr. Paul, to send your servant, Juan, away for the next two, three days. Let the gourd man think you're alone. Maybe he'll make a move and we can put an end to this shit. Trust me, brah.

Talk about stroke jobs. This one belonged in the *Guinness Book of Records*. Mr. Paul swallowed every word.

Later on Manoa would have to ask Mr. Paul about this Kasumi woman Mrs. Bendor was getting herself worked up over. The detective had left his room to come to the top of the stairs and listen to the conversation between Anami and the old broad coming from the dining room. Interesting. Something about the *gaijin* and a woman who was supposed to be dead, but who wasn't dead after all. The woman's name was Kasumi and according to Mrs. Bendor she was on her way to being dead real soon. Kasumi lived in Los Angeles and had a bad heart. The *oyabun*, Mrs. Bendor said, really loved this Kasumi and would give anything to know she was still living. Now ready for the weird part? Mrs. Bendor was planning to use Kasumi to lure the *gaijin* to Los Angeles so she could waste him. No wonder he wanted that old broad taken out.

It was after Manoa returned to his room that he said, "Holy shit," because suddenly he remembered what the *gaijin* had been doing in Honolulu last week when he'd been spotted by Mrs. Bendor. He'd been at a *Bon* festival, where he'd gone to honor a dead woman. Could she have been the same woman now dying in Los Angeles? The only person who'd know for sure would be the *gaijin* and he'd have to fly to California to check it out. Would he do something crazy like that? He might, especially if Mrs. Bendor wasn't around to cause trouble. In any case the *oyabun* ought to be grateful when Manoa told him about Kasumi. Very, very grateful.

Manoa, in *aloha* shirt, jeans, and running shoes, picked up the shopping bag, left the veranda, then crossed the room and cracked the door. All clear in the hallway. He stepped from the guest room and quietly closed the door behind him. Then he crossed the hall and slowly opened the door to the master bedroom. Mr. Paul was curled on his side and sleeping like a baby, thanks to the sleeping pills Manoa'd insisted he take.

The detective pulled the door shut, then walked back across the hall to Alexis Bendor's room. He opened the door slowly, taking his time, not rushing things. When he heard her slight snore, he relaxed. The *mana* had said do it now and the *mana* had been right.

Manoa entered the room, closed the door behind him, and tiptoed over to the bed. There she was, lying on her back, mouth open, curlers in her hair, and dead to the world. Comin' at you, mama. Manoa had his hand in the shopping bag when Alexis moved. She turned away from him and rolled over on her stomach. The detective, who'd been holding his breath, exhaled. Then he took a strangling cord from the shopping bag and placed the bag on the floor. The cord, thin, gray, and slightly over three feet long, was almost one hundred years old and had once belonged to Manoa's great-grandfather, a bodyguard to Queen Liliuokalani, last royal ruler of Hawaii before the United States took the islands away from her by force.

Manoa waited a few seconds more and when Alexis Bendor didn't move, he did. He pulled back the mosquito netting, closed his eyes and heard the *mana,* then opened his eyes and leaped on the woman. He quickly wrapped the strangling cord around her neck two times, jammed a knee between her shoulder blades, then gripping the cord at either end pulled back hard.

The old woman came awake gasping for breath, fingers tearing at the cord, her legs thrashing about as though she were swimming. She tried to raise herself up and throw Manoa off, but she was wasting her time. He jerked back on the cord some more, lifting her head and shoulders off the bed, hearing her rasp like somebody trying to clear her throat, and then Manoa stopped because the *mana* told him to. The *haole* was almost dead, but not quite. The *mana* demanded she be alive when sacrificed.

The detective pulled handcuffs from the small of his back, cuffed the old lady's hands in front of her, and slung her over his shoulder. No problem. He could carry three old broads her size twenty miles if he had to. Picking up his shopping bag, he left the bedroom, walked downstairs and through the house until he reached the sliding glass doors leading outside. He pulled back the active door, stepped onto the patio, and closed the door behind him. Not a peep out of Mrs. Bendor. The second she made a sound Manoa was simply going to punch her out until she quieted down.

He circled the edge of Paul Anami's property, keeping away from the moonlight and walking in the shadows cast by eucalyptus, pine, banyan, and gnarled hau trees lying between the well-tended grounds and a surrounding woods. When he reached Anami's private dirt road Manoa began walking toward the highway. He was humming "Just a Closer Walk with Thee." After a quarter of a mile he stepped off the road and walked several yards until he found the clump of eucalyptus trees where he'd hidden the Mercury he'd borrowed from the *yakuza.* He threw the still unconscious Mrs. Bendor and the shopping bag into the trunk and locked it.

After backing the Mercury out onto the road he drove down to the highway, then headed east. Toward the Koolau Mountains.

Manoa took Alexis Bendor to a *luakini heiau* that had been abandoned for 150 years. Rats, wild pigs, and bats were the only things that came here now. There was the occasional *haole* backpacker who sometimes stumbled across the outdoor temple by accident. But being *haole* meant he was ignorant of Hawaiian history and what he saw had no meaning for him. Manoa reached the temple through a little-known secret passage in the sheer rock face of the cliffs forming the Koolau range. He had to fight the trade winds constantly blowing across the mountains; they were so strong that a man could lean against them. Hang-gliding enthusiasts were drawn to the cliffs even though a few of them got killed every year when the winds slammed them into the side of the mountains.

With Alexis Bendor slung across his shoulder, Manoa, flashlight in hand, followed a zigzagging course through the green-and-brown cliffs. Tonight the wind was crazy. It was strong enough to literally make his hair stand on end and it blew the old woman's caftan in his face, blinding him a few times and causing him to stumble and almost fall against rock walls sharp enough to cut him like a straight razor. Fucking rats. They were everywhere. Manoa wasn't afraid of them. He shone the flashlight on them and yelled like a mad man, sending the rats running in all directions.

After several hundred yards he came out into a small hidden valley, emerging in front of an abandoned sugar mill and the ruins of what had once been a prosperous sugar plantation. The federal government owned the land now and wasn't doing shit with it. It had taken control of the land when cane prices dropped and the owner couldn't pay his taxes. Beyond the mill and plantation lay an almost impenetrable rain forest. Manoa had all the privacy he needed.

The *heiau* itself was at the base of the cliffs, just feet away from the passage opening and separated from the mill and plantation by dark red powdery earth. It was an outdoor enclosure 150 yards long and 50 yards wide, with a stone altar at the top of a small terrace in the center. Manoa had rebuilt it alone and by hand, using lava stones, pili grass, and ohia timber, as the ancient Polynesians had done. But for the temple to become spiritually alive, blood had to be spilled here.

Manoa placed Alexis Bendor on the altar, then picked up four torches he'd hidden under the altar and stuck them into the sides of the cliffs. When he lit the torches, the rats appeared in the temple, their eyes tiny pinpricks of light in shadows cast by the flickering flames. They scurried back and forth, keeping their distance from the altar and Manoa.

Chanting in Polynesian, the detective crouched down beside the altar and reached into the shopping bag, and that's when Alexis Bendor sat up and smashed him in the face with her cuffed hands, catching him near the left eye and cheekbone, surprising the hell out of him, hurting him and knocking him down.

He landed on the stone terrace.

Alexis rolled off the altar and hit the ground running, down the terrace steps and heading toward the rain forest. Manoa got to his feet and ran after her. The old broad could motor. She tore across the red earth, kicking up dust, with the caftan flowing behind her like a cape. If it wasn't for the caftan flying around her in the moonlight, Manoa might have lost her in the darkness.

She was screaming, but with her damaged throat the sound came out like a croak. Dumb. Nobody around here to hear her and then the wind started up again, stronger than earlier, and it completely drowned out her voice.

If she made the rain forest he'd have a tough time finding her. He tried to run faster, feeling his chest burn with the effort, and then when he thought he might lose her, that she might get to the forest and disappear, a gust of wind wrapped the caftan around her and she tripped and Manoa had her.

He was on her before she could untangle herself and get to her feet. He kicked her in the stomach, the side, the back, then grabbed the cuffs and yanked her to her feet. He slung her over his shoulder, angry now because she was vomiting, and he heard her moan, but he didn't give a shit 'cause the bitch was gonna pay.

Minutes later she was back on the altar, legs drawn up to her chin and groaning with pain. Manoa, stripped to the waist, wore the gourd mask. He pushed her on her back and, using a piece of charcoal, tattooed her forehead with tiny dots. The dots were the mark of a *kauwa*, an outcast, those fit only for blood sacrifice. The old woman was crying and coughing because her ribs hurt where Manoa'd kicked her.

He finished the tattooing, then began chanting an ancient Polynesian prayer, ignoring her pleas, her questions, and when the chant ended he tore open her caftan, exposing her breasts. She begged him not to do it, but Manoa couldn't hear her. In the shrieking wind he heard only the *mana*.

When he spoke he used the words of a *mu*, the executioner who sacrificed tribal outcasts and prisoners of war to Ku, the war god. Finished, he brought his hand from behind his back and with a shark's-tooth knife made an incision on Alexis Bendor's bare chest. The incision was directly over the heart.

Twenty-Four

Simon Bendor walked onto Paul Anami's patio shortly before
eleven o'clock in the morning. He placed Kasumi's diary and
his mother's bifocals on a teakwood table, then sat down in a
wrought-iron chair. The chair next to his—Erica's—was empty.
She was at the far end of the grounds, smoking and staring at
the hau trees. And thinking of Molly.

Simon reached for a pitcher of papaya juice and refilled his
glass. His mother's purse and one of her pink plastic curlers lay
on his lap. He drank the cool, orange liquid with his eyes
on Paul Anami. Paul was edgy but doing his best to stay
calm. And doing his best to help Simon by translating the
tapes. At the moment he was listening to Japanese voices on
the portable cassette recorder in front of him. Paul's elbows
were on the table, hands over both eyes. Concentrating.
Maybe trying to block out what had happened to him during
the past two days. The *gaijin* had Manoa playing hard ball all
the way on this one.

Simon asked Paul if there was anything new, anything
they'd missed the first time. "Negative," Paul said. Rupert
de Jongh was still laying down the law to his godson Frankie
Odori, letting him know that an *oyabun* was to be obeyed
without question. Like it or not, Frankie was to be at the
Lauhala Hotel no later than Wednesday, today. Two days
later, Friday, Frankie was to take delivery of $50 million in

rare stamps, property of some very important officials in the
Republic of China. Frankie was to stop offering excuses or
objections and do as he was told.

Sir Michael Marwood of the British Foreign Office would
check into the Lauhala on Friday with the stamps. Time:
approximately 1:00 P.M. Frankie was to remain at the hotel
until Detective Manoa brought him the stamps. After a twenty-
four-hour wait Frankie was to check out of the Lauhala and
leave for Los Angeles. From there he was to fly to Mexico
City, then on to the Cayman Islands, where bankers would
convert the stamps to cash.

Paul told Simon that the *gaijin* was coming down hard on
Frankie for dragging his feet about going to Hawaii. Frankie
had to remember that the godson of an *oyabun* must set an
example. Disobedience or disrespect by Frankie was a signal
for others to do the same. "Don't take advantage of the
special place you have in my heart," the *gaijin* said. "From
the time I met your father, Omuri, at Oxford," he told
Frankie, "until his death twenty years ago, I never saw him
disgrace himself by refusing to obey a superior. Walk in his
footsteps, Frank-san, and be proud."

Simon watched Paul take a vial of pills from his shirt jacket.
When he'd washed two down with papaya juice Anami said,
"The *oyabun* takes the old ways seriously. He's like those
feudal samurai, who in the old days would slice you in half
for stepping on their shadow."

Paul tapped the cassette recorder. "Right now de Jongh is
explaining to Frankie why he doesn't want him to go near
Marwood. Apparently Marwood's diplomatic status makes
him the *yakuza*'s most valuable courier, bar none. Wouldn't
do to have Frankie be seen talking to him, especially since
Frankie's suspected of being *yakuza* by the American police."

Simon said, "De Jongh's a man who thinks ahead. Anything on when Manoa's taking the stamps to Frankie?"

"That's more or less up in the air. It's to be done that same
Friday, but after Manoa's meeting with Marwood. Marwood's
supposed to spend an hour or two with the people from the
British consulate and one or two reporters. Manoa will be
there as a one-man Hawaiian welcoming committee. The
gaijin's letting him decide when to hand over the stamps.
Frankie has to wait until his phone rings."

"Frankie's going to love that."

"Marwood's looking forward to Honolulu. According to the tape, he's stopping off here for a five-day holiday after some high-powered talks in Hong Kong about the colony's future. Lady Marwood's supposed to be joining him on Saturday."

"Everybody wants to catch the rays at Waikiki." Simon felt Erica's arms around him. He kissed the palm of her right hand, then drew her to the seat beside him. She looked drained, ready to pass out. Wrong time to get on her about smoking. He said to Paul, "The part about Kasumi. Go over that again for me, will you?"

Paul put the tape into reverse. "It's at the beginning. De Jongh talks about the old ways, festivals, rituals, about how important they are and about how the younger Japanese are forgetting these things. Too much Western influence, according to de Jongh. The old music being played on electronic instruments, taped music being heard in temples. De Jongh thinks it's disgusting."

Simon watched Paul press stop, then play. Paul's nerves were holding up fine. So far. Then again, who knew what was going on inside of the man? "Okay," Paul said. "Here's Frankie kidding his godfather. When de Jongh reaches *koki*, what the Japanese call rare old age, seventy years old, Frankie's coming back to Japan and throw him the biggest party the country's ever seen. Dancing girls, heavy-metal bands, door prizes, music videos, the works. 'My kind of celebration,' Frankie says. He's only teasing him, of course."

Erica stubbed out a cigarette in an ashtray. "Good old Frankie. He's a real card."

Paul held up one hand in a stop signal. "Here. De Jongh says he plans to light the *okuri-bi* this Sunday. That's a special bonfire the Japanese light in front of their homes in connection with the *O-Bon* festival. The fire furnishes light for the dead, who've returned to earth during the *Bon* celebrations, to find their way back to paradise. De Jongh's fire will be for Kasumi. He'll do it Sunday night in front of his Yokohama home."

Erica reached for Simon's hand. "I thought the *Bon* festival was two weeks ago," she said. "That's when Alexis saw de Jongh here in Honolulu."

Paul said, "*O-Bons*, which is another name for them, actually go on for close to a month. They start around the middle of July and last until the middle of August. Different Japanese provinces and communities have their own *O-Bons* during that time.''

He chewed on a thumbnail. ''You have to understand, the Japanese worship their dead. They look upon them as gods. The living and the dead depend on one another. The living keep the dead alive in memory. In return the dead help them by performing special favors from beyond the grave. I guess that's what de Jongh expects Kasumi to do for him.''

Simon asked Paul if he was absolutely sure about the bonfire for Kasumi. Any chance he could be mistaken? Paul shook his head. De Jongh had asked Frankie to say a prayer this coming Sunday night in memory of his own father. The *gaijin* would offer prayers at the private altar after the fire was lit. On that night let Frankie think of the fire burning in front of his godfather's Yokohama home.

Simon picked up his mother's bifocals. ''You said Alexis just disappeared during the night. Walked off without telling you where she was going.''

He watched Paul chew his lip, frowning. ''I can't understand it,'' Paul said. ''When I mentioned it to Detective Manoa this morning all he said was these things happen.''

''When he's around they happen. And he heard nothing?''

''He told me he dozed off for a couple of hours and didn't hear a thing.''

''She arrived here by taxi. How did he think she was going to get out of the valley?''

Paul shook his head, then coverd his eyes. He was having trouble coming up with answers that made sense. Push him too hard, Simon thought, and he goes over the edge.

Simon deliberately kept his voice even, nonthreatening. ''Her purse is still here. So's her luggage, keys to the house, keys to the bookstore.'' He picked up Kasumi's diary. ''Hard to believe she'd leave this behind. Hung onto it for years. Close to forty years.'' He flipped through the pages. ''Manoa know about the diary?''

Simon looked at Paul's face, seeing him torn between wanting to put Manoa out of his mind and trying to remember what he and the detective had talked about this morning. When Simon had told him Manoa was the man in the gourd mask, Paul had literally collapsed. Some ice cubes at the back of the neck had brought him around. Simon had also given

Paul a promise: "Manoa won't hurt you anymore. I can tell you he won't." Still, it had been a while before Paul could bring himself to listen to the tapes.

Paul said, "I don't think I mentioned anything about the diary. Hard to remember."

"I know."

"Before you and Erica arrived he was asking me about Kasumi and the *gaijin*. He said he'd overheard Alexis and me talking about them last night and it sounded like an interesting story. He was just curious, he said. Come to think of it, no, the diary didn't come up. Just didn't occur to me to mention it."

"You heard the tapes. You know Manoa works for the *gaijin* and has been ordered to kill me and my mother."

Paul looked away and began rocking back and forth in his chair. "And he said he's using one of your friends to do it."

Simon took mirrored sunglasses from a shirt pocket and put them on. "Like I said, don't give too much thought to Detective Manoa anymore."

Erica said to Simon, "Where's Kasumi's photograph, the one Alexis sent you?"

"Upstairs on the night table in her room. I left it there along with her note. Left them where Manoa can find them."

He felt his forearm being grabbed by Paul, who said, "You don't know him."

Simon waited.

Paul said, "Yesterday I told him I had to go away for a few days, just like you wanted me to."

"You mention my name?"

Vigorous shake of the head. "No, no. But he wouldn't let me leave, you see. I mean he didn't keep me here by force, but he—he dominated me. That's the only way I can put it. There's something about him, some sort of power. Very primitive. Simon, if I have to face him again—oh, God."

Simon stood up. "You won't. We're leaving, all of us. The *yakuza* probably know I'm not in New York anymore. Sooner or later they'll figure out I'm here."

Paul smiled. "You dressed up as a mailman. I'd pay to have seen that."

Simon handed the tapes to Erica, who put them in her shoulder bag. "I guess I did look spiffy in my blue uniform, leather bag, and pith helmet. Walked right out of my apart-

ment building in New York, strolled over to Central Park
West to make sure I wasn't being followed, then hopped into
a cab and went to Kennedy. Two hours later Joe shows up
with Erica and the two of us take off. This time Joe also made
sure he wasn't being followed."

Erica lit another cigarette. "At the airport in Honolulu,
Simon goes into the men's room and comes out in his pony-
tail, mustache, and granny glasses. Talk about your aging
hippie. Then it's separate cabs and here we are."

The telphone rang and a nervous Paul Anami knocked over
his glass, sending papaya juice splashing across the table.

No one moved.

Simon said, "Manoa."

Paul fingered the Maltese cross around his neck. "How do
you know?"

"I know."

The phone kept ringing. Simon asked about Juan, the
Filipino houseboy.

"Gone for a couple of days," Paul said. "Manoa's idea. I
had to look vulnerable."

Simon said he was going upstairs to put his mother's purse
and bifocals back on the night table. After that they were
going to his home to pick up a few items.

The phone continued to ring.

Simon placed his hands on Paul's shoulders. "When you
don't answer, he'll come out here looking for you. He has to.
You're the key to the Bendor family." He jerked his head
toward the garage. "Get the car. I'll be down in a minute."

"I guess I should take a few things with me, maybe make
some calls."

"No time. Manoa has to take me out as soon as he can.
Gaijin's orders, remember? You can call from my place. Oh,
I want you to call Juan. Tell him you changed your mind and
would like him to show up for work today as soon as possible. Don't say anything else. Just let him do what he always
does. Clean, gardening, whatever it is. Okay, old buddy, get
a move on."

As Paul walked toward the garage, Simon picked up the
pink curler. "Doesn't look good," he said to Erica.

She took it from him and stared at it. "I don't understand."

"I only found one in her room upstairs. Just one. The rest
were gone. Alexis wouldn't go anywhere with curlers in her

hair. If she left here wearing them it was because someone
forced her to do it. Her hair had to be just so, to cover the area
where she'd lost the ear.''

"Manoa."

"The *gaijin*'s number-one goon here in paradise."

Simon turned toward the house and the ringing phone.
"See you soon, Officer," he said softly.

Twenty-Five

Joe D'Agosta put down his coffee cup, then looked through the window of Olly's Lounge and across the street at the Corona Subway Yards. In its unending war on graffiti artists, the city had recently spent $2 million to surround the yards with a new chain-link fence topped by razor-sharp metal coils. Security guards now patrolled the grounds accompanied by nasty-tempered German shepherd dogs.

Jake Otto was telling D'Agosta this in a small, empty bar while a jukebox played country-and-western and the two of them sat at a wobbly table whose weak leg rested on a copy of Brendan Behan's plays. Tall, skinny Double O, who at 11:35 in the morning was drinking boilermakers, chasing each shot of Johnny Walker Red with a Budweiser. And who was telling D'Agosta that Irwin Tuckerman was poking around the coin dealer's life and trying to prove he was dirty.

Jake Otto said, "Tuckerman's only started to ask questions." He eyed what remained of his third beer and scotch. "Decided to get off my ass and become gainfully employed. Got tired of sitting at home pounding my pud, so I go over there." He nodded toward the subway yards. "Security guard, dispatcher, night clerk. Right now I'll take anything. Some broad wants to come along and pay me to let her sit on my face while she eats prunes, I'll take that. Except I don't know about working with those dogs they got over there. Dogs have teeth, lots and lots of teeth.''

He polished off the beer. ''I got a contact over there. Security. Ex-cop, what else? He's the one who told me about Feighen. Walter X. Feighen, to be precise.''

D'Agosta poured more coffee from a Plexiglas pot. ''Tuckerman's boy. His chief investigator and sometime bodyguard.''

''You got it, big guy. Feighen's bird-dogging you. Now ask me how I know.''

''How do you know?''

''Sol Birnbaum.'' Otto aimed a finger at the subway yards. ''He's my contact over there. I think you know Mr. Birnbaum.''

D'Agosta did indeed know Mr. Birnbaum. He'd been one of the shooflies who'd gone after D'Agosta and his partner, eventually driving them from the force. Five years ago Birnbaum himself had been forced to resign over the matter of some grand jury information that had ended up in the hands of the mob. With the help of an expensive lawyer and a promise to keep his mouth shut, Birnbaum had landed on his feet, coming up with a nice job in the city transit system and a chance at a second city pension. All D'Agosta could say to that was, ''Shit floats.''

''Birnbaum doesn't like you from your last movie,'' Otto said. ''The man absolutely, positively couldn't wait to tell me the good news about you and Tuckerman. Seems Tuckerman wants to know if you're dealing in stolen goods. Now where would he get an idea like that?''

Because the prick wants to know why Molly was stashed at my place, D'Agosta thought, instead of being stashed somewhere else. Anywhere else. Because the *yakuza* have connected Simon and me and if Tuckerman can prove I'm a fence, then it's a sure bet Simon's the thief who hit Tuckerman's house last week. Because Tuckerman's been around long enough to know that when it comes to stolen goods, check out antique dealers, flea markets, jewelers, and coin dealers.

D'Agosta said, ''Maybe Tuckerman suddenly decided he likes guineas and he's willing to let me swim in his private beach if I promise not to leave an oil slick.''

''I see.'' Jake Otto looked around for the bartender, caught his eye, and held up an empty shot glass. ''So far Mr. Feighen's not come up with too much. But he appears to be interested in anyone who ain't too fond of you. You know the routine. Start with a man's enemies. Ask if he still beats his wife, does he eat shit and bark at the moon? Does he go around smelling girls' bicycle seats.''

D'Agosta watched the bartender place Jake Otto's boiler-maker on the table, then walk the length of the bar to the jukebox. After punching several buttons the bartender, a size-able mick with receding salt-and-pepper hair, returned to the bar and a television set showing "The Price Is Right." On the jukebox Merle Haggard sang about an outlaw fleeing a posse.

Jake Otto said, "The only good thing Reagan did. He pardoned Merle Haggard."

D'Agosta raised both eyebrows. "No shit."

"Reagan was governor of California at the time and Merle was in the slammer. I think it was San Quentin, I'm not sure."

Jake Otto, cadaverous-looking in a shiny blue suit, white shirt, no tie, knocked down half of the beer and cocked his head at an angle to stare at the new subway yard fence. If the subject of Tuckerman and his curiosity about D'Agosta the dago was closed, so be it.

As for D'Agosta, he had no doubt that Tuckerman had probably watched Molly die, as he'd watched Teriko die. Molly was the reason Tuckerman was poking into D'Agosta's life. She didn't know Simon was a thief, but she'd seen him operate in Japan and knew he wasn't just your average citi-zen. Now the *yakuza* and Tuckerman knew it.

Molly's disappearance two days ago had made D'Agosta return to being supercautious. If nothing else, the police would be back the minute Molly's body appeared, and D'Agosta had better be ready for them. So he'd stopped using the phone in his shop and all calls with Simon would be done over the scrambler. That's also why he'd decided to meet Jake Otto somewhere other than Astoria. No reason for the cops to be watching D'Agosta, but after being taken by the *yakuza* the other night it was time to be more careful.

He said to Otto, " 'Preciate hearing about Tuckerman. If you don't connect with Birnbaum, I know a few people. Give me a holler. I'll see what I can line up for you."

"You have my undying gratitude for at least the next ten minutes."

D'Agosta took out his wallet, removed four twenties and

three tens, and tucked them into Otto's handkerchief pocket.
"We never had this little talk, you and me."

"What talk? And who the fuck are you anyway and what
are you doing sitting at my table? Jesus, they let anybody in
this place."

They toasted each other, coffee cup against shot glass. The
jukebox was playing the Hank Cochran tune "It Ain't Love,
But It Ain't Bad." Surprised the hell out of D'Agosta when
Jake Otto started singing along. Son of a bitch knew all the
words. D'Agosta thought of Molly January and the few hours
they'd spent together. No, it hadn't been bad at all.

Long Island City. In the basement of an abandoned chewing gum factory, Irwin Tuckerman stood in the shadows,
back to a crumbling staircase. Damn factory was falling
apart. All the windows were broken, a portion of the roof had
caved in, and anything worth stealing had long since disappeared. Vandals and vagrants had been having a field day
with the fucking place. Frankie Odori owned it. Owned the
surrounding empty acreage, too. And wasn't doing shit with
that, either. The land had become little more than a dumping
ground.

That was Frankie's problem. The putz just couldn't make
decisions. He preferred the soft life. The man didn't have the
onions to come out there tonight and watch his people do
Molly January. Well, Tuckerman did. He'd found a dry spot
in the flooded basement, away from puddles of rancid water
and oil, away from moldy newspapers and rat shit, and he'd
watched it all.

First time he'd made this kind of scene had been out in Los
Angeles, fruit-and-nut city, where else? Some young guy in
frizzed hair, tailored work clothes, and cowboy boots, a
so-called record genius in debt to the La Serras for three-
quarters of a million dollars, had invited Tuckerman to watch
a twelve-year-old Mexican girl die. The girl was a nobody,
courtesy of a Mexican pimp who collected girls like her in his
country and sold them to anyone in America who had the
money. The record genius, Tuckerman, and a few others had
watched the girl die in the record genius's Bel Air mansion.
Tuckerman had never been more sexually aroused in his life.
Right after the killing everybody had taken off their clothes
and really had a party. Right there in the room with the dead

girl. Everybody fucking their brains out. Tuckerman hadn't enjoyed himself so much in his life.

He'd have loved to jump Molly January, but it was important to look good in front of the Japs. So all he did was watch the four *yakuza* rape her again and again and again. After a while she stopped screaming and just cried. When they finished fucking her, the Japs used pliers to pull out her teeth. And they used the flame from a cigarette lighter on her genitals. Payback for the death of their man in Tokyo. That's what happened when you made the *gaijin*'s shit list.

Then the Japs used the electric drills on Molly January and Tuckerman couldn't tear his gaze away. He wanted to look into her eyes at the exact moment of her death, but he had to be careful of the blood. Jesus, it was everywhere and he was wearing $300 shoes. Fucking Japs would have to hose down most of the basement when they were finished.

Tuckerman had his Polaroid ready and when it looked like Molly January couldn't hang on any longer, he took a chance and inched forward, camera to his eye, and then when he got closer he forgot all about his shoes and just started snapping pictures.

Twenty-Six

Rupert de Jongh felt confused, dumfounded and, unusual for him, dazed beyond words.

This was a highly upsetting state of mind. He found it so unpleasant and disagreeable that he insisted on being left alone in his walled garden to think. Under no circumstances was he to be disturbed. Just minutes ago he had received the photograph of Kasumi and her husband, Arthur Kuby, who now called himself Oscar Koehl. Detective Manoa had described the photograph over the telephone, but that had not prepared de Jongh for the shock of actually seeing Kasumi's face. The blow to his equilibrium had been a violent one.

She's alive, Manoa had said. He'd gotten his information by eavesdropping on a conversation between Alexis Bendor and Paul Anami in the latter's home. De Jongh's reaction: eyewash and poppycock. Manoa's report was more like the ravings of a lunatic and nothing to be taken seriously. The *gaijin*'s warning to the detective: continue playing silly buggers with a memory I hold sacred and you face very painful consequences. But Manoa had persisted. He'd definitely heard Alexis Bendor plotting to kill the *gaijin* with the unwitting help of this Kasumi Koehl, now seriously ill and on her death bed. Mrs. Bendor knew of de Jongh's vow to bury a lock of Kasumi's hair in Japan. When the *gaijin* came to America, as he must, Mrs. Bendor would be waiting for him.

Implausible? Quite. Then again, Alexis Bendor was no
ordinary woman. If truth be told she'd been a better cryptanalyst
than de Jongh, who hadn't exactly been small beer in the
matter of codes and ciphers. He'd defeated her only through
the treachery of her weak-willed colleague, one Michael
Marwood. Give her credit; she was an intelligent and tenacious woman and quite courageous in her own way. Had
Kasumi survived the war, the one person who might have
located her again would have to be the redoubtable A. Bendor.
The same A. Bendor adroit enough to know of the vow de
Jongh had made to Kasumi forty years ago.

It was when Manoa had mentioned the name Arthur Kuby,
a name he might not have known under ordinary circumstances, that de Jongh had ordered the photograph and note
containing Kasumi's address to be hand-carried to him here in
Japan. Let the messenger leave Honolulu immediately. A car
would meet him at Tokyo Airport and bring him directly to
the *gaijin*'s Yokohama home.

In his walled garden de Jongh, wearing a summer kimono
and *geta*, sat on a stone bench facing dwarf bamboo trees,
and by the red light of a setting sun looked at the black-and-
white photograph. *Hai*, it was his beloved Kasumi. No words
from Manoa had the impact of seeing that face once more.
The righthand corner of her mouth was pulled up in a half
smile and there was the same sweet sadness in her eyes. Time
had been extraordinarily kind to her. Her exquisitely fine
beauty had matured without losing its delicacy. De Jongh
wept. The hideous old man, as Baudelaire called time, had
indeed returned with his devilish retinue of memories, regrets, fears, anguishes.

Kasumi was alive. And about to die.

De Jongh tilted the photograph to allow the fading sunlight
to fall on Arthur Kuby, known in his new incarnation as
Oscar Koehl. Herr Kuby, once the fair-haired boy of the
Abwehr, German World War II counterintelligence. De Jongh
snorted. Time had not been so kind to dear Arthur. He had
less hair, more flesh about the face and neck, but still possessed the arrogance to be found in a member of a wealthy
Prussian family that had produced two German field mar-
shals. The knowledge that Kasumi had been alive all these
years and living with Arthur Kuby left de Jongh frustrated,
angry, and with a great deal of animosity toward the German.

Alexis Bendor must have known about Kasumi's existence all along. And together with fate and Arthur Kuby she had conspired to cheat de Jongh out of the happiness that should have been his. Who else but Mrs. Bendor could have smoothed the way for Kasumi and Arthur Kuby to find a hiding place in America. Damn her eyes. Well, the late unlamented Mrs. Bendor was no longer a factor in anyone's life. Manoa had disposed of the old dear, removing a not-so-minor nuisance and leaving her remains in a makeshift grave located somewhere in the mountains of Hawaii. Highly unlikely she'd be waiting in Los Angeles when de Jongh showed up at Kasumi's bedside.

He rose from the stone bench and walked along the garden's path of stepping stones until he came to the red-lacquered teahouse that had once belonged to Hideyoshi, Japan's legendary spy master. De Jongh stared at the small house, thinking of Hideyoshi, whom he had always admired. The feudal warlord was an espionage genius whose skills had unified Japan. His almost unbroken string of military victories had been the result of an uncanny ability to obtain intelligence on his enemies. Troop strength, harvest reports, the condition of bridges and roads, a warlord's relationship with his soldiers, the number of fortified castles, the amount of rainfall in a given area. No information was too small or too large to be overlooked. Hideyoshi had long been one of the *gaijin*'s role models.

A scowling de Jongh looked at the wall, toward the direction of the center of town. Even though his Victorian mansion was on the Bluff, the pine-covered hill overlooking Yokohama harbor, he was still able to hear the bloody noise. Drunks, tourists, and overenthusiastic Japanese, all celebrating their own version of the *O-Bon* festival and using it as an excuse to debauch themselves. Disgraceful.

This week a pair of inebriated pranksters had found their way to the Bluff and lit a fire in front of a Swiss businessman's home and invited the Swiss out to join them in a toast to the dead. A few *Bon* dancers had found their way to the forest on the hill, bringing with them recorded traditional music played obscenely loud. De Jongh had sent someone out to chase the stupid sods away when they'd gotten too close to his property.

De Jongh walked over to Hideyoshi's teahouse and touched

its roof as though drawing strength from the tiny ancient house. *Hai*, he would go to Los Angeles to see Kasumi and bring her back to Japan. Or bring back a lock of her hair, as he had once vowed to do. But not before his men confirmed the existence of Mr. and Mrs. Oscar Koehl. And confirmed their address, business address, and the name of the hospital where Kasumi was being treated.

Arrangements would also be made to deal with Simon Bendor. He'd dropped out of sight, but chances are he'd been in contact with his mother. Quite a brazen young man, our Mr. Bendor. And always to be regarded as dangerous. Suppose, just suppose that he, too, was aware of Kasumi's existence and was waiting for de Jongh to make an appearance. Why shouldn't a devoted son do his mother's killing for her? He had not hesitated to assume the role of cutthroat on behalf of another woman, Erica Styler. Surely he'd do the same for his old mum.

When crossing a bridge a cautious man counts every stone. De Jongh would count every stone on the bridge between him and Kasumi. As for whether or not Simon Bendor might take up his mother's blood feud, assume that he would and act accordingly. One generation builds the road; the next generation travels on it.

Teki ni yotte tenka seyo. Meeting your enemy. Make the techniques and tactics the enemy is trying to use your own. Strength against strength, pliancy against pliancy. Answer regular attacking tactics with the same, a surprise attack with a surprise attack. Young Bendor believes in fighting his women's battles. And it is unlikely that he is in ignorance of his mother's plans. Therefore he will attempt to trap me, thought de Jongh. But it is I who will trap him.

The Englishman walked over to the carp pool and looked down at the large gray fish gathered at the pool's edge and patiently waiting for him to feed them. During his early days in Japan he had impressed *judokas* and fencers with his skill. He'd been quite proud of his ability, confident that he could give a good account of himself when called upon to do so. One day Baron Kanamori ordered him to practice kendo with a frail-looking old man who was gray-beared and minus most of his teeth. The doddering old party didn't appear able to hold a *shinai*, the bamboo fencing sword, let alone wield one in combat. A slightly contemptuous de Jongh wondered how in heaven's name he could avoid harming the old codger.

The fight was an eye opener for de Jongh. He could not lay a hand on the rotten sod, who gave him one of the worst defeats of his life. It was so humiliating that de Jongh was almost reduced to tears. The old man's skill was demonic and he used the *shinai* with a ruthlessness de Jongh found terrifying. When the fight was over both de Jongh's body and ego were extremely bruised.

Over cups of sake, and with the old man looking on with his village-idiot smile, the baron explained the purpose of the encounter. "Physical strength is not the most important factor in the martial arts," he said. "In any fight between a strong body and a strong mind, the mind will win because it will always find the weak point."

Simon Bendor had a strong body, but the *gaijin* had a strong mind. For now, all problems with the villainous Uraga were pushed aside. Nor did de Jongh give any thought to the $50 million in stamps being transported from Hong Kong to Hawaii by Sir Michael Marwood. The immediate problem was how to deal with Simon Bendor, who would surely be waiting for de Jongh in Los Angeles.

The *gaijin* thought, He expects me to come to him. Or rather to Kasumi. What he does not expect is for Kasumi to come to me.

De Jongh leaned over and dipped a hand in the pool. He stroked the fish, who were used to his touch. It could be done. Find out first if Kasumi is alive and after that draw up the plan of attack. An ambulance was necessary, along with a discreet and highly skilled doctor, because de Jongh intended to have his men take Kasumi out of the hospital and bring her to where he would be waiting in Los Angeles. And there would be enough *yakuza* on hand to keep young Mr. Bendor entertained when he showed up.

Sunday night's *O-Bon* celebration here in the *gaijin*'s Yokohama home would go on as scheduled. Not in honor of a dead Kasumi, but as a prayer to the gods that she be kept alive until de Jongh could see her. If the Los Angeles *yakuza* confirmed Alexis Bendor's intelligence that Kasumi had indeed risen from the dead, de Jongh would leave for America immediately after the *O-Bon* ceremony.

Only Simon Bendor, son of the tiger, posed a threat to the reunion. A dead tiger, however, was as harmless as a lamb.

Twenty-Seven

Erica Styler sat in the office behind the antique shop co-owned by Paul Anami and Simon and allowed Simon to turn her into someone unrecognizable. Smoke screen, he called it. Her disguise had to be perfect, he said, because if it wasn't "we've bought the farm, all of us." His words made Paul, who was watching the makeup job, go for his pills.

Unless Erica could walk into the Lauhala Hotel two hours from now and not be recognized, Simon's chances of stealing the *gaijin*'s stamps were between slim and none. His chances of dealing with Raymond Manoa and Sir Michael Marwood would be about the same. How did Erica feel about Simon killing those two men? She didn't. Marwood and Manoa belonged to the group that had taken Molly. Erica didn't give a shit what Simon did to them.

The disguise. She had to fool them all: Hollywood Frankie, reporters waiting to talk to Marwood, the *yakuza* who'd seen her photograph, vacationing gamblers she might have played cards with. And most important of all, she had to get into Marwood's suite, which meant getting by the bodyguard, Alan Bruce.

Scared? The fear hung on Erica so thick she could have scraped it off with a stick. "The all overs," her father used to call it. A sick feeling from top to bottom. Upset stomach, headache, sweaty palms, nerves. Simon sensed it and stopped working; he took both of her hands and said that the trick was to be afraid and still push on.

Erica said, "Like Alexis?"

He nodded. "Like Alexis."

Erica was so touched by his concern for his mother that for a time it took her mind off Molly. Yesterday, with Paul Anami, they'd left Nuuanu Valley and driven to Mount Tantalus to pick up some items Simon said he'd need during the next few days. Erica had watched him go into Alexis's room and silently walk around, a hand touching a bureau, the closet, a photograph of the two of them, a gymnastic medal he'd won and presented to her years ago. It had been too much for Erica. She'd turned away, tears hot on her face.

They're close, Paul had told her. *Sometimes it's as if the two of them have just one heart between them.*

When the three left the house Simon had taken a photograph of his mother with them.

Simon found a place for them to spend the night: his Honolulu health club, where for dinner they ate the fruits and veggies at the salad bar and slept in the manager's office. At dawn Simon awakened Erica and Paul, saying they had to be out of the club before it opened to the public and that it was better to move about while the streets were empty. Before leaving the club Simon telephoned his home and Paul's for word of Alexis. She had not called either place.

In the back of the antique shop Simon worked on Erica while he listened to the taped conversation between Raymond Manoa and Frankie Odori discussing the plan to kill Alexis. The tape was making Erica even more nervous, but she didn't have the heart to tell Simon to turn it off. Eventually he did, selecting an all-news station and turning it down low. It was a few minutes before Erica realized he had no interest in the news. He was listening for word about Alexis.

The disguise.

Erica watched her skin color change. Simon did it by using what he called "soft grease," a dark foundation that he applied to her face and neck, setting it with face powder so that it wouldn't smear. Then he shaved away part of her eyebrows and used a brown eyebrow pencil to reshape them entirely. A touch of shadow pencil under the eyes added years to her age and her chin was darkened to make it appear more fleshy. The eyebrow pencil was used to brown her teeth and a bit of sponge edged between her lip and gum changed the shape of her mouth.

Simon wasn't finished with her mouth. He made it bigger by drawing in a larger one with pencil and filling it in with coral lipstick borrowed from Alexis. A touch of moist rouge on the nose reddened the tip and gave her the look of a woman who liked her liquor. The nose itself was reshaped, lengthened with highlighter and brown shadow.

Hip and bust padding was next. Then a long-sleeved, floor-length blue-and-white muumuu. Topping it all off was a waist-length human-hair wig, grayed with silver color spray. Paul sent his clerk out to buy platform shoes, adding inches to Erica's height. When she looked in the mirror she was shocked. The word was gruesome. She looked like Quasimodo in drag, a combination of all three Lee sisters—ugly, beastly, ghastly. And older, Christ did she look older. Simon had done a remarkable job. The more Erica looked at herself in the mirror, the more fascinated she was with the new her. Paul said she looked like a Polish homecoming queen.

"One more time," Simon said to Erica. "Tell me what you're supposed to do at the Lauhala Hotel." She closed her eyes and recited from memory the instructions he'd given her earlier. When she finished he said good, then turned to Paul.

"Change of plans," Simon said. "You're leaving Hawaii."

The Japanese fingered the Maltese cross hanging from his neck. The nervous tic near his left eye had started up again. "I don't understand. I thought you wanted me here in case Alexis called."

Simon looked down at the floor. That's when Erica realized he'd accepted the idea that his mother was dead. Simon said, "Shit's gonna hit the fan when Manoa dies. I don't want you around when that happens."

He smiled at Paul. "Didn't know what you were letting yourself in for when you pulled me out of the ocean, did you?"

They embraced.

Erica, thinking of her makeup, tried not to cry and failed.

An hour later Simon stood in front of the door to the presidential suite of the Lauhala Hotel. He wore a policeman's uniform, red wig, and red mustache. His cap was pulled low and touched the top of his mirrored sunglasses. In one hand he held a device resembling a portable tape recorder and there was an attaché case at his feet. He looked left and right. The corridor was empty to his right, but there were people to his left. Fortunately they were at the far end of the hall and paying no attention to him. He knocked on the door for the fourth time to be sure. No answer. Well now.

The lock. It was a good one, a digital alarm panel, with an alarm pad that resembled the dial on a touchtone phone. With this kind of lock you punched in a code number to enter the room and to turn the alarm on or off. No keys to lose or have stolen. Either you knew the number or you didn't. Simon was going to know the number within seconds.

What he held in his hands was a small computer, a random digital selector. He looked left, saw the couple still waiting for the elevator and told himself to go for it anyway. Hotel management or security could be on the way to make sure a heavy like Marwood received the best of Hawaiian hospitality. Mustn't forget the aloha spirit, the famous welcome for all visitors. Mustn't forget Alexis Bendor either.

Simon connected a two-foot-long wire from the digital selector to the alarm panel, then aiming the selector at the panel used his thumbs to press two buttons. He kept his eyes on the selector's small screen. Just like playing a slot machine. Numbers whizzed by too fast to read. Then a 5 appeared in the screen's lefthand corner and stayed there. More numbers whizzed past the five and suddenly a 2 clicked into place beside the 5. Fifteen seconds later Simon had the five-figure code that had been programmed into the lock. Wasting no time, he punched it into the digital alarm panel, turned the knob, and the door opened. Quickly disconnecting the selector wire, he stepped inside and closed the door behind hin. He took a pair of black leather gloves from his back pocket and put them on.

Superdeluxe. High ceilings, chandeliers, a grand piano and a small bar in the living room. Another bar in the conference room. Private kitchen, two double bedrooms, and two bathrooms, one containing an ultraviolet sun bed, a large pea-pod-shaped device for indoor tanning. And a lanai, a veranda overlooking two swimming pools and a saltwater lagoon nineteen stories below. Marwood believed in living well. The Lauhala was one of Waikiki's newest beachfront hotels, twenty-five floors of pink stucco surrounded by tropical gardens,

with a view of Diamond Head and the ocean and with a glass
elevator running up the side to a rooftop restaurant that was
the most expensive in Honolulu. One more monstrosity to
block out the sun, Alexis had said of the hotel.

Simon checked out every room, which is exactly what
Marwood's bodyguard Alan Bruce would do. That was Bruce's
job. He'd poke around, ask questions of the hotel staff, and
do his best to make sure nobody was hiding in the suite ready
to do bodily harm to his employer. No crouching under the
bed or crawling behind the couch with someone like Bruce
around. Simon was going to have to disappear somewhere in
this suite and make a good job of it.

He walked out on to the lanai and stared northeast at the
Koolau Mountains. He found himself staring at them for a
long time without knowing why, feeling a strong sadness
come over him, but then he snapped out of it. Seconds later
he'd found a place to hide, the last place Alan Bruce or
anyone else would think of looking.

Sir Michael Marwood stood facing Raymond Manoa on the
lanai of the Lauhala's presidential suite, sipping a gin and
tonic and forcing himself to make small talk. Marwood wore
a Gieves & Hawkes pinstripe suit and a blue silk tie from
Sulka's in London to complement the off-white Turnbull &
Asser shirt given him by his wife for his sixty-sixth birthday a
month ago. The diplomat looked worn out and depressed.
The flight from Hong Kong had been brutal, not helped in the
least by the showing of an American coming-of-age film
featuring adolescents with exalted notions about the joys to be
found in each other's genitalia.

Minutes ago Marwood, pleading fatigue, had gotten rid of
the last of the unofficial welcoming committee: embassy personnel, top hotel staff, reporters. He wasn't here to save the
bloody world, he was here on holiday, plus a bit of business
for the *gaijin,* and the sooner that was settled the sooner he
could be alone. He'd chase the dragon, perhaps play a Chopin
étude or two, and have dinner out here on the lanai. Alan
Bruce was in one of the bedrooms unpacking the luggage,
laying out the stamps for Manoa to see, at the detective's
insistence, and, of course, hiding Marwood's supply of heroin. Which left Marwood on the balcony, sharing a marvel-

ous view of the oceans and various mountains with the aboriginal Detective Manoa.

Years of experience around the conference table in a score of countries had taught the Englishman to be ever mindful of the slightest nuance in another's behavior. His true impression of Detective Manoa? The Hawaiian was in the early stages of human evolution. It was there for anyone alert enough to see it: the thickness of the man's features; the cold watchfulness in his hooded, cobralike gaze; the coarse manner in which he ate his food. And there was the lack of compassion shown in talking about Alexis Bendor, whom Manoa had murdered only days ago. No human feeling in the man. A decent person would have refused to bring up the subject in the first place.

Just the memory of Manoa's entrance was enough to make Marwood cringe inwardly. The Hawaiian had worked the crowd like a flash politician, using one tawdry mannerism after another—back slapping, smiling, hand shaking, arm around the shoulder and glad to see you. Pressing the flesh, in the grotesque American phrase. Doing his godawful bloody best to win friends and influence people. Then he made his way to Marwood, grabbed him painfully by the elbow, and whispered he'd taken care of Alexis Bendor three nights ago. Said it with pride. Revolting, really.

On the lanai Marwood attempted to steer the conversation away from Alexis. He asked Manoa questions about the hotel, Honolulu's rising crime rate, the rooftop restaurant, Manoa's wife. In turn the detective noted points of interest— Diamond Head, Pearl Harbor, the general direction of the luxury hotel being built by Rupert de Jongh in partnership with the nefarious La Serra brothers.

The detective pointed east. "Koolau Mountains over there. That's where Mrs. Bendor's buried."

Marwood rolled his eyes up into his head. "Good God, man. Do you have to mention *that?* Let her rest in peace."

"She wouldn't be restin' at all, bruddah, if you hadn't helped out. Man, she was one tough old lady. Look here. She did this." Manoa pointed to a swollen area near his cheekbone. "Hit me with my own handcuffs. Man, I got pissed after that, know what I mean?"

"I can well imagine." Marwood swallowed the rest of his drink. He turned to face the Koolau Mountains. He whispered, "I knew her for such a long time. Such a long time. Very forceful woman. She's up there, is she?"

"Oh yeah. Ain't nobody ever gonna find her no matter how long they look. There's a special Hawaiian temple near an abandoned mill and plantation—"

"If you don't mind, I'd rather be spared the details. I'd rather not know about it."

"Lots of things you don't know about, bruddah." That Cheshire grin again.

"Such as?"

"Such as the *gaijin*'s gonna be comin' to America. Did you know that?"

Marwood used a hand to steady himself against the balcony. "Rubbish. There's absolutely no reason for him to do such a thing."

Manoa's pride in himself was infuriating. He said, "You ever hear of a woman called Kasumi?" He told Marwood about the Japanese woman now living in Los Angeles and married to one of the *gaijin*'s old war buddies. Somebody named Arthur Kuby.

Marwood was in a state of shock. "And you say Alexis turned up Kasumi's whereabouts? God, that woman is amazing."

"Was, bruddah, was. That old lady's history. Did I tell you I'm plannin' to go into politics? There's a few things I'd like to ask you about how you're supposed to act."

Marwood walked away from him. Of course Alexis Bendor was dead and a part of Marwood had died with her. Difficult to think of her in the past tense. She was so alive, so energetic. One of the few women he had any respect for. He didn't like being reminded of her death, and as for Manoa entering the world of politics, spare me. Marwood had left the lanai because he wanted to get away from this cretin, this dim-witted imbecile. In the living room Marwood called Alan's name. Loudly.

Simon hung beneath the lanai.

He lay in a crude rope swing hastily rigged by wrapping the rope around his waist, then tying it under either end of the balcony. For backup he gripped two smaller lengths of rope tied to the balcony behind his head. He was in agony. Hands, arms, shoulders, and back burned from the pain of hanging onto the ropes nineteen stories above the ground. Veins had popped out in his forehead and neck. He was dizzy from the effort of controlling his breathing so that the two men standing inches away could not hear him.

Simon, however, heard them. Heard every word.

He shook his head gently, clearing the tears from his eyes and not wanting to believe what he'd just heard about his mother, and then the rope supporting him broke. He swung free, fighting panic, and then his body dropped, yanking his arms, and the pain was so intense he almost let go. Now only the two short ropes lay between him and dying.

One short rope unwound itself, broke free, and dropped past him toward the ground. He'd tied both short ropes tightly to the underrailing, but his weight was now too much for them. The backup ropes weren't strong enough to do the job alone. He felt the second rope loosen, felt himself sliding down.

He was spinning, being lowered, and then he gripped the short rope with both hands, pulled up with all his strength, forgetting the pain, using thoughts of his mother to will himself to live, and when he was within inches of the balcony he caught the bottom with the fingertips of his right hand, then got a stronger grip as the second rope came loose and floated toward the ground.

He brought his left hand onto the balcony, swung forward, back, then got a leg on the balcony, pulled himself up, climbed over the railing, and crouched behind a potted palm. He closed his eyes, shivered, saw his mother in his mind, then took the radio from his belt and contacted Erica.

"Now," he said.

He hooked the radio back on his belt, looked at the mist-shrouded Koolau Mountains in the distance, then used his fingertips to wipe the tears from his eyes.

He looked into the living room. Empty. He waited.

There was a knock at the front door. Then a second and a third. Seconds later Alan Bruce entered the living room from Simon's left, still in a jacket and tie and eating left over canapés. At the door he paused to push the last bit of food into his mouth and unbutton his jacket. His hand was on the gun as he asked who was at the door.

Simon stood up, took his black gloves from a back pocket and put them on, then walked from the *lanai* into the living room. Slowly, as though he belonged there, he began walking toward the bedroom, making no noise, keeping his eyes on Bruce's back, and willing himself to remain unseen.

Erica slipped the hand radio into her shoulder bag, picked up a clipboard from the stairs, and walked across the landing to the exit door. She hesitated, took a deep breath, then opened the door and stepped into the corridor. She wore a hotel name tag reading IDA RUBY and she did her damnedest to look as though she worked there. Her eyes, hidden behind a pair of dark glasses with rhinestone-studded mother-of-pearl frames, could not stop blinking. Like Martha and the Vandellas sang, nowhere to run and nowhere to hide.

She told herself, it's poker. All you need is a cool head, then you make your bluff.

She walked to the door of the presidential suite and knocked once, twice, three times before somebody answered.

"Ida Ruby," Erica said in response to Bruce's question. "I'm from Mr. Berlin's office. The manager?"

"I know who he is, sunshine. What I'd like to know is who the hell might you be." Thick Scottish burr and mean as a junkyard dog.

"Miss Ruby, his assistant. He was supposed to give you the new code for your lock when he was here, but I guess he forgot. And he doesn't want to give it out over the phone. I'm sure you understand. I—he told me to bring it to Sir Marwood personally."

She took an envelope from the clipboard and held it to the peephole. "We like to change the combination for each guest. It's a security precaution we've decided to adopt as a policy."

"Sloppy sort of business if you ask me. Bloody jerk should have done it earlier. I've half a mind to call down and let him know what I think about the way he does his job."

Erica closed her eyes. And opened them when she heard the door open.

Alan Bruce, grim, unsmiling, stood in front of her, hand outstretched. "Well, let's have it then."

"I'll have to show you how the lock operates." She held out the envelope. And dropped it when he reached toward her. Bruce muttered Jesus and crouched down to pick it up.

Erica reached under a sheaf of papers on the clipboard for the hypodermic Simon had taped there, then stepped close to

the hunched-over bodyguard and plunged the needle into the
left side of his neck, remembering Simon's words: "Shove it
in deep. And if you can't get the neck, go for the stomach."

Bruce, needle jutting from his neck, grabbed her left wrist
and yanked her into the suite. Erica hit him in the face with
the clipboard and kicked his right ankle as he spun her
off-balance. His right hand was inside his jacket when his eyes
turned up in his head and he dropped to his knees. Erica took
the gun from him, then closed the door. She turned in time to
see the bodyguard pitch forward, one arm slamming onto an
imitation Louis Quinze end table, bringing the table and a
vase of red and yellow hibiscus down on top of him.

A voice from the bedroom. Marwood's. "Alan, what was
that? Alan?"

Erica, back to the door, jammed her hand in her shoulder
bag and fumbled for the magnum.

Simon headed toward the bedroom, toward the sound of
Marwood's voice. He walked along a carpeted corridor whose
walls were hung with original watercolors of island landscapes and when he heard Marwood call to his bodyguard
again, Simon flattened himself against a wall and froze. He
waited. But not for long. He carried no weapon; his weapons
were surprise and nerve. Alexis used to say, "You got sand,
kid. Mucho panache." *Alexis.*

Simon moved away from the wall and walked to the bedroom. Back against the wall once more, he edged forward
and peeked through an open doorway. Marwood and Manoa
had their backs to him. Both men stood near the bed, looking
down at rows of stamps that had been placed between plastic
sheets taken from photograph albums. Marwood was pointing
to a particular sheet and explaining something about it to
Manoa, who nodded his head.

Simon pulled back from the door. Closing his eyes, he
placed his hands back to back, fingers pointing toward the
floor. Then he interlocked his fingers, brought the palms
together over the fingers, shutting them inside the hands. He
aimed the ring and little fingers forward. His thumbs were
extended. *Tai,* the fourth sign in the *kuji no in.* Designed to
strengthen the fighting spirit, to concentrate his mind for
combat. When he had drawn the nine lines in the air, he
willed himself to be unseen. To be silent. To be powerful.

Then he thought of his mother. Seconds later, he stepped into the doorway.

Marwood and Manoa. Both men faced the bed, their attention still on the stamps. Simon walked soundlessly across the room, stopped less than two feet from the pair, *and still the Englishman and the Hawaiian did not turn around.* Simon thought, Manoa first. He's the most dangerous.

Quickly Simon swung his right leg in a roundhouse kick, aiming low, driving his shin into Manoa's right thigh. Then he jammed his right heel down hard on the detective's left achilles tendon, tearing it, making Manoa scream, and when the detective sat down hard on the rug, Simon stepped close and with his right fist punched him at the base of the skull. A strong punch, strong enough to stop the screaming, to put Manoa on his back and almost knock him out. But not to kill him. Not yet.

Simon bent over Manoa, pulled the .38 Smith & Wesson from the detective's belt holster, then looked at Marwood.

Marwood took a step back and whispered, "Good lord, no." Then he called for Alan.

Simon stood up. "Alan won't be coming. On the floor, please, face down."

"You're no policeman, I know that much. I'm calling hotel security."

"I said on the floor."

Marwood's eyes went to the doorway and his face became slack. Simon didn't bother turning around. He said, "Erica?" She entered the room, magnum in a two-handed grip and aimed at Marwood.

The diplomat crouched slowly, suddenly much older than his years, knees creaking, hands on the carpet, then laboriously stretching himself out beside a tortured Manoa.

No marks, Simon told himself. No marks on Manoa. He walked to one of the double beds in the suite, reached behind the headboard, and pulled out his attaché case.

Back at Manoa's side he removed the detective's shoes and socks. But when he went to unbuckle the detective's belt a weakened Manoa tried to push him away. Simon reached between the detective's legs, squeezed his testicles and kept squeezing for a few seconds. Manoa, teeth clenched and perspiring heavily, inhaled loudly and fell back.

Simon unbuckled Manoa's pants, then removed them, along

with his boxer shorts. Marwood, head raised from the carpet, watched with wide-eyed fascination. Simon opened his attaché case, removed a hypodermic case, and selected a needle containing a colorless liquid. Then he leaned over Manoa and injected him just above the penis, pushing the needle deep into his pubic hairs. The detective screamed. Marwood closed his eyes and dropped his head to the carpet.

After putting the needle back in the attache case Simon stripped Manoa of all his clothes. No resistance from the detective this time. His eyes were glassy, his muscles slack, and saliva ran from a corner of his open mouth. Simon said, "The injection won't kill you. But it will paralyze you. You won't be able to move for eight, ten hours. Then it gets worse. It affects the brain. Pretty soon you won't be able to think."

Manoa blinked and tried to speak. His eyes followed Simon, who leaned over him until they were face to face. "I'm Alexis Bendor's son."

Marwood said, "Dear God," and turned away.

Simon stepped behind a naked Manoa, gripped him under the armpits and dragged him from the bedroom to the bathroom next door. He lifted him into the ultraviolet tanning bed, made sure the bed was plugged in, then switched it on. Manoa got the max. Maximum heat. Maximum time. For a full minute Simon watched the detective think and when he saw that Manoa understood, he nodded. You're right, this is exactly how you're going out.

The inside of the bed turned pink, then a deep red. Simon, standing a few feet away, felt the heat. He watched Manoa use all of his strength to force his mouth open. But nothing came out.

John Kanna had taught Simon a knowledge of poisons. Some kill, Kanna had said. Others paralyze a man, attack only the brain, or make him go blind. Poisons are as much of a weapon as a knife or a sword. Or your hands and feet. Learn to make your own from raw fish, scorpions, from the seeds of apples, plums, almonds. Poisons that attack quickly and leave no trace. Simon had used them in Vietnam with great success.

He watched Manoa's skin break out in perspiration, saw it turn pink, and saw Manoa plead with his eyes. Simon walked away.

In the bedroom he crouched over Marwood and gently turned him on his back. The diplomat was weeping. "I'm terribly sorry about your mother, really I am. I was quite fond of her, you see. We met during the war and got along quite well."

He didn't resist as Simon removed his jacket, loosened his tie, then rolled up his left sleeve. "Brilliant woman," Marwood said. "Absolutely brilliant. I introduced her to your father, you know."

Simon pushed the diplomat back to the floor and reached for the hypodermic case. He removed a second needle, then picked up Marwood's left arm. The diplomat offered no resistance but continued speaking. "Had no choice, really I didn't. You don't know de Jongh. The man's diabolical, not of this world, actually. 'The Devil as a roaring lion, walketh about, seeking whom he may devour.' Peter, chapter five, verse eight."

Simon injected him in the crook of the left elbow. Marwood, eyes on the ceiling, stiffened. Simon made two more puncture holes, then watched Marwood push himself to a sitting position, look at his arm, then at Simon.

"Heroin," Simon said. "My mother told me you were a user."

Marwood frowned, then smiled. "Really? Now how did she learn that, I wonder. No matter. She always was too clever by half."

Marwood sighed with pleasure. "Never tried it this way before. I—"

He twitched, clutched his heart, and gasped.

Paul had picked up the heroin last night from a gay bar on Hotel Street. Simon didn't know what it was cut with and didn't care. Milk sugar, baby powder, powdered milk, any one of a dozen laxatives. It didn't matter. What mattered was the strychnine he'd added himself. Alexis kept it around the house to kill rats. In minutes it would kill Marwood.

Simon picked up Manoa's clothing, took it to the bathroom, and left it neatly hung on a chair in front of a makeup table. He left the detective's .38 there, too. Manoa's skin had started to smoke. Simon checked the gauges on the tanning bed, saw they were still on maximum, and left.

In the bedroom he lifted Marwood onto the bed while Erica placed the plastic sheets of stamps—there were almost two dozen of them—in one of Marwood's small suitcases. Simon took his police cap from the attaché case, put it on, then removed three nickel bags of heroin, two empty glassine envelopes, a burnt spoon, a disposable cigarette lighter, and set them on the night table within Marwood's reach. Then he removed Marwood's belt and wrapped it around the diplomat's left bicep, pulling it tight, helping Marwood to tie off like every good little junkie did before shooting up.

The Englishman lay unmoving on the bed, eyes closed, right arm dangling over the side. "Forty years too late," Simon whispered.

In the living room Erica, holding the suitcase, watched while Simon dragged Alan Bruce to a couch and poured vodka in his mouth and over his chest. The bodyguard wasn't dead and wasn't paralyzed. He was unconscious and would stay that way for a few hours. When he came to, explaining the liquor would be the least of his problems.

Simon walked to the house phone, telephoned the front desk, and said he was Alan Bruce and that Sir Marwood did not want to be disturbed until further notice. Hold all calls.

Then he walked over to Erica, squeezed her hand, and nodded toward the door. She left first. Simon waited ten minutes before following her.

Twenty-Eight

LOS ANGELES
AUGUST 1983

Joe D'Agosta and Simon Bendor stood under a Mexican fan palm tree, the two of them staring across the sidewalk at the hospital where Kasumi Koehl lay dying. D'Agosta wore a short-sleeved white shirt and blue polyester pants. Simon wore white jeans and a green satin warmup jacket. D'Agosta looked up at the sky, said it was a cool night and maybe he should have brought a sweater with him from New York. He'd worn a jacket but had loaned it to Erica, who stood talking with Paul Anami at the top of the hospital stairs.

D'Agosta said, "Jesus, when I saw Erica at the airport I fuckin' couldn't believe my eyes. I almost plotzed. Surprised my lunch didn't come up. Then she goes into the ladies' room and comes out looking like herself, which ain't bad. If you hadna told me it was her, I'd never have known."

Simon blew into his cupped hands. "She stayed cool the whole time. Wasn't for her, I couldn't have pulled it off."

"You goddam made a believer out of me. You whacked 'em like you said you would. Fucking beautiful." D'Agosta shook his head. "Sorry about Alexis. She was a stand-up guy. She didn't just do it for herself, you know. There were those three guys with her, the ones who got taken out by de Jongh. She did it for them, too. That's the beauty of it. She never forgot them guys."

He saw the tears in Simon's eyes and said, "Me and my big mouth. I'm sorry. Should have kept quiet."

Simon shook his head. "No. Maybe that's the point, what you just said. You can't just live for yourself, the way I've been doing. Once in a while you have to do something for somebody else. I just wish I'd picked up on this a little sooner. Like when she first came to me—"

He looked at the ground and shook his head. "Should have picked up on it sooner."

D'Agosta waited, then said he thought they'd found Molly back in New York. A fishing boat in Jamaica Bay had pulled in a floater. The torso of a Caucasian female. Head, arms, legs missing. Age between twenty and twenty-five. There was no positive I.D., but D'Agosta felt it was Molly.

Simon looked at Erica. "If we don't know for sure, don't tell her."

D'Agosta sighed. "Maybe you're right. One more thing. You might find this interesting. Tuckerman got himself smoked yesterday. Two in the heart with a twenty-two."

"Yeah?"

"Whoever did it used a silencer." D'Agosta rubbed his arms. "Really shoulda brought a fuckin' sweater. I thought it was supposed to be warm out here. Anyway, the shooter catches Tuckerman on the Staten Island Ferry, when the shyster's goin' to work in the morning like everybody else. Catches him in a crowd of commuters. Nobody hears a thing, nobody sees a thing. Fact is, Tuckerman was sittin' at the end of the boat, reading the *Wall Street Journal*. That's how they found him."

"Didn't Tuckerman have a bodyguard?"

D'Agosta shrugged. "Only part-time." He looked down the street at the *Los Angeles Times* building, which took up an entire block. "You can't carry a bodyguard with you everywhere. Ain't practical. The cops, they think it might have been one of Tuckerman's friends or business associates or clients, none of whom are what you might call regular churchgoers."

D'Agosta watched a battered Buick pull up to the curb. A Mexican man and young woman got out and helped a pregnant Mexican woman from the car. As the three walked up the stairs D'Agosta said he thought the reason Tuckerman got smoked is because he was asking around about a fence and a thief who were involved with a young lady who'd been recently kidnapped. The way D'Agosta heard it, Tuckerman was getting close to connecting the thief to a robbery at his house. The thief had also been linked to the kidnapped woman and it was D'Agosta's opinion that if Tuckerman had continued digging, he might have gotten lucky.

Simon looked up at the sky. "Like you said, it's interesting. One thing: the gun. That's not hanging around anywhere, is it?"

D'Agosta slowly shook his head. "Long gone, goombah. Broken down and the pieces dropped in a couple of sewers and in a local Astoria river."

Simon smiled. "Beautiful."

"My pleasure. By the way, you know we're being watched, don't you?"

Simon rubbed the back of his neck and waved to Erica and Paul. "Two cars. Toyota at the corner behind you. A Ford diagonally across the street and not too far from the bus stop."

"Not bad, not bad. De Jongh's people are on the ball."

"For sure, as they say out here. You packing?"

D'Agosta patted the .38 beneath his shirt front. "Don't leave home without it. Gonna have to get a new backup to replace the twenty-two, but that can wait."

Simon stretched his arms overhead. "Let's get the show on the road, goombah."

Simon and Erica entered the hospital with their arms around each other. Paul and D'Agosta followed.

Outside in the darkness the *yakuza* watched the hospital in silence.

In a second-floor hospital room Simon and Arthur Kuby looked through a window at a darkened courtyard. Behind them Kasumi lay sleeping in an oxygen tent.

Kuby said, "He's coming? He's actually coming to America?"

Simon said, "Yes. He knows she's alive and that she's married to you."

"What makes you think he'll kill me?"

"Because you've taken away something that should be his. My mother knew de Jongh better than anyone and she said he'd come to Kasumi under any circumstances."

''And Alexis is dead, you say.''

''Yes.''

Kuby turned from the window to look at Simon. ''With all due respect, you and your mother have no right to enter our lives.''

Simon's voice was a hiss. ''You entered my mother's life forty years ago. And you weren't invited. I don't want to hear a goddam thing about what I have a right to do. De Jongh's coming here to take away your wife and to kill you. *De Jongh is alive.* And he knows where you are. Now, how long do you think you have to live?''

Kuby's shoulders dropped. ''Your mother was a great woman. My condolences to you. She was the strongest of us all, the best of us all.''

The German looked at his sleeping wife. ''The inevitability of history. Right back to square one, aren't we? De Jongh, Kasumi, and me, with me as afraid of him now as I was then.''

He looked at Simon. ''What do you want me to do?''

Twenty-Nine

Rupert de Jongh entered the *butsuma*, the small altar room on
the first floor of his Victorian mansion, and slid the rice-paper
door closed behind him. He walked across the mat-covered
floor to one corner and placed Kasumi's fan, the doll head,
and the photograph given him by Manoa on the *butsudan*,
family altar. He wore a summer kimono of white silk, a matching headband, and a *tabi*. A slight flare of the nostrils was the
only sign of his anger.

There was the matter of the stolen stamps, combined with
the unexplained deaths of Marwood and Manoa. De Jongh's
telephone hadn't stopped ringing since the Chinese had learned
they were out fifty million American dollars, a fact he'd been
forced to share with them when it became apparent that
bankers in the Cayman Islands wouldn't be depositing money
in the Chinese accounts. A general in the Fuzhou Military
Region, the coastal area protecting China against a naval
invasion by Taiwan, told de Jongh that he expected his
money to be in his Caymans account three days from now.
Excuses of any sort would be totally unacceptable. A Communist party official in Peking sent word that his millions were
to be returned to the Baoqin Bank in Hong Kong by tomorrow morning.

Two Japanese government officials called on behalf of
important Chinese who had entrusted their money to de Jongh.

The stolen stamps could affect relations between China and Japan, de Jongh was told. China's Communist party took a dim view of those in power who attempted to get rich outside official channels. Such a practice was called "socialism with Chinese characteristics" and was usually discouraged by shooting anyone caught doing it. Should any such executions occur due to the stolen stamps, de Jongh, and by extension Japan, would be considered to be at fault. To avoid any embarrassment, the *gaijin* would have to recover the stamps as soon as possible or find himself minus support from Japanese friends in high places. Put bluntly, de Jongh's own life could well be forfeit.

He did not tell anyone that he was fairly sure who had the stamps. To wit, the unspeakable urchin who had sprung from the loins of Alexis Bendor. Who but Simon Bendor was clever enough to pull off such a robbery, while making the deaths of Marwood and Manoa appear accidental. Bizarre and accidental. Marwood grabs his harp as a result of a taste for heroin, and Manoa, for reasons known only to himself and God, fries himself to death in a bloody tanning bed.

At first the *gaijin* had suspected Alan Bruce of going into business for himself and he had ordered Frankie to question him. Which Frankie had done, resulting in Mr. Bruce's departure from this vale of tears. Before going on ahead, Mr. Bruce had vigorously denied any collusion in the death of his employer and Detective Manoa. The Hawaiian press, and the world press for that matter, were having a field day with what had been described as "a baffling mystery, worthy of Agatha Christie at her most intriguing." So far, there'd been no mention of the *yakuza* in all of this, but de Jongh, being quite pragmatic, wondered how long this benevolent state of affairs would last. *How on earth had Simon Bendor learned about those stamps?*

De Jongh turned from the altar and looked at a shuttered window blocking out a view of the Foreign Cemetery. Minutes ago, raucous music had erupted from the cemetery, only yards away from the altar room. It was an earsplitting din of taped *O-Bon* music coming from portable cassette players. Disgraceful and sacrilegious. And on top of that there were fires in the cemetery. Not small ones, but dangerous fires undoubtedly set by some of the drunken louts staggering through the streets of Yokohama. There had been a great deal of drinking during these two weeks of *Bon* celebrations, with more to come during the next two weeks. Locals, foreigners living here, tourists. All fried to the tonsils and drunk as a fiddler.

The *O-Bon* celebrations were turning into an excuse for swinish behavior. Every night hundreds danced in the streets, temples, parking lots, dancing around large or small platforms containing a drum. People in summer kimonos and eating roasted corn, barbecued squid, and weaving colored lanterns and drinking sake. Well, let them dance through town, but keep them away from the Bluff, de Jongh's private patch. And definitely keep the drunken sods out of the Foreign Cemetery, which was practically his back door.

He still had two men on guard at the front of the house, but he'd been forced to send three into the cemetery to stop that infernal racket, the recorded music that made it so difficult for him to meditate in front of his altar. Perhaps most important of all, de Jongh wanted those damned fires put out. They were too close to his home. A spark might blow across the wall and catch, and what then?

De Jongh had men going about the house shutting the windows so that he could pay tribute to Kasumi without being smoked out of his altar room or having his eardrums shattered by the recorded noise. *Hai,* she was alive. His people in Los Angeles had confirmed that she was in a hospital there, that she was indeed married to Arthur Kuby, or Oscar Koehl, as he now called himself. And they had confirmed that Simon Bendor was waiting for de Jongh to come to Kasumi. Mr. Bendor and his associates—one Joseph D'Agosta, one Erica Styler, and one Paul Anami—were all staying at the hospital. Arthur Kuby had cooked up an interesting little fiction on their behalf. All were related to him or his wife, he'd said, thereby paving the way for all to have rooms on her floor.

The ambulance that would bring Kasumi to the *gaijin* would lure Simon Bendor to him as well. Staying close to Kasumi was Bendor's only chance at the *gaijin.*

De Jongh would leave Japan tonight, arrive in California late tomorrow, and the business of the missing stamps would be settled not long thereafter. And he would either bring Kasumi or a lock of her hair back to Japan, something he must do himself, for it was he who had made the vow. Keeping that vow would mean everlasting honor and glory for many lives to come. He was at the age when he must think of death.

He was being given a rare opportunity, a second chance at greatness. To bring back a lock of Kasumi's hair was to honor all that he held dear in this world and the next. He must not fail. With this act he would leave behind a name that would be venerated for years to come. It would be a memorial to his life as a samurai. Not even $50 million could buy him such a gift. Kasumi was his key to immortality, to meeting old friends like Baron Kanamori in the next world with honor and having them know that he had been true to all he held dear, that he had been true to them, to Japan, his *yakuza* house, and to Kasumi.

Zazen. Meditation.

De Jongh sat on a *zafu,* a small blue cushion, and crossed his legs in the traditional lotus posture—left foot on right thigh, right foot on left thigh. He kept his body straight, eyes half closed, wrists on his thighs with the palms up. The left hand rested on the right, thumbs gently touching. He slowed his breathing down, inhaling gently but breathing out with strength.

He kept his breathing natural, unforced. And he made his concentration strong, closing out everything but Kasumi. Nothing, not the music and shouting from the cemetery, not the smell of smoke from fires only yards away, was to be allowed to intrude on this moment. His soul reached out for Kasumi. In his mind they were young again and the vision warmed him, nearly lulling him to sleep.

Minutes later he opened his eyes and looked at the altar. He saw the rice cakes, tea, and sweet bean jam he had placed near her picture as an offering. He saw the doll's head, her fan, a photograph taken of the two of them at a Shinto shrine before leaving on the ill-fated mission to Switzerland.

And he saw her diary and a lock of her hair.

He shook his head in disbelief, rubbing his eyes to clear them. The shock glued him to the spot. His hand shook as he reached out for the diary. It was real. And so was the hair. He wasn't imagining things. He opened the diary, turned the pages, saw her childish handwriting, read her words, and tears filled his eyes. Something dropped from the diary and he leaned forward to pick it up.

A photograph. De Jongh and Frankie's two children.

Behind de Jongh a voice whispered, "I used her to get to you."

De Jongh turned around slowly to see a figure in black standing over him. The *oyabun* saw with his eyes, but his mind refused to accept the sight of an intruder in his home. No one was that bold. *No one*. He saw, he heard, but he refused to believe and in that instant his reflexes failed him.

Simon said, "Fire and noise. A nice diversion."

He reached out with his left hand, grabbed the front of de Jongh's kimono and yanked him to the floor, on his stomach. And then he was on the Englishman's back, a knee pushing down between de Jongh's shoulder blades, a left hand pressing his head into the mat, and with the right hand Simon jammed an ice pick into de Jongh's right ear, pushing it in until the handle touched the ear.

De Jongh shivered, then relaxed. Then he sighed once and died.

Simon removed the ice pick, wiped it on his trousers and looked to see if any blood was leaking from de Jongh's ear. When he saw none he stood up. He walked to the altar, blew out the candles, then walked to the rice-paper door. He inched it open, saw the corridor was empty, and slipped into the shadowy half-light.

He moved toward the back of the house, toward the flames and smoke, visible through an open window. He heard the Japanese cursing outside as they tried to put out the fires and shut off the portable cassettes he had wired to tombstones and in the tops of trees.

He tiptoed down the hall to the window, climbed through to the ground, and did what he had done all his life. He ran toward the fire and smoke, toward the men shouting at each other among the gravestones and memorials. He ran toward the danger.

Epilogue

KOOLAU MOUNTAINS, OAHU
SEPTEMBER 1983

The storm began with a crack of thunder and a warm rain. With the rain scores of narrow waterfalls suddenly appeared, to drop hundreds of feet along the gouged face of the cliffs. Toward the western part of the range strong winds blew waterfalls back into the air, creating a mist that the cliffs wore as a lei. In the east mynah birds, sparrows, and doves fled the cliffs for the shelter of a rain forest. They flew through a red haze that was wind-stirred powdery red dirt at the base of the cliffs.

Here the red dirt also blew through what remained of an abandoned sugar mill and plantation now home to stray cats, wild goats, and mongrels called *poi* dogs. Trash—pineapple husks, beer cans tossed away by back-packers, darkened banana skins, wet leaves from the rain forest, pages of old newspapers—were blown by the wind into the semicircle formed by the stone-and-wood enclosure that was a *heiau*. One newspaper page, plastered against the side of the altar by wind and rain, contained two stories on Japan's leading *yakuza* group. Both stories were a week old.

The first told of the elaborate funeral of a legendary underworld figure named Yamaga Razan, also known as the *gaijin*. Over a thousand *yakuza* had attended the services for Razan, who had died of a brain hemorrhage and was said to have been the most powerful gang leader in postwar Japan. Rumors that Razan might actually have been a Westerner were never confirmed. He was buried in a closed coffin guarded by members of his group, Shinanui-Kai, whose ten thousand members made it Japan's largest crime family.

A current gang war was expected to heat up as rival *yakuza* leaders sought pieces of drug, gambling, prostitution, and money-laundering rackets long controlled by Razan.

The second *yakuza* story told of U.S. Justice Department interest in a series of taped telephone conversations now in the possession of the newspaper. The tapes linked Shinanui-Kai with a New York crime family, a former Korean CIA official, and with an English diplomat and a Honolulu police lieutenant, both of whom had recently died in Hawaii under mysterious circumstances. According to Tokyo police, the deaths of the diplomat and the police officer may have been tied in with the theft of $50 million in rare stamps that had somehow found their way back to the rightful owners. Sources in the Japanese underworld were said to have told police that highly placed government officials in both Japan and China insisted the affair of the stamps be considered a closed issue. The disappearance of Frank Shiba Odori, an alleged *yakuza* living in New York, was believed due to his refusal to go along with this.

The rain began coming down harder, pelting the newspaper page until it darkened, and then the wind tore it from the altar and carried it toward the top of the cliff.

As the page flew away a lone figure stepped from the rain forest wearing a hooded poncho and combat boots. He stopped to check a compass, then walked past the decaying plantation and mill, across the wet red dirt, and stopped just outside of the *heiau*. He shaded his eyes with one hand, spied the altar, then walked toward it.

On the terrace the figure crouched at the base of the altar, removed a letter from under the poncho, and shielding the letter with his body, looked at it briefly. The letter, from the Sunday *Times* of London, was addressed to Mrs. Alexis Bendor.

Dear Mrs. Bendor:

This is in reply to your letter of July 16, 1983, in which you correctly called our attention to several errors in our account of the third Kasparov-Korchnoi chess game. 5 P-Q3 should have read P-QR3; 20 Q-Q4 should have read 20 Q-Q4 ch; 34 PXR. We regret any inconvenience this may have caused you and would like to take this opportunity to say we appreciate your interest and stand in awe of your powers of observation and penchant for truth. Again, our deepest apologies.

Sincerely,
Philip Tibber
Features Editor
Sunday *Times* of London

Simon Bendor folded the letter and tucked it under the altar. "You were right, ace," he said. "As usual."

He touched the altar and, head bowed, wept for a long time.